3 5674 00562110 8

DETROIT PUBLIC LIBRARY

DETROIT PUBLIC LIBRARY

BL

DATE DUE

THE WAY UP
The Memoirs of Count Gramont

Books by Sanche de Gramont

THE SECRET WAR

THE AGE OF MAGNIFICENCE:
The Memoirs of the Duc de Saint-Simon

EPITAPH FOR KINGS

THE FRENCH:
Portrait of a People

LIVES TO GIVE

THE WAY UP:
The Memoirs of Count Gramont

THE WAY UP

The Memoirs of Count Gramont

A NOVEL BY

Sanche de Gramont

G. P. Putnam's Sons
New York

c 1

Copyright © 1972 by Sanche de Gramont

*All rights reserved. This book, or parts thereof, must not
be reproduced in any form without permission. Published on the
same day in Canada by Longmans Canada, Limited, Toronto.*

SBN: 399-10978-1
Library of Congress Catalog Card Number: 72-80340

PRINTED IN THE UNITED STATES OF AMERICA

BL DEC8 '72

To all the members of the Gramont Family,
and to one in particular

Zestful French rake recounts in
intimate detail his escapades at
the Court of Louis XV.

Introduction

B EFORE the reader meets the star of this production, I would
like to introduce the supporting players, that is to say,
the other Gramonts: those who by preceding him made
possible his existence, and those who by following him made possible the discovery of his memoirs. Readers uninterested in sex, violence, and diabolical intrigue can skip this brief curriculum vitae
of the Gramont family.

The name Gramont comes from the land. It is an exaggeration,
being, not a mountain, but a rather low, commonplace hill surrounded by ditches. The first Gramont was the son of the viscount
of Dax, a powerful family in the Pyrénées, directly descended from
the dukes of Gascony. His name was Bergon-Garcia, and he lived
in the first half of the eleventh century. His father left him the
property of Gramont, on the left bank of the Bidouze River, about
fifteen miles from Bayonne, and he adopted the name. The spelling
appears as "Agramont" in twelfth-century Latin texts, and the
Basque form was "Agramuntek." The original castle, of which
nothing remains, was built by Bergon-Garcia at a spot now called
Viellenave-sur-Bidouze. The family motto, which began to appear
in thirteenth-century documents, is *"Gratia Dei, sum id quod sum"*
(thanks to God, I am what I am). It is taken from an epistle where
Saint Paul explains his conversion from paganism to Christianity.
Taken out of context, however, his words of gratitude became a
profession of smug self-satisfaction.

From the start, the Gramonts were quarrelsome. One of Bergon-
Garcia's sons contested a gift of land his father had made to a local
monastery and spent most of his life suing to reclaim it. The first
girl mentioned, Elvire, scratched out the eyes of a young nobleman
who had killed one of her cousins. The family's initial allegiance
was not to France, but to the Basque kingdom of Navarre. My
own name, Sanche, was the traditional name of the early kings of

7

Navarre, who minted a coin called the *sanchette*. In 1203, the Gramonts became the suzerains of the King of Navarre. They paid him taxes and fought in his wars. A Gramont accompanied King Thibaut I of Navarre on the Sixth Crusade. During the Hundred Years' War, their precarious geographical situation made it necessary for the Gramonts to shift their loyalties in order to keep their lands. They were allied by turn with the Navarre kingdom and with the English who occupied much of southwest France. They reflected the inconsistency of the times and were successful in their principal aim, which was to survive them.

The end of the Hundred Years' War confirmed the power of the Valois kings. The Gramonts, ever alert to the balance of power, rallied to their side and fought in their ill-fated Italian campaigns. Jean de Gramont, nicknamed The Thunder of Italy, fought with the famous Chevalier de Bayard at Ravenna in 1512 and was killed, along with thirty-eight other captains.

The sixteenth-century wars of religion brought out pious vocations in the family. Two brothers, Charles and Gabriel, became, the one, Archbishop of Bordeaux, and the other, Archbishop Cardinal of Toulouse. This religious zeal contributed to a crisis in the family. The two archbishops could leave no heirs (even though one had a natural son), and in 1528, the head of the family, Jean II, the son of their elder brother, died childless at the age of twenty-nine. That would have meant the end of the Gramonts had it not been for a fairly commonplace practice in those days, the adoption of the family name by one of its female members. The head of the family became Jean's sister, Claire, who had, with the dispensation of Pope Clement VII, married her cousin Menaud d'Aure, vicomte d'Aster. He consented to adopt his wife's maiden name, preserving the family's continuity.

The first offshoot of this new branch was Antoine I, baron de Gramont, born in 1526. François Ier made him Mayor of Bayonne at the age of nine. The wars of religion were still raging, and Antoine I displayed a dangerous partiality for the new beliefs. A whispering campaign at court threatened to compromise his position, and he renounced Protestantism to remain on good terms with the king. One lesson the family history teaches is that principles can be discarded when interests are threatened.

The Gramonts' fortune rose with his son Philibert, born in 1552, the first to make the transition from feudal lord to courtier. He lived under Henri III, who insisted on a regulated court life,

and who liked to surround himself with handsome young noble-
men whom he called his *mignons*. They were favorites, bodyguards, perhaps lovers, and some had political influence. Being a
mignon did not prevent Philibert from marrying the thirteen-year-
old Diane d'Andoins, the richest heiress in Gascony, in 1568. She
soon changed her first name to Corisande, the name of the heroine
in a popular *roman de chevalerie*, as if, by adopting a romantic
name, she were announcing her availability for a romantic destiny.
In 1580, Philibert left for a campaign against the Huguenots and
was killed at the siege of La Fère, at the age of twenty-eight. Henri
III wept when he heard the news.

Philibert left a beautiful, rich, intelligent, twenty-six-year-old
widow. It seems established that her love affair with the future
Henri IV of France did not begin until two or three years after her
husband's death. Henri was recovering from an illness at his sister's castle in Pau in the spring of 1582, when he renewed a childhood friendship with Corisande. For once, he was romantically
uninvolved, and he began to consider her in a new light. In Henri
she found the knight-errant she had seemed to be seeking when she
called herself Corisande.

He was more errant than knight, for as chief of the Huguenots,
he was busy conducting the War of the Three Henrys, and he
pursued other love affairs wherever his campaigns took him.
Their passion soon subsided into a friendship that was carried
on mainly by correspondence. When Henri III died in 1589,
stabbed in the stomach by the fanatical monk Jacques Clément,
Henri of Navarre pressed his claim to the crown. Five years later,
having made the famous remark that "Paris is well worth a mass,"
he entered the capital as Henri IV of France.

Corisande, who had loaned Henri twenty thousand pounds to
pay his troops, and who had recruited horses and men for him
throughout the Béarn, saw him several times in Paris after he was
crowned, but only as a background court figure. In 1610 Henri IV
was assassinated by the religious fanatic Ravaillac. Corisande out-
lived him by eleven years, which she spent closeted in her castle of
Hagetmau, seeing few friends, and worrying over the extravagant
behavior of her son, Antoine II.

Born in 1572, Antoine II was a pivotal figure in the Gramont
history. He was the first duke, and yet his behavior was anachro-
nistic, far closer in temperament to a rebellious medieval baron
than to an obedient courtier. In 1601 he married Louise de

Roquelaure, the daughter of another powerful Gascon lord. Three years later, she gave birth to a son, another Antoine, the future Marshal of France.

One day in March, 1610, Antoine returned to Bidache unannounced after a hunt to find his wife in the arms of his equerry. This is enough to try the patience of the most even-tempered man, and for someone as quick to anger as Antoine II, the results were predictable. He sent the equerry to "enjoy the other world," as he put it. His wife fled and found asylum in a convent, but Antoine II snatched her from the protecting arms of the nuns and locked her in the Bidache dungeon. He considered himself absolute sovereign of Bidache, with the traditional feudal right to dispense justice. He put his wife and her dead lover on trial and pressured two local lawyers and four "village judges" into serving as a jury. He began by trying the corpse of his equerry, who, to no one's surprise, was found guilty and sentenced to death, posthumously. The sentence was carried out by chopping off his lifeless head with an ax. The father of the bride, Antoine de Roquelaure, petitioned the Queen Mother, Marie de Médicis, to rescue his daughter from the Bidache dungeon where she languished. Such requests took time, and meanwhile, Antoine II went ahead with the trial of his wife, respecting all the formalities of judicial procedure and drawing up written interrogations and cross-examinations.

After a brief deliberation, the improvised court ruled that she was guilty. In October, an emissary finally arrived in Bidache to tell Antoine that the Queen Mother urgently wanted to see him. He did not set out for court until a month later, after leaving instructions with the head of his household that the execution of his wife should be carried out once he was under way. He was, as many Gramonts since have been, a firm believer in the *fait accompli*. On November 9, as Antoine II was making his leisurely way to Paris, Louise was put to death.

By the time Antoine reached Paris, news of his wife's death had preceded him. The Queen Mother's reaction was surprisingly mild. A decree voided the Bidache trial. The jury was ordered to appear before the King's Council. Antoine II's two sons were removed from his custody to be brought up at court. Antoine was ordered to pay child support. A royal decree exonerated him from "all crimes for which he might be accused," without going into further detail. He was, in effect, pardoned for the murder of his wife.

In 1643, the year Louis XIII died, Antoine II, despite his anti-social behavior, was made a hereditary duke and peer. The royal warrant was signed by the childish hand of the five-year-old Louis XIV. It was an honor Antoine enjoyed but briefly, for he was already seventy-one, and he died a year later. He was an anachronism, a throwback to the times when feudal lords minted their own coin, availed themselves of the *droit de cuissage*, slept with their horse and their coat of mail in their bedroom, and kept the oil boiling behind the castle's crenels. The surprise ending to his life was that he married again. The intrepid lady was Claude de Montmorency, and she gave him a son named Philibert, who was to make his mark in both the French and English courts.

Born in 1621, Philibert had already earned a reputation for gallantry by the time Louis XIV was born. He developed a passion for a lady the king was interested in. The lady complained, and Philibert was exiled to England, where he met the twenty-two-year-old Elizabeth Hamilton at the court of Charles II. They were married in 1663 in what may have been a shotgun wedding. Rumor has it that Philibert was riding hard on the Dover road when his path was blocked by Elizabeth's brothers, who wanted to know whether he had forgotten anything. "Yes, gentlemen," he replied, "I have forgotten to marry your sister. Let us go back."

Philibert was allowed to return to the French court a year later, and became known for his expertise in English affairs and for his quick tongue. He was a professional courtier, a careerist, acquisitive, unsentimental, and unscrupulous. Court was a competitive society. One rose for the same reasons one rises in a business community, through hard work and stubbornness and contacts. One of his favorite sayings was: "Only fools die." He became foolish in 1707.

Antoine III, Philibert's elder half-brother, was born in 1604. The story of his life becomes confused with the long list of battles in the Thirty Years' War. He was wounded in 1635 while defending a bridge on the Rhine, and six years later the king gave him his Marshal's baton. He came home between campaigns just long enough to conceive a son. In 1645, he was wounded and taken prisoner at the battle of Nördlingen. Three days later, he was exchanged against an English general.

When the match between Louis XIV and the Spanish infanta was arranged, Antoine III was sent to Spain to fetch the bride-to-be. Entering Madrid, he spurred his horse to a full gallop to keep up the pretense of the king's impatience. The queen mother, Ann of Austria, had asked him to let her know frankly what the infanta looked like. Antoine III tactfully wrote back: "The qualities of her body could not be more to my taste." Antoine III came as close to as his father Antoine II had been distant from the seventeenth-century ideal of the *honnête homme*. One of his contemporaries wrote that "he was one of those men who, wherever they are, do more honor than it is possible to do them." He was such a faithful courtier that when he died in 1678, he was a duke and peer, a Marshal, a knight of the Saint-Esprit, a Colonel in the French Guards, a Porte-Oriflamme of France, the Sovereign of Bidache, a Minister of State, the Governor of Béarn and Navarre, and the Governor and Mayor of Bayonne.

The lives of these seventeenth-century Antoines seem cast from one mold. They were good soldiers, attentive courtiers, and bad husbands. They seldom traveled abroad except at the head of their troops, and they displayed no cultural interests. They were religious out of duty, brave out of habit, and contemptuous of whatever lay outside their restricted field of vision. Antoine IV had a life-span almost identical with that of the Sun King—born in 1641, he died in 1720—and was named Ambassador to Spain. Antoine V was a member of the Regency Council in 1718, after the death of Louis XIV. Antoine VI was derelict in the first obligation of his rank. He had no male offspring. The title of duke went to his brother Louis, who was born a year after him, in 1689. Louis inherited the family trait of rashness and became famous for charging the enemy against orders, at the battle of Dettingen, in 1743. He had three sons: Antoine VII, born in 1719, Anaxagoras, born in 1725, and Alfred, born in 1731. There is no point in discussing them in this introduction, for one is the author of the memoirs that follow, in which the other two are dealt with at length.

But a word should be said about Antoine VII's second wife, who was a close friend of Marie Antoinette and a sister of the minister Choiseul. She could have emigrated when the revolution broke out, but chose to stay by the queen's side. She remained in Paris even after the king and queen had been guillotined in 1793. Perhaps she thought the worst was over. In March, 1794, she was arrested under the Jacobin Law of the Suspects. Questioned by the public prosecutor, Fouquier-Tinville, who wanted to know whether she had ever sent funds to the émigrés, she replied: "I was about to say no, but my life is not worth a lie."

"When the gods are thirsty," the official family historian writes, "a noble answer will not slake them."

She died on the guillotine on April 22 and seems to have been the only Gramont casualty, with the exception of the castle of Bidache, which burned down in 1796. Abandoned by the family, it had become a *bien national* administered by a government-appointed curator. He embezzled the funds for the castle's upkeep, and when he heard that he was about to be investigated, he set fire to the library. Fire, water—once the castle was destroyed, the curator drowned himself in the Bidouze River.

The son of Antoine VII having died before him, the title of duke came eventually to the son of his brother, Antoine VIII, born in 1755. Antoine VIII commanded the guards unit outside Versailles on the night in October, 1789, when the Paris populace came to claim the royal family. Too compromised to remain in France, he emigrated to Rome and then to Austria. He did not return to France until 1814, with Louis XVIII. His son, Antoine IX, was born a month before the Bastille was stormed and grew up in exile. In England, he joined the regiment of the Prince of Wales, and fought in many of the European campaigns against Napoleon, choosing the interests of his class over those of his country. When Louis XVIII was restored to power in 1815. Antoine IX, who was still duc de Guiche,* became the favorite of the Bourbon court. He was handsome and dashing, and with his *ancien régime* manners and intense royalist convictions, he helped maintain the illusion that nothing had changed. Everyone called him *le beau duc de Guiche*. He married the comtesse d'Orsay, a great beauty who counted Balzac and Disraeli among her admirers. He became duke at his father's death in 1836, and died in 1855, having lived through the revolution of 1789, the first republic, the first empire, the Bourbon restoration of 1815, the revolution of 1830, the constitutional monarchy of Louis-Philippe, the revolution of 1848, the second republic, and the second empire. He deserves a medal for endurance.

His eldest son, Antoine X Agénor, born in 1819, was the first nonmilitary head of the family. True to tradition, he attended the École Polytechnique, an elite military school, but he disliked barracks life and resigned from the army as soon as he could. Tall,

* The eldest son of the duc de Gramont bears the title duc de Guiche until his father dies.

blond, and handsome, he had the good fortune to be loved by three of the most famous courtesans of his time: The actress Rachel, who was credited with giving him a taste for literature; La Paiva, who kept him locked under guard in her apartment for a week; and finally, Marie Duplessis, who became better known as The Lady of the Camellias. A banal love affair was raised to the level of legend by the combined talents of Dumas the Younger and Verdi, who used Dumas' book as the libretto for *La Traviata*. Dumas called the ill-starred lovers Marguerite Gautier and Armand Duval, but Armand's description, "as blond as a German, as impassible as an Englishman," fits Antoine X Agénor, who will hereafter be referred to as Agénor. The Lady of the Camellias was so named because she always carried a bouquet of those mournful flowers, a white bouquet twenty-five days a month, a red bouquet the other five. Like Marie Duplessis, Dumas' heroine was consumptive, "and led a life not destined to cure her." She tells her lover: "Since I am sure to have a shorter life than others, I have promised myself to live more quickly."

The love affair began while Agénor was at Polytechnique. He preferred, the family historian writes, to the ballistic studies of the God Mars, the arrows that were fired by the archer Cupid. In Dumas' book, Armand's father goes to Marguerite and begs her to give up his son, "before it's too late." Describing the dangers of their liaison, he says: "Armand may grow jealous, challenge a rival to a duel, and be killed. The sister he loves dearly is about to marry an honorable man, who, having learned of Armand's conduct, threatens to break off the engagement. The future of a child who has done you no harm, and who is entitled to a future, is in your hands."

Marguerite is so moved by the father's eloquence that she promises to break with Armand. She tells him she has found a new love. Soon after, she falls ill. She begins spitting blood. She tells her maid: "I did not know a body could suffer so."

A priest summoned to give her the last rites says: "She lived like a sinner and will die like a Christian."

The book is factual up to a point, since it was Agénor's father who convinced Marie Duplessis to give up his son, who would be sent on a grand tour in order to Forget Everything. After much weeping, Marie Duplessis agreed to give up Armand. But she was careful not to spill any tears on the check. Nor did she have Dumas' gift for expressing her feelings. In the only remaining note from Marie to Agénor, the spelling is more heartbreaking than the sentiment: "Goodby my deer angel. Dont forget me to mutch. Think somtimes of the one who loves you." The European tour was a great success. Agénor fell in love with a Finnish girl named Hilda Arnold in Vienna and had an illegitimate daughter by her.

When Agénor reached the age of thirty, his father suggested that the heir to the family name should begin to think about perpetuating it. He traveled to England and Scotland, and to everyone's surprise, this Don Juan who had had his pick of the most alluring women in Paris chose a rather dour, athletic Scottish woman named Emma MacKinnon, who was eight years his senior. Her passions were golf and riding, and her ancestry could be traced to the invasion of Scotland by the Saxons. Agénor brought his Highlands bride to Paris and settled down to the unapplied life of a gentleman.

Two years later, Napoleon III came to power and, seeking to surround himself with *ancien régime* types in the hope that it would make his title of emperor sound more authentic, asked Agénor to become his minister to the German principality of Hesse-Cassel. To the rest of the *ancien régime* nobility, Agénor's acceptance was a betrayal. The Bourbon pretender was in exile and a Gramont was willing to serve the usurper. He grandly told his critics: "The king is not in his place, but that is no reason why I should not be in mine." His career was a success. He was named Ambassador to the Holy See and to Vienna, and became Minister of Foreign Affairs just in time to espouse the cause of war with Prussia, at a time when Bismarck was determined to forge German unity at the expense of a war with France. After 1870, he became the scapegoat for France's defeat. He was so bitterly attacked that he took refuge in England. He spent the rest of his life clearing his name, and died in 1880, a broken and penniless man, who had spent his wife's fortune to keep up his various embassies.

My grandfather, Antoine XI Agénor, was born in 1851 and spent his childhood in the embassies where his father was posted. He was clever at mathematics and came out third in his class at Saumur, the military academy for the cavalry. He fought in the brief campaign of 1870, as a nineteen-year-old second lieutenant in the Fourth Hussars, and successfully defended the town of Bapaume against the Prussians. After the war, he suffered from the resentment against his father, which was so intense that his own uncle refused to sponsor him for membership in the Jockey

Club. He liked to hunt, but was not invited anywhere for weekends. He complained that "there was nowhere I could go in September to shoot a few rabbits." Moreover, he was penniless. He lived on his lieutenant's salary. From his father, he had received only his blond good looks. Fortunately, they were sufficient to capture the heart of a young heiress, Isabelle de Beauveau. Antoine XI Agénor (whom his friends called Agénor) was introduced by his father to Isabelle's father. "Agénor puts his foot in his mouth," his father said, "but he won't go into debt." With that paternal endorsement, they were married in 1874. A year later, the young bride gave birth to a daughter, Elizabeth, and died in the process.

Several years later, Agénor met Marguerite de Rothschild, one of the five daughters of baron Charles of Frankfurt, at a ball. He danced with her once, he danced with her twice, he conquered her simple heart. Three of the daughters had married their cousins, as Rothschilds will, and their mother wanted the last two to marry titled Frenchmen. Agénor defied the conventions of the Faubourg Saint-Germain, and Marguerite went ahead even though her father threatened to disinherit her for marrying outside her faith.

They were married in 1878 after she had converted to Catholicism. Two years later, Agénor became duke and resigned his army commission. An enormous fortune descended upon his shoulders when his father-in-law died. He bought a mansion on the Champs-Élysées, on the corner where the cinéma Biarritz now stands. He attended the important auctions in order to furnish and decorate his town house, but he had to get around his wife's frugality. He wanted to buy Caravaggio's "Gamesters," one of the few pictures of the Italian school that does not represent a sacred subject, from the destitute prince Colonna, but she balked at the expense. As a consolation, he was allowed to buy a Gobelins tapestry representing the "Toilet of Psyche," which hung in the drawing room.

Agénor was finally able to satisfy his passion for hunting. In 1892, he bought the property of Mortefontaine, in the Oise, twenty-five miles north of Paris—four thousand acres of woods, ponds, ferns, and rocky hills. Surrounded by the Ermenonville forest, it was ideal for hunting. From 1892 to 1894, a castle modeled on Azay-le-Rideau was built on a site overlooking a large pond, said to be the pond Watteau painted in "l'Embarquement pour Cythère." Called Vallière, the castle was comfortable for its time; each of the thirty bedrooms had its own bathroom. There was a kennel, a stable, a stud farm, a pheasant farm, and an orchid hothouse. The grand dukes Cyril, Boris, and Vladimir hunted at Vallière. Everyone raves about the beauty of Vallière, the islanded lakes where Rousseau strolled, and it is customary to say: "One would think oneself in Scotland, and yet one is only twenty miles from Paris." But I have always thought that this cumbersome imitation of one of the loveliest of Loire castles was conceived in a parvenu mentality. Here was an authentic duke living in a fake sixteenth-century castle, like Hearst in San Simeon. I still find Vallière as drafty and inhospitable as a provincial museum, and the landscape melancholy and insipid, like a yellowing, faded daguerreotype.

In 1905, Marguerite née Rothschild died. She had given Agénor three children, two boys and a girl, and he also had Elizabeth from his first marriage. He needed a wife to run his household and manage his children. His only method of discipline was to bark at an unruly son or daughter: "I disown you." He was lonely. He heard about a charming widow in Rome named Ruspoli, and went there to court her. At dinner at her home, he found himself seated between the widow and her nineteen-year-old daughter Maria, who had just finished her convent studies. With the bluntness of the hussar lieutenant he had been, he announced that it was the daughter he wanted.

He took her for a carriage ride and asked: "Would you like to marry me?"

"Oh, yes sir, thank you very much," Maria replied in her best convent manner, as though she were being asked whether she wanted a cup of tea.

Maria's mother decided that if she could not be a bride it was better to be a mother-in-law than nothing at all, and she graciously agreed to the match. In 1907, Antoine XI Agénor, fifty-four, married Maria Ruspoli, nineteen, my grandmother. He wrote his children by former marriages, all of whom were older than his bride: "I'm marrying dona Maria Ruspoli. Consult the Gotha, page so and so." Paris wits said he had married his first wife mademoiselle de Beauveau *pour l'écu* (for the escutcheon), his second wife fräulein de Rothschild *pour l'écu* (for the gold crowns), and his third wife signorina Ruspoli *pour le cul* (for the pleasures of the flesh).

Maria had been brought up in a cloistered environment that still seemed closer to the *Rinascimento* than the *Risorgimento*. Within the framework of her upbringing, she showed considerable independence. As a girl, she had to read the *Messaggero* to her father in the morning as he sat on his *chaise percée*. She read the head-lines, and knew whether or not to go on according to his grunts. Maria attended the Trinita del Monte convent school, which was visited each year by a cardinal. One year, she won the recitation contest, and as a prize, she was allowed to walk in the garden with the cardinal. His Eminence, making small talk, asked her about the food.

"Abominable," she said, "it is a Calvary to swallow it."

This was said with such accents of passion that the cardinal told the Mother Superior: "You must do something about the food. I understand it leaves a great deal to be desired."

. Her chat with the cardinal did not endear her to the nuns, who began looking for an excuse to expel her. They found it shortly afterward, when one of the nuns sneezed during a class, and Maria said, *"Salute figli maschi,"* which is the Italian equivalent of Ge-sundheit, but means, literally: "Congratulations on having a male child." Because of her family name, however, the nuns had to take her back. After her first communion, with two other little girls from well-known families, she went to the Vatican to receive the blessings of Pius X. In their white dresses with veils, like tiny brides, they strolled with the holy father in the flowered paths of the Vatican gardens.

She adored her tall and handsome older brothers, and when one of them fell ill, she promised to make an embroidered cushion if he got well. She worked at the cushion but did not have the patience to finish it. In those days, at the Trinita del Monte, while in one section of the school the daughters of the Italian nobility learned the history of the Catholic church, in another section the daughters of the poor were taught sewing. Maria gave her cushion to one of the poor girls to finish, promising to pay her ten lire. When she presented the cushion to her brother, the whole family was amazed at an industriousness she had never before displayed. Every day at recess the girl who had made the cushion asked Maria for her ten lire. Maria went to her mother and confessed, saying: "You should know that I could never finish something like that." As someone who squandered several fortunes during her lifetime, and who al-ways had a mysterious relationship with money, which tends to disappear and reappear in her pockets like a magician's colored scarves, she remembers that incident vividly, because, she says: "It was the first time I ever went into debt."

One could not say that she was interested in money, any more than the driver of a car is interested in engine oil. For her, money was lubrication, it made life advance more smoothly, it made the engine of her needs turn, and was taken for granted until the engine began coughing. Bribery never worked with her. One of her lovers once swore that he would get her to eat snails, which she detests. He took her to a Paris restaurant and ordered a dozen. He then pulled from his pocket a velour jewelry case, which he opened to reveal a gold and diamond clip from Cartier in the form of a snail. The clip would be hers, he said, if she ate the snails. She never got it.

Contempt for material things in her case means that she has as few qualms about taking them as she has about losing them or giving them away. One time on the Vallière golf course, she was watching my father and my uncle Gratien play when a sapphire ring worth a great deal slipped from her finger into the rough. "Don't interrupt the game," she said, "it's such a small sapphire." The corollary to this anecdote is that when my mother married Maria's son, she was given a ruby ring by her mother, which Maria much admired, saying: "What a shame it's loose on your finger. I know a little Italian jeweler on the rue de la Paix who will fix it for you in a day." The day turned into a week, the week turned into a month, my mother never saw the ring again.

"Say something to her," she told my father, "she's your mother."

My father asked Maria if she had seen the ruby ring.

"Oh, the ring," she replied, with the bored indifference of someone being asked to recall trivia from the distant past, "the maid took it."

But I am getting ahead of myself. Maria grew up a devout Catholic and a hopeless romantic, who believed in Héloïse and Abélard as fervently as in the infallibility of the pope, which had recently been pronounced. She knew that perfect love existed.

Maria, secretly nurturing dreams of elopement with a Renaissance prince, found, instead, my grandfather. A Florentine secretiveness was bred into her. It was a matter of survival, first with an authoritarian father, then with an authoritarian husband who was the same age as her father. The husband was paunchy, balding, with walrus mustaches, a foreigner who spoke only a few police phrases of Italian. Her father's favorite dictum had been: *"Moglie e buoi, paese tuoi"* (spouses and beef should be obtained from one's own country).

On their wedding night in Dieppe, Agénor took a suite in the best hotel, with separate rooms. Food was brought up by a battery of servants, and after a copious meal, Agénor said good night to his young bride and retired. She did not know what was worse, nothing happening, or something happening. The next day her mother called and asked how everything had gone. There are two versions of her reply. Truth is too linear to circumscribe Maria. According to one version, she was too proud to admit her disappointment and told her mother that everything was fine. In the other version, she pleaded with her mother to let her return to Rome. "You didn't like the convent either," her mother told her, "but you got used to it."

Toward noon, the duke appeared, pink-cheeked and refreshed, and asked: "Well, good lady, what would you say to lunch in the country?"

"What a good idea," Maria said.

When he was pleased, he called her "good lady" (*bonne dame*). When he was delighted, he called her signorina.

Thanks to one of those irrational reversals by which we come to begrudge the objects of our good fortune, his marriage to Marguerite de Rothschild had made my grandfather violently anti-Semitic. He warned his new wife against his children, particularly his daughter Corise, who was not more than four feet tall, with flaming red hair, and who had married the duc de Noailles. "Watch out for her," Agénor said, "there is nothing worse than a red-headed Jewish midget."

Maria fulfilled her most important task by giving my grandfather two sons in the first two years of their marriage, my father Gabriel, and my uncle, Gratien. Breast feeding would have interfered with the duke's social life, so they were turned over to wet nurses. She settled down to six months of intense social activity in Paris and six months of equally intense entertaining in Vallière. In Paris, she became famous for her beauty. She was painted by Augustus John and admired by Proust, Jean Cocteau, and countless others. She started wearing her pearls backward, hanging down her back, after someone remarked: *"Elle a la plus belle chute d'épaules de Paris et de toute l'Europe."**

Activities at Vallière revolved around hunting and eating. Every morning the chef arrived in his starched hat to present Maria with

---

* She has the most beautiful shoulders in Paris and all of Europe.

the day's menu. As a concession to her nationality, there was a second chef in charge of pasta. Agénor had a third chef brought from England and put in charge of breakfast. "The French don't know how to make muffins," he explained. One of Agénor's ambitions, never realized, was to shoot more than a thousand pheasants in a single day. He was furious when he heard that the Rothschilds had shot thirteen hundred in their neighboring property of Armainvilliers.

When he fell off a horse and broke his leg, he was forced to give up both riding and hunting. Maria had to substitute for him and report in detail where the stag had been taken, by whom, under what circumstances, and what the exact role of each member of the hunting party had been. There were also annual theatrical productions at Vallière. The officers of the Second Hussar Regiment, garrisoned in nearby Senlis, were recruited for minor roles. Usually there was a musical review, or a comedy by Sacha Guitry. The theatrical tradition continued until World War II. The nineteenth century ended in 1914. *La vie de château* continued until 1939.

Antoine XI Agénor was the last do-nothing duke. Looking after his properties and receiving his guests filled his life, and although he had long since left the army, he continued ordering everyone about as if they were soldiers. When World War I broke out, Agénor, who was sixty-three, requested a commission, and fell into a deep melancholy when he was turned down. He ruminated over the defeat of 1870 while following the dispatches of the war to end wars. He died in 1925. I never knew him. Both his sons from his Rothschild marriage conducted themselves meritoriously in the war. Armand, a young but already brilliant physicist, designed the gunsight for the French fighter planes. Louis-René, an infantry officer, was wounded in the trenches, much as one of his ancestors had been three centuries earlier.

Antoine XII Armand, the physicist, was born in 1879. As a five-year-old boy he heard the Invalides cannons fire to announce the start of the funeral procession for Victor Hugo. As a ten-year-old boy he saw the Eiffel Tower go up, its square iron legs slowly rising from the green Champ de Mars. He had a talent for drawing, and when his secondary studies were over, he told his father he wanted to enroll in the Beaux Arts school.

Agénor exploded. "You'll spend all your time chasing girls in Montmartre," he said.

"All right," Armand replied, "I'll study physics."

"You'll never get anywhere," Agénor prophesied, "but if that's what you want."

Armand became an outstanding physicist, elected to the Academy of Sciences, inventor of optical devices like the gastroscope, which enables a doctor to photograph the inside of a patient's stomach, founder of an optics company, and developer of the first French mass market camera, the Foca. He was the first of the Gramont dukes to break out of the confining limits of his caste. Instead of the family motto, "I am what I am," he adopted Montaigne's "What do I know?" He would have achieved recognition had his name been Dupont or Durand. He was also remarkably handsome in a spats-and-cane turn-of-the-century way, with silken mustaches, aquiline features, and a voice that combined warmth with a slightly rasping quality. As a young man he met the writer D'Annunzio, who told him: "I've seen you before."

"Where?" asked Armand.

"At the Uffizi in Florence," D'Annunzio said, "where Titian painted your portrait."

D'Annunzio was right. The resemblance between Armand and Titian's "Man in Black" is startling.

In 1904, he married Elaine Greffulhe, the daughter of the agate-eyed comtesse de Greffulhe, famed for her beauty and her salon. Elaine was an introspective girl who grew up in the shadow of her beautiful, energetic mother. She was resigned to being an ugly duckling who would never turn into a swan. When I knew her, in middle age, she wore a red wig like an ill-fitting wool helmet over her own thick, black hair, and was given to overeating. Elaine's match with Armand was the most talked-about Paris wedding of 1904. Gabriel Fauré composed a wedding march, which he played himself at the organ of the Madeleine church. Proust's wedding gift was a pearl-handled revolver inside a painted case on which had been inscribed several of the verses the bride had written as a girl. The wedding night was less brilliant than the ceremony. Armand had indigestion and Elaine's first conjugal duty was to administer an enema.

Armand's friendship with Proust began in 1901. At that time, Proust was not taken seriously as a writer. He was considered a dilettante who wrote precious articles in *Le Figaro* under the pseudonym Horatio. Literary critics said his prose was mildewed. Armand met him at Anna de Noailles' and was struck by his intelligence. He helped introduce Proust to the families he would later portray.

He also saw the society Proust described collapse with the coming of World War II. Vallière became a relay for German armored units, and later, a weekend retreat for the general staff. The cellar was depleted, as was the rare book collection. Seventeenth-century frames were used for kindling. Two of Armand's four sons were taken prisoner. Armand himself moved to Biarritz in the early stages of the occupation, with his daughter Corisande. Soon after renting a villa there, he was called on by three Gestapo men in plain clothes, who spoke fluent French and asked seemingly aimless questions. But behind the aimlessness Armand detected a line of questioning intended to bring out that he was linked to left-wing political parties.

"In our family, we have always kept our distance from these parties," he said.

"Family proves nothing," one of the Gestapo men said. "The prince of Baden was a Red."

They then began to talk about the Freemasons, and asked to see his mail. He led them to his study, trying not to betray his concern, for he had received, via friends, several letters from the new batch of émigrés, including Robert de Rothschild, who were outspoken in their opinion of the occupiers. Upon reaching his study, he was relieved to see that the incriminating correspondence had disappeared. His daughter, hearing the Gestapo car stop in front of the house and seeing three unknown men get out, had shredded the letters and flushed them down a toilet.

The Gestapo men finally left, and the reason behind their visit did not become apparent to Armand until 1946, when a total stranger offered to sell him a family document that had vanished from the Gramont archives for one hundred thousand francs. Armand told the man that he would give him four thousand francs for his troubles, and that if he did not accept the offer he would press charges for theft. He recovered the document. It was a diploma of membership in the Freemasons that had belonged to his great-grandfather, Antoine IX, the one who was born a month before the Bastille was stormed, and spent years of exile in England. While there, he became a Freemason. A century later, his membership in that secret fraternal order caused his great-grandson to come under the suspicion of the Gestapo. Thus do the lives of our ancestors come back to haunt us.

Armand was a man of exquisite refinement and urbanity, a scientist, the distillation of the best that centuries of overbred Gramont blood, mixed with the more recent but inbred Rothschild blood, could produce. Yet in all of us the beast emerges. No woman who visited Vallière was safe unless she locked her door at night. When my grandmother first arrived there as the child bride of Agénor, she had to fight off the advances of her stepson, who was ten years her senior. One night he came into her room through a secret door, "in a visible state of excitement," according to my grandmother. His father was snoring in the adjoining bedroom.

He fell to his knees and pleaded: "Only you can help me."

"I told him," my grandmother said, "that if he came one step closer, he would never set foot in Vallière again."

It must be said that my grandmother was forever fighting off advances of this nature. She became famous for her legion of lovers, but although romantic, she was not sensual, and once told me: "I was never that interested in appendages." Men seeing the lovely young duchess on the arm of her wintery husband thought the hunting season was open.

When Agénor died in 1925, Vallière and the bulk of the Gramont fortune was left to his children by his Rothschild wife. My grandmother, his third and last wife, received only a small share of the inheritance. There were some obscure negotiations I have never really understood, which resulted in her signing over all claims to property in exchange for a cash settlement. What with accounts in the major couturier houses, and meals brought up from the best restaurants in Paris, and feeding live trout from Fouquet's to the seals in the Jardin des Plantes, and buying diamonds as if they were rhinestones, the cash soon ran out.

Maria then married the great-grandson of Victor Hugo, François Hugo, with whom she shared the condition of total penury. In François she found a husband ten years her junior, as if she was trying to establish an average that would correspond to an ideal mate more or less her own age. She had a child by François when she was forty-five or forty-six years old—the exact age is difficult to establish, since Maria long ago took the precaution of changing the date of birth on her passport. No longer wealthy, no longer a duchess, she was forced, at an age when most working women are looking forward to retirement, to earn her living. She came to the United States at the start of World War II and became an assistant to Elizabeth Arden. She also opened the Hugo Gallery, where she showed the works of Max Ernst and Jean Cocteau. She was still a great beauty, still youthful. Her son Gratien, bald and overweight, looked older than she did. When they were together, and he was asked how they were related, he would say: "She is a very distant mother."

In the early fifties, with the proceeds of a painting Max Ernst had given her, she bought a 150-acre property three miles outside Aix-en-Provence, with a view of the Mont Saint-Victoire. She told me that while walking there amid the thyme and the lavender, she had a vision. My dead father appeared and told her that this was the place where she must spend the rest of her days. Maria is so secretive that she prefers to get her advice from the dead because she knows they won't repeat it to anyone else. In any case, she has with her magic wand turned a primitive Provençal cabin into a home of great charm, which has also increased in value a hundred-fold. Now in her mid-eighties, she still occasionally walks the six miles to town and back. Another sign of her vigor is that she continues to go into debt.

My memories of my father, Gabriel, are confused with the stories I have heard about him. The French ambassador Saint-Quentin, under whom my father served in Washington, called him a mixture of Joan of Arc and Don Quijote. He was quixotic about matters small and large. When he was nine years old, his father fired his pretty English nanny and he threw himself from a third-floor window in Vallière, fortunately landing in a bed of roses. When he was preparing for his foreign service exams, he complained there was too much noise at home. He went to the local police commissariat, carrying his books under his arm, and asked to be locked up. The police pointed out that he had not broken any law. He went outside and began throwing rocks at a lamppost until they convinced him to go home.

The weight of evidence was never heavy enough to deter my father from whatever he had set out to do. Golf was one of his passions. It would be raining hard in Paris, and my mother would watch him take his golf bag out of the ground-floor hall closet and put on his golf shoes and his visored tattersall golf cap.

"But it's pouring outside," she would say.

"Not in Mortefontaine," he would reply, for the golf course in Mortefontaine was twenty miles away.

With the same unshakeable conviction, and despite all evidence to the contrary, he believed in 1939 that France was going to win the war. Two years earlier, we had arrived in Washington, my father's first diplomatic post, and when he saw that war was likely, he began to take flying lessons. When it was declared, he took us all back to France. He was assigned to an escadrille near Caen, but the armistice was signed before he could be sent to the front. He joined De Gaulle in England and arranged for us to go back to America. He was sent to South Africa, to flight school, and on the way back to England his ship was torpedoed off Mozambique. He reached shore in a lifeboat, and got back to England in time to take part in eight bombing missions before he was killed in a training flight in 1943.

My father was probably the Gramont family's first professed atheist. The Gramonts were always Catholic. It was part of being a loyal subject, when it had nothing to do with religious conviction, and later it became a matter of social convention. One day, when he was nineteen, on the train to Vallière, my father suddenly announced that he no longer believed in God. I used to tell myself: My father lost his faith in the Gare Saint-Lazare.

He was equally controversial in his choice of a bride. He spurned the rich and titled French girls who were thrust upon him and fell in love with a pretty Greek girl from an old but untitled family of distant Venetian origin, the Negropontes, whom he met in a tuberculosis sanatorium in Davos, Switzerland. My father had been sent to the sanatorium suffering from parathyroid complicated by pneumonia. My mother was there with her mother, who eventually died of a heart attack complicated by tuberculosis. In the magic mountain atmosphere of the sanatorium, the courtship began. Sanatoriums in those days tried to maintain a cheerful façade through organized social activities. I have some old photographs that show the sanatorium guests at a costume ball, their doomed consumptive overfed faces hidden behind masks or smiling above the ruffles of a harlequin costume.

Their parents were not happy about my parents' engagement, but the opposition they met only strengthened their feelings. They were bound to marry, if only in order to have their way. One of the wedding presents was a Nash sedan, and my father became determined to teach my mother how to drive, despite her evident lack of aptitude. She crashed into a tree on the way to Vallière, shortly after the wedding. A dog traveling with them was killed and they were both disfigured, so that I only know my parents' original faces from photographs. They spent most of their honeymoon in the hospital, their faces swathed in bandages, with slits for the eyes, nose, and mouth, holding hands across their white iron beds.

My uncle Gratien, my father's only full brother, never married. In his youth he was what the Greeks call a *meraklides*, an enjoyer of life. He was a scratch golfer at eighteen, and could support himself by playing bridge. He played most games so well that he saw no reason to work. It was his tragedy to have inherited all the accouterments of wealth, like the gout, and a taste for fine things, and the capacity to be happy doing nothing, and to find himself poor at the age of twenty-one. He was everyone's favorite guest at country houses all over Europe. For one season, he was the golf pro at the Palace Hotel in Saint Moritz. Then polio cut short his golf career. In the thirties, he was part of the Montparnasse scene. At one point, fifteen women had keys to his apartment in the Rue Delambre. He was famous for his cocaine-assisted bedroom performances.

He began selling cars for a living, but always dreamed of the unattainable blue flower, the marvelous scheme that would bring him the wealth he should have inherited. One scheme involved a mirror gadget that allowed a golfer to watch himself swinging and see his mistakes. It was called the Magic Eye, but it was an eye that never opened. Another was a product called Firezone, which was added to automobile oil like a vitamin, as though oil were inadequate. I remember visiting Gratien at the Paris automobile show in the unheated Grand Palais, where he sat shivering behind the Firezone stand, the only one that was deserted. Whenever I saw Gratien, he was busy marketing a gadget that couldn't be sold, working on a movie that would never be produced, or a real-estate deal that never materialized. He taught me that failure can be more interesting than success. On the rare occasions when he did conclude a duel, he was unabe to collect his commission. His flaw was that he was physically incapable of asking for anything for himself. He lived on promises, while considering it normal that they would never be kept. He is my favorite Gramont because he understands the fragility of existence. When he was twelve, after a lovely summer day at Vallière with my father and my grandmother, he said: "Let's stop a moment and think, because we may never again know such happiness."

The range of Gratien's life has been broader than the rest of the family's. He has avoided the middle register, and those who know him well know that his life has been adventurous, that he has gone from thresholds of great pain to thresholds of intense pleasure, while always keeping his vision of life ironic. Now in his early sixties, he has retired to the South of France. No more get-rich-quick schemes, no more three-star restaurants and all-night bridge games. Gratien says he has found the secret of happiness. "I have eliminated everything," he says, "desire, activity, ambition, responsibility, enthusiasm (very tiring, enthusiasm), passion, jealousy, friendship. I vegetate."

The latest and present duke, Antoine XIII, was born in 1907 and inherited the presidency of the optics company founded by his father. He also keeps up the charity foundation set up by his mother. Such is the life of a dutiful elder son: To maintain what his parents founded. He goes to Vallière out of a sense of duty, for its days of splendor are forever gone. Never again will musicians play for fifty weekend guests; never will the hussars of Senlis be asked to take minor roles in the annual play. I am not sure there are any hussars left in Senlis. Today, Vallière, with its vast halls and high-ceilinged tapestried drawing rooms, is a drain on the family fortune. Its future probably lies in the hands of a real-estate developer.

In the meantime, Antoine XIII has done what he could to make Vallière pay for itself. The woods bring a small income, as does the right to fish in its ponds and streams. The biggest income producer, however, is a track rented by Simca to test its automobiles. Antoine is open to any new idea, short of opening the castle to the public, à l'Anglaise. In 1949, Antoine surprised those who said he would never marry by taking Odile de Lenoncourt as his wife. She likes to do things differently. She insists, for instance, on driving a car with a right-hand steering wheel in Paris, and curses all the other drivers for their wrongheadedness. Beneath her gruff exterior, she is a woman of warmth and generosity. She has a son, also named Antoine, the future Antoine XIV, who, when I last saw him, wanted to be a fireman when he grew up.

Antoine has three younger brothers, two of them identical twins, and a sister. One of the twins, Jean, is a talented interior decorator. The other, Henri, was commercial director for the candid camera business founded by his father and since discontinued. Both of them, while not wanting to live in Vallière itself, have, in a fine display of atavism, built homes on its grounds, smaller, satellite castles in its shadow. The twins are different in temperament, but their lives seem in many ways symmetrical. They own twin buildings, numbers four and six in Paris' rue d'Astorg, and they married sisters who were not far apart in age. With the years, their faces have taken on different casts, like two caryatids unevenly worn by varying winds. Henri has always reminded me of Louis XIII, who would draw a reluctant courtier into an alcove and say: *"Ennuyons-nous."** But he is the most generous of all the Gramonts. The other son, Charles, did not have to build a house on the grounds of Vallière, for he inherited from his Greffulhe mother the splendid castle of Boisboudran, renowned for its hunts. He rents the hunt to keep it up, but since he has no children, it seems doubtful that it can remain in the hands of one person. Charles' sister, Corisande, inherited her father's scientific gifts and slightly rasping voice. She is a physicist of some repute and works in the family optical works.

In this chronicle, I have mentioned only the most important members of the family among the dead, and only those whose lives are more or less rounded among the living. I have left out the younger generation, including my two brothers, for they are still in the process of becoming the men and women who will someday be written about. My own position in the family is one of distance. I have been geographically distant, nomadic where they were sedentary, repeatedly transplanted where they were rooted in their inherited properties, unattached where they were bound by the conventions of their class. I was born a displaced person, in the multinational cow pasture called Switzerland (my father had quixotically moved to Geneva for a year to sell Bugatti cars), and I was reared, a creature but not a victim of family circumstance, in Spain, Belgium, France, Mexico, Canada, and the United States. Over the years, I have been able to convert my sense of rootlessness from a feeling of being at home nowhere to a feeling of being at home everywhere. There is something to be said for air plants. They require little care. Their roots are not in the ground, but inside themselves. They are the most nearly self-sufficient of all living things, since they obtain their nourishment from the most available of all natural resources. And they travel well. I have also been distant from the family's center of power and wealth, the eldest son of a younger son. My grandfather had married three times, and there were children from all three marriages. I was a

---

* Let us bore ourselves.

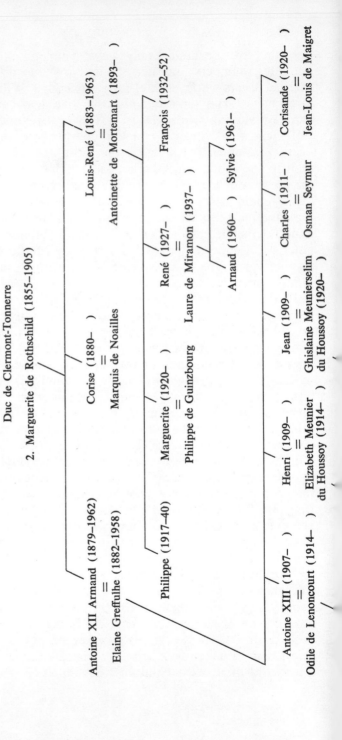

ANTOINE XI AGÉNOR (1851–1925)
=
1. Isabelle de Beauveau (1852–75)

Elizabeth de Gramont (1875–1954)
=
Duc de Clermont-Tonnerre

2. Marguerite de Rothschild (1855–1905)

Corise (1880–   )
=
Marquis de Noailles

Louis-René (1883–1963)
=
Antoinette de Mortemart (1893–   )

Antoine XII Armand (1879–1962)
=
Elaine Greffulhe (1882–1958)

Philippe (1917–40)

Marguerite (1920–   )
=
Philippe de Guinzbourg

René (1927–   )
=
Laure de Miramon (1937–   )

François (1932–52)

Arnaud (1960–   )   Sylvie (1961–   )

Henri (1909–   )
=
Elizabeth Meunier
du Houssoy (1914–   )

Jean (1909–   )
=
Ghislaine Meunierselim
du Houssoy (1920–   )

Charles (1911–   )
=
Osman Seymur

Corisande (1920–   )
=
Jean-Louis de Maigret

Antoine XIII (1907–   )
=
Odile de Lenoncourt (1914–   )

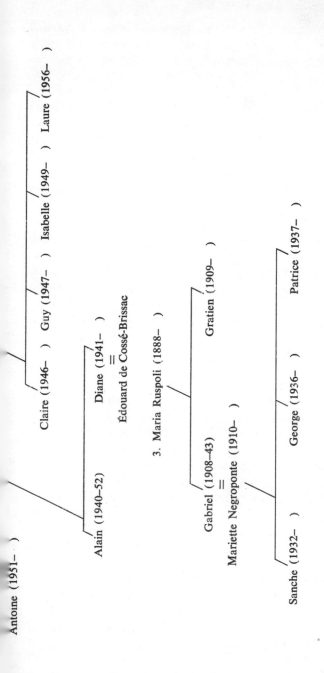

Note: In this chart, = means married to, and / means son or daughter of.

twig on the lowest branch. The title of duke and whatever power lay within the family were as distant from me as the grapes from La Fontaine's fox. Wealth had been injected into the family via my grandfather's marriage with a Rothschild. Again, I had been by-passed.

While pondering the injustices of birth, I once drew up a chart to calculate, in my own version of *Kind Hearts and Coronets*, how many of my relatives I would have to do away with to come into the title of duke, with its still-resounding echoes of glory and vast properties. The chart listed the last four generations of Gramonts, going back to my grandfather Antoine XI Agénor, and traced his offspring through his three wives. It came out like this:

It was apparent from this chart that to press my claim to the leadership of the Gramont family, I would have to dispose of nine male members who preceded me in lineage. Four sparrows huddled on the highest branch, the four sons of Antoine XII Armand, Antoine XIII, Henri and Jean (the twins), and Charles (who liked to hunt). None of them had any conspicuous vices through which they might be laid low. But their occupations and hobbies could be turned into the agents of their demise. Henri, for instance, was a golfer. Every weekend he sliced his way across the golf course at Vallière. I have never been able to abide golf. Why spoil a good walk? But it would be a simple matter to hide in the bushes, replace the ball he was bound to send into the rough with one filled with nitroglycerin, and run for cover as he connected with it, and his body was scattered like a handful of flung bran across the green. I could hear his golf cronies discussing him in the locker room: I told him not to use a six iron on that shot.

Antoine was less of a sportsman, more of an indoor man. He was, however, a gifted amateur painter. I had once admired a pair of Braque lemons in his living room, only to be told that they were a copy by Antoine. He preferred to copy famous painters, rather than develop a style of his own. I remembered that Clare Boothe Luce had been poisoned by ingredients in the painted wood roses in the ceiling of her ambassadorial bedroom in Rome, and I discovered that paints could be mixed with strong asphyxiants which, in a closed room—and Antoine was terrified of drafts—would dispose of the artist in less than an hour. He would be found crumpled over his easel, an unfinished brushstroke dribbling off the canvas in untidy drops.

As for Charles, he had inherited Boisboudran from his Greffulhe mother and kept up the tradition of the hunt. Nothing was easier to arrange than a hunting accident. They were commonplace, part of the day's fun. As the beaters drove the game toward the path in the forest where the hunters waited in a line with their double-barreled shotguns crooked under their arms, the first hare would leap across the path and the firing would begin. When the volley ended, two crusty hunters toting up their kills would come upon Charles' body. "He's mine," one would claim. "I beg your pardon," the other one would say, "but he was nowhere near you. He was right in my line of fire." And on they would argue, as hunters will, about poor Charles. It would be a fitting death. Who knows? He might even end up with his head mounted in someone's living room. Guests would admire the trophy and ask: But where are the antlers?

Jean was an interior decorator, a profession with few hazards. His specialty was doors that looked like paneled bookshelves, with the spines of bound books pasted on for realistic effect. I would ask him to decorate my apartment. It would be appropriate to find him strangled in the silk cords of a curtain. Or else he could be impaled on his shears while falling from a stool he had climbed on to regulate one of the indirect lighting fixtures he was famous for.

That left, among the adults, my uncle Gratien, my father's only full brother, and my cousin René (son of Armand's younger brother Louis-René), with whom I shared memories of a misspent youth. I was extremely fond of both of them, but can a man's purpose be swayed by fondness? I thought of all the great ships of enterprise that might have foundered in the shoals of affection, but had sailed on to reach their destination. Gratien and René would have to go like the rest, and I would weep at their funerals, as they would have wept at mine. They were, alas, all too easy to dispose of. Gratien suffered agony from gout, but like Oscar Wilde, he could resist everything but temptation. It would be expensive, but if I shepherded him regularly to two- and three-star restaurants, and if I sent him the bottles of *cognac, poire, framboise, mirabelle*, and *armagnac* which he did not have the willpower to leave unopened, he would soon become a victim of his palate, his liver, and his gout.

René had once been a tireless ladies' man. I was with him on one occasion when he followed a pretty girl into a first-class compartment in the subway. We had to pay a fine because we had second-class tickets. In those days, he was always ready to make sacrifices in the pursuit of love. But marriage had on him the same effect saltpeter has on the inmates of French boarding schools. He became a man of ordered and regular habits, and transferred his passion to books. The femmeophile became a bibliophile. While leafing through a history of the Borgias, I found several examples of books transformed into lethal weapons. One concealed a small pistol that fired when the book was opened. Another had the tip of a tiny pin dipped in poison protruding from the binding. For a man who hunted down rare books with the same frenzy he had once employed to chase women, I thought there could be no happier death than to be poisoned or shot by one of his *plein veau* eighteenth-century first editions.

That disposed of the adults. But there was another problem I had conveniently set aside until I had to face it—the children. Jean and Antoine had teen-age sons, and René had a son about the same age as my own. When my mission had been in the planning stage, abstract and on paper, I thought I could summon the necessary callousness to dispose of all the Gramonts who stood in my way. But now, when it came to actually carrying out the murders of children, I found my resolution faltering. The death of adults is often a relief to those around them, and even to themselves. It is that much less garbage to be picked up by the sanitation department. But the death of children is an unfair interruption in the fermentation process.

I began to wonder whether I could go through with it, which led to the following rationalization: The Gramont youngsters were not healthy, they were thin-blooded and overbred, they would disappear from natural causes without my interference. A peritonitis here, a pneumonia there, an Asian flu epidemic to flush out and carry off the phlegm-coughing, hollow-chested, sparrow-shouldered stragglers who lingered on in this world against the advice of their doctors. Yes, I could count on the biological inability of these *fin-de-siècle* remainders to resist illnesses and germs. I could sit on the sidelines and watch them float softly down from the family tree like dead leaves and be raked away.

To help me decide whether to take an active part in the extinction of my male relatives, I visited, as I would have visited an oracle, the Gramont castle of Bidache. But no counsel came from those pitted, moss-covered, fallen stones. The drawbridge was permanently down. The great Louis XIV gateway was a yawning frame, leading into a weed-invaded courtyard and a dungeon littered with rusty sardine cans, shriveled condoms, and empty wine bottles. Two mullioned windows with broken pediments had been reassembled and flanked the gate, forever open to the Béarn sky. Had I expected this heap of rubble to summon forth a ghost who, like Hamlet's father, would tell me what to do? Bidache was mute and dispiriting, the land it lay on fallow, returned to nature, burrowed by moles.

Across the road from the castle stood the commons, where I would spend the night, fed and attended to by an elderly housekeeper whose cheerful disposition was based in equal parts on the ample cellar and the rareness of the family's visits to its damaged seat. The commons, a low building of substantial yellow stone, remained habitable, while the castle, with its broken towers and parapets and crenels, was a vacant lot littered with parts that needed assembling, like a children's kit for a medieval castle. I suppose there is a lesson there somewhere, I thought later that evening, when, drowsy with Jurançon wine and *Piperade*, I climbed the stairs to my room, carrying a candle protected by a glass shield: The survival and endurance of humble folk, the caretaker's cottage intact and the castle ruined, a populist morality tale. It had been an accident, really. The fire started by the embezzling administrator in 1796 had not spread to the commons. It was as simple as that. A hot brick had been placed in my bed to warm it, the commons still being, in the matter of modern comfort, entrenched in the eighteenth century.

I quickly dropped off to sleep in the brick-warmed bed, but was awakened some time later by odd sounds downstairs, which seemed to my sleep-numbed brain like the rumble a troop of cavalry makes as it prepares for battle. I lit the candle, put on the white terry-cloth robe that hung as standard equipment on the back of my door, and went down to take a look. I checked the ground-floor windows. They were all closed. I opened one. It was not a windy night. The noise resumed. It seemed to be coming from the alcove off the dining room, a small paneled study furnished in the Béarn country style, with two eighteenth-century salt chairs, a wooden-framed sofa upholstered with straw, and a buffet of light wood with carved garlands on each of its two doors, and a white marble top. On the walls hung engravings of Gramonts of different periods, all looking remarkably alike, with thick silken mustaches, cupid-bow lips, and sleepy, slightly protruding eyes. They were lined up like soldiers in formation, in parade uniforms, their chests studded with Croix du Saint-Esprit and other royal decorations, and they seemed to be staring sternly at me, like judges. Again I heard the rattling, this time behind me, and I wheeled around expecting to see one of the engravings come to life and challenging me to a duel for having disturbed their peace, but there was nothing except disembodied noise. It is tricky to locate sounds; they bounce off walls and pass through solid objects and scurry around corners and play acoustic tricks on you. I continued to hear them, like ten swords rattling in ten scabbards, but I could not pinpoint them, except that they came from somewhere in the small study.

I placed my ear to the wall and slowly made my way around the room. Anyone coming upon me at that moment, a wide-eyed, rumple-haired figure in a terry-cloth robe, holding a candle and slinking along the walls with my cheek pressed against the oak paneling, would surely have thought my senses had deserted me. I tapped on the paneling, but there was no resonance. For the sake of thoroughness, I pulled out the buffet in order to auscultate that side of the room as well. The rattling now seemed louder, like the sound of approaching troops. It gave me the uncanny feeling that I was in some Flemish valley and that on the top of a hill, on the horizon line, there had suddenly appeared a dark line of horsemen. Again I knocked, and this time there was a barely perceptible, hollow echo. I ran my fingers along the molding, expecting to find a hidden latch that would spring the panel open, but there was none. I knocked harder, to make sure there was a space behind the panel, and I decided that there are cases where vandalism is justified. I made a mental sign of the cross in gratitude that the most violent thunderstorm could not have disturbed the housekeeper's wine-induced slumber, and I took my candle to the kitchen, where in the back of a drawer I found a hammer and a sharp chisel. It pained me to pierce the fine old paneling, but soon I had gouged out a hole big enough to look through. A space the size of a pantry dumbwaiter had been fitted into the wall and was stacked with folders and what looked like piles of letters.

I broke away enough of the paneling so that I could remove the folders from their hiding place. Once I had emptied the secret compartment, I took another long look, wondering whether I might find the source of the mysterious rattling. Had it been one of my engraved ancestors summoning me across the expanse of lost centuries? I was romantic enough to believe it. Had it been some kitchen noise that I had invested with significance? I was practical enough to believe it. But no explanation was satisfactory, since a glance at the folders proved that the noises had led me to the cache where the prerevolutionary archives of the Gramont family, believed destroyed in the fire of 1796, had been stored for one hundred and seventy-five years.

I carried the treasure to my room in a state of great excitement and spread the folders on the bed. Soon I was yawning again, for family archives are boring stuff, inventories, tax receipts, contracts, land deeds—in the year 1523 sieur Hubert de Montmirail did sell to the comte de Gramont three hectares of land planted with barley, on the edge of the forest known as La Voisine, by the stone wall near the road from Bidache to Puységur, for the sum of two hundred *écus*—that sort of thing. Nothing there would have interested anyone outside the family, I thought; in fact it barely interested me. There were no love letters, or revelations, or accounts of battles. It was then, as I mulled over the disappointing contents of the secret compartment, that I noticed for the first time three notebooks bound in green calf, about the size of a newsmagazine, which had been lying beneath the larger paper folders. Each one was clasped shut with a tiny, intricate, heart-shaped lock. I picked one of the locks with a safety pin, and after some coaxing, it snapped open. The unlined pages of rag paper were covered with a long, narrow, sloping handwriting which the years had turned reddish-brown—it was as if the writing, exposed to air, had rusted.

Except for the annoying practice of writing the letter *s* like the letter *f*, the handwriting was surprisingly legible, and what is more important, sympathetic. By that I mean that I have the same reaction to a handwriting as I have to a face or a voice; some attract and some repel. There are handwritings that reveal personality disorders, or vain and superfluous natures, or announce a love of deceit. In our handwriting we give away secrets that we take great pains to conceal in every other aspect of our public personality. At first glance, the handwriting now before me showed a man who combined the two qualities most appreciated in his own time, intuition and intelligence, the first then thought of as an attribute of the heart, the second as a quality of mind. I liked the man even before studying the contents of the notebooks, for when one studies a handwriting, one is attentive to the shape and spacing of the letters and words, and not to their meaning. On the title page of the first notebook, I saw: "Memoirs of my life and times, to serve for the instruction of future generations, by Anaxagoras de Gramont (1725–   )." The parenthesis was closed, but the date was not filled in. The only thing a memoirist cannot include about himself is the date of his death, which must be added by a survivor. In this case, no one had bothered.

I flipped the pages of the notebooks, raising small puffs of dust as I did so, and soon became convinced that I was in the presence of an exceptional life story. I was struck by the tone of absolute candor. Here was no touched-up portrait, presenting only, like the one-eyed duke of Montefeltro's head by Piero della Francesca, the good profile with the sound eye. This was the whole man, blind spots, warts, blemishes and all, without a trace of false modesty, or even, it seemed at a cursory reading, shame. Here was a man fond of mocking others, but capable of self-mockery, aware of his failings, and aware also that his awareness could neither excuse nor remedy them. Here was a man making his final statement, and disdaining to use it as a platform to justify his life. As I had liked his handwriting, I also liked the style of a man who had never collected sufficient moral capital to become sanctimonious, who made no excuses for himself, and who now seemed to be calling from a hilltop across the valley of time: "Read this, all of you whose lives are a lie, but judge me not, for I have been my own defendant, judge, and jury, and I have passed sentence on myself."

What was most remarkable, my unexpected visitor from the past had written these pages without the slightest thought of publication. My discovery put me in a position to repair this loss to history. I resolved to forget all other preoccupations and devote myself to the publication of the memoirs. I would give up my plans to dispose of the male members of my family, in order to rehabilitate an obscure ancestor. It was not only that I was fascinated by the memoirs and felt that I had been mysteriously elected to bring them to light. It was also, I felt, my responsibility to the international community of scholars, who would now be able to enrich and revise their appreciation of the period thanks to this new material. And finally, it would be a major contribution to eighteenth-century French letters, bound to be, I felt sure, studied in the classrooms of lycées and universities alongside such other great court writers as Madame de Sévigné.

The present edition, the fruit of two years' unremitting labor, was translated by me from the French. I have tried to be faithful to the flavor as well as the meaning of the original. Certain passages that might seem overly explicit about physical love or that use words unacceptable in polite society have been kept by me at the risk of offending delicate readers, for I feel that bowdlerization is a worse sin than impropriety. I have added some explanatory notes for the general reader, in the hope that these memoirs, so crowded with the life and excitement of their times, will not find their appeal limited to specialists. Those scholars interested in consulting the original manuscripts in my possession can make an appointment to do so by writing me in care of my publisher. They must, however, make known their request before June, 1973, at which time the manuscripts will be donated to the Bibliothèque Nationale. I would also like to add that Professor Jean Guerreau, who has taught eighteenth-century French literature at the University of Toulouse for more than twenty years, is preparing a critical study of these memoirs, entitled: *Un Gentilhomme Écrivain à la Cour de Louis XV*.

SANCHE DE GRAMONT

Childhood

I Am Born and Brought Up

I SUPPOSE I should begin with my birth, an event that took place without my being consulted. From that early injustice I believe I learned fairness of mind. Give the other fellow a chance, let him say his prayers before you run him through, to ensure a safe journey to the void from whence we came. I was impatient to arrive in the world, don't ask me why, and my mother gave birth while still in her farthingale. That was near midnight, on the third of April, 1725, ten years after the death of the Sun King. Like Caesar, I was born under Aries, and although I don't hold with astrology, I have on occasion found a resemblance between a man and the animal representation of his birth sign in the zodiac: A Cancer moving sideways, crablike, a Scorpio with a hidden sting, an inoffensive, secretive Pisces, an elusive Capricorn, forever climbing out of reach onto the next rocky ledge. Christ was a Capricorn, and they are always doing the unexpected, such as resurrecting. My private curse is that the ram charges with its head down. Its horns are in position, but it cannot see where it is going.

I was named Anaxagoras after a Greek philosopher my father much admired, probably because he was the only man in history as wrongheaded as himself. Anaxagoras believed that the sun was made of white-hot stone and that the moon was a discarded lump of earth. These notions appealed to my father for their concreteness and simplicity. Anaxagoras was not only wrongheaded but contrary, another quality that endeared him to my father. He wanted no part of the four elements, but insisted that every object was composed of an infinite number of particles, like sand on a beach. My father favored the particle theory as explaining the high percentage of fools to be found on the planet. There had been a mistake in their combination of particles, which were at war with one another, a fact evident from their daily behavior.

While my brothers were given the honest Christian names of

Antoine and Alfred, which conferred automatic membership in the community of their peers, I grew up bearing the burden of an unpronounceable, five-syllable cognomen that made teachers gag and schoolmates jeer. Since it was not included in the royal registry of first names, my father had obtained special dispensation from the archbishop of Bayonne to have me baptized. The dispensation cost him a new slate roof for the archbishopric. It must be said to his credit that on those occasions when his miserliness was at odds with his stubborness, he paid without a grumble.

I grew up pushing my name ahead of me like Sisyphus his rock. The effort had to be repeated with each person I met. Anax what? How do you spell it? In school I had to defend it, as though a maiden's honor, against attempted violations. The only way to avoid being called *ananas** or *gorille* was the promise of a bloody nose for whoever tried it first. To that effect, from the age of nine, I always carried in my pocket a cloth roll of sous, coins small enough to fit in my fist. By the time I was eleven, I had enforced the use of the nickname Ax. It was short and had a cutting edge.

In those days, the notion that children should be taken care of by their parents did not exist. A child's lot was an odd mixture of parental neglect and close supervision. My father showed as much interest in me as in a piece of furniture. I came with the house, although my utility was more debatable than, say, a chair's. At least you could sit on a chair. But what could you do with a curly-haired, monkey-faced, gangling boy, a noise surrounded by dirt? He only noticed me when I interfered with his routine, when I lost the page in his book or mislaid the garden shears when he wanted to trim the roses, or borrowed one of his canes for a musket when he wanted to take a walk. He took scant interest in my schooling, except when my governesses complained about my laziness. On those occasions, he would say: "I can see the asses' ears growing on you, sir."

History, philosophy, and mathematics, however, were to him frivolous pursuits compared with riding, weapons, and fencing. He had me on a horse from the age of five, and often took me out himself on the grounds of the castle, stiff-backed on his roan mare. The first time I fell, my horse having deliberately carried me under trees with low-hanging branches, so that I dropped off to avoid being knocked off, he waited silently as I picked myself up, then

* French for pineapple.

said: "A man must learn to ride well, for a horse is not a courtier; it does not flatter."

He had a soldier's contempt for the court and professed to prefer the trench of a siege to the apartment at Versailles he seldom occupied. He was determined that I should follow in his footsteps, which did not keep him from repeating that I would be a discredit to the family name. I had a terrible time with numbers, for I have always been partial to the tangible, and when I hear six or seven, I want to know, six or seven of what, princesses or piss-pots?

"What is the use?" I asked my father.

"You must know arithmetic to do army drills," he said.

One morning when I was seven, my mother awakened me and said: "An angel has brought you a baby brother. Do you want to see him?"

"I want to see the angel," I replied, expressing a precocious but healthy skepticism.

Several weeks later, as a result of my brother's birth, my mother died. In my eyes, the equation was simple. If my brother had not been brought by the angel, my mother would not be dead. The angel had not done a very good job. I could not see what I had gained in the exchange. I resented my brother's existence. Because of this drooling, wrinkled, goggle-eyed intruder, I had lost a familiar presence.

It was only when my mother was dead that I realized my father had loved her. He had his drawing room and bedroom hung in black. The wide, canopied bed was burned in the garden, and he brought in a military cot, also covered with black material. He said he would remain in mourning for a year, and he did, hardly leaving his room. I remember very little about my mother, except that she was lovely, warm, and kind. I think of her, and her face is blurred, but I see a smile, and forgiving eyes, and a brow incapable of frowning.

She often took my side against my father. When I was caught drinking sacramental wine in the chapel, my father made me copy one hundred times a Latin phrase that said: Of what use is it to know the Christian religion if we live like pagans? My mother wrote most of it herself. It was a curious punishment, for my father had very little use for the Christian religion, and only went to mass on Sundays in Bayonne to keep up appearances. On weekdays a priest came to say mass in the castle chapel, but my father did not attend. One year he scolded the servants for giving the priest wine when he came to preach the Lent sermon. "Beer is good enough for those people," he said. He always referred to the clergy as "those people."

The only emotion I ever saw my father express was anger. He must have felt that to show affection in some way diminished him, and would make him lose forever an essential defense against the world at large. Soon after my mother's death, I came into his study, in itself an act of boldness, and asked: "Why do people die, Papa?"

He grunted, and put down the magnifying glass through which he had been examining some new species of insect he had found in the garden, and he said: "The machine runs down, the mortal coil uncoils, and we are separated from someone we love very dearly— ourselves. And what is more, we never get over it." That was not the answer I had wanted. His avarice extended to a refusal to share his grief.

In later years, I was to come unexpectedly upon new information about my mother, which made me keep revising the image I had of her, like a landscape painted from memory that must be touched up when we see it again. There were areas of my parents' marriage I had never meant to explore. It had never occurred to me that my mother might have had the normal desires of a woman, that she might have been, in situations quite foreign to those in which I customarily saw her, not the maternal Hera but the temptress Astarte. Such possibilities were beyond my imagination.

One evening in Paris, I was invited to the salon of a famous but aging courtesan who had reached the period of her life when, instead of adding to her collection of lovers, she was taking inventory. I had come with a friend and had not been introduced, for she always sat on a sofa by the fire, and one had to wait one's turn to approach her and hear the latest chapter in her anthology. In any case, I was standing behind the sofa and heard her say: "The lady I most admired in my youth was the duchesse de Gramont, the one who married that eternal adjutant Louis, because every time she did it she fainted." I flushed until I imagined I must be the same scarlet as her curtains, and I left lest someone ask me what was wrong. It was a double revelation, to learn the derision in which my father was held for his soldierly ways, and that my mother was passionate.

I told myself that the important thing was not that my mother fainted when she made love, but that she fainted in *his* arms. For again, it was unthinkable, even in an age that defined love as the contact between two epiderms, that my mother had ever been in any arms but his. This blind spot was left over from a childhood conviction that love must always be exclusive. Just as a child had only one mother, he would have only one love to whom he would be true. That seemed to me a rigorously logical proposition. So that when I heard my father refer to his brother's escapades, I stammered, incomprehending: "But I thought he loved Aunt Marie."

"That has nothing to do with it," my father snapped.

Once again, I had been caught underestimating the needs of the human heart. Love was like the pyramids, now rough and porous stone, but once covered with tiles of gold.

I Settle Accounts with Alfred and the Governess

After my mother's death, my younger brother Alfred and I were reared by that hybrid species, part sergeant at arms and part witch, called governesses. My brother Antoine, six years older than myself, was a military cadet who only came home on holidays. My father did not think he had the makings of a military man, for as a boy he could not sleep without a tallow candle in his room. The most flattering thing my father ever told me, which I treasure even though it turned out to be wrong, was: "Antoine will be killed in battle, for you have the look of an heir."

One day when Alfred was not quite two, I came upon him in the small drawing room, momentarily unattended by his governess. There he squatted, his face blank as usual, staring up with its blue china eyes. Within his chubby reach, on a low table, stood a blue Sèvres porcelain vase with an arabesque design, part of a collection much prized by my father. I tipped it over, and it fell almost soundlessly on the carpet and did not break. I took a heavy silver paperweight from a nearby desk and smashed it. It lay in precious pieces on the carpet, a foot away from Alfred, who watched with an interested expression. I ran into the garden, leaving Alfred to be discovered by the governess next to the broken vase. When I returned two hours later, he was still crying, and his face was red from being slapped. It was the perfect crime. He did not have the vocabulary to protest his innocence.

I took Alfred's defense as a way of showing that I was no more than an interested observer. "It's not his fault," I said. "He didn't do it on purpose."

"Clumsiness is no excuse, and there's no excuse for clumsiness," said the governess, who was given to aphorisms of this sort to justify her native cruelty.

Rather than remorse over what I had done, I felt I was testing one of the first principles of life, which distinguishes man from the lower animals. Instead of saying that man is the only reasonable animal, I would venture that he is the only one capable of betrayal. For he is born as the result of the only permissible betrayal, the charming betrayal of love. The first gesture he feels is a slap. When he wants to pull on his nurse's rosebud, he is given a finger or a rattle. And after having been betrayed in this manner a thousand or more times, he emerges from infancy in order to be betrayed in more important matters, by teachers who do not believe what they teach and priests who counterfeit piety, so that he responds by pretending to learn and pretending to believe. It was a principle one had better learn while young. It went along with lying, the child's defense against grown-ups. The lie was my only trump in the parent-child game. For me, as for the ancient Greeks, lying was a virtue. The liar was three times wise, for he knew the truth, he dissimulated it, and he presented the dissimulation of the truth as if it were the truth. Lying was a great help whenever my father made me feel that he could see through me. It made me opaque.

After Alfred's came the turn of the governess. She was a Pomeranian named Martha, with the same foxy muzzle, hairy face, and servile eyes as the dog of the same name. She had been hired for the same qualities an overseer of slaves is chosen on a West Indian plantation. When my face was dirty, she washed it with a pumice stone, giving it a permanently bruised, pinkish glow. She had long fingernails whose points I felt on my arms or in my neck at the most unexpected moments. One of her methods was to immerse my head in a vat of water that was used for laundry, and hold it under until no more bubbles rose to the surface. She would then release her hold, and I would take hungry gulps of air. I hated the dunking more than I hated her, and to this day, I will not allow my head to be covered with water. I resolved to disprove the moral in the La Fontaine fable that says the reason of the strongest is always the best.

One of my mother's treasured possessions had been a sewing box, a wedding present from her mother, containing a solid-gold darning egg. Now that she was dead, my father kept the box on

one of a series of shelves in his bedroom. The shelves were an altar
to her memory, with portraits and drawings, framed letters, favorite books, a well-thumbed missal with holy pictures to mark the
pages, her tortoiseshell comb, her gold *nécessaire*, the silver mirror
that had daily reflected her face, the silver knife with which she
had opened letters, the *toile des Landes* shawl she had worn in the
winter, even a pair of brocaded slippers. It was a veritable museum, and my father let no one come near it. The maids were not
allowed to dust. It was a sacred shrine that no infidel must see, and
he was the only noninfidel.

In any case, one morning after breakfast, when my father was
out riding and Martha was gossiping in the kitchen with the cook,
I went into his room, which in his absence was kept unlocked only
for the hour that its cleaning required, and I took the darning egg
from my mother's sewing box. I went to Martha's room under the
eaves and placed the gold egg in one of the lavender-scented drawers where she kept her clothes, wrapping it in one of her night-
gowns at the bottom of the drawer, so that if she opened it to
remove something she would not feel it. Each day, my father made
a close inspection of all the ex-votos in his shrine, and I knew it
would not be long before he noticed the darning egg's absence.

Less than a hour after he was back from his ride, I heard him
shout from the top of the stairs: "Everybody in the dining room,
on the double. And that means everybody." The maids, the cook,
the gardeners, the coachman, the scullery wench, dog-faced Martha, Alfred, and myself, all assembled in the dining room and
awaited my father's harangue. His voice, punctuated by the whistle
of a riding crop, took on the tone reserved for the eve of great
battles. "All right, you men," he said, forgetting that half of us
were women, "deploy through the house in searching parties, by
twos. I don't want to see any malingering. Continue the operation
until it is found. Dis-missed!"

The cook, a large woman whom my father did not actively
dislike, owing to her obsequiousness, had the audacity to ask:
"Begging your pardon, your lordship, but what are we meant to be
looking for?"

"You know perfectly well," my father shot back, and stormed off.

The servants went off by twos, the gardeners together, the upstairs maid with the downstairs maid, the cook with the coachman,
and bilious Martha holding little Alfred by the hand. I paired off
with Lisette, the pimply-faced scullery maid, whose body had

raced ahead of her mind in attaining maturity. She was four years
older than I was. At ten, I had already felt pleasant stirrings,
particularly in the morning. I had mentioned these to the family
confessor, more out of curiosity than in need of absolution, and
had been told that sleeping on my stomach was sinful. Once I had
watched my father separate a pair of coupled greyhounds. "They
are having a fight," he explained, but I knew better. Lisette's bright-
red mouth was always moist. She constantly passed her tongue
over her lips, which she let me kiss in exchange for the cake and
candy I was able to bring her, sometimes stealing Alfred's portion
from his afternoon *goûter** tray. Once, I found a small box of
chocolate-covered cherries in the music room, on the lid of the
harpsichord, and offered them to Lisette if she would show me her
breasts. She led me into the pantry and unbuttoned her linen
blouse and shook her torso and they came tumbling out of their
nest, full and high and alive with her breathing. She laughed at my
gaping face and said, "They're nice, aren't they?" as though talking about something that did not belong to her, something she had
seen in a shop. I tried to touch them but she slapped my hand and
said, "Down with your paws, you're too young."

I had picked Lisette because we were already, in a mild way,
conspirators. I did not trust her, for our dealings up to then had
shown that she was guided by a narrow conception of her own
interests, but I knew I could rely on her lack of imagination. As
the searching parties fanned out, looking behind chairs and under
beds for whatever it was that my father had neglected to tell them,
Lisette yawned and said: "What a waste of time. Have you got any
money on you?"

I happened to have a silver crown my father had given me for
placing third in a children's steeplechase the week before. Astonishment at his generosity had kept me from spending it. I dug into
my pocket and held the gleaming coin in my open palm. To her, it
must have represented a month's wages, and I thought I saw the
pupils of her eyes dilate, the way a cat's do. "Let's pretend to be
looking and find someplace private," she said, "and I'll let you
look at them again." I was not about to content myself with mere
looking in exchange for the princely sum at my disposal, and I
bargained for more substantial advantages. "Oh, all right, you
dirty little urchin," she said.

---

* The *goûter* is a French version of high tea.

I looked offended and said, "It was your idea," making as though to walk away, but she pulled me back and said, "Come on, don't be so thin-skinned." I suggested that since the other members of the searching party had concentrated on the ground floor, we should go under the eaves. I led her to an alcove near Martha's mansard room, and there I felt at will of what is often referred to, in those licentious books I was later to read with one hand, as the "milky globes." Until that moment, I had thought that the sense of touch was a poor cousin to the other four, but now that I was learning to make some practical use of it, it was redeemed. I wondered at the change in the nipple when I touched it. That tiny bit of stiffening flesh established, in a way more real than anything I had yet experienced, the fact of my manhood. Lisette, annoyed that her breasts, with a will of their own, were responding to the fumbling of a ten-year-old boy, said, "Come on, we haven't got all day." She snatched the silver crown from my pocket and buttoned herself up.

As we passed Martha's room, I said: "Did you know that Martha keeps dirty books in her room? Have a look."

Lisette giggled, put her finger to her lips, and opened Martha's door. She rummaged through the dresser drawers, saying, "Oh, that Martha, what a hypocrite, she looks as though you could give her absolution without confession," and when she reached the bottom drawer, her hand stopped and she said, "Here, what's this?"

"What?" I asked.

"I feel something hard under all these stiff nightshirts she wears," she said.

"Pull it out and let's see what it is," I suggested.

She extracted the gold darning egg from its linen nest and stared at it.

"That's from my mother's sewing box," I said with a show of great surprise. "My father keeps it in his room with a lot of other stuff of hers and won't let anyone touch it. It's probably what everyone's looking for."

"My heavens," Lisette said, "and to think I found it, who wasn't even looking."

"You'll get a reward for this," I told her. "Take it back to him on your own, without attracting any attention. If I go with you, you'll have to share the reward."

She didn't have to be told twice. She ran down the stairs two at a time, like a child who has found a chocolate egg in an Easter hunt.

That evening, when Martha came to draw the curtains in my room and blow out the candle by my bed, her pale eyes were red from crying. She said nothing until she had almost shut the door of my room, and then whispered through the crack: "Someday you will be punished, you horrid boy." Her admonition did not keep me from sleeping the sleep of the just. The next day she was gone, and her name was never mentioned again. As for Lisette, she was so handsomely rewarded by my father that she had enough for a small dowry, and three months later she married a sailor who took her to La Rochelle. I felt that I deserved to be godfather of her twelfth child.

I Pursue Knowledge

I continued my schooling, treating knowledge as I treated butterflies, seizing their wings with two fingers and then letting them fly off, so that they left only a thin layer of yellow powder on my fingertips. My conscience was so rubbery you could bounce it like a ball. At the age of twelve I hid a copy of Aretino inside my history book, and wondered, not at the miraculous way Saint Geneviève saved Paris from the Huns, but whether it was physically possible to enjoy the lady depicted in the illustration, who rolled along the floor, holding two little handles on either side of a wheel, and whose spread legs were lifted by a standing man in what Aretino called the wheelbarrow position.

On Sundays I pretended to be sick in order to miss mass. I never had much faith; all I had to do was look around me, and see that in a society founded on injustice and greed, where the poor died of malnutrition and the rich of indigestion, there was no room for divine Providence. I wanted no part of a God who could allow a single child to be beaten to death by a drunken father. I lost my faith at the age of twelve, in the same way that others have had theirs confirmed, in a vision. I was sitting under an oak when a strange light appeared before me, blinding me with a brightnses that outshone the sun's, and a voice spoke and resounded in my head, and what it said was: Nothingness. The voice spoke to me of the void in so convincing a manner that disbelief became for me an act of faith. I have an absolute conviction that God does not exist. It is not that I am dissatisfied with the various proofs of His existence, whether Cartesian or Aquinan; it is that I have an intense and positive sense of His nonexistence. I know in my heart of hearts that God is a hoax man has had to make up so that he can hope for other cards than those he has been dealt.

I knew my father had me earmarked for a military career, for I spent more time with the riding master than with my books. One morning he called me into his room, where I found him sitting in an attitude of profound concentration on his *chaise percée*. This chaise had been a wedding present from his practical joker of a brother. Its sides were made to look like bookcases, and the leather spines of the books had titles like *Travels in the Lowlands*, *Styles in Stools from Medieval Times to the Present*, and *The Final Push*. My father, mounted on the chaise in his wrinkled nightshirt, his fist filled with tow, his powdered wig askew, looked like the disheveled ruler of some kingdom of the mad. I tried to keep a straight face as he asked me: "Well, sir, what do you want to be in life?"

The question was rhetorical, since I would have no say in the matter, and I replied without hesitation: "Amusing."

He choked and coughed and ranted about fops and courtiers, and said it was not enough to be well born. "Some of the best names in France end up on the wheel," he warned.

My father straddled two centuries, having been born in the seventeenth, the age of faith, in which it was held that men of different religious beliefs could not live peacefully in the same kingdom, and having died in the eighteenth, which somewhat presumptuously placed itself under the wing of the goddess reason. From the century of his birth, he retained a negative faith, for he believed only in the punitive powers of an Old Testament God, wrathful and vindictive, the God who brought drought and defeat. Heaven, populated by fat cherubs sitting on violet clouds, did not seem real to him, but he could feel the flames burning the sinners in hell. Hell was easier to believe in because it was more convincingly presented. The devil always has the best lines. From the century of his death, coexisting uneasily with the fire and brimstone, he derived an interest in science, in experimental knowledge and observable phenomena. For men of that time, the laws of nature seemed a treasure chest to which the keys had finally been found. It was theirs to open, and to marvel at the glittering precious stones therein.

My father threw himself on knowledge as the daughters of Lycomedes threw themselves on Odysseus' jewels. He once spent six months locked in his study, emerging only once a day for his meal, and sleeping on a cot. No one knew what he was up to. It developed that he was dissecting a bee's intestines, with instruments so tiny he had to look at them through a magnifying glass. Those were the times when he was happiest. "I have found a fly whose offspring are at birth the same size as their mother," he told me, "and an insect composed of a chain of rings hooked one into the other. I saw the hooks. When they talk about miracles, that is what they are talking about."

I nodded, for disagreement was a provocation, but I knew that he was pursuing science with the same visionary gleam as those explorers of old who had sought the Golden Fleece. Couched in the new language of scientific evidence was an equally impossible quest. He wanted to find proof for everything, but proof was elusive, proof was in hiding because of its debts. Even then, I knew that proof is a rascal who owes everyone, who has given promissory notes by the thousands to well-intentioned men like my father who spend the rest of their lives trying to collect.

There occurred a period of several years when Europe was at peace. My father's services at the head of his guards' regiment were not required, and he was able to spend all his time at home, pursuing what he intended as his great work, his personal contribution to progress, which would make him remembered wherever scholars gathered: The squaring of the circle. After laboring three years to discover what had eluded the great minds of the past, from Euclid to Copernicus, he sent his memoir to the Royal Academy of Sciences, asking that following their scrutiny it should be shown to the king. He was so sure of his demonstration that he left ten thousand francs with a notary and announced in the gazettes that the money would be given to "whoever can find a chink in my armor." Luckily, no one took advantage of the offer.

My father's memoir is brief enough to be quoted here as a tribute to his memory, for surely he never cared for his lands or his family as intensely as he did for the proposition that the circle could be squared.

"PREAMBLE: Knowing full well that a man who reveals his predecessors to have been in error is branded a heretic, and that Hippasus of Metapontum, who first made public the theory of incommensurability between the side and the diagonal of the square, perished in a shipwreck, for, having revealed a secret of nature, he was destroyed by nature, lashed to the waves as Prometheus was delivered to a vulture, I nonetheless make bold to present to the distinguished members of the Royal Academy of Sciences, in the hope that this work will fall beneath the gaze of our beloved monarch, a modest demonstration concerning the two fundamental geometric shapes, the square and the circle.

"THE SQUARE: The square, some will say, is monotonous, with its four equal sides, like a story endlessly repeated. But to a child who cuts along the diagonals of a cardboard square to make a windmill it is not monotonous, nor is it to a chess player who uses a square board, nor is it to a navigator, who must know the four cardinal points, or to a farmer who depends on the four seasons and the four phases of the moon. Four, it will be readily perceived, is the ideal number, comprising the number of limbs, the number of letters in the name of the first man, and the golden number of the human anatomy, for a man's breadth with his arms outstretched is equal to his height, thereby forming the base and height of an ideal square. The square is found in nature, in iron pyrites. The organic growth of certain conch shells, as well as the arrangement of sunflower seeds, follows the curve of the logarithmic spiral that derives from the square. My ancestors wore a silver disk with a square cut into it as an amulet against the plague. And what is the infinite but a square without angles?

"THE CIRCLE: The square, then, is human, but the circle is divine, eternal, without beginning or end. God is a circle. The universe is a circle. The scheme of life is a circle. From a circle, one can trace a polygon with an infinite number of sides. A circle is orderly, it is always in place, it has no right and wrong side, all the points of its circumference are at equal distance from its center. The human species instinctively follows this inclination to circular order, as in the circular theater of the Greeks, or the way spectators watching street jugglers spontaneously form in a circle. The circle is also ideal, for no one can draw a perfect circle, and magical, as witness the magic powers of the ring and the immunity conferred by the halo. The square is static, but the circle is all motion, whether in the workings of a clock, the wheels of a carriage, or the course of the planets. The signs of the zodiac are represented in a circle, for life itself is an eternal renewal.

"DEMONSTRATION: For centuries, sometimes without knowing it, man has been trying to square the circle, but has never succeeded. In the Nile valley, when yearly floods erased the marks the peasants made to indicate the boundaries of their properties, geometry helped redefine them, for they knew the shapes of their lands. Areas bounded by curved lines, however, were impossible to redefine, so the Egyptians tried to convert those curved boundaries into straight lines, making this the first known attempt to square the circle, for if a square with the same area as a circle could be drawn, by measuring the area of the square you would also know the area of the circle. This, then, is the first proposition: To describe a square perfectly equal to a given circle.

"The second proposition is that in geometry, a whole has two distinct parts, geometrically and numerically equal to the whole. This leads us to a law of organic growth: From a square one can obtain a rectangle by lowering the diagonal between the center of the base and an opposite corner onto the prolongation of the base. Attach to this rectangle another square based on the longer side to obtain another rectangle. Continue to attach squares to the longer side of the rectangle and you obtain a figure composed of squares making a spiral form around the pole O, which is the point of intersection of the diagonals of the successive rectangles. If we draw a curve through the points of intersection of these diagonals with the successive squares, the curve will be a logarithmic spiral, an imitation of nature by science, for it is the very same curve that is found in conch shells.

"From this proposition we can advance to the third and final proposition, the definition of the squaring of the circle, which will appear (oh, marvel of science) to be the real shape of the earth. For as has already been shown, a circle is a curve which, when completed, will pass through any point in the square. Since this reasoning applies to any point in the square, the logical conclusion is that the curve must fill the whole of the square. Those mathematicians who thought it was axiomatic that every curve have a tangent committed the cardinal sin, I am not afraid to say it, for this is a curve that does not admit tangents at any point, since it fills up the entire area of the square, and for that reason can only be represented by a square black patch. This, then, is the solution to a problem that has baffled mathematicians for centuries, and which will have innumerable applications, particularly in the military field, in the computation of ballistics tables. As a soldier and a Frenchman, I am proud to present this discovery to my king and country."

My father was certain that he would be hailed as the new Pythagoras, and the reply that came from the Royal Academy of Sciences, after four months of anxious waiting, was the keenest disappointment of his life.

"Having given your report two readings," this distinguished body wrote, "the Academy has noticed several manifestly false propositions, others that are unintelligible, and a frequent abuse of terms. We confess we are baffled by your demonstration. A curve inside a square that fills up a square and can only be represented by a black patch, is, in the unanimous opinion of the members, another square, while a curve that has no tangent belongs in the realm of spiritualism, not geometry. The Academy has concluded that the problem of the quadrature of the circle still remains to be solved."

The gloom that fell upon the household when the news came compared with the period of mourning for my mother, and would doubtless have ended with my wearing black for my father had it continued. I felt sorry for the old boy, whose faith in his ideas was forever shaken. I resolved never to believe anything too fervently, as a good soldier must always keep an escape route open. Fortunately, the peace that had descended on Europe like a pall ended abruptly when the Fifteenth Louis made known his claim to several thousand acres of barren Flanders fields, which no one could have wanted except to dispute another's right to them, and my father was summoned from his melancholy to lead his regiment in a campaign against the English. It was one of those wars the king periodically started to relieve the boredom of life at court and impress a recent mistress with his heroic behavior on top of a hill overlooking the battlefield, out of range of enemy shot.

I Fight My First Duel and Almost Lose My Virginity

At the time, when I saw him leave, in his blue velvet guards' uniform, with the scrolled gold braid of a general's rank on the sleeves, waving his plumed hat as he galloped down the driveway between the rows of elms, followed by the six Bayonne soldiers who constituted his personal guard, I heard stirring martial music rustle through the leaves. I had reached the age of thirteen, the hinge of childhood. I still played with toy soldiers, and as news of the campaign reached me, I deployed my little painted lead figures on the floor of the music room, the red-coated troops of George II advancing across the parquet lowlands ever closer to our own. At the same time, I felt ashamed to be on my hands and knees moving my miniature combatants when I knew that lads my own age were in real battles as drummer boys. It weighed heavily upon me that at the advanced age of thirteen, only three years younger than the great Turenne when he had been named a general, I had accomplished neither of the two main rites of manhood. I had never fought a duel or enjoyed the favors of a woman. I resolved to put those matters right at the earliest opportunity.

It may seem archaic in the enlightened eighteenth century still to be talking of duels, it may even seem irrational to give personal honor such importance, but to me honor is a mixture of conscience and pride stronger than faith or love. That is a damaging admission to make, I know, but it is a true one. I have never tried to excuse it; it is one of my failings, like taking snuff. Whoever insults me marks his superiority over me and must be challenged. It is not that I like to fight; it is that I am physically unable to disregard provocation. The Biblical injunction to turn the other cheek is not in my nature. Having proffered the first cheek is already too much to bear. I have fought my share of duels, because no tribunal is the guardian of a man's honor, and, in doing so, I have saved myself the cost of lawyers and the delays of court procedures. What is more, duels are seldom mortal. Death is usually the result of clumsiness, for killing an adversary is not important; it is showing him that you are the better man that counts. A man must prove in a duel that he is not what he is accused of being, just as in the days of antiquity suspects were thrown into an arena with a lion or made to walk over hot coals to prove their innocence of a crime.

I must have fought fifty duels in my time, and I learned something about bravery and something about strategy. Bravery has nothing to do with physical strength, and shows up in the most unlikely candidates. I once crossed swords with a well-known pederast who had made a disobliging remark about my father and whom I provoked by saying: "I know you are accustomed to turning your back on gentlemen." Despite his rouged cheeks and mincing ways, he fought like a tiger, and ran me through the shoulder after one of my sword thrusts at his neck was deflected by an amber necklace he was wearing.

The strategy I learned, at the expense of a bullet in the thigh, was the importance of being the one who is challenged, for whoever does the challenging must give the other fellow the choice of weapons, and a duel can be won or lost right there. The basic lack of fairness in this system is that the man who provokes the duel with an insult and is challenged has the choice of weapons. Whereas the man whose sense of honor forces him to make the challenge in the face of an insult loses all initiative, even though a duel may have been the furthest thing from his mind. The only way to avoid challenging and thereby retain the choice of weapons is to reply to an insult with a denial rather than with a direct challenge. Say someone calls you a sniveling, cowardly whoremonger, you reply by saying: "You lie like a villain," which is not a counterinsult, since it does not directly accuse the man of being a villain, but only compares his behavior to that of a villain. His only recourse is then either to lose face or challenge you, giving you the choice of weapons. For someone like myself, who has never been able to put the bullet where he puts his eye, and therefore has a marked preference for rapiers, the choice is essential. It is therefore preferable to provoke the duel with a man whom you are destined to fight by insulting him before he has a chance to insult you.

The insult, I may say, is the easiest and most satisfying part of a duel, as it so often flows effortlessly from the lips, with exactly the right blend of contempt and indifference. Those unfamiliar with dueling are amazed at how little it takes. Forgetting the name of a man one knows is enough—"Pray be good enough to remind me of your name." An accusation of illegitimacy, a taunt about a physical defect, almost anything will do. There are of course degrees. It is far worse to call a man a traitor, which is an offense against the honor of his country, than a cuckold, which concerns only himself and his wife. Cuckoldry, in fact, has become so widespread that it has ceased to count as an insult. Call a man a cuckold and he may laugh in your face and ask you who is not. It is like calling someone a subject of the king or a member of the human race.

In my youth, I sought out duels, for I was no taller than the average, which made me prompt to prove my physical prowess, and I was a Gascon, which made me the butt of regional jokes and caused me to develop a touchiness to slights that were often imaginary. Gascons are known as quarrelsome, and if I was going to be poured into the Gascon mold, then I would be quarrelsome. In those days, when I first came to Paris, I would fight over whether a man had a hair more or less on his mustache, or whether his hat was worn at a certain angle, or whether he had coughed in the street. There were also more serious reasons. Once a man claimed that my mistress had no pubic hair. How did he know? I once fought over the respective merits of La Fontaine and Corneille, in defense of the author of the fables, for I have always liked stories about animals. The ground was wet, my adversary slipped, and he

literally impaled himself on my rapier. We did our best to save
him, but the loss of blood was too great, and his last words to me
were: "Is it possible that I am dying in the prime of my life for an
author I have never read and would not have understood if I
had?"

In any case, at thirteen, I was determined to fight my first duel,
and I knew that I would find a reason. My older brother Antoine
was home on one of his irregular visits, for he had as little fondness
for life in a country castle as he did for my father's alternate
silences and outbursts. He had recently married and was busy in
Paris spending his wife's dowry on gifts for actresses and champagne suppers with oysters brought at great expense, on ice, from
the salty beds of Marennes, to nourish his male vigor. He came to
spend a week with us, in my father's absence, to try and sell his
inherited share of a provincial tax on wine bottles to the merchants
of Bayonne. As the eldest son, he would inherit the peerage, and
would probably have sold that too if he could, for money burned a
hole in his pocket, and no matter how much he had, it was never
enough. He was always full of plans that did not work out, like a
man churning water to make butter. That was not my concern,
however, and I got along with him, because he did not have one of
those personalities with separate drawers that open one under the
other; he was all of a piece, hewn from a single block of wood.

The family motto, *Soy lo que soy*, inherited from a distant Spanish ancestor of limited imagination, suited him perfectly, for he
would never be anything else than what he was, rough-edged,
bluff, even-tempered, pleasant drunk or sober, irresponsible with
money but totally without malice, like a dog who takes the food
from one's plate if one leaves it within his reach, and whom one
cannot punish because he does not know any better, and one
should not have tempted him. He hated the court, claiming that he
suffered a physical deformity that prevented him from bending at
the waist, and he was only happy with his social inferiors, tavern
keepers, cardplayers, minor artists, Pont-Neuf jugglers, all the
dubious marginal types who wore down the Paris sidewalks in
search of a quick fortune and never knew at breakfast how they
would pay for dinner. They were his drinking companions, the
only sort he wanted, and there was more than one tavern in Paris
where his name had become a byword. "When will we have an
honest king," the saying went, "when Gramont takes to water."

"Here, you anointed rascal," he told me one afternoon after

downing two bottles of good Médoc at lunch, clapping me on the back and sending me halfway across the room, "you are the father and mother of idleness. Why, you are as lazy as a Brazilian devouring his lice. What do you do with yourself to look so ragged, beat the dummy a dozen times a day?"

"I was up at six, riding," I said, "and did not see you about at that hour."

"That's neither here nor there, you little brigand," he said. "You look as though you could be strung through a needle. What you need is an outing, to take your mind off dreams of silken thighs. I can see those dark smudges under your eyes. It's Bayonne for us tonight. They're playing one of those endless boring tragedies by Corneille. Just the thing to put ballast in your brain."

We occupied the family box that evening, and as I gazed at the other spectators before the curtain went up, through the lorgnette I had borrowed from my father's room, I saw a young man in the yellow and blue uniform of a cadet de Gascogne, who seemed to be trying to call attention to himself. He would point at someone in another box, and whisper in the ear of the lady sitting next to him, and laugh loudly, and then point again, as though the spectacle was in the audience instead of on the stage.

During the intermission I saw him again in the foyer, long-jawed, with protuberant eyes like a frog's, strutting like a turkey. He was a good head taller than I, looked about twenty, and since he was a cadet de Gascogne, wearing rapier and spurs, I assumed he was an experienced swordsman. I did not care, for a rush of blood to my head told me this was my man. His fatuousness was a challenge. Walking up to him, I ground my heel in his foot. He did his best to keep his composure, but I saw his eyes water.

"That little fellow is clumsy," he said to the lady he was with, who looked at me through violet eyes as large as oysters.

Being called little has the same effect on me as eating a mixture of mustard and pepper. "It was no accident," I said. "I didn't like the way you looked at me."

"I never even saw you," said the gangling cadet, stifling a feigned yawn with a lace handkerchief.

"That is even worse," I said, "and if you are a man you will challenge me."

He laughed and told his lovely companion: "I would have to drop on my knees to fight this imp."

I must have looked like David provoking Goliath, for several men within earshot laughed as I put my hand to my rapier, which was nearly touching the ground, and tried to assume an expression of suitable ferocity. But there must also have been steel in my voice when I said: "Find a second and come outside at once, or I will run you through right here and provide a new ending for tonight's tragedy," for he replied: "You need to be knocked down a peg."

At that moment, Antoine came looking for me, for the three blows had sounded,* and when he saw me facing the cadet, my hand gripping the pommel of my rapier, he shouted: "What's this, you blundering jacket-duster, don't you see he's twice your size and reach?"

"It's too late to argue," I said. "Come along and serve as my second."

The cadet invited his lady companion to be his second, saying: "This will not be nearly so interesting as what we were watching, my dear, but it will be shorter, and I will have you back in time to see Augustus pardon Cinna."

The four of us descended the marble stairway into the carriage-filled street and crossed into a poplar-lined square, lit by the bright chandeliers that festooned the theater's pediment. The cadet sliced the air with his rapier to impress his pretty second, with one arm folded behind his back, darting forward, parrying imaginary thrusts, showing off the clever footwork he had learned at the military academy. I was an able swordsman, but the night air having cooled me down, I could see that I was no match for this giraffe, whose arms were twice as long as mine.

Antoine measured out paces in the center of the square, shaking his head and mumbling to himself. "Tell my adversary to remove his spurs in order to avoid stumbling over them," I said. Antoine relayed my suggestion to the cadet, who nodded, sat on the edge of a low stone vase that served as a fountain, crossed one knee over the other, and began to untie the lanyards that attached his spurs to the short, musketeer-style boots he affected, with flaring cuffed tops. While he was thus employed, I pulled my rapier from its scabbard, shouted "On guard, sir," and ran him through the right shoulder, from which blood spurted to stain his pretty uniform. He jumped up and seized his own weapon, but his weakened arm could not hold it. "Out of my sight, sir, else you will join those

---

* Three blows in the French theater meant and still mean that the curtain is about to go up.

Italian singers they call *castrati*," I said, thrusting my rapier close to his groin. He did not need to be told twice, and ran off in such a hurry that you could have corked his ass with a canary seed.

The whole thing happened so fast that the lady, who had been sniffing roses in a flower bed while waiting for the duel to begin, missed the crucial moment. She arrived as I threatened her wounded cadet, and saw her escort for the evening flee without taking the trouble to bid her farewell. Blinking her enormous violet eyes, she asked: "Where has Gaston gone?"

"He was outmatched, madam," I replied, "and he preferred to leave the field of battle rather than be sent to another world."

"But what about me?" she asked. "He promised we would see the end of the play, and I was counting on his carriage to take me home."

"Please do me the honor of counting on mine," I said, bowing and flourishing my hat as I had learned to do in dancing class. "The comte de Gramont is your servant."

"Aren't you a bit young to escort ladies?" she asked. "I don't want anyone thinking I'm your mother, that would be too awful."

"He was not too young to pink your friend and send him running," said Antoine, entering in the game, "and as for the rest, you are far too fresh a flower to have this strapping lad for a son."

I crooked my left arm, held it out, the ravishing creature took it, and the three of us went back into the theater to watch the denouement of the play from our box. She sat in the front chair, and I negligently let my arm rest on its back, my hand brushing her neck's satin skin. She did not draw away. Antoine, chuckling over the duel, could not concentrate on Corneille's Alexandrines. "Why, you little apostate," he whispered admiringly, "you are as false as a policeman's handshake." I asked him to excuse himself before the curtain fell, so that I might return the lady to her lodgings unchaperoned. Encouraged by my first success, I felt the evening required me to win a duel of another sort. I was young, but it was time I was de-oafed,* if I may be allowed to use an expression that is hardly apostolic. Antoine graciously vanished, and when the play was over, I bundled the lady into my carriage.

Her name, she told me, was Madeleine de Rethy, and she was visiting a maiden aunt in Bayonne. Her husband, a notary in Paris, was a man somewhat older than herself. The cadet, she insisted,

---

* A literal rendering of the French *déniaisé*.

was no more than a *sigisbée* during her stay in our fair city. In the carriage, I took her hand, but she withdrew it, making further references to my tender age. I kept up a running commentary of ready-made phrases I had learned in books, to give an impression of greater experience than I in fact had. We reached her gate, and I said that the thought of leaving her was cruel.

"It's past your bedtime," she said, laughing.

I clasped both her hands in mine and said: "Madam, you see a man disabled by your beauty. I could in former times have called you an angel, but nowadays one sees far too many in paintings, and they are dwarflike chubby creatures who hardly do you justice. Circe changed men into pigs, madam, but you are her opposite; you have changed a raw youth into a man. Thanks to you, madam, I am feeling for the first time the mysterious tremors of a heart that beats in echo to your footsteps." The translation of these remarks being: "To the victor go the spoils."

I could see she was touched by my words, but her condition required her to show further resistance. "This is madness," she said. "I am twice your age. If we were seen together in public, I would be arrested for corrupting a minor."

Seeing you in private is enough, I thought, as I bent my head to kiss her hand, lifting it and rubbing it gently against my eyes, which reddened them. I thought of a dapple-gray mare I had had to shoot the year before after she broke a leg, and the memory of those large, brown, trusting eyes as the muzzle touched her ear brought tears to my eyes. Raising my head, I said: "Madam, you are a witness to the first tears I ever shed for love."

Surprised and full of pity, Madeleine brought her lips closer to taste the salty evidence of my emotion. "Ah," she said, "you are all the more dangerous for being so young and vulnerable," and soon her lips were performing another duty than talking. I have often noted since that first encounter that tears are the fuel of love, they help one advance, and I have had occasion to use them more than once. To cry on demand is merely a question of practice, one has only to think of something sad, such as gambling losses or the death of a beloved horse. It is surprising how many women it softens, for it seems one of the two unmistakably sincere tributes a man can offer.

Madeleine invited me to come in "just for a second, to dry your eyes." The fortress was half stormed, the moat was crossed, there were left only the locks of the entrance gate to pick. We slid silently past the aunt's room and into her own apartment. She threw her evening cape on the bed and sat in a lounging chair, where there was only room for one, creating a new breach between us. I closed the breach by falling to my knees, a posture devised to show respect, but not always faithful to the intentions of its founders. From this new position, I examined the field of battle: A bed, covered with pink and silver damask, seemed an altar raised to the gods of love. Madeleine had lit two candles and placed them behind curtains of green taffeta, which seemed to be there to enshroud defeated virtue. I maintained a tone of natural gaiety, for I had been told that love is a child who likes to laugh, but as I tried to take possession of the fortress' two most advanced towers, I began to meet resistance. "Well, sir," she said, "is this part of our pact? You promised to behave. I took you for a man of your word."

Better at this point to be a man of few words, I thought, deciding to press my advantage and make the final assault. I picked her up in my arms and carried her to the bed. She was slight, and wasp-waisted, and I expected her to be as light as lace, but I had miscalculated my own strength, and had to make a herculean effort to reach the bed without dropping her. I groaned with relief as I released her like a sack of meal on the counterpane.

"What is this extravagant behavior?" she demanded. "What do you have in mind? Where did you get such manners? Is this the way a very young man behaves toward a married lady of condition? Enough now, what impudence. What if my aunt came in? I haven't even locked the door."

I wasted no time in the midst of this tirade, which left her breathless, and which I ended with a burning kiss. She returned my kiss with just the right degree of ardor for a woman of the world. I removed her shawl, as jealous a sentinel as the dragon who guarded the Hesperides, and threw it on the floor, where it could no longer conceal the apples of the garden of love. Her large violet eyes expressed a thousand emotions in an instant. My maneuver allowed her to touch the truth of what I was advancing, so that she could find me in a state proper to the execution of my desires.

"Ah," she went on, "for heaven's sake, enough. I've said it for the last time. I am going to lose my temper. You cannot have imagined I was that sort of woman."

I silenced her with my lips, sliding an agile and flexible organ between the opening grille of her teeth. At the same time, I slid a hand between her breasts, wishing I had several mouths to do proper homage to the side altars of her cathedral. My mouth remained glued to hers. I did not dare remove it for fear that if she caught her breath she would order me to leave or cry for her aunt. Had I been in a less excited state, the discrepancy between her words and her deeds would have been more apparent. I now momentarily abandoned her breasts to test the final, best defended bastion, and, after some trouble groping for the hem of her dress, I slid my hand under it and up a calf and a thigh that were like warm, palpitating alabaster. Instead of resisting, she moved her body slightly to make the passageway more accessible, and my fingers reached the moist orchid in its silken wrapping. The swiftness of my success, however, made me so exceedingly agitated that, while triumphant on the one hand, I secretly defeated myself on the other. I was both victor and vanquished. I was in the fortress, but spent, unable to receive the marks of possession.

Madeleine did not realize my predicament, for when I sat up, she continued to moan: "Pray, sir, I beg you, I am lost," and other implorations of that nature; but as she protested she clung to me all the more tightly. Until, by virtue of rubbing against me, she discovered my condition, and shedding the airs and vocabulary of the violated maiden, she shoved me off the bed with a strength she had not previously demonstrated, and shouted in a voice that contrasted shrilly with her sweet objections: "You came in your pants, you little bastard."

"Madam," I said, trying to preserve some semblance of self-respect, "one drop of water cannot put out a fire."

"That's what I get for bringing home thirteen-year-old boys," Madeleine said. "On your feet, you little wretch, and out. This isn't a home for stray adolescents." She was shouting now, taking no precautions not to wake up her slumbering aunt, and I could see there was no way to redress a situation that had so badly deteriorated. It was no use explaining that it was the first time, and that youthful ardor rushes out of step. The lady was in a state of dissatisfaction bordering on physical distress, and I thought it best to withdraw from the field, and write the evening off, in dueler's parlance, to one *"touché"* and one "nothing either way."

I Am Married

In the next five years, my education continued. I learned to win duels without trickery and make love to women without racing ahead of them. The secret in both cases was a matter of timing, of reflexes that had to be, in the first case, sharpened and, in the second case, dulled. I gained a modest regional reputation for my skill with pointed instruments. In those years, with my mother dead and my father seeking glory on Flemish battlefields, my natural impulsiveness was allowed to course unchecked, and my life was a series of incidents for which I deserved to be punished. But there was no one in residence who could handle that assignment. I studied when I felt like it, that is to say, never. I took advantage of my rank with some of the village girls, in meadows or haylofts, like the shepherds in pastoral prints. I lost count of the number of pranks I played, none of them memorable. One summer a judge came from Bayonne to obtain my signature, in my father's and my elder brother's absence, for a new cadastral survey that would include some of our property, and I pretended to mistake him for a tailor come to take measurements for a new coat.

"First, we must find a room with a tall mirror," I said.

"Well, of course, if you like," the judge said, standing there uneasily in his black suit, holding a bulging leather case under his arm.

"I was thinking of a velvet coat, for the fall," I said, taking him into the music room, where there was no comfortable place for him to sit except the harpsichord stool.

"Ah, yes," he said, thinking I was making small talk, "the season will change soon enough."

"Full in the sleeve, with two vents down the back, a high collar, and porcelain buttons," I said.

"Well, what I came about . . ." said the judge, clearing his throat.

"I know, I know," I said. "You will go on about the cost of velvet, but don't worry, the account will be settled in full by the end of the year." I stood in front of the mirror with my arms spread out. "Well, are you ready?" I asked.

"Yes, of course," he said, thinking by this time that he must be dealing with a madman. "Just let me find these papers . . ."

"Never mind the papers," I said. "Did you bring your measuring tape?" And so it went, in the classic *quid pro quo*, until the poor man left in a daze, feeling fortunate to have got away alive.

My brother came to spend Christmas the year I was eighteen, for Christmas in Paris meant creditors at his door, and announced that my father would soon be home. The king had wearied of the

Flemish campaign and signed a truce. Antoine told me I had reached an age where I must decide what to make of myself. "You must choose, little one," he said, "between the only two roads open to you. Whether, by entering the church, you wish to possess the goods of this world without having to work for them. The principal advantage of a religious vocation being that you can avoid marriage. Or whether, with a wife to keep, you wish to lose arms and legs in order to be the *fructus belli* of an insensitive court, and, toward the end of your days, reach the dignity of a camp marshal, with a glass eye and a peg leg."

I was sure of only one thing: My salvation did not lie with the church. That left a military career, and I awaited my father's return, mustering up the courage to ask him for the capital to purchase a regiment. The campaign had aged him. His hair was white, and his face was as lined as the exercise paper I used in class. He was full of stories about the war. At a Bavarian village called Dettingen, on the Main River, he had charged an English force three times the size of his cavalry and routed them. "They fled into the river like rabbits at a hunt," he said, "and we sliced them up into food for the fish." The king, he said, had praised his gallantry. "I was only doing my duty, sire," he had replied.

A delegation from the Bayonne parliament came to the castle and read a proclamation about my father's gallant conduct. A high mass was sung at the cathedral to celebrate his return. My father played the modest hero as if born to the part, insisting gruffly that in his line of work, bravery was a matter of self-preservation. Rumors sprang up that he was being considered for a *maréchal's* baton, but he said he was just an old soldier growing stiff with rheumatism who wanted nothing more than to die a natural death.

The first thing he said to me upon his return was: "I expected to find you married, sir. We'll have to attend to that."

I was stunned. I wanted to buy a regiment, and he wanted me to find a wife. "Why should I marry?" I asked. I could think of nothing more brilliant to say.

"Because man was not made to live alone, that's why," he replied.

"I once heard you say that marriage is the end of life," I said.

"Eighteen is too young for the end of life."

"Don't worry," he assured me, "it's not the husband women want, it's the wedding."

I was disconsolate, for marriage reminded me of two pythons

eating the same pig from either end. Eventually, the two ravenous reptiles meet in the middle, and the larger python swallows the smaller one as well as the pig. The smaller python remains inside the larger python along with the half-digested pig. Since my bride was to be chosen for her wealth, I would be the smaller python.

I knew it was pointless to discuss the matter with my father. What I wanted was irrelevant. He simply took me to a house where there were quite a few young women—I suppose you could have called it an elegant version of the Bayonne livestock market—and told me afterward that my chosen one was among them. Not knowing which one she was, I might as well have been playing blindman's buff. A week later, I was taken to meet the young lady, who resided in a large manor near Pau. As I had expected, nature in its equity had withheld its benefits in proportion to those she had inherited in the way of property.

"Is she not beautiful?" my father asked, doubtless seeing vineyards and granaries instead of the features of her face.

"Very," I replied, "in the fashion of the day." She limped a bit, but not without reason, for one of her legs was shorter than the other, and her eyes were set as close together as the eyes of a gibbon. Her complexion was ideal except for a field of closely planted pockmarks which a special lotion helped disguise. Her mouth was perfectly shaped, and surmounted by a dark hirsute shadow said to announce a passionate nature, and her nose, while of pleasing proportions, seemed borrowed from another face. Her long brown hair partly concealed two ears that stuck out from her head like gargoyles from the wall of a cathedral. Her smile was adorable, from a distance, for closer up, her breath was like the stink of a bronze chamber pot.

"This is Thérèse," my father said, all honey and lavender in his role of matchmaker. "Why don't you two children go and sit somewhere and get to know one another? We have business to attend to." I took the creature off and mumbled a few banalities, while my father sat down at the bargaining table for the dowry negotiations with my future in-laws, a marquis of recent vintage who had made a fortune hoarding grain, and selling it in times of famine at four or five times the market price, and his wife, who looked force-fed with the very grain he kept from others, and whose silhouette alarmed me in that it announced the appearance of her daughter at some future time.

I could hear snatches of the negotiations when the voices rose, and it dawned on me that my father, so long removed from the ways of the world in the sepulchral quiet of his study, had allowed a keen business sense to lie fallow. "What?" my mother-in-law-to-be exclaimed. "Does he need a fortune to sleep with my daughter?" Even though I knew it was said for the sake of argument, my father's reply made me shudder: "Don't forget, madam, that he will sleep with her tomorrow, after tomorrow, and on each and every night." While the bickering over the property value of our respective persons dragged on, I took Thérèse into the garden and asked her to identify the flowers. Fortunately, the garden was large, and this task kept her busy and relieved me from the strain of making conversation.

When I returned from my hour of horticultural instruction, being now quite clear on the difference between weeds and daffodils, it seemed from my father's hearty, satisfied tone that they were about to conclude. "Let's not be so mysterious, now that we're all one big family," he said. "All we want is the happiness of our children. It's all a matter of yes or no. Does my son suit you? That is the item. As for property, he will have an income of ten thousand pounds and a cavalry regiment. Now that we're all agreed, we can sign the contract tonight, publish the bans on Sunday, and the wedding can take place a week from Monday."

The old soldier's haste, in this case, would not lose a battle, but commit his son to a prison worse than Bicêtre.* The news of the cavalry regiment almost made up for the sacrifice I was making. I no more believed the talk of annual income than I believed my toad of a wife would turn into a fairy princess, but the regiment was an item on which he could not renege.

And so it was that, a week later, we were married. I was eighteen, three years older than my wife, and had been a bachelor since earliest childhood. We had hardly exchanged a word. I did not feel the slightest inclination toward her. Indeed, in my dealings with her, my principal effort was to overcome an overwhelming sense of revulsion. And that is how I accomplished what is claimed to be the most important act in one's life.

The invitation to the nuptial blessing, a work of art by a local master, showed two angelic young people kneeling in tunics at the foot of Married Bliss, with Time, chained by a garland of roses, having momentarily rested his scythe on a horn of plenty.

* Bicêtre was the Paris prison for the destitute.

There was one true detail in this representation, for the match was a triumph of family solidarity. Cousins by the hundreds turned out in Bayonne cathedral and showered us with enough gifts to establish several households. It took Thérèse a week to write thank-you notes in her cramped child's hand. The archbishop spoke in a vibrant voice of the duties of marriage, as if, after one look at the bride, he had decided that it was pointless to discuss its pleasures. I can truthfully say that Thérèse was never lovelier than on that day, for she was veiled. I heard a tiny voice, buried under a silver brocade gown garnished with mother-of-pearl and precious stones, pronounce the word "yes" without realizing its implications. And I heard my own distant, disembodied voice pronounce the same word, wondering at the disparity between the effortlessness of the gesture I was performing, and the tentacular, binding network of obligations I had thereby created for myself.

Afterward, the women of both families kissed by order of kinship, and a valet brought a basket filled with fans and tassels and other favors, to be distributed among the guests. My father must have noticed my glum expression, which I thought I could pass off as a solemn church face, for he took me by the arm outside the cathedral and said: "Cheer up, you are a husband, but you also command a cavalry regiment."

It was decided that we would set up house in a small château in the Bigorre, at an almost equal distance between the residences of my father and my in-laws, so that we might remain under their mutual surveillance. Thérèse was an innocent, who had gone straight from the hard narrow cot of the convent to the marriage bed. Still faithful to the disciplines of convent life, she rose at six and spent long hours telling her beads. I did not wish to disrupt such pious dispositions, and asked only that we each keep our own bedroom, since our hours were different. She seemed to expect no more from marriage than sharing the same roof, like two members of a religious community who might meet at meals or in the hall, and had brought her governess to keep her company and help her with the duties of running a house. I made no attempt to initiate her to the mysteries of married life. It was not a mere absence of desire. I really could not think of a way to shake her out of her convent manners. She seemed quite happy remaining a lay nun, and I had no reason to change her. This *modus vivendi* lasted several months. I regularly visited the warm welcoming bed of a chambermaid rather than disturb the slumber of my child bride, all the while leading a quiet country existence as I waited for news of my regiment.

But the calm of our household was shattered one morning by a visit from my mother-in-law. Thanks to my little chambermaid, whose two essential talents were shaking a man's loins and eavesdropping, I learned the gist of the mother-daughter conversation, which I set down as follows:

"Well, are you pleased with your husband?"

"Yes, Mother."

"When are you going to give me a grandson?"

"I don't know."

"Do you notice any change?"

"Change? Am I subject to change?"

"I mean, since you have become a woman. I hope you don't find my questions indiscreet. Please don't be embarrassed by my frankness. Does your husband do his duty?"

"Oh, yes, Mother, every day."

"That's all to the good. But you must be careful."

"About what?"

"You must not overtire him. After all, at eighteen, he is still growing."

"Overtire him how?"

"I mean you must not too often want . . ."

"Want what?"

"What we are discussing, my dear. Men, even young men, can easily wear out until there is nothing left of them."

"Wear out?"

"There are exertions that women tolerate better than men."

"Because he does his duty? But he looks none the worse for it."

"All the better, but be careful."

"Don't worry, I tell him what I want."

"And he obeys?"

"To the letter."

"Splendid, but be reasonable, for you must know that a young man risks his health trying to satisfy a very young woman with immoderate appetites."

"What makes you think my appetites are immoderate?"

"You said yourself that you insist on your husband performing his duty daily. That seems to be all young women think about these days. You must promise to give him a day's respite now and then."

"Why should I not do today what I did yesterday?"

"If you look at it that way, my dear, there is no saying how it will end. I despair of putting any sense into your head."

"Then don't talk to me as if I were a child."

"Do you sleep in the same room?"

"Never."

"Does he visit you in the evening?"

"After supper, for five minutes, to say good night."

"How does he say good night?"

"He kisses me."

"Where does he kiss you?"

"On the brow, the eyes, and the chin."

"That's all?"

"I think that's quite enough."

"And on your wedding night, didn't he lie next to you in bed?"

"Yes, Mother."

"And afterward?"

"He said good night and left."

"He didn't . . . move closer to you?"

"No, Mother."

"He didn't . . . put his hands under your nightgown?"

"What an idea."

"He didn't press his body to yours?"

"I would ask him to leave if he did."

My mother-in-law could contain herself no longer. "What an insult," she cried. "To leave her a virgin is to let us know that her flower is not worth picking."

The expected summons from my father came two days later. Thérèse's parents threatened to begin annulment proceedings. An ecclesiastical tribunal, after the proper mixture of theological discussion and medical examination, would certify that she was still a *virgo intacta* and that the marriage had not been consummated. This would be the greatest dishonor in the family since Antoine II had murdered his wife in 1610. I was a shame and a discredit to him, and what is more, my manhood was now in doubt.

I informed him that the situation had changed since my mother-in-law's visit. I had been up the entire night making good the marriage contract. Like a cellar worker come upon a moldy, disused cask, I had to tap the bunghole more than once before it would open. We both cried from the pain, and Thérèse said that if she had known what marriage was like she would have stayed in the nunnery. "And my mother wanted to know whether I did this every day," she moaned. I privately resolved that if she was fertile, once a year would be enough to keep up appearances and occupy her with a growing belly. I found that I was only able to keep my end of the bargain by thinking of horses, of their graceful legs when they passed from a trot to a canter, of their long silken tails swinging rhythmically and their brushed manes rising with the breeze. I would give this mare of mine a fine brood, I thought, in order to have to ride her as little as possible. Later, when my duties called me to Paris, the court, and foreign battlefields, I would return long enough to bestride her, pat my latest colt on the head, inspect the family stable, and leave her to foal once again.

My own home became as unfamiliar to me as any house where I might spend a week as a guest, being careful not to depart from established custom, ask for changes in the menu, or claim any privileges which my temporary presence did not justify. Thérèse seemed pleased with the arrangement, or at least showed an even disposition that could be interpreted as an absence of displeasure. Perhaps I had married the right woman after all, since she made no demands on me, and I had none to make on her. Indifference seemed as solid a ground to build a marriage on as passion, more so, for it did not ferment into bitterness.

I Lose My Father

Three months after the defloration of Thérèse (uprooting would be a more proper term), a footman arrived from Bidache to tell me that my father was in the worst way. An attack of gout had felled him. In those days, and times have not changed that much, it took very little to kill a man. A friend of my father's broke an arm raising his carriage window and died of that. My uncle Armand died of an excoriated rectum, as the result of giving himself too many enemas. My father, having survived the shot and shell of a dozen campaigns as well as the bile of his own disposition, was dying of an affliction he had done nothing to deserve. Gout is associated with lack of temperance, but my father drank wine very moderately, never took spirits or snuff, and had, as far as I know, stayed clear of loose women. He had inherited the gout, as in the Biblical prophecy, "The fathers ate green grapes and the sons had indigestion." His father had consumed a bottle of Burgundy at every meal without ill effects, and had simply passed on the consequences of his thirst to his son. And now, the son, instead of being rewarded for his own moderation, was dying the death his father should have died. If there was a God in heaven, where was His justice?

The confessor, the one who preached the annual Lent sermon, had been summoned, and came up the stairs and down the hall with that noiseless ecclesiastical shuffle that seems designed for occasions of family grief. He was always trying to get on my father's good side, and even now, when I led him in, he said: "Oh, you're looking so much better. Someone in heaven must be saying prayers for you."

My father's gouty foot was propped up on cushions. His whole leg was numb with the infection. He was thinner than I had ever seen him; the skin was stretched as tight over his cheekbones as canvas across a frame. "I'm dying and you know it," he said.

"Not at all, not at all," the confessor said, spraying holy water about the room with an aspergillum, as if disinfecting it. "A Carmelite nun, blessed with stigmata, who is in direct communication with Saint Theresa of Lisieux, has prophesied your recovery."

"Don't talk rot," my father said.

"Well," the confessor said, miffed that his optimism had been rebuffed, "if you are so sure you are dying, I must hear your confession and give you the last sacraments. You must begin by forgiving your enemies."

"I have no enemies," my father roared. "They are all dead."

"Come, come, now, a man in your position . . ."

"You are my only enemy," my father shouted, half-rising from his bed. "Out of here, you dribbling simoniac." He reached for the sword hanging from a hook behind his bed, and waved it at the priest, who picked up the skirts of his cassock and scurried out.

"Poor young fellow," he told me once he was safely outside, "I share your sorrow. The last act is always sad, however brilliant the play has been. The curtain falls, the costumes are put away. The fullest lives must end, we are all the same. A little earth to cover us, and we are ready to face eternity."

My younger brother's weeping governess interrupted us to say that Alfred was in his room arranging flowers, his favorite pastime, and that he refused to come out to attend his dying father. I went to his room to fetch him and found him cutting the stems of blue and white irises. "It's very strange," he said as I entered. "What makes one iris bloom weeks later than another, in the same garden, in the same flower bed?"

Alfred was remarkably self-possessed for his age. He was only twelve, but dressed like an adult, wore velvet trousers, jerkins, and frock coats, and since he had a tendency to roundness, he looked like a stunted beadle about to announce the hours of Sunday office, full of portly self-importance. There was in him none of the tentative quality that children usually have; his speech and gestures were as deliberate as a town crier's. He made me feel that he was older than I was. I would have taken any other twelve-year-old boy by the scruff of the neck and dragged him to my father's sickroom. But Alfred's mock adulthood was an effective defense that made one reason with him.

"Don't you think you could leave your flowers for a moment and pay your father a visit?" I asked. "He may not last the night."

"I don't like that sort of thing," Alfred said. "It's nasty."

"What sort of thing?"

"Bedpans, chamber pots, clammy sheets, half-empty cups of chamomile tea."

"Alfred, it's your father," I said.

"He never paid any attention to me," Alfred said.

"If you don't come at once, I'm going to knock over your vase," I said. Abandoning reason, I had resorted to a childish threat, confirming the feeling that I was the younger of the two. Alfred sighed, as if humoring some form of lower species, and came with me, but when we reached my father's room, he was dead. The confessor had shut his eyes and was mumbling Latin phrases over his body. Alfred took the scene in at a glance, said, "You see," and walked out. Whatever my own feelings were, they were overridden by the need to make practical arrangements for the burial. The dead, like the living, create obligations to prevent us from seeing them distinctly.

I buried him. What else could I do? He was dead. It was while going through his papers that I found an envelope addressed to me. It contained an account of that famous battle of Dettingen where he had routed a superior English force. The report was the result of a royal investigation on the reasons why the king's army had lost the battle. I include it here in full:

"The army in Bavaria, forty thousand men under the command of the maréchal duc de Noailles, had as its strategic objective to prevent the junction of England's King George II with Prince Charles of Lorraine. George II was advancing along the Main River toward Frankfurt, with his son, the Duke of Cumberland, and Lord Stair. Noailles caught him in a narrow defile between the river and the Spessart mountains, near the town of Aschaffenburg. His artillery held the heights and a stunning victory was within his grasp. The English were caught in a mousetrap. The only retreat was through the village of Dettingen. The duc de Gramont, under his uncle Noailles, was in command of six battalions of guards and the troops of the king's household, roughly ten thousand men.

"At 1 A.M. on June 27, 1743, the duc de Noailles was informed that the enemy was advancing on his right flank, and moved his troops to Seligenstadt, where they could cross the Main over two bridges. He massed his cavalry and artillery on the banks of the Main, in order to outflank the enemy, and pushed his troops as far as Dettingen, a little farther along the same bank. At the foot of this village a mountain stream crosses an impracticable swamp, and there are only three points of passage, one through the village, one over a wooden bridge, and one over a stone bridge at the foot of the mountain.

"The village of Dettingen, like the cork in a bottle, sealed off the British troops. Noailles ordered that it be occupied by infantry, and that the cavalry should back up the infantry, behind the plain. Gramont was in command of the troops that were to occupy Dettingen. It was four in the morning when he received the order. The sky was whitening, and he gave his officers the order to saddle and bridle at once. Gramont at this time was hoping for the opportunity to perform an exceptional feat of arms that would earn him a maréchal's baton. Noailles told him to take his troops and occupy Dettingen. Gramont replied: 'I will keep going until I meet the enemy.' Noailles asked him to exercise caution and not go beyond the village. Reaching Dettingen with his men and finding it deserted, Gramont decided to move on. This meant crossing the stream with his infantry and cavalry.

"One of his officers told him: 'It may be very inconvenient to cross the river and be caught on the other bank.'

"Gramont was furious at the suggestion and said: 'When I want your advice, I'll ask for it. I know what I'm doing.'

"Meanwhile, Noailles, having taken his dispositions, again crossed the Main to see what effect his artillery batteries were having. The enemy was caught in an artillery barrage between the mountains and the Main. Noailles was astonished to see that, against his precise instructions, the troops defending Dettingen were leaving the village and crossing the stream, without waiting for the rest of the army. He dispatched a messenger to Gramont to order him to stop his advance, return to the village, and occupy it.

"When Gramont saw the order he disregarded it, saying: 'I am taking it upon myself. Great acts are never successful without great risks. Let history be the judge.' Having crossed the stream with his ten thousand men, Gramont found himself facing an English force of forty-five thousand. The English infantry was massed four deep on the edge of a large wood. He was too close to the enemy to be supported by his own artillery. Oblivious to the imminent disaster, blinded by the vision of the maréchal's baton he thought was now within his grasp, he galloped along the front line of his cavalry, shouting: 'It's time to have at them.'

"From his observation post on the side of the mountain, Noailles watched Gramont's forces move into range of the British infantry's muskets. He decided to let them go on, as there was little he could do to stop them. Also, as sorry as he was to lose a favorable position, he preferred to let them attack rather than cover the king's troops with shame by ordering a retreat, which might have led to panic since the only way back was across the stream. Noailles watched Gramont's cavalry ride up in close formation until it seemed that the horses' breastplates were touching the muzzles of the extended English muskets. He heard the redcoats fire together, so that it sounded like one loud report, and he saw the French line break, horses crumple, riders thrown off, and islands of resistance forming that were soon cut off from his view by the smoke and dust.

"Now it was the English cavalry's turn to charge from its hidden position behind a hill, and they rode through the French infantry as though through barley fields. Gramont's troops were outnumbered and in an untenable strategic position. The infantry panicked, broke and ran for the river, throwing away their muskets and knapsacks in order to speed their return across the river. Twenty officers dismounted and formed a square to save the regimental flag, fighting with incredible bravery, holding off repeated cavalry charges, and finally making their way back to their lines with the colors safe. Gramont could be seen trying to regroup his shaken forces, galloping from one end of the field to the other, shouting at men who were beyond hearing him, shaking his sword and miraculously escaping enemy fire. When Noailles saw that the situation had degenerated into a retreat, he used his artillery to prevent the British from following Gramont's troops across the stream.

"Gramont was able to reach Dettingen with what was left of his men, a little more than half the original number. The casualty rate was particularly high among the officers. Dettingen could not be called an important defeat for the king's army, because the English did not pursue their advantage. However, thanks to Gramont's foolhardy attack, a decisive victory was transformed into a costly skirmish.

"The king's reaction, when he received Gramont's list of vacancies in his regiment, was surprisingly laconic. Not a word of criticism was addressed to Gramont. Indeed, Gramont wrote the king that he had, as a result of Dettingen, made several useful observations that would improve the conduct of his regiment. One of these was, that since so many of his officers had been shot off their horses, they were forced to march with the infantry. This, said Gramont, was a useful tactic to adopt in the future, for with the officers marching on the end, the infantry lines would remain in closer formation. The king congratulated Gramont on having discovered this tactic, which apparently has also been used successfully by the King of Sweden.

"In Gramont's regiment, however, discontent seethed. The men felt they had been sacrificed in a useless action prompted only by their general's thirst for personal glory. The musketeers held a mock trial in which a straw dummy of Gramont appeared before a panel of judges. Gramont was defended by a musketeer dressed up in the gold braid of a brigadier. The judges sentenced the dummy to death for his 'atrocious bungling.' The brigadier appealed for leniency. 'The man on trial before you,' he said, 'is a member of one of the most glorious families in France. His ancestors have left a trail of blood in the service of the king.'

" 'Our blood more often than theirs,' a judge said.

" 'The Gramonts have been military men from father to son,' the defense said.

" 'That is precisely what we are reproaching them for,' a judge said.

" 'What of my client's advancing years?' the defense asked.

" 'Age has never been an excuse for criminal stupidity,' the judges said.

" 'I see that I cannot move such implacable judges,' the brigadier concluded. 'As a last argument I appeal to your sense of clemency for the imperious reason that my client is not worth the rope it would take to hang him.'

"On those grounds the death sentence was commuted to tossing the straw effigy of Gramont in a blanket.

"The sentence was executed one night in front of a bonfire, with much hilarity and most of the regiment looking on, as they drank toasts to 'our straw general.' It ended Gramont's effectiveness as a regimental commander. In France, ridicule kills. A man who has been laughed at by his men cannot expect to be obeyed. Even though he had not incurred the king's displeasure, Gramont's military career was over. He was banished from the army by his men."

So this was the great feat of arms that the city of Bayonne had celebrated. Here was the hero unmasked. He had devoted his life to arms, and been undone by them. And yet he had to maintain the illusion that he was a great soldier. It did not matter what happened in the field; when he came home, he had to be covered with wreaths of laurel like a Roman emperor. The real defeat was not in battle but in the eyes of those close to him. As long as he could keep me believing that he was a great general, he remained one. I might never have learned the truth if my father had not left it for me to discover. This was the most curious: that after having gone to such pains to maintain his reputation in my eyes, he would now leave me a document that canceled it all out. In dying, he was settling his accounts. While alive, he had wanted me to think of him as a famous soldier, but that required lying. Now, he was making up for the lie by showing me the truth, posthumously. I discovered him for what he was, a vainglorious, foolish old man who had disobeyed an order and snatched defeat from the jaws of victory. I would not remember my father as a hero, but as a man who had devoted his life to reconciling the impossible. He had wanted me to think that he was a great general, and then he had to give up that posture in order to prove that he was not a liar. Even in death, he was still trying to square the circle.

Court

I Leave for Paris

M Y FATHER'S will made clear that my coat of arms might as
well represent an empty purse falling through a hole in
my pocket. He had barely left enough to settle his debts
and pay for my promised regiment. The annual income promised
my in-laws as a lure in the marriage settlement was nonexistent. I
could not count on my wife, for her parents kept a lynx-eyed vigil
over her purse strings. I left for Versailles to claim my regiment
without knowing how I would make ends meet. I hardly had enough
to pay for the clothes I would need to cover my provincial awk-
wardness. I had only my luck to count on, and a face that several
ladies had found pleasing; ten campaigns give a man the right to a
regiment, ten years in the seminary give him the right to a bishopric,
but a single day in the service of love can determine one's fortune.

After bidding my child bride farewell, I set out in a carriage
laden with my few belongings, on the long road that would lead to
the royal court. It was a fine day, and the sunlight passing in shafts
between the poplars made golden-dappled designs in the road
that seemed to be signposts showing the way to Versailles, while
the sound of the coachman's whip flicking the horses, and the
rhythmical pattern of their hooves on the packed dirt sounded like
a corps of drummers announcing my arrival. I sat back and
watched the green fields fly by, and imagined I saw friendly crowds
by the side of the road, cheering me on and wishing me Godspeed.
But all I did see, before we had gone ten leagues, was a surly
peasant in a stocking cap beating a donkey with a thick staff. The
poor animal was braying with its head down, and its back legs
were spread, for it was pissing from fear. I knocked to make the
coachman stop, for I cannot bear to see animals mistreated, they
are the true innocents of our planet.

"Have you no conscience, then, to berate this poor beast?" I

83

asked. The peasant removed his cap, held it in his two hands, bowed low, and said with mock reverence:

"Pardon, sir donkey, I did not know you had protectors at court."

I shouted for the coachman to start up, secretly flattered at being taken for a courtier, but when I looked back thirty meters later, the fellow was at it with greater gusto than before, breaking his stick over the donkey's back. One could have the best intentions in the world, it did no good. I found myself longing for the days of chivalry, when one could slay a dragon, cleave in twain a giant, fight against hopeless odds, seek the Holy Grail, and carry a beauteous damoiselle on the crupper of one's horse after rescuing her from villains. Times had changed, and today, it was all one could do to keep a peasant from mistreating a donkey.

As I crossed the land from south to north, I found such differences from my native Béarn, where our good Henri IV had kept his promise to put a fowl in every pot, that I could scarcely believe I was still in the same country. Beggars on the side of the road wore such encrusted rags that they would have been more seemly naked. Curled under trees, grimy and unshaven, like dogs licking their sores, they awakened at the sound of my approaching carriage to trot alongside, pleading for a crust of bread their toothless mouths could not have chewed, their whines turning to curses as I sped on. In many places, husbandry seemed no more advanced than among the Hurons. Women, if the sexless, bony-faced, barefoot creatures I saw could be called that, plowed with a pair of mules to sow barley, gathered chestnuts for their dinner, or picked weeds with which they filled their ample aprons, for their children or their cows, I knew not. Their houses were miserable mounds of thatch-roofed dirt, and I crossed stretches of uncultivated, unpopulated land so wild that I would not have been surprised to be set upon by savages brandishing tomahawks. I marveled at the desolation that was France, and now saw confirmed the stories I had scoffed at about peasants who ate roots and grass and baked their bread but twice a year, breaking it with a hammer and soaking it in water before they could eat it.

Reaching Lyon after four days, I found it a fine city, with many substantial houses overlooking the river, and I put up at an inn called the Smoking Dog, whose proprietor gave me a room with a view of the cathedral spires and promised me a fat capon and a bottle of good Mâcon wine for my supper. The tavern room was crowded with men of all conditions, drinking, smoking, and throwing dice, but despite the smoke and noise I settled down with a hearty appetite.

I was not to remain long alone, however, for upon hearing a feminine voice ask, "And who's this fine young fellow?" I looked up from my plate and saw that the remark was addressed to me. Standing in front of me, hardly higher than the top of the table, was a girl with a pretty, rosebud face and a misshapen body, like one of those flowers that grow in a swamp. Where her back should have been there was a great hump, and she was bent almost double under its weight. She had no waist, her body was one continuous lump, twisting out of alignment at the hips. She looked like a porcelain figurine that has misfired in the oven, leaving only the pretty, painted face intact. Taking my hand in hers, she asked: "And do you want your fortune told, and the names of the girls whose hearts you'll break?" I said I was in too great an awe of the future to want to know it in advance, and withdrew my hand. She then suggested I should accompany her into a back room for purposes that remained vague, an offer I declined as politely as I could. Turning her hump toward me, she said: "Don't you know that touching it brings you luck? Come on, only a crown."

"Madam," I said, "I am not insensitive to your charms, but I am bound for Paris, and still have a certain number of leagues to put behind me this day."

"Oh, Paris, my heart's desire," she said, batting her eyelashes flirtatiously. "Take me with you."

"I regret, madam, that I have not got room for you," I said.

"I don't need much room, young lord," she said. "I can fit in any corner."

"I regret to say that will be impossible," I said, turning my attention once again to my half-empty plate.

To my astonishment, the creature began to shout that she had been insulted, and had done nothing to deserve being called such vile names, that it was not her fault she was deformed, God had chosen to cripple her at birth, and was that a reason to treat her so cruelly?

Two men who had been drinking at a table in the corner, one a black-bearded, strong-shouldered fellow with a walleye, the other shorter, curly-haired, round-faced, with a reddish complexion that announced a nature given to excesses, came up and pushed her aside. The red-faced one said: "Why did you insult my sister?"

"Are you addressing me, sir?" I asked.

"Don't waste your fine manners," he said. "What did you say to this poor girl?"

"I turned down several requests for closer acquaintance," I said.

"Don't you know it isn't nice to make remarks about a physical handicap?" he said.

"You look like you went to school," the black-bearded one said. "Didn't they teach you how to talk to ladies? What's your name, anyway?"

"Count Gramont, at your service," I said, hoping the title would impress them, as, rising, I added: "If you will excuse me . . ."

The black-bearded one pushed me back on the bench and said: "Gramont: A great mount, in other words a fine horse, probably five-gaited."

"Ah," said the red-faced one, "but look at his emerald-green coat, there is a horse of another color."

The black-bearded one laughed, and unsheathing his sword, waved it and shouted: "A great mount, a great mount, my kingdom for a great mount."

My face flushed with anger, and I said: "Gentlemen, I confess that I have never appreciated plays on names, they remind me of the classroom and announce the barracks. It's a bit too easy . . ."

"Well, look, Blackie," the red-faced one said, "the young lord's upset. Do you think he's going to cry?"

"Get something to blow his nose," the one called Blackie said.

"I've got just the thing," the red-faced one said, pulling from under the sacklike coat he was wearing an evil-looking pistol with two small barrels. He cocked back the hammers and said: "On your way, or I'll blow your nose and your face off with it."

Since the innkeeper had made no move to assist me, I gathered that these two cutthroats were the highest court in that establishment, and, seeing no way I could retaliate against their very evident intentions, I made a strategic retreat, with their laughter echoing in my ears. As I rode off, I wondered what had provoked the scene. The explanation did not come until I reached into a pocket for the diamond and gold watch left by my father to a lady in Paris, which I had appropriated, for I saw no reason to respect his wishes when he had never respected mine. It was gone. I was sorry to lose it, not because of the precious stones, but because of a Latin inscription on the inside of the lid that said: All hours wound, the last one kills.

My troubles were not over, for on the following day I was stopped by two men on horseback who blocked the road, one in blue and one in red. They said they were officers and had orders to take me back to Lyon. I explained that I was on my way to Versailles to take command of a regiment purchased by my father, but it did no good. The man in red, who was no taller than myself, with a long pale face and a head that leaned forward, as if trying to catch a word he had missed, said he was very sorry, "but when a gentleman has orders he must execute them." I consented to that to which I could not object, asking only to see his orders. He replied most politely that he would impart them to me at the earliest opportunity.

"You have nothing to fear from us," he said, as he took a place beside me in the carriage, leaving his horse in the care of his colleague. "We are not highway robbers. I am a gentleman like yourself, the son of a provincial nobleman in the Garonne, raised by the Jesuits, God-fearing, a seminarian for five years before poor health made me throw my cassock to the nettles and enter the king's service. I was prepared for the military life by the discipline of Saint Ignatius: *Perinde ac cadaver.** But alas, I joined the service too late, and, as is well known, *tarde venientibus ossa.†* You see, my Latin is still serviceable, what the Jesuits teach stays with you. I speak six other languages as well, I am a cultivated man, not one of your sodden, unread barracks hounds."

He went on in this inexhaustible vein as we rode on, directing the coachman to take narrowing country roads until I no longer had any idea where I was. The bark is deceitful of the nature of the tree, I thought, and asked again to see his orders. "I will show them to you soon enough," he said, "for we have almost reached our destination."

"Why are we going off the main road?" I asked.

"It's a shortcut," said the officer. "We are sorry to impose on you and want to take as little of your time as possible. After all, we are fellow officers, we understand what life in the field can be, here

* A reference to Saint Ignatius of Loyola's dictum that one should obey one's superiors "like a corpse."
† Those who come to the table late get only bones.

today and gone tomorrow. *Memento, homo, quia pulvis es et in pulveram reverteris.*"*

We reached the edge of a forest, and the officer called for the coachman to stop. I asked the reason for the halt, and he replied: "I must confirm your identity and inspect your trunk. Please give me the keys."

"You told me we were going back to Lyon," I said, "and instead you take me to the middle of nowhere and want to search my things. I find your behavior most peculiar."

"You are right," he said, "I am remiss in stopping you here. It is too late to reach Lyon by nightfall. We can take rooms in the village in yonder valley and continue tomorrow. I will leave you with my friend and see about it at once. But first you must turn over your sword."

I realized now, that despite their manners and fine phrases, I was in the hands of two unscrupulous ruffians. I thought of all the jests I had heard on the theme of "your purse or your life," and decided they were not funny. I was not to be given a choice. I handed over my sword, and the officer in red galloped off in the direction of the village, where the band's headquarters probably were.

The second fellow, obviously subordinate, from the way he deferred to the other, had a sad, long-nosed face and would have been well cast in the role of professional mourner. It had grown dark very suddenly, the moon was concealed behind clouds, and the forest sounds, crickets and owls, made him nervous. "Damn that son of a whore for leaving me without a light," he said, to no one in particular. Pulling the coachman roughly from his seat, he ordered him in back with me, "where I can keep an eye on you."

The coachman was a lad from Bidache, no older and no taller than myself, who was to deliver me to Versailles in style and then bring the coach back to the castle. He was trembling with fright and kept crossing himself. "Don't worry," I told him, "we'll get out of this." I was not at all sure about the plural, but that was another matter.

"Oh, my sainted mother," he said, "What did I do to deserve this? I'm just a poor country boy."

"Be quiet," I said, annoyed by his craven complaints, "listen carefully, and try to keep your teeth from clicking."

---

* Remember, man, that powder you once were and to powder you shall return.

I told him that our only chance lay in my getting away and finding help. To do that, he would have to act as a decoy. We would exchange coats, and he would remove his high-crowned coachman's hat and put on my powdered wig. I would say I had an urgent need to satisfy, and he would step out of the carriage in my green coat and wig and, escorted by our guard, move as far away as the man would let him, giving me a chance to slip away. "And what will he do when he finds you gone?" the coachman asked.

"He will do one of two things," I replied. "More likely, he will follow in my pursuit, leaving you unattended, to get away as best you can. Or he will wait for his friend to return, which is a way to buy time while I find help."

"Why don't you stay, and I'll get help?" the fellow asked. Fear had made him quite forget the distance between us, and for the first time in his life, he was addressing me as an equal.

In a situation like this, ordering him about would only paralyze him. I had to invoke the goddess reason. "They might not listen to you," I said, "whereas when they see who I am, I can convince some soldiers to come back here." He kept raising objections, that the brigand would recognize him even though he wore my clothes, that it was too late to find help, that he would be punished for helping me escape. Finally, at my patience's end, I took fifty crowns, half my entire fortune, from the chamois bag where I kept it tied to my waist inside my trousers, and offered it to him if he would go along with my plan.

"A lot of good it will do me," he grumbled, but as he had never in his life seen a like sum all at once, he took it.

"Hey there, friend," I called out, "I must relieve myself."

"Can't it wait?" the brigand asked.

"One moment more, and this carriage will stink like an outhouse," I said.

"All right," he said, "come outside, and I'll go with you, to keep you from any tricks." Out stepped the coachman, in my wig and coat, with stiff strides to keep his knees from knocking, and walked down to the edge of the forest with our guard.

I stepped out of the other side of the carriage and unhitched the lead horse as silently as I could, praying that the beast would not begin to neigh at being separated from its companions. I had neither saddle nor stirrups, but I did not let that bother me. I slid the horse's head out of his harness and coaxed him gently away from the carriage. I could hear the brigand telling my coachman, "All right, then, don't be all night about it." I jumped onto the horse's bare back, dug my heels into his sides, and he made across the field as if to the steeplechase born. I had not gone fifty yards when I heard a cry for help, followed by the crack of a single shot. I neither stopped nor looked back. It was too dark to see, and I knew what had happened. The poor fellow had been the brief owner of a fortune of fifty crowns, but had not had time to spend a penny of it.

The genuine sorrow I felt was submerged by the awareness of my own predicament. Hearing no hoofbeats behind me, however, I guessed that the fellow was waiting for his friend instead of setting off after me. After all, they had my belongings, half my fortune, even my wig. I had set out full of high expectations and a youthful faith in my own good fortune, hopeful that the gates of the court would open before me as they had in distant Arabia for the Forty Thieves, and I had so far succeeded only in being robbed of all my personal belongings, and almost of my life.

I Arrive in Paris and Make a Friend

Five days later I was in Paris, after spending more of my dwindling capital on a saddle and bridle, and I forgot the tribulations of my trip, feeling as overjoyed as a sweepstakes winner at reaching the capital. I had not realized one could feel happy just by arriving somewhere. The people of Paris seemed to be members of a secret fraternity, who knew more about the pleasures of life than other mortals, and whom I was joining by my mere presence in the capital. Every cobblestone, every gleaming window, every smoking chimney on top of every slate roof, spoke to me of future delights.

I rode in on the rue Saint-Jacques into the Porte Saint-Michel, where I saw a scaffolding up and a good-sized crowd waiting for some spectacle to start. A Punch-and-Judy show, I expected, and tied my horse to a hitching post to watch the puppets.

But this Judy was alive, and naked to the waist, and riding a donkey backward, so that her head pointed in the direction of its tail. She wore a straw hat, and around her neck hung a sign that said: PUBLIC PROCURESS. The crowd laughed as the puzzled donkey was poked across the scaffolding, and some threw rotten vegetables at the woman, who soon had the juice of overripe tomatoes running between her breasts. One man held the donkey, and another, bare-chested like the woman, flicked a cat-o'-nine-tails and began to raise rows of welts on her back, giving her twenty lashes as she howled and clutched the poor animal's tail more fiercely than she had ever embraced a lover. Another of her attendants, who had been crouched over a brazier, took the place of the man with the whip, and applied a red-hot poker to her upper arm, leaving the fleur-de-lis imprint that one recognizes in brothels as the brand of the debased woman. The crowd seemed to find the display amusing, and although my admiration for the Parisians did not diminish, I tempered it with the thought that urban life breeds callousness. As for myself, I reflected on the number of women at court preserved from wearing the lily emblem only bceause they procured for men outside the reaches of the law.

Continuing my way, I crossed the Pont-Neuf, which was more like a densely inhabited castle than a bridge, with its white towers, parapets, semicircular balconies, and the greatly motley crowd that swirled there and made it almost impassable, a mixture of merchants and students, soldiers and whores, dog barbers and jugglers, and street criers who added to the din with their musical cries of "Here comes the live mackerel, burning-hot potatoes cooked this very day, and Portugal, Portugal,* here's the ladies' pleasure."

The Seine was covered with a web of cordage and bobbing masts, so dense that its waters could hardly be seen. Barges laden with wheat, wine casks, and manure were towed by teams of horses on the banks, who, their heads bent by their labor, pulled through a swarm of longshoremen, criers, day laborers and coal carriers. Here was the great artery that regulated the beat of the city's pulse. I decided to find rooms near the Tuileries gardens, which my father had once described as "embroidery," having heard that it was a lively center of the capital, and hard on the Palais-Royal, where single ladies strolled in search of chance encounters.

I made my way to the elm-lined terrace of the Orangerie, overlooking a large round basin where children with their nurses sailed miniature clippers, which afforded a fine view of the recently finished, gold-domed Invalides, and I joined a group of men who were gathered around a portly fellow in a frog-green cape and a three-cornered hat covered with gold braid and piping. The tail of

---

* A reference to Portuguese oysters, then, as now, a Paris delicacy.

his wig was imprisoned in one of those little taffeta bags called toads. Two gold watch chains crossed his bulging stomach, and in one hand he waved a cane with a gold pommel, while in the other he held a lacquered tobacco pouch. His air of prosperous elegance was tempered by stockings full of runs and buckled beaver shoes badly scuffed by the Tuileries sand. "Pompadour is fading," the man announced with fanfare, as if delivering news of the greatest importance. "She vomits often. Yesterday she threw up a bouillon she had taken ten minutes earlier, her fever never lets up. The king came to see her after mass but stayed no longer than it takes to say a miserere."

"And it's for the likes of her we're bled white," a man in the crowd said. "If more Parisians were like me, they would march on the markets and take the bread."

"What news of the famine?" someone else asked.

"None that I know," the orator said.

"We live like animals," the first man said. "We never know anything."

Seeing that the discussion was taking a rebellious turn, the orator announced news of the war in Holland, and went into a long harangue that dealt with the immediate origins and distant causes of the conflict, dates, facts, names, treaties, and fresh information from returning soldiers. The king had flown from conquest to conquest, despite a lack of supplies because the country was so narrow and covered with dikes. "The fields are lower than the level of the sea," he concluded, "no mountains, and every house is washed daily outside and inside. And the husbands aren't allowed to beat their wives . . ."

He was immediately contradicted by an elderly fellow dressed in what seemed to be parts of the uniform of several armies, as though he had gone scavenging after a battle involving the entire European coalition. "They've made a terrible mistake," he said. "The whole army is bogged down in lowland swamps. I know what I'm talking about, war is not foreign to me. I've worn the soldier's knapsack and loaded a musket with the best. I learned the hard way. No, they can't pull the wool over my eyes."

The discussion broke down into two camps, those who agreed that the king was winning in Holland, and those who took a bleaker view. The orator stepped down from the bench on which he had been standing and pushed outside the circle of debaters. I followed him down the path and fell into step with him. "Is it true, sir," I asked, "what you said about the marquise de Pompadour?"

"It's true today, my young friend," he replied. "It may be less true tomorrow. My information comes fresh, like day-old eggs, and is subject to change. But what is your interest in the matter?"

I told him I had just arrived in the capital, and was preparing to go to court, meet the king, and claim my regiment.

"Most excellent," he said, clapping me heartily on the back. "I see before me an embryonic courtier, one who will make fans flutter and gossip mills turn. We must see more of each other. I will keep you notified. My friendship with great lords teaches me what to think of events, and supplies me with information not to be obtained elsewhere. Thanks to my entree at court, I have gained a certain reputation for the judiciousness of my analyses. Yes, you will often hear it said, what Roger la Trompette does not know is hardly worth knowing. The king himself sends emissaries to listen to my reports in order to learn what is happening at his own court. Trials, feasts, the outcome of battles, the siege of a city, the infidelity of a mistress, the first night of a play, why the king replaced a minister, what prince of the blood has gone to Plombières for the cure, you will find it all under here." And he tapped his gold-braided hat with a finger.

"Every day at noon I'm on duty on the same bench, disseminating information, like a farmer feeding hens," he went on. "I venture to say there is not a *nouvelliste** in the Tuileries with as large and faithful a following. Anyone listens who wishes, including police informers, and the deaf repeat it to the others. Believe me, it doesn't take much to make Paris run, a ribbon, a rumor, or a baboon's ass. But where are you off to?"

I explained that I was seeking rooms in the neighborhood, and he insisted on introducing me to the proprietress of the tavern where he lodged, called the Tonsured Monk. Her name was Maggie, and her small ferret face rose above huge breasts, reminding me of the hawker I had seen in the Tuileries, whose face was almost hidden behind the helium balloons he sold, and upon which, Roger said, she was able to balance two liter tankards of ale. "You'll never want for company in this place," he added, "and if you're late with the bill, Maggie will take it out in trade."

I promised myself that even if I had to go hungry, I would pay promptly for my room, which was small but afforded a view of the

---

* The *nouvellistes* constituted a form of oral press, since there were few newspapers, and the best ones had quite a following.

gardens. I thought of going to see my brother Antoine, who had come into the title of duke since my father's death. It had not changed him, he was drunk most of the time, and in debt, and I feared that rather than help me, he would ask me to help him. I knew with what contempt he was regarded at court, and I did not want his reputation to rub off on me. What is a duke, after all, but the eldest son of a duke?

I Learn About Court Usage

I had one letter of introduction, written by my father before his death to a friend he had grown up with, who had risen in the ecclesiastical ranks to the eminence of cardinal. At the time, I had asked my father if he could not provide me with other letters, to men more active at court, since Cardinal de Noirot was ill and seldom left his bed. "That one will be enough," my father replied. The cardinal lived in a house in Versailles, near the palace, where the court came to him. He was said to be a man of such subtlety and discernment that I found myself wondering why he had accepted my father for a friend. I resolved to go and see him at once, remembering my father's injunction that, due to the particular nature of his illness, he only received in the evening.

The next morning, fortified by an excellent breakfast of herring and porridge brought to my room by Maggie, who walked on her heels to balance the weight of her great melons, I set out for Versailles in one of those convenient and economical carriages called chamber pots. Drawn by eight horses, the carriage accommodated twenty persons in a long sausagelike wicker cage, which one reached by climbing an iron staircase with a banister. The four leagues took six and a half hours because of frequent stops, but cost a mere twelve sous.

The road from Paris to Versailles was lined with modest, thatched cottages separated by the green rectangles of vegetable gardens. It was autumn, and walls of dust formed on either side of us, dust which I imagined turned to mud in the winter. Dust and mud, I thought, and this the path to wealth and honor, the great road of world history, trod by so many passions, successes, and failures. I wished I could ask this silent thoroughfare what had become of the white powder that rose in small clouds over the dazzling carriage trains. That elm on my left saw it all pass, but lightning had struck it, and it would not reply. The passengers changed, the landscape itself withered, only the destination remained, the resting place between the old age of one king and the youth of another.

I found the cardinal's house without difficulty, in one of those truncated Versailles streets where during the day lackeys sell leftovers from the king's table, while at night servants with torches precede the slowly advancing carriages of gentlemen, calling "Make way, make way." I knocked at the door, which was answered by a valet who introduced me into a small drawing room where a fire was prepared in the chimney, although it was not lit. I was to wait in this room often in the months to come, as my visits to the cardinal became an almost daily event.

The valet Nicholas always wore the same soiled, homespun jerkin, which exactly matched the color of his listless hair, and I came to realize that the unlit fire in the chimney was intended to give the impression that one's visit was unexpected, and to imply that it was in the nature of an intrusion, even though, after my first visit, I always sent a note by messenger well in advance of my arrival. According to this familiar scenario, Nicholas would wait ten minutes, enter the drawing room, and say: "Monsieur le comte will excuse me, I did not think to light the fire," and proceed to do so. So that in the short time one waited, on those damp autumn evenings, one always felt uncomfortable. Nicholas would then slowly ascend the stairs to his master's bedroom, groaning audibly to call attention to the extra effort he was being asked to provide, and return to announce in sepulchral tones: "His Eminence awaits monsieur le comte, if monsieur le comte will take the trouble to follow me." Passing through the narrow unlit corridor that led to the room, Nicholas invariably said: "Monsieur le comte cannot see very clearly, I should get the lamp for monsieur le comte," the mention of which possibility dispensed him from carrying it out.

On this first occasion, as I wondered whether the cardinal would receive me in such an impromptu manner, Nicholas came in to summon me with his graveyard voice, and I entered the room to find Cardinal de Noirot sitting up in bed, propped and bolstered and lifted by a number of pillows of varying sizes, his pink face beaming from their midst, so that he looked like the conventional representation of a cherub surrounded by clouds that one sees in the paintings of Boucher. His round face had the same pink peppermint-candy smoothness, and his lips were those of an aging cupid, moist and fleshy. His bejeweled hand motioned wanly in the direction of a small settee upholstered in Genoa velvet of "liturgi-cal blue," as he called it, and he said, in that slightly rasping voice which always brought to mind a steaming mug of hot buttered rum: "Dear boy, what a pleasant surprise. I was so sorry to hear about your poor father. Did Nicholas light the fire for you? I hope you weren't too cold. As you can see, I am chained to my bed, and must receive my friends this way."

His illness, as I learned, was of an undetermined nature; it al-lowed him to banish the bores from his life and receive only those persons he wanted at hours that were convenient for him, for he suffered from insomnia, and preferred to stay up at night rather than wait for sleep that did not come. Between others and himself stood the screen of his unidentified illness, which absolved him, like a plenary indulgence won through long years of piety, from the chores and obligations at court. At the same time, since he so seldom left his bed, he loved stories of court life, and those who could brought an anecdote or a snatch of gossip as they might have brought a bouquet of tulips and roses, a basket of cher-ries, or a box of liqueur-filled chocolates. As for me, I was there to listen, not talk, and during my visits I received the education I had so long resisted in my native Béarn.

Cardinal de Noirot did not speak to convince, or even to be heard, but as a farmer sows, with the easy natural gesture of throwing handfuls of grain. The quality of his mind lay not only in the experience gained in long years at the elbow of the power-ful, but in the seductiveness of his associations, in the way his thoughts passed to others through a process of irradiation. He never insisted; he seemed always to propose, to suggest, to expose for one's approval. It was never his presumption to instruct, but only to remind one of what one almost certainly knew. He was as supple as Grenoble gloves. He was like a guide showing one an unknown city and increasing one's familiarity with it by presuming that one has been there before. It was part of his strategy to fade behind his suggestions, so that one never had the uncomfortable feeling that one's faculties were being tested. It was never "Let me tell you," or "You may not know this," or "I have always been convinced," or "Experience has shown me," but always "Perhaps, does it not seem to you," "I am sure that you have already heard," "I don't have the right to say what I am not completely sure of myself," or at the extreme limit: "Perhaps I am wrong to tell you what will not please you, for you will not interpret it as I had hoped." This manner of presenting his thoughts conferred upon them a reassuring delicacy. They came, as it were, wrapped in cotton. He sometimes concealed in his phrases judgments from which there was no appeal, but it was like being pricked with a needle so sharp one only felt it later, when one noticed the mark.

Our first meeting was like the first act of a play, when the character of the principal players is exposed. He took pains to reveal that behind the red hat and the ringed hand kissed by the faithful there was a man who had, while remaining faithful to the conventions of his office, held highly individual beliefs. "The great moments of our life," he confided, "do not come from important events, but by surprise, starting with trivial, unforeseen circumstances that give rise to multiple associations, and these are rich and precious.

"For instance, the other day at Champlâtreux (contrary to appearances, I do sometimse venture outside this room), I was strolling in the garden after lunch when I saw the youngest Noailles girl. She must be thirteen or fourteen, in the first flush of adolescence; she always seems a bit breathless, as if she had been running, and indeed she is running, to catch up with all that life still denies her. I saw her in a swing, her wayward sunbonnet tied to her neck with a yellow satin ribbon, filling with air like a sail on the swing's downward course, and her light-brown curls framing her face. Her eyes were shut, as they will be one day in moments of (let us hope) equally intense pleasure, her lips were slightly parted, her legs moved rhythmically to maintain the swing's momentum, and her hands, tightly holding the two ropes, seemed to be claiming them as one might claim a partner. Her arched back, her swaying body, and the barely perceptible ruffling sound that her silk petticoats made as the swing described its parabola, all these confused perceptions sent a shudder through these old bones and brought to mind with a peculiar vividness some of the most sensuous moments of my young life, so similar was this young girl's innocent swinging to certain cadences of the act of love."

I expressed my congratulations that the clerical collar had not been a yoke, and his pale-blue eyes narrowed in his currant face, so like a face that had been painted with oils, since it was rarely exposed to the sun, and he said: "I, the confessor of kings, will make a confession to you, my young friend, because I can see we are going to become friends, and that, despite your recent arrival in the capital, you are not one of our provincial prigs, all starch and saltpeter. I never really believed. In the seminary, my favorite words were '*Ite, missa est.*' Or rather, I believe in the church as a great human institution. I consider myself a servant of the state, and after all, one can be a cabinet minister or a general without believing. I resolved to concentrate my faith on the visible church, and it has returned my efforts. God has never interfered with my advancement, and I wear the *cappa magna* to His greater glory. The amethyst on my right hand is kissed in His name, and for years, I accompanied the king at Lent to hold the water basin as he healed the scrofulous. Such was their strength of conviction that a few were actually cured. What then is the difference between a man who believes and a man who pretends to believe? Their hands are no less joined in prayer, their knees are no less bent, their eyes are no less reverently closed when they receive communion.

"The church is the external representation of a transcendence which may or may not exist. I believe in liturgy, I believe in vestments, I believe in cathedrals, I believe in Latin, I believe in crucifixes and holy images, and, yes, the indulgences that Luther fought. I am an old man, and I have based my life on these beliefs and risen in the ranks of my chosen profession. Not because I loved God, but because I served an institution created by man. And I know how to get along with my fellow man. I will always prefer tact to piety. Preserve me from saints, they are troublemakers; when everyone else is quietly reading the epistle for the day, they will be lying facedown in front of the altar with their arms stretched out in the shape of a cross. I serve my king and I serve my Pope, and I leave it to them to converse with the Almighty."

Not wanting to prolong my first visit, I excused myself, telling the cardinal with all sincerity that introducing me to him was one of the best things my father had ever done. The cardinal asked me to return as often as I liked, for he had the fruit of his experience at court to impart to me. "To know the sesame," he said, "all is there, for every person and every situation possesses its sesame, more or less secret, or easily guessed at. One must always find a person's hidden low doors."

On my subsequent visits, the cardinal gave me what I can only call my court breviary, as essential for my own time as Castiglione's *The Courtier* was for his. All my troubles, my eventual loss of favor and the burden of exile, came from not following the advice I had been privileged to receive. I was like a man who holds the secret of turning lead into gold but does not take the trouble to use it. It was not that I did not prize what the cardinal told me, but when practical situations arose I behaved in accordance with my impetuous nature rather than his teachings. Indeed, I set such store by his principles that I took the trouble to set them down, and hereby pass them on to those who would be armed against the pitfalls of court life.

Courtier is a profession, he told me, a career; one must prepare for it as carefully as for the profession of navigator on the high seas. There are simple things to be learned, but they must be learned so that one does them without thinking. Never express an opinion contrary to that of your king. When he asks for advice, tell him what you think he wants to hear. To sense what that is will be the measure of your judiciousness. For when a prince asks for advice, what he is seeking is endorsement.

Speak well of everyone. If you must speak ill, limit yourself to saying: He does not pass for a man of quality. Be the friend of everyone, which amounts to being the friend of no one. It will take time for you to realize that there are no friends, there are only moments of friendship.

Never contradict the opinion of a superior, for that gives offense, or of an inferior, for that places him on the same level as yourself.

Make your flattery seem the natural outpouring of a bluff, soldierly independence of mind. A gift for flattery can fill an empty purse. Hide your cleverness behind a mask of buffoonery. Better for people to say, "He is more clever than he appears," than "He is a fool pretending to be clever." Never ask a favor for a friend; keep your credit for your own advancement.

Envy: We do not envy the wealth of someone unknown to us, in India or China, but of a companion. We do not envy the man who has always been above us, but the man who, having been our equal, has risen above us in a short time. Emulation is a benign form of envy.

Anxiety: Remember that most problems are two-handled vases, which taken by one handle seem heavy and by the other seem light.

Passion: Passion is repetitive. One passion drives out the other the way one nail drives out the other.

Lies: The value of the lie depends upon the trust we place in the liar, and of his intention, for if we flatter to please, or to avoid unpleasantness, or to gain some advantage, that is excusable. Dissimulation is like the antidote to an illness, which in small doses cures and in large doses kills.

Promises: Beware of those who promise easily, for they hope that in time something will intervene to deliver them from their obligation. Use promises as you use salt, sparingly.

Opportunity: At court, every dog has his day, for the prince needs people of all kinds. He who was thought useless suddenly finds himself indispensable. Wait, and the occasion will arise.

Ruse: A common ruse is to trip someone so as to have the opportunity to help him rise, thus creating an obligation.

Ambition: Open ambition offends those who could do the most to help you if you proceeded otherwise. It is best to imitate a man in a rowboat, whose back is turned on his destination.

Hope: All hopes are false hopes, in that we form a false opinion from our expectations.

Will you be disposed to flatter the great and sometimes the valets, to court porters who have kept you half an hour counting the hinges on a door, to never speak your mind, until you have forgotten that you have one? Of all the arts, the most difficult is crawling, which is why the courtier learns it as a child, reaching a degree of excellence that leads to high honors. Snakes reach the tops of mountains that defeat the most spirited horses. A good courtier must know the price of all those he meets; he must be ready to bow to the chambermaid of a favorite, to caress the dog of a minister; his life is a long sequence of contemptible tasks. Remember that everything at court is fortuitous. When a courtier complained that he had received no favors, Emperor Sigismund offered him the choice between a gold and a lead box. Needless to say, the courtier chose the lead box.

Etiquette: We laugh when we hear that the king of Bakongo takes his meals in two different houses. Are our customs any less ridiculous? Never forget that you are governed by etiquette as a ship is governed by a rudder. It is etiquette that places the *chaise percée* in the midst of courtiers and that dictates who among them will proffer the cotton. Etiquette is a rampart that keeps back an infinite number of unwanted claimants. Follow it blindly. We all do. It is because of etiquette that dead kings are served hot meals. Humankind is immersed in forms, and every state has its own. It is more important to know when the king rises and sets than when the sun does.

You must know about usages; they are the ironclad laws of life at court. No matter how foolish they seem, they must be observed. The duc d'Uzès, the ranking peer, passes ahead of the duc de La Trémoïlle, the ranking duke, at sessions of parliament, while at court ceremonies the order is reversed.

A few things it will be useful to commit to memory: The sons and daughters of the king are the sons and daughters of France; the sons of the dauphin are the dukes of Burgundy, Anjou, and Berry. The eldest of the Condé princes is Monsieur le Prince, and his eldest son is Monsieur le Duc. *Entrées* go down and not up. That is to say, when you have an *entrée* with the king, you automatically have it with the other princes, while the reverse does not hold true. When you leave the king's bedchamber, it is the height of civility to go first, giving an advantage to whoever follows you and has a longer time to enjoy watching him. You will hear a great deal of talk about the divine *tabouret*, and you will be surprised to learn that this most sought-after of honors is no more than a lady's right to rest her rear on an uncomfortable four-legged wooden stool in front of the king or queen. Make no mistake, fortunes have been spent and marriages have been contracted for that right. There are women at court who would kill for that right. Etiquette consists in the exact observance of trivia. It is a turning inside out of the coat of human values, in which the superfluous becomes essential. On the simple matter of pronunciation, a man can betray himself. Remember, and don't ask me why, that Berwick is pronounced "Barwick," Croÿ "Crouy," Bracciano "Brachane," Coislin "Coalin," La Trémoïlle "La Trimouille," and Sully "Suiyi." Finally be careful of the word. A man who puts his foot in his mouth does not have to be garrulous; a single word is enough.

Such was Cardinal de Noirot's advice, dispensed over a series of visits which became for me, like Sunday mass for a good Catholic, days of obligation. The gospel he dispensed had nothing to do with faith and charity, and did not end with a crucifixion. It was a manual for survival in the jungle of the court.

The only problem of these visits was saying good-bye. The cardinal was ready to stay up all night talking, while I often had business in Paris and had to make the six-hour journey in a chamber pot, catching up on my sleep during the trip. Leaving the cardinal was not a departure, but the final movement in a symphony. One could not leave abruptly, that was an affront; it meant that the evening had been a failure, that the magic had not operated, that the fragile link of friendship had been severed. One had

to leave gradually, in stages, rising, sitting down, expressing surprise at the lateness of the hour, saying "Can your clock be right?"
listing the pressing obligations of the following morning, agreeing
to stay a few minutes longer, and thus, imperceptibly, disappearing
without having to mouth anything so brutal as a farewell.

One night, however, I had a midnight engagement with a young
lady I had met outside the palace, strolling with her mother. I had
been struck by her beauty, her long blond hair rippled out from
under her bonnet like a field of buttercups, and I doffed my hat to
the mother, who replied with a smile. I eventually suggested a
further meeting, but alas, the mother thought it was her I had in
mind and whispered, "Not in front of my daughter." This misap-
prehension made my task more difficult, but I finally managed to
have a moment alone with the daughter, on the pretext of showing
her a detail in the palace grille, and she agreed to meet me on a
night when her mother would be away. I grew increasingly nervous on the appointed night as I sat listening to the cardinal, watching the clock, and imagining my sweet Caroline, for that was her
name, waiting for me and finally giving me up for lost. The vision
of those blond curls disappearing forever made me jump to my feet
and blurt out: "I quite forgot the time, I must leave immediately."

"Oh," the cardinal said, "the evening must have seemed very
long. How I regret having kept you."

"Not at all," I said, trying to make my departure as graceful as
possible. "It's simply that with you one does not notice the time
pass."

"The tedium of the evening must have been too much to bear,"
he said.

"I promise that I have never been so entertained," I replied. "It
was just that I felt I must be importuning you."

"In that case leave, my dear, yes, leave at once, if you must. I
won't keep you. I only regret that your departure is so sudden."

I had never met anyone so touchy. He seemed eager to interpret
the most legitimate impatience as a rebuff. I made a gesture as if to
stay, but he waved me away and said: "No, no, you must leave,
you are already late for an appointment, I sense it, I see what it is.
You must not keep her waiting; if you are late she will blame
me."

Excusing myself a thousand times, I left, and rushed to the inn
where Caroline was waiting. My impatience was not in vain, for
she agreed to join me in the room I had reserved. She said she was

a novice, and that I could do with her what I wanted. I proceeded to instruct her in the use of the machinery with which nature has provided us. Whoever has seen that portrait of Coypel in which a nymph, lying on a bed of flowers next to Jupiter, is handling his thunder, will see what I mean, for she and I were a perfect copy of that masterpiece.

Alas, my night of love had two disturbing sequels. The first was a note from Cardinal de Noirot, delivered to my room at the Tonsured Monk. I was being punished for my hasty departure, and for having preferred the company of a ripe untutored lass to his own. "I don't think I will be able to continue our friendship much longer," he wrote, "or as long as I had hoped, for you do not correspond sufficiently to the idea I had of your sensibility. Every day there are new aspects of your character that surprise me, aspects that you took care to bury when we first met, and I no longer find you consistent with the original idea I had of you. I regret it desperately, but there is nothing to be done. To persevere in a friendship that cannot last will only serve to spoil the pleasant memories we can still preserve."

I threw the note into the gutter with a shrug, for I had obtained what I wanted from the touchy old fool, and toward the end, he had been growing repetitious. I recalled the advice he had given me: There are no friends, there are only moments of friendship.

The second discovery, however, could not be so easily shrugged off. Caroline, far from the novice she claimed to be, had given me my first dose of what Cardinal de Noirot called the ecclesiastical grippe. I had stung her with such gusto that I had forced her to plead for mercy. Alas, I could not know that between her thighs I had pumped in the vemon it takes six weeks to get rid of. Where one sins, there one is punished. It's not for nothing that Valentine's Day and venereal disease share the same initials. I was spotted over like a Nigerian leopard, and when I passed water it was like liquid fire. Bent over double from the pain, like a little old hunchback, I was joining a long line of sufferers, beginning with the syphilitic Job, it's written out for all to see in the Bible. I took some of Kayser's pills. The instructions on the box said: "For all of you who follow the tender laws of Venus, do not allow the fear of blame to trouble your love of life and the course of your amorous exploits: Kayser is watching when love forgets." Alas, Kayser was not watching closely enough. All the juice of my generative parts remained corroded. I also tried urethral antivenereal candles, a secret which its French inventor had refused to sell to the English for patriotic reasons, misguided ones. I then engaged the services of a reputed phallustine who was said to do marvels with ointments, but all he did was spread the itch.

Alas, I had to take the mercury cure at Plombières, spend a month in the dark for fear of going blind, and two more weeks taking the waters with the lame, the halt, the amphibious animals of the church, hypochrondriac lords, Paris tarts with dyed hair and insincere laughs, two bearded Jews, young dandies posing as Englishmen, bishops with their nieces, a midwife, a dentist, a dancing master dressed like a Russian major, Dutchmen looking up currency exchange rates in the gazette, Knights of Malta, ancient duchesses with canes, incognito princes, three Brandenburgian electors in Tyrolean native costumes, liverish generals retired for their wounds, all of them religiously charting the progress of their disturbed organs. How was your bath today, was the water too hot? Has your fever gone down? Are you digesting the waters? Has your excellency's liver been able to absorb them? I have the honor of informing your excellency that I perspire from eight to ten in the evening, and that from ten to midnight I am in a perfect sweat.

I vowed that I never would touch another woman, the cure was too long and painful, and I kept my promise a full eight days. My first task upon returning to Paris was to seek out the lady who had seeded me. She had given me the names of the dance halls she frequented, and after three nights of fruitless wandering, I found her, identifying her easily despite the black domino she wore. Between dances, I approached her stealthily and tied to the back of her domino an object commonly known as an English riding coat, which hung from her nape like a disused hairnet. She danced several times without noticing it, provoking a hail of laughter and offcolor remarks, and I considered myself avenged.

I Meet the King and Turn a Reproof into a Reward

I was now ready to make my first appearance at court, armed with the cardinal's axioms and an increase in my fortunes, thanks to the good Roger la Trompette. I had formed the habit of meeting him in the evening in an establishment called Au Coup de Rouge, easily identified by a sign over the door representing a naked Bacchus astride a barrel, lifting a silver goblet. When I told Roger

I could not afford to buy the carriage I needed to go to court, he said: "My boy, there are a hundred ways to make money in Paris. The trouble is, most of them are dishonest."

I said I was not overscrupulous, but wanted to avoid trouble with the police. "You could become a police informer," he suggested. "The trouble is, you haven't been here long enough. Or you could run a string of girls. But that takes capital. Or you could let Maggie support you for a while." I made a face. "Then there is gambling," Roger said, thoughtfully draining a glass of *gros rouge*. He pulled from his pocket a cloth bag and emptied it on the table. Out came tumbling six or seven pairs of dice. He chose a pair, and threw them three times. They came up five each time. "Weighted with quicksilver," Roger explained. "I keep these as protection when I go out among the dice rattlers and whoremongers. It's the only way an honest man can defend himself against professional gamblers."

I asked him whether the gambling houses would let patrons use their own dice.

"These dice are perfect copies of the ones used in some of the best-known establishments," he said. "The trick is substituting yours for theirs. This set of four dice, with pared corners, is called the bones of the four thieves. This other pair of staghorn is heavier above than below. Take your pick and try your luck."

I chose a pair that Roger called Dutch dice. The sides with the fives and sixes were filed down, so that if one gave them what was called the Amsterdam spin, they came up that way. Roger said he would take me to Blondeau's gaming academy on the Place Royale, where those particular dice could work wonders at trictrac. The next night found us at the trictrac table at Blondeau's, an elegant place crowded with fine ladies and gentlemen, where a liveried lackey opened the door. I had expected a hidden den up a dark alley, and said to Roger, "I thought gambling was illegal."

"It is," he said. "From time to time the police 'hail on the parsley,' that is, they arrest a house manager in arrears on his police protection, to set an example, and posters proclaiming the arrest are pasted up on every Paris street corner, at the same time that the Controller General's mistress is losing twice his wages at Blondeau's."

I soon got the hang of trictrac, and in an hour, thanks to my Dutch dice, amassed a small pile of gold louis that was enough to pay for five carriages. Each time I threw, a tiny devil rolled from my hand with the dice to guide them. An Italian who kept betting against me lost heavily, and, giving in to the exuberance of his race, lost his temper, not at me, but at the tapestry of Cleopatra on her throne that hung above his head. Climbing on a chair, he pulled a pair of nail scissors from his pocket and, before anyone could stop him, cut out Cleopatra's nose. *"Porca Madonna,"* he cried. "For two hours that bitch's nose has brought me bad luck."

We left without tarrying, for the attendants were beginning to whisper about my run of luck, and watched me more closely, and I was afraid they would catch me palming the house dice and using my own. I wanted to give Roger half my winnings, but he would have none of it, saying only that I could pay him back some other time. I was able with the proceeds of that night to pay my tailor, my back rent, and my bill at Au Coup de Rouge. I had ample funds left over to buy a carriage with my coat of arms painted on the doors, and to hire a coachman who answered to the name of John and wore a livery of blue and gold. Thus decked out, I prepared to meet the king. This was accomplished, however, more suddenly than I had expected. I decided to celebrate my winnings with a night at the Opéra, which I had, until then, felt too poor to attend. I did not know that only princes of the blood had the right to bring their carriages into the dead-end street behind the Opéra, and, proud to show off my carriage and coachman, I headed straight into that forbidden alley. I was late, and annoyed that I would not have a chance to show myself off in the foyer before the performance began. The street was narrow, and a carriage coming in the opposite direction blocked mine. I stuck my head out the window and shouted at its coachman: "Move back, lummox, you're blocking me."

"Sorry, sir, I am blocked myself," the man replied.

Furious at this contretemps, I leaped from my carriage and seized the bridle of the other coach's horses to start them up.

"Help," the coachman said, clicking his whip defensively in my direction. Cursing the unwiped pissant, I drew my sword and struck him two blows on the back with the flat of it. The man began to howl, and the audience deserted the Opéra lobby to watch the goings on.

A cool voice from inside the carriage called me: "Sir," it said, "there is no need to bludgeon my man. I would be glad to give you the right-of-way, for I see you are new to our ways." Not even thinking who the man might be, and increasingly annoyed by a situation that exposed me to ridicule, I said, stating as accomplished facts what were still intentions:

"No, sir, I am not new, sir. I have fought in the king's troops and held his banner, sir, and slain his enemies. There is no newness there."

"I did not mean a lack of military experience, but a lack of manners," the man said. "I will retire, sir, and let you pass, since you seem to be in a great hurry."

"You will not let me pass. I will affirm my right to pass," I said.

"From your melodious accent, I would make you out to be a Gascon," the man said.

"And proud of it," I replied.

"All the Gascons I ever met were loudmouthed braggarts," the man said, "from the one who said he slept upon a mattress stuffed with the mustaches of slain enemies, to the one who claimed to have killed ten men with a single shot, and, when asked where the bodies were, said he had reduced them to powder. You have the right-of-way, sir, so use it while you can."

The man slammed the door of his carriage after telling his coachman to let me by. I decided against pursuing the argument, for there was in his voice a cold assurance that chilled me, and I was already late enough.

Two days later, a messenger from the palace turned up at the Tonsured Monk with a summons from the king, who wanted to see me in connection with the incident involving the prince de Croÿ at the Opéra. I wondered how I had been identified. Obviously the king's police were efficient. The prince, if the man in the carriage was indeed he, knew I was a Gascon, and had probably recognized my coat of arms—two greyhounds, three vertical arrows, and a lion rampant. I decided to take heart against adversity, put on my blameless morning face, and left for Versailles at once.

After being led down a succession of halls by a succession of ushers (in one great mirrored hall, orange trees grew in solid silver pots), I was shown into the king's study. The king, then thirty-five years of age, was in his prime, robust without being fat, of middle stature, without being short. He had lustrous black eyes, with long, curling lashes, set closely on either side of his generously proportioned Bourbon nose, and a mouth that could not have been improved by the finest painters of his court. He was dressed simply, in a suit of brown velvet. Gold buckles on his shoes were the only decoration he allowed himself. A wig of brown curls fell below his shoulders, and added several inches to his height. He had a natural majesty that made his every gesture seem ceremonial. If he had wiped his nose in front of you, he would have convinced you that it was part of an elaborate ritual. I was led in by a gentleman of the bedchamber, who whispered as he opened the door, "You've been a bad boy," and found him seated at his desk, pressing his ring into a lump of soft red wax on the back of an envelope.

As I entered, I removed my hat with a flourish, knelt on one knee, and said: "Your humble servant." I had practiced the gesture the night before in front of a mirror, trying out the various phrases that seemed apt—"Your servant," too short; "Your most humble and devoted servant," too long; "I lay myself at your feet," too fawning; "Your servant who has fought for you and is ready to die for you," untrue and bombastic; "Your most loyal, faithful and devoted servant," redundant. I decided on "Your humble servant" —matter-of-fact and to the point.

The king rose and waved his hand, a gesture that managed to be at the same time a blessing, a scolding, and an invitation to make myself at ease. I stood like a penitent before his maker, with my head bowed and my hat in my hand. "So you are the young man who charged the carriage of a prince of the blood and attacked his coachman," the king said.

"Your majesty," I replied, with a bow so low that the top of my wig scraped the carpet, "allow me to declare that the honor of being in your presence far outweighs in my eyes the unfortunate circumstances that have brought me here. As, in warfare, the decoration makes the wound worthwhile, my presence here is an undeserved reward for my rashness. I have but recently arrived at Versailles, determined to pay my court, and have done so as assiduously as your gentleman of the quarter would allow, but always from a distance. I am, sire, if I may attempt a mild paradox, both ashamed and rejoiced that my blunder has narrowed that distance."

"Yes, but what of the prince?" the king asked. "You should know that only I can claim the right to be rude to princes of the blood, and I never avail myself of it. And what is worse, the princess was with the prince, and as you know, she is my cousin, so that if you were rude to him, you were rude to her, and if you were rude to her, you were rude to me."

Just my luck, I thought, that the vague shape in the back of the carriage, a shape I had hardly seen, should turn out to be the instrument of my doom.

"Ah, the princess," I said. "I would fall on my hands and knees and kiss the ground her carriage has covered between Paris and Versailles. I would draw and quarter any knave who dared call her less than perfect. I would walk to Ispahan to fetch her back a rose. In short, sire, I did not know that was the prince's carriage, nor that the princess was in it. His coachman was uncivil, and I come to a boil as quickly as milk." My imagination, racing ahead of my words, suddenly saw a way out. "My impulsiveness was put to better use at Dettingen," I added.

"So you were at Dettingen," the king said, in a more amiable, almost fatherly tone.

"In the fourth Hussars, sire, as aide-de-camp to my poor father. I came against his wishes, so he probably did not mention me to you, but once I was there, the soldier overruled the father and let me stay. I helped retrieve the regimental banner from the waters of the Main when the standard-bearer received a musket shot full face, and I ran through two Englishmen as I climbed back on the bank. In fact, my main reason for coming to Versailles was to ask your majesty for the regiment my father gave me before he died, in order that I may continue to serve you."

"Yes," the king said, with a faraway look in his eyes, "our men seldom fought so bravely. Had it not been for the difference in numbers . . . You're a brave lad, and your father was a gallant soldier. Ah, well, let's talk no more of this carriage business. A man in my position has to listen to complaints every time a princess stubs her toe. What was it the Pope wrote me the other day? 'Son in un sacco qui.' I will instruct the gentlemen of the bedchamber that you are to attend my retiring tonight."

And thus it was that not only was I allowed among the handpicked courtiers whose privilege it was to watch the king retire, but that those experienced bed watchers were astonished to see the king that night hand me the candlestick that lit his way.* The king was sitting in his *ruelle*,† with a hat on his head. Against the baluster I noticed the duc de Bouillon whispering to a short man with a pointed nose. I performed a deep bow in front of the king, who doffed his hat and handed me the candle. I was warmed by that attention, and as I left his apartment with the others, I said to the

* To be handed the candlestick was a great honor.
† The space between the bedside and the wall.

man with the pointed nose: "I hope he gets a good night's rest."

"Ha," he replied, "it's easy to see you haven't been here long. After a decent interval, he will leave the royal bedroom through a door concealed in the paneling and join more pleasant company in a more cheerful bedroom up a private stairway. Kings are fortunate in this respect: They may dispense with the chores of courtship."

"But that is where the pleasure lies," I exclaimed.

The short man shrugged and introduced himself as the duc de Lauzun. Taking me into his confidence, he painted a discouraging portrait of the monarch. "He is a king, that I grant you," Lauzun said, "by birth and by deportment, but he is not the man his grandfather was. He is secretive, melancholy, and cruel. As a child, he liked to torture cats. He has a morbid streak. He is always inquiring about who has died, or what illness one is suffering from. To any man over thirty, he says: 'At your age, death is always around the corner.' He once heard me cough, and said: 'This cough has the scent of pinewood.' "

"He is concerned for the health of his courtiers," I said, coming to the king's defense. Lauzun shrugged and went on as though he had not heard me:

"He is not lazy, but he has strange pastimes for a king. Last Christmas, he made tobacco pouches, bits of hollowed-out wood with the bark still on them. Ugly as they were, it was a penalty to be seen without one. He likes to discuss botany, physics, and astronomy, but if the conversation goes beneath the skin of the subject he is lost. The only education that stuck was the course in lubricity taught by a mistress twice his age when he was fifteen. He respects the external signs of faith, hears mass every day, never misses morning and evening prayers, never raises his eyes from his Book of Hours, while his lips move to prove he is reading it, attends vespers, sermons, and has an absolute hatred of unbelievers, which is why, although he admires his talent, he cannot stand the sight of Voltaire. He is not so much devout as superstitious, and with every new mistress, thinks only of appeasing heaven."

"Does he exhibit them publicly?" I asked.

"The castle of Choisy* is the secret sanctuary of his orgies," Lauzun said, with the air of a man who has been there. "He in-

---

* Choisy-le-Roi, in Sceaux, was built by Mansart in 1635 for Mlle. de Montpensier, and Louis XIV had it entirely rebuilt. Rouget de Lisle, composer of the "Marseillaise," died there. It was destroyed in the Revolution.

vented a moving table, a marvel of mechanical ingenuity, which brings the dishes up hot from the kitchen. This is how the pernicious habit of serving oneself, one of the many signs of a crumbling society, came into being. At this time he had two mistresses, sisters, one so plump she was called the hen, the other so thin she was known as the lizard, and he slept between them and spent the night going from the fat to the lean.

"When these ladies needed money, they had only to send notes with the amount and their initial, countersigned by the king, to the royal treasury. Love turns him to quivering jelly, he is ready to grant anything. One would think a man who can bed down any woman in the kingdom for the asking would be less softheaded about cunt. And yet when he's had enough, he gets rid of them with as little fanfare as if they were beginners at the Opéra. The blue silk bed at Choisy is called the revolving bed. It must be said for the king that the queen often reduced him to conjugal unemployment, pretexting religious holidays, vigils, and saints' days. The saints became more numerous and obscure, and the king one night wrote on a mirror, after blowing on the glass: 'Her Majesty is a prude.' After the king publicly began to take mistresses, the queen told her ladies-in-waiting she was terrified he would pass on to her a virus she could do without."

"And who does he have at present?" I inquired, my curiosity growing at this portrait of the king's frivolous side.

Lauzun shook his head sadly. "A commoner," he said. "At least the sisters I have mentioned were *de ce pays-ci.** This one comes from the dregs of the people. Her name, if you can believe it, is Poisson.† She had to be taught manners by the abbé de Bernis before she could be shown at court. And now they've found an abandoned castle called Pompadour to make her the marquise of. I'm afraid this one will not soon be thrown off the revolving bed. The king has given her brother an office, and when he starts doing favors for relatives, watch out, it's good advice to stay on her good side. There are already casualties."

"Courtiers who displeased her?" I asked.

"Exactly," Lauzun said. "The king's bedroom at Choisy is on the ground floor, with a secret staircase to the blue room on the first floor. Last week, through a mix-up, the blue room was given

* *Ce pays-ci*, or, literally, "this here country," was the way courtiers referred to the court.
† Fish.

to Madame de Chevreuse. La Poisson, trying to be tactful, asked Madame de Chevreuse: 'Can't we change rooms?' Madame de Chevreuse is such a prig she pretended not to know what was involved. 'I can't change with you,' she said, 'without knowing the king's will.' Now she knows it. She has been asked not to come to court for six months."

The principal talent of a courtier, I soon gathered, was to be seen as often as possible. As Lauzun said, a courtier is someone who spends his life going up and down stairs. His whole being is in his legs. Having been granted permission, I went to each of the king's *levers* and *couchers*. The king took careful note of those who had the permission and did not use it. When Lauzun was absent several days running, the king told him: "You could come more often without tiring yourself, for I am a late riser."

I too was sorry not to see Lauzun, for he was about my age, and amused me with his commentary on other courtiers, recited *sotto voce* as they entered and bowed to the monarch sitting on the edge of his bed. Of the prince de Conti, he said: "He is an obelisk. As he rises, he grows smaller, and ends in a point." It was true, the prince de Conti had a pear-shaped body and a tiny head. Of the duc de Bouillon, he said: "He is the biggest miser around. To know him is to know the marriage of hunger and thirst." Of La Trémoïlle, a stooped young man with a low brow, he warned me: "He works underground like a mole." Of the strutting duc d'Aumont, whose heels were an inch higher than the king's, he said: "He is living on his reputation, like the Romans besieged in the Capitol who threw bread from the windows even though they were starving."

He also warned me about the duc de Gesvres, who devoted his life to hunting down infractions to usage, which he then made a great fuss about. No sooner had Lauzun spoken than the little duke, whose nose twitched like a ferret's, came up with his latest tempest in a thimble. He was highly agitated, darting his eyes and mopping his brow. "A crisis this morning," he announced. "The queen found dust on the counterpane of her bed and summoned the valet in charge of upholstery, who maintained, can you believe the fellow's impudence, that it is not the upholsterer's duty to make the queen's bed, having made it to begin with, but the responsibility of the gentleman of the wardrobe." Whenever he could, the duc de Gesvres would corner you and describe at length the latest blow to manners, always ending with a phrase that called attention to his own vigilance in the face of general indifference, on the order of: "I don't know what the court is coming to, one might as well be living in a field with gypsies for all the attention that is paid important matters."

I was also present at the king's dinner, which generally took place at two in the afternoon. He almost always ate alone. The queen had her own attendants and kitchens, and spent a good deal of time by herself. It was rumored that she had strange habits. She was, it was said, afraid of the dark, and always kept a candle lit beside her bed, inside the skull that was said to have once encased the tiny brain of the famous courtesan, Ninon de Lenclos.

Five gentlemen were appointed to serve the king, and I took my turn with the rest. One was a sort of taster. If the roast was poisoned, he would have the honor of sacrificing his life for his prince. When my turn came, I was passed snippets of each dish, and munched them with a thoughtful air. Two others brought the food to the king's table, and a fourth served as wine steward. He did not taste the wines, however, limiting his office to throwing a drop off the decanter and scouring the king's glass before he filled it. The fifth served the king, handing him knives and forks, picking up his napkin if it fell, and taking away the plates when the monarch indicated satisfaction, with a wave of the hand or a discreet belch.

There was little conversation at these meals. The courtiers were as solemn as storks standing in a field on one leg, and sometimes the king addressed them. He was known for his ability to slice the top off a soft-boiled egg with one blow of the knife, and they were often on the menu. Once when he had performed this feat, and the runny white was sliding down the side of the decapitated egg, he turned to me and said: "Listen to where an egg can lead you. The poor duc d'Ayen asked for hard-boiled eggs for lunch. He ate between twenty and thirty, went hunting, was attacked by a shrinking of the intestine. His stomach grew hard as a rock, and an inflammation ensued." The king dipped a piece of bread crust in the egg, retrieved it moist and yellow, swallowed it with satisfaction, and added: "His doctor could do nothing for him."

On one occasion, a young woman with a flirtatious manner was summoned by the king as he ate and given a morsel from his plate, as one might throw a scrap to a dog. I asked Lauzun who she was. "Someone the anti-Poisson forces are trying to foist upon the king," he said. "Her name is the Countess of Lawner. She looks as though she had escaped from an Arabian harem, is devoured by hemorrhoids, and has been had by half the footmen in Versailles, and half the upstairs maids as well." The king's interest was short-lived, however, for La Poisson continued to reign supreme, even though it was reputed that she was cold-blooded and feigned *la petite mort*.*

I Am Loved by Two Ladies

I kept trying to arrange another interview with the king, but he was always surrounded. The ministers themselves had to lie in ambush for days to discuss affairs of state. My chance finally came at the end of a morning when he had been receiving ambassadors who seemed to have been chosen for their appearance, for the Swedish ambassador was stern and pale, the Swiss ambassador was a leathery mountaineer, with the beginning of a goiter, and the one from St. Petersburg had slanted Tartar eyes, a bushy beard, and the rollicking manner of a confirmed drunkard. The reception was brief. The king was seated in his armchair with his hat on. When the Russian ambassador came in, the king removed his hat, then put it back on to hear the harangue of the ambassador, whose hat was also on. There was a little ballet of hats. After the harangue, the master of the wardrobe brought the king the crossbelt. The ambassador called for his square. The king said: "Get on your knees." The ambassador normally knelt and the king passed the crossbelt around his neck. But the Russian, who probably felt that he represented a country as great as the king's, even though it is populated mainly by savages, only bent his knees instead of kneeling. After he had gone out, the king turned to me, for I was, as usual, in close attendance, and said: "We will write that he knelt and he will write that he did not."

Seizing the opportunity, I said: "Your Majesty, let me now kneel to implore you for my regiment. I burn to be in the field, defending your banner."

The king looked displeased at my boldness. "How can I please a hundred postulants with only twenty-two available regiments?" he asked. "There are some people who would not be content were I to hand them my crown."

* The little death, a popular euphemism for orgasm.

I let a week go by, and decided to write a memoir, for Lauzun had told me this was the correct procedure. Again I made my request, drowning it in flattery.

It began: "If your majesty is willing to lose a quarter of an hour of the time he employs so well to win the love of all those to whom he deigns to make himself known," and continued in the same appalling vein. But no reply was forthcoming. I resolved that an oblique course of action was preferable. If the front door was shut, I might find an open side door. I looked for a chance to make myself agreeable to the marquise de Pompadour, who had become the chief dispenser of favors. Her conversations with the king, instead of love, now turned on: "We must do something for that young colonel, his merit is known to me, and what of that young abbott? How surprising he is not a bishop yet; he comes from such a good family, and I have heard glowing reports of his virtue."

The chance soon came thanks to Lauzun, who had been asked by the king to invent for the marquise a genealogy to match her rise in station. He came to me for advice. "Simple," I said. "Her name is Poisson, give her a coat of arms with fish in it. If that smells to you of the central market, remember that the sovereigns of the house of Bar had in their coat of arms fish and a silver bar. Let it be known that this *poisson* is a junior branch which in ages past displeased its senior and lost its bar." The idea pleased Lauzun, and he commissioned an artist to draw a coat of arms with a castle and a fish. What is more important, the marquise was delighted, and ordered a set of Sèvres plateware with her new blazon on it. Lauzun told her whose idea it was, and she asked to meet me, kept me for an hour in her apartment, treating me most kindly, and promised I would have my regiment within a week.

A week went by, then two weeks, until, champing at the bit, I went to see her one afternoon, and found her alone, looking like a governess with her hair in a bun, wearing a simple brown cotton dress, and working on petit point. "You enter blustering like the spring," she said, looking up from her work. "I have just been thinking about what I can do for you."

"Madam, you have done too much already," I protested.

"Well, no," she said, "you see, I forgot I had promised you the horse guards, and I have given them to another deserving young man, for his dowry. However, I will make it up to you."

I was crestfallen. "Madam," I said, "it is no longer the regiment I am pleading for, it is my honor. For in depriving me of it, you will be dealing me a deathblow. Being sure of my success, I wrote my brother the good news, and he has told all of Bayonne that I had your word. My wife and her family have also spread the news. Two provinces know about it, and I have praised your generosity in Versailles as in Paris. At this point, madam, no one will believe that you gave to someone else a regiment you formally promised me. Everyone knows you have a thousand ways of helping whomever you wish. I will be accused of bragging, of bad faith, of lying, to my eternal dishonor. Madam, I have lived in indigence, but I cannot live in shame. Pray remove from this other protégé a regiment which a momentary lapse made you promise twice. It is easy for you to find him something more advantageous, whereas my deprivation would be irreparable."

Touched by my sincerity and eloquence, she promised to put the matter right. I professed eternal devotion, and took my leave as quickly as decency would allow to tell the news to my dear duchesse de Villiers. I found her wandering in the garden, near the equestrian statue of the Sun King dressed in the garb of a Roman emperor, seized her hands, and told her: "The old bitch is giving me the horse guards after all; that means, by selling the lieutenant's commissions, two thousand pounds a year without lifting a finger. On honeyed tongue, oh, wily and resourceful fellow, if only you were ambitious." The duchesse laughed and congratulated me. I should explain that since coming to court, I had become a fashionable toy. Duchesses fought over me, and let me know in no uncertain way that if I was not yet a man they would help me become one.

I had learned the subtlety of expressing desire in a manner once removed. I was attentive, but not overeager, for that smacks of adolescent drooling. I made every gesture seem natural: "Remove this palatine, it must be uncomfortable indoors." "Your throat is covered with powder. Here, let me dust it with my handkerchief." "What a lovely emerald. May I see the ring?" There are a hundred pretexts for touching a woman without offending her.

I grew so versed in love's small labors that I soon had two of the most desirable ladies at Versailles hopelessly in love with me, the duchesse de Villiers and the Countess of Lawner. The duchesse de Villiers looked more English than French, with hair the color of Normandy butter and eyes the exact tint of bluebottles. She had a convent complexion, and an Attic profile, her small straight nose continuing without interruption the line of her brow, like the profiles one sees in coin collections. Her eyes were not set horizontally in her face, but at a slight upward tilt, so that, seen full face, she had a feline look. She could stare in the superior way that cats do, when they seem to be saying: I saw the fall of Memphis and the fall of Thebes, and I was by the pharaoh's side when the great pyramid of Cheops was built. But the strange look that sometimes came into her eyes was softened by a mouth that was quick to laugh. Of her figure, it is enough to say that in an evening of charades she portrayed Aglaia, the first of the three Graces, and so outshone the other two that I was reminded of the Spanish proverb: If there were no ugly women, there would be no beautiful women.

I had paid my court to her as to the others, but thought her beyond my reach, admiring her beauty without making any overt declaration. One morning I was gossiping with Lauzun in the hall of mirrors, between two orange trees. The duchesse de Villiers came toward us, and I whispered something in Lauzun's ear. She went directly up to Lauzun and said: "You must tell me what Gramont just said."

"I beg you, madam, to allow me not to satisfy your curiosity," Lauzun mumbled in embarrassment.

"But I insist," she said, turning her blue eyes on me.

"Then, madam, I must obey," I said, with a slight bow. "I was saying, madam, that if you were a dancer at the Opéra, I would give my last sou for you." I met her eyes as I spoke, and she was unable to sustain the directness of my gaze. She walked on without further comment, leaving me convinced that I had offended her.

Later that day, however, as I played cavagnola at the queen's table, she looked in, and seeing me there, stood beside me as if watching my cards. Moving quite close, so that I could feel the organdy ruffle of her gown against my leg, she said in my ear: "I have just applied for an audition at the Opéra." The phrase was a summons, and a proof that while we flatter ourselves with the illusion that we choose women, they are more often the ones who choose us, for in our role of courtship, we must roam like bees from flower to flower, until we find one that opens and receives us.

In the days that followed, the duchesse de Villiers and I acted out the charming charades of the body, the leaning head, the half smiles, the fan whose coming and going, like a pigeon's fluttering wing, scans courtly conversation. I employed the conventional exaggerations, "astonishing," "miraculous," "divine," "I am in despair, prodigiously obsessed, unable to eat and drink, ready to fling myself from a window." She told me that I learned my fine speeches by heart and recited them like a lesson. I fell to my knees to convince her that my heart dictated words I had never said before. She burst out laughing and called me a liar.

This was part of the game and it had to be played out, although we both knew its outcome. A man of the world pretends passion when he feels desire. A woman of the world accepts the pretense for what it is, opposing it with the pretense of resistance. She protests faithfulness to a husband she has scarcely seen since the first six months of marriage, when a more experienced lady told her she was making a spectacle of herself by spending too much time at his side: "You have been married for six months and still love your husband? Your cleaning woman loves her husband, but you are a duchesse. A gentleman finds you attractive and you blush. At court, only the rouge brush should make you blush. Is it true that you go to vespers? Listen to other sermons, never those that convert. The day will come when your husband will disappear a little more each day, until you no longer see him at all behind the screen of your admirers." Such was the advice the duchesse de Villiers had heeded, and was now passing on to other ladies of more recent vintage, as an experienced soldier tells a young recruit as much about survival in battle as can be taught and is not part of instinct.

Love at court was always tied to power, to favors given and intricate webs of influence. A man had to look upon the woman he was courting with vows of eternal love as a potential enemy. This was the first lesson I learned from the duchesse de Villiers. I managed one morning in a crowded anteroom to place a love letter in her fur muff, and that evening she handed me the reply. I went into an adjoining room to read it, and she followed me, waited until I had read the note agreeing to receive me in her apartment, snatched it from my hand, and threw it into the fire. When I expressed shock at her lack of trust, she laughed and said I would learn. Later, admitted to her bedroom, I praised everything in it, as an indirect way of praising her: "By heaven," I said, "what a superb fireplace. These Chinese lacquered cabinets are charming. And this porcelain shepherd playing a flute is wonderfully made."

To the cat curled in her lap, I said: "The gods who reign above us, among the stars, have a seat less enviable than yours."

Again she called me a liar, but did not protest when I sat next to
her, displacing the cat. When I kissed her she slid her lips away at
the last moment, adroitly slipped out of my embrace, and said:
"You will not want a prize too easily won." Even as she said this,
however, she complained about the heat and loosened her muslin
bodice. I sped to her side, and pressed burning kisses on her lips,
which she returned with just the right degree of ardor. But when I
lowered my lips, she pushed me back. "Enough for now," she said.
I pretended love made me deaf, and pressed against her so that
there could be no ambiguity about my intentions. She wrenched
herself free and rose to her feet, standing behind the chair. Her
breath came as hard as if she were being chased by a bear through
a forest. She put the back of her hand to her brow and said:
"Please leave me, I don't feel well."

In every battle, there is a decisive turning point that decides the
day, and the good officer's virtue lies in knowing how to recognize
it. I picked her up in my arms, silencing her with kisses, put her
down on the bed, lay beside her, and proceeded to fully disclose
my intentions. "Be gentle," she said, and our bodies in unison
began a soft rocking, until the mind receded to give way to the
rainbow arch of fulfillment. We spent hours of such delight that I
forgot to count them. As I left her room in the small hours of the
morning, as dazed by the intensity of pleasure as a man who has
been too long in the sun, she turned lazily in her bed, and said, in a
voice that tried to sound stern: "Come and see me tomorrow, I am
not through scolding you."

After that, I visited the duchesse regularly. She was my mistress
and my confidante; we freely mixed the two functions of the
mouth, kisses and conversation. She was always delighted when
the conversation stopped. Most women love to make love, but
their modesty will not let them admit it. They think secretly about
it, and wait with a muffled impatience for the man who will solicit
them. One must go resolutely toward them, and not treat them like
lifeless porcelain figurines. Their senses are always in a state of
watchfulness; they are hoping to find, thanks to a man's guidance,
the form their capitulation will take.

Less than a week after my affair with the duchesse de Villiers
had begun its happy course, I was in the small apartments with a
group of courtiers who were weathering the latest tempest of the
duc de Gesvres. Tiny patches of foam appeared at the corners of
his mouth as he said, his arms stiffly moving like those of a wind-

mill: "I was able to correct a grave impropriety yesterday at chapel. You know of course that when the queen is occupying the little round oratory, the one with gilt wood columns, the rule is that no one should lean against the banister, even while kneeling. Well, I found the cardinal of Auvergne kneeling there, as still as a stone statue. I told him he should not be there, and he replied in a very civil manner that he had not known and would not do it again. You would think he of all people would have known. In this place, one has to tell cows about milk."

I was listening with one ear, my arm resting on the back of an armchair where a woman was sitting. To occupy my hand as the little duke rambled on, I caressed the top of the sculpted molding of the armchair, when, lowering my gaze, I realized that it was the nape of the lady's neck I had been rubbing for over a minute, with all the ardor one can summon when touching a finely made piece of wood. To stop would have meant admitting my error (terribly sorry, madam, I thought the nape of your neck was the back of a chair), so I continued, more gently, finally removing my hand. Curious to see who it was I had been surreptitiously caressing, I moved in front of the chair. It was the Countess of Lawner, the lady the anti-Pompadour cabal had tried to press on the king. I nodded, and she smiled in a way that seemed to be saying: "You rascal, we have hardly exchanged two words, and you already have your hand down my dress."

The Countess of Lawner was a beauty in her own right, although slightly too Mediterranean for my taste. There was a softness in her face that would turn to overripeness. She was now in her prime, with skin like lavender honey and large, liquid-brown eyes. Her mouth was full, and I noticed that she did not rouge it entirely in order to brush in a bow shape that it did not have. At one corner there was a delightful mole, a tiny sentinel, and her oval chin was agreeably dimpled. She managed to look always languorous, like those paintings of odalisques reclining on piles of cushions, gazing seductively through heavy-lidded eyes moistened with belladonna. I later learned that the Countess of Lawner's romantic gaze was due to myopia. Her eyes were always out of focus, looking past one. No one knew precisely how she had arrived at court. The source of her income was equally mysterious. It was whispered that she had carried the bastard of an English prince, who now provided for her, so long as she remained out of

England. She was the sort of woman whose footsteps are dogged by a murmur of scandal.

My neck massage earned me an invitation to dinner. I could not turn it down. It is hard for a man to say no. The word is a weapon grown rusty from disuse. He is expected to be always available. If he rejects a lady, he not only insults her, but raises doubts about his manhood. At court, it was better to juggle five mistresses than to spurn four to keep one, for in the first case one had five allies while in the second one made four enemies. I therefore went that same evening, after telling the duchesse de Villiers that I had to see my brother in Paris, to the Countess of Lawner's lodgings in a small house near the palace.

In her silk-tapestried dining room, a table was set with various *pâtés* and a bottle of champagne on ice. There was no sign of servants, and the countess was dressed as if ready for bed, having removed her wig, with her luxuriant brown hair falling about her shoulders, in a patterned robe that opened generously to reveal the two cupolas of her chapel. "Madam," I said, "you honor me more than I can say. I would be mortified to abuse your hospitality."

Abandoning her earlier languorous manner, she said, in a voice accustomed to command: "Spare me your compliments. They bore me. You are here because I want you here."

My mouth dropped open in surprise. "What is it?" she went on. "Am I making you miss some rendezvous? You should see yourself. You look as if you had seen an angel pass."

"Ah, madam," I said, "how can I tell what pitfalls lie behind your forthright manner?"

"Don't be a fool," she said, pointing at the chair she intended me to sit on and spreading *pâté* on a slice of *brioche*, which she handed me. "If one had to reject all advances, one might as well bury oneself in the desert."

I reflected that the advances thus far had come from her, with the exception of my initial mistake. But I decided to play the role for which I had been cast, and went through my repertoire of tender phrases.

"For God's sake," she said, "no vows, they drive me to distraction."

I was silenced, and turned my attention to the food. She fed me morsels, moving her chair closer to mine, and whispered words that I would blush to set down here. When my plate and glass were empty, she led me by the hand into her bedroom, stood before a full-length mirror, and threw off her robe, standing before me as she had been made, in the garb of Eve. "This is what you came for. Why pretend?" she asked.

As she spoke, she began to unbutton my jerkin, and I was soon as naked as Adam. The countess took control, giving me orders like a soldier at drill: Kiss here, touch there, squeeze here, rub there. I had to concentrate to the utmost to obey her directives. I must say to her credit that she knew what she wanted; she had none of the vaporous lapses many women experience in the midst of lovemaking. When I was particularly responsive, she commended me with an "Ah, yes, that is it, exactly," spoken in the tone of a schoolmistress congratulating a pupil on having recited his multiplication tables without error. After I had manipulated her for a considerable time, she announced that she was ready, told me to lie on my back, and straddled me, introducing my *qu'importe** into her as if it were disconnected from my body. I lay there motionless, feeling as though it was out on loan, as she rode up and down on it, her eyes shut in concentration, guiding it with one hand as with the other she continued those caresses I had begun. Her head was thrown back as it might have been in a strong wind, and her parted lips moaned the same words repeatedly. Straining to hear, I finally made out the name David. While using me, her thoughts were on another man. I might as well not have been there at all. I could have left, if that were possible, the part of me she needed, and come back for it later. Moved to a paroxysm by the thought of the unknown David, she collapsed and bit my shoulder until it bled. Suddenly composed again, she said: "That worked out very well."

I was allowed a fifteen-minute intermission, and then had to go through my paces again. The second time, I derived some pleasure from it too, for she was warmed up, and I did not have to tune her clavecin quite so long. To pay her back in kind, I cried out, at the moment of passion, the name Elizabeth, which was the duchesse de Villiers' first name.

Later, as she helped me apply a poultice to my gnawed shoulder, she asked me who Elizabeth was. "And I might ask you the same with regard to David," I replied.

"How right," she said. "There is no need for further explanation. You have someone else, and so have I, to whom we have left

* Literally, "What does it matter?" an eighteenth-century euphemism for the male organ.

our hearts in trust. But we have kept our bodies, and continue to use them."

I let her believe what she wanted. My heart was still my own, and I meant to keep it so. The Countess of Lawner proceeded to give me my days. On Tuesdays and Fridays I was to visit her little house and service her. I did not ask how many pigeons came to her dovecote on other evenings. I decided to comply, for she had become a figure of some note at court, her name had at one time been linked with the king's, and it might advance my own affairs to have it linked with mine. On other days, the duchesse de Villiers and I played the game of love as if we had invented it. But the court is a village where no secret can be kept, and it soon became known that I was enjoying the favors of two of its most sought-after ladies.

Lauzun said: "I hear you are burning at both ends a candle with one brown wick and one blond one." I did not deny it. I was flattered to be winning a reputation as a libertine, for constancy in love is like having a terrible itch that no one's allowed to scratch, and there were no clauses guaranteeing fidelity in the contracts I had signed.

Several weeks later, spurred by oysters and champagne, I performed four times for the Countess of Lawner. She rewarded me with a gold horseshoe scarf pin studded with four pearls. I thanked her and asked: "The first time we met, what were you looking for?"

"Pleasure," she said.

"And from whom did you expect to find it?"

"The first one to come along. You men want to be allowed everything. We have only one way to reconquer our rights, and that is to do secretly what you take pride in doing in public."

"Oh, so you have one of those," Lauzun commented when I wore my horseshoe pin on one of our morning rides through the forest of Rambouillet. "One sees quite a few of them around. A Moldavian hospodar, a giant of a fellow, with forearms like wine kegs, holds the record—seven pearls." After hearing that, I no longer wore mine. It was a badge of membership in a far from exclusive club, where one had no say in boycotting undesirable candidates.

I made the mistake of wearing the pin once when I was meeting the duchesse de Villiers, and she said: "What a lovely pin, Ax. Did it cost a great deal?"

I could tell from her tone that she knew more than I had toid her. Candor was part of my nature, and I wanted to tell each of my mistresses about the other, but that would have spoiled the delicate balance, and I was forced into attitudes of deceit. Neither of the two ladies was really in love with me, but vanity made them believe they claimed my attentions exclusively. If one learned about the other, would she accept the apportionment, or play the fury? I dreaded the day of reckoning, and yet was unwilling to give up the arrangement, for each of my mistresses provided a welcome contrast to the other: The Countess of Lawner's bluntness refreshed me from the duchesse de Villiers' persiflage, and the duchesse's tenderness was a relief after the countess' military drills. I was like a man with two houses, one a stone medieval castle, unassailable and dominant, with a view over fields and mountains, the other an enclosed country manor filled with fruit trees, climbing roses, fragrant lilies, and pink and white carnations. I went from one to the other, finding in each a separate pleasure.

A Duel Is Fought over Me

Such was the state I was in when the king announced a masked ball, to be held in the large drawing room near the chapel, the one painted by Le Moyne. The expense was estimated at two hundred thousand pounds, and there were to be twenty-four thousand candles. A masked ball, I thought, is an excellent device, a feminine occasion that corresponds to the woman's love of double registers, the done and the undone, the said and the unsaid, the putting on and the taking off. Masked, everyone is equal, the king, the princes of the blood, great ladies and courtesans, a lord and his valet. The blue ribbon of the highest order is concealed under Harlequin's quilt, the archbishop comes as Tom Fool, and one never knows whether one is talking to a princess or a shopgirl. With a strip of black satin over her face, a woman will dare anything.

I decided to come as a Spanish grandee, for in the Béarn of my birth, I had learned the language, and could easily pass myself off as one. My mask of black velvet lined with white taffeta had a thin silver wire with a glass ball on the end of it, as large as a hazelnut, which, when I introduced it in my mouth, served the dual purpose of holding up the mask and disguising my voice. With my false mustache and beard, my short velvet cape, and my disguised Spanish voice, I was confident I would not be recognized.

I arrived with a group of young courtiers including Lauzun, who was blasphemously clad in the robes of a cardinal. The advantage of arriving in a group was that if one came alone, the ushers would ask one to remove one's mask so that they would know who one was, whereas only one member of a group had to unmask.

Chandeliers and silver candelabra in the embrasures of the windows brightly lit the room. The strains of the first courante came from the drawing room where the dancing was to be conducted. On the far side of the room, tables were set and guests sat sipping champagne and exchanging the banter of piercing one another's disguises. The room was a blur of color, with, at the other end, the king and queen's armchairs, across from the fireplace, with their backs turned on the large Veronese. The ambassadors were seated in tiers on the king's right, and the last row of each tier was covered with girandoles. The king and queen were not in their armchairs, however, but mingled with the other masks. The queen was easy to recognize; she wore a simple domino, a white dress with twisted gold columns sprinkled with embroidered flowers, and a necklace that included the famed Cenci diamond. The word spread that the king, with seven or eight others, was costumed as a bat, and was bumping into people as evidence of his supposed blindness. The bats made a game of it, asking everyone where the king was. Since no one knew which bat wore the crown, they were all in demand as dancers. It was fairly easy to recognize some of the masks, the duc de Gesvres, from his stoop, as a lawyer in a long black robe, and the price de Croÿ, the one whose carriage had given me the right-of-way at the Opéra, as the jack of hearts. As a knave, and a valet, I thought, he is perfect. The most farfetched costume was the duc d'Aumont as a wicker mannequin, his head topped by a windmill. Thanks to a system of strings, he made the arms of the windmill move from left to right and right to left.

Someone dressed as Don Quijote engaged me in a conversation in rapid Spanish. I gave as good as I got, and the fellow went away none the wiser. Others approached me with a cryptic word, or called me by another name, and I shook my head. I felt my disguise was a great success. I sat at a table to drink in the entire spectacle, and an anonymous white satin slipper brushed my buckled shoe. I did not pursue the invitation, for, seeing a flurry of activity at the door, I rose in time to observe the entrance of a group of ladies dressed as the seven capital sins. They wore white dominoes, and costumes assorted to each particular sin. It was whispered that the leader of the group was the marquise de Pompadour, in a dress covered with a matting of peacock feathers that represented pride.

It did not take me long to recognize two of the loveliest sins, despite the masks that matched their high, pearl-festooned wigs. Envy, this time, was not, as Beaumarchais has written, rapacious-fingered and sallow-skinned, but a vision of loveliness, to be envied by every other woman in the room, the duchesse de Villiers, who wore, as the only emblem of her sin, a bright-green satin gown. She was followed by lust, in the most pleasing form of the Countess of Lawner, cast in the role of Messalina, the wife of Claudius, who played the strumpet by night, haunting taverns to fornicate with men of low extraction. I flattered myself that I had committed with her the sin she represented, for she was ravishing that night in a diaphanous Roman gown cut to reveal her bosom above the nipples.

The entrance of this charming coterie, who made the sins we commit worth burning for, announced the official start of the ball. The king removed his bat's head, took the queen's arm, and led his guests down the two terraces and into the grove, which had been covered with a tent and turned into a theater.

We watched a pretty ballet with a great many musicians, and a chorus that sang the second act of *Scandenbeg*, which begins with: "Obscure the memory of our sultans." Then came a compliment for the king, the gist of which was that, like the sun, which sometimes conceals the brilliance of its rays behind clouds, he preferred to hide his splendor. After the compliment was over, the minuets began, with the king naming those courtiers he had recognized.

I was standing near the cupid's fountain at one end of the tent, and was startled to hear a voice behind me say: "I know you, *beau masque.*" I turned to meet the soft blue gaze of the duchess de Villiers, and replied in Spanish that I had not understood. I introduced myself as the conde de Lopez y Basualdo, from the city of Toledo, where I raised fighting bulls, on my first visit to the court of Louis XV, where I had found the most beautiful women in Europe, more beautiful even than our own fiery, olive-skinned Andalusian señoritas. She laughed at my thick-tongued Spanish, for I still had the glass pebble in my mouth, and, without replying, took hold of my left hand and fingered my signet ring. I had not thought to remove it, and she of course had recognized my coat of arms.

"You have found me out," I told her. "Pray do not share your knowledge."

At that moment, the Countess of Lawner, seeing a masked figure in close conversation with the duchesse de Villiers, came up and said, in her peremptory way, "I know you, Ax, remove your mask." I resumed my imitation of a Spaniard, saying I did not have the pleasure of having met her. She grew more furious as the comedy was prolonged, and suddenly flicked out her hand and tried to snatch my domino, but my head was quicker. That made her even angrier. "Don't you think I know you well enough to recognize you with a mask on?" she said. "You can grant me the next minuet."

Elizabeth spoke up and said: "That dance is already promised, madam."

"Indeed it is, madam," said the Countess of Lawner, "and to me." As she spoke, she held my left arm in a proprietary manner.

"I mean, madam," said Elizabeth in a voice that remained dispassionate, "that this matter was decided before you arrived. The comte de Gramont asked me for the next dance. Tell her, Ax."

Having lost the advantage of my disguise, I was in the unpleasant position of Paris, I had to make a judgment. But to choose one was to offend the other. I preferred to sit it out and watch the epic struggle between envy and lust. How well I knew the way different sins compete for dominance inside one. I was now seeing the battle waged before my eyes.

"Ladies," I said, "despite my desire to satisfy you both, I am afraid I have pulled a muscle in my calf and am unable to dance at all."

"Well, madam," the Countess of Lawner said, "you have not heard the end of this."

"I have heard quite enough," Elizabeth said. "Madam, you have my permission to leave."

I discreetly disappeared, hoping that their quarrel would abate in the absence of the object of litigation. Alas, I heard two days later that it had not. I was leaving the king's *coucher* when Lauzun came running up and said: "You are lucky, my friend, they are both out of danger." I asked him what he meant. "Do you mean you don't know that your two mistresses fought a duel?" he asked. I told him that if I had known I would have prevented it.

He had just heard the news from the duc de Cossé-Brissac, a

young fop who had agreed to serve as the Countess of Lawner's second. Apparently it was she, on the day after the masked ball, who provoked Elizabeth by slapping her face with a glove. I could not believe that Elizabeth would take up the gauntlet. After all, it was easy for a woman to turn the offer of a duel to derision. Obviously, however, she had agreed, perhaps because she did not wish to seem less brave than her rival, or saw in the duel a way of eliminating her. She had chosen the weapons, pistols at twenty paces, perhaps counting on the Countess of Lawner's nearsightedness.

They had gone to Paris that morning at dawn, in the hope that the event would not become known at court, and met in the Bois. A faint mist hung over the woods, and the grass was wet with dew. They chose a secluded field near the boating pond, and their seconds examined the pistols. I could not imagine how my poor Elizabeth had even the strength to lift hers, much less load and fire it. The Countess of Lawner wore the trousers, boots, and broad-brimmed feathered hat of a musketeer, while my poor darling, loath to costume herself as a man, wore a simple white cotton dress that provided an excellent target against the dark backdrop of the trees.

The ladies emerged from their carriages and stood in the center of the clearing. Elizabeth's second, one of her cousins, had the good sense to ask whether excuses would suffice. The Countess of Lawner insisted that she wanted reparations on the field of honor. The pistols were removed from their cases and examined by both seconds, who handed them to the ladies. They stood thirty steps apart, holding their pistols in the air unloaded, and in the hazy dawn light, they must have seemed like two Tanagra figurines in stylized attitudes, holding a common utensil, a comb perhaps, or a closed fan. The seconds filled measuring cups with powder and loaded the pistols with the necessary quantity. They then lodged a bullet in the bored barrel of each pistol, placing it with a small iron mallet, and pulled back the hammer. The Countess of Lawner's second gave the order "March," and they slowly advanced across the grass, the Countess of Lawner with her pistol at her side, while Elizabeth walked with her arm outstretched, already sighting.

At twenty paces, they waited for the order to fire at will. When it came, the countess called out: "Fire first, and if you value your life, don't miss."

I doubt that Elizabeth had ever handled a firearm before. From the way she wrenched the trigger, it seems unlikely. Her shot lopped off a branch from a tree ten yards away from where her rival stood. "Anger made my hand tremble," she said.

Now the Countess of Lawner slowly raised her right arm, sighted carefully along the top of the barrel at her rival who stood in the clearing, swaying a bit, like a fragile white lily, disabled and defenseless, and, after what seemed like enough time to rout an army, fired. A tiny delicate particle flew into the air, no larger than a teardrop, but traveling upward, and blood streamed from Elizabeth's lobeless left ear and stained her white dress. Her second stanched the blood with the juice of nettles squeezed between two stones, and the wound was bandaged with her cambric handkerchief. The Countess of Lawner, shaken by the sight of blood, and conscious of the consequences had the bullet's path deviated only an inch to the right, announced that she had obtained satisfaction. The seconds agreed that the adversaries had been reconciled on the field of battle.

Elizabeth, faint from loss of blood, and probably delirious, said, as they started the trip back to Versailles: "So you think a woman can only risk her life by giving birth? I was ready to give my blood to the last drop for the most lovable gentleman in the kingdom."

All this, recounted by Lauzun, made my own blood stir, and I rushed to my wounded darling's apartments to inquire after her condition. She was in bed, with her head bandaged like the veteran of a Flemish campaign, looking at herself with a hand mirror. When she saw me she burst into tears. I commented that she should be glad to see me after such a narrow escape. "Oh, I am, dear heart, I am," she said through her sobs.

"Then what is it?" I asked.

The question unleashed a new cataract. In a broken voice, she said: "My earrings. How will I wear them now, with only one lobe? I am ruined."

I told her she had more urgent worries, not the least of which would be the king's reaction when he heard about the duel, for the prohibition on dueling was strictly enforced. His reaction, when it came, was a relief to both of us. He had a good laugh and said: "It's only forbidden for men."

As a result of this incident, I stopped seeing the Countess of Lawner. In winning the duel, she had lost me. It was the excuse I needed to terminate an affair that had been more of the groin than of the heart. Or so I thought, for I was still unaware of the secret passions that smoulder in a woman's heart. I had not realized that beneath her blunt exterior there was a nature quick to surrender to the most severe melancholia at the least reversal, a nature given to irreversible extremes. Two weeks after the duel, a portly bailiff knocked on the door of the small apartment under the eaves of the palace that the king had seen fit to grant me, and informed me that I was summoned at once to 3 rue de la Petite Faisanderie in Versailles. This I recognized as the Countess of Lawner's address, and I asked why my presence there was required. The bailiff had the stiff, constrained air of a bearer of ill tidings. "She has killed herself by swallowing a mixture of perfume and belladona," he said. "You might say she died of an overdose of cosmetics." The fellow was not without wit. He handed me a note and said: "This was found by her side."

"Farewell," the note said. "You who did not love me in life, pity me in death. As always, all I have is yours." The most romantic thing she ever said to me, I thought, and all the while I thought she loved someone called David. How impenetrable women are!

The bailiff drew me from my reverie. "She left you everything," he said. "You are the executor of her estate."

At her house, servants with expressions suited to the occasion were covering the furniture and drawing the curtains. I accompanied the bailiff to her bedroom, where her still-warm body lay. My hand rested on the bed, and I thought: Many a bounce I had on this mattress. I looked at her face in its final repose, the honey-eyed skin turned pallid. "Poor darling," I thought, "if you had known what you would look like you would not have done it."

"Does your lordship wish to take inventory," the bailiff asked, "or is he too upset?"

"I will try to control myself," I said. "Whatever is not worth selling we'll give to the Found Children Hospice."

As an assistant wrote with a quill pen in a ledger, the bailiff intoned: "One Saxe porcelain figurine representing a shepherd holding a cage with a bird inside it.

"One gilt clock enclosed in an ebony case, with the glass in the shape of a heart."

"How could someone with perfect breasts have had such dreadful taste?" I could not help from asking. The bailiff went on: "A thermometer and a barometer with motifs of love."

"The higher the fever, the greater the passion," I said.

"A fireguard of embroidered Chinese satin; a miniature of count

S., who is said to have ruined himself for her; sixty volumes bound in calf."

"Of which she never read a page," I said.

"Two bedside tables in precious wood inlaid with mother-of-pearl and gilded copper; eight small porcelain statues representing the Muses."

I counted them and said, "One missing, doubtless Erato, flown to more hospitable surroundings."

"A fireplace grille ornamented with four copper apples."

"The apples of discord," I said.

"A bed with four carved oaken pillars surmounted by a 'duchess' canopy."

"A bed?" I asked. "How prosaic. The throne of a goddess, Cleopatra's barge."

"A marquetry bureau with eighteen drawers, some of them containing love letters."

"And others containing unpaid bills," I said.

"A silver inkstand in the shape of a Cupid riding a dolphin with its jaws open."

"Horrendous," I said.

"Six jabots of Malines lace."

"Whose were those, I wonder?" I asked.

"A pastel of a lady whose dress is fastened at the shoulder with an emerald."

"False," I said.

"A series of engravings. The first is called 'The Empty Quiver.' In an elegant Louis XV interior, a young man is sitting on a couch, talking to a young lady seated before her *bonheur-du-jour*. The second is called 'Oh, Do Let Me See.' A couple in a garden is passing in front of a statue of Pan, and the young man hides his priapus with his hat."

"For God's sake, man," I interrupted, "if you describe each one, we'll be here all day. The titles should suffice."

The bailiff nodded, cleared his throat, and continued: " 'The Stolen Kiss,' 'The Shepherdess Surprised,' 'The Rejected Flower,' 'The Charms of the Morning,' 'The Unexpected Fall,' 'Cupid Raising Venus' Smock,' 'The Sweet Illusion,' 'The Discreet Governess,' 'The Warm Hand,' 'The Pleasures of the Country,' 'Useless Regrets,' 'The Sleep of Love,' 'You Have the Key but He Has Found the Lock,' 'She Bites on a Grape,' 'The Friend of the House,' 'The

Contented Husband,' 'Sweet Conversation,' 'A Rose in Danger,' 'The Monk and the Nun.' "

"Her taste leaned more to subject matter than style," I said.

"One enameled snuffbox."

I picked up the snuffbox and found it so beautifully worked that I decided to keep it, and told the bailiff to sell the rest and pay the poor wretch's debts, if she had any. Small as it was, the box summed up for me the hypocrisy of courtly love.

The scenes, painted in enamel, were as follows: On top, a miniature representing the "School of Love." Mercury is giving the cupids a lesson in the presence of their mother. Some are writing on rolls of parchment, others are reading, all are studying. Venus is seated, and upon her kneees rests a whip made of roses. She seems determined to punish unruly pupils. Mercury, seated on a tree trunk, is writing letters with a stylet, for the benefit of a cupid who is touching his teacher's parchment with the index finger of his right hand, while with his left hand the little libertine is playing with himself. On the front of the box, "Love Punished." Venus is holding the little Cupid across her knees and lashing him with her rose whip. The ground is covered with fallen petals and rosebuds. The underside of the box showed "Love Comforted by the Graces." Cupid is bouncing on the knees of one Grace, has his arms thrown around the arms of the second, while the third is caressing his little red rear with an expression of solace. Venus still holds the whip, but her arm hangs loose, and she looks tired. The right side of the box showed "The Loves Who Did Well in Their Work Rewarded by Venus." Venus is distributing bows, arrows, and quivers, while in a corner, the little whipped Cupid looks sadly on. The left side of the box showed "Mercury Distributing Garlands of Flowers to the Good Cupids," while the back of the box showed "The Cupids' Recreation." They have suspended one of the parchment rolls from the branch of a tree and are firing arrows at it. A final scene inside the box departed from allegory, goddesses, roses and cupids. This scene was the height of realism. It showed a naked man lying on his back with a large appendage sticking up, like a flagpole, the tip of which was lost inside the mouth of an equally naked lady who knelt over him, while a second man, standing, and wielding a whip that was not made of roses, bent back his arm to lash her plump and pink *derrière*. This scene would only be seen by the owner of the box when he ran out of snuff.

I Am Sent to the Bastille

I was not given time to feel sorry for the Countess of Lawner, for news came that my regiment had been chosen. The marquise had been true to her word. I was to command the 5th regiment of horse guards. My uniform had been ready for months, and on the appointed day, I rode out to review my men, who were presenting arms in the great square between the palace and the stables. They formed a rectangle open on one side, where the ironwork grille stood. The drums rolled, and the king appeared through the gate, flanked by the regiment's other officers. "You will recognize the comte de Gramont as your colonel," he said, "and you will obey him in whatever he orders you for my service." I admired the pertinence and brevity of his remarks. When he was gone, I gave my first orders, had the regiment line up in order of march, by company, and set out on the road to Paris to show my men off to the populace, as was the custom.

That night, a celebration in my honor was held in the officers' quarters of the guards regiments, attended by several commanders of other regiments, such as Lauzun, De Noblet, and a Bulgarian adventurer who had joined the king's service, named Panitza. This last was a champion drinker, who could fill his boot with wine and empty it in one draft. He was cheered as he did so, and proceeded afterward to put the boot back on, stand on a table, and perform one of his native dances, in which there was considerable spirited kicking. The merriment was unrestrained, the wine flowed as freely as a mountain spring, and the guests rivaled as to who could tell the bawdiest tale.

Lauzun thought he had won the prize with his discourse. As I remember it through a fog of wine, it went something like this: "There are no two alike, you know, each has its distinct personality. You can recognize them just as you can faces; line them up and I'll tell you one from the other, make no mistake. Some are as curly as a baby lamb, others as long and silky as a Saracen's mustache. I once encountered hair so pointed and sharp that it was like being stung by cactus. One lady I know kept hers so long she tied it in pigtails with red silk ribbon. Others keep it as close-cropped as a monk's beard. Some have such a wide opening you would mistake it for the entrance to the Sibyl's cave. Some have lips so long and pendulous they look like the crest of an angry rooster, while others have an opening as small and narrow as the eye of a needle. The gates of heaven can be puffy and red, or as brown and leathery as a saddle, or as pale as the moon that dictates the female temperaments, or as damp and luxuriant as an African rain forest." He went on in this vein until we were all rolling under the table with laughter, but the rest of his description escapes me.

As guest of honor, I could not let Lauzun outdo me. Inspired by champagne, elated by the new command, I strained my lyric gifts to the utmost, and recited an ode which those gathered agreed was as good if not better than Lauzun's diatribe. It went like this:

> Like a Gironde lamprey it has no bone,
> Its shape is something like a cone.
> At attention it can stand
> At almost any lady's command.
> The envious, prone to criticize,
> Make fun of its prodigious size.
> Why, sir, they say, for that great thing,
> Do you not require a sling?
> Will something so large
> Not protrude from its garage?
> Does it weigh more than a pound
> And reach the ground?
> Are you not worried, when strolling through town,
> That its great weight will drag you down?
> And are you then so fond of sparrows
> As to provide for them a perch with your marrow?
> Why, that's no human part,
> But a hat rack, a bowsprit, a broomstick, by my heart,
> A fearful thing to present to a maid.
> Have you thought of getting spayed?

The entire assembly cheered my ode, which made up in the vigor of its theme what it lacked in prosody. Many toasts were drunk in honor of its subject, which someone christened Gulliver, in honor of that celebrated English giant. Panitza leaped from his chair, worked the cork off a bottle of champagne with his thumbs, and when it popped and the foam came pouring from the bottle, shouted: *"Ejaculatio praecox."*

Toward the end of the evening, when everyone was singing, for in France, everything from a mass to an execution ends with a song, someone thrust a scrap of paper in my hand and asked if I

would read it. I could hardly make out the writing, the letters
jumped over the paper like frogs in a pond, but I called for silence
and applied myself to reciting a work that the author was too shy
to read himself. I had no idea what it was about, or who it dealt
with, and only remember that it produced applause and general
hilarity. I do not even recall how the evening ended, except that by
then it was morning, and I was dragged by four friendly arms over
cobblestones, under stars, in the cool night air, and thought there
was no finer thing than the comradeship of soldiers.

The next morning, I looked in the mirror, and what I saw reminded me of the ghost of Christmas past. My head felt as though
a game of *boules* was being played inside it, and to that confounded
noise was added a knock on my door. I threw a robe over my
shoulders and opened it to find one of the sententious ministerial
clerks who haunt the palace on their missions of gloom. I was
wanted at once by the prince de Croÿ, the first secretary in charge
of censorship, and the very fellow who had called me to the king's
attention over our little misunderstanding with the carriages.

"What's it all about?" I asked the clerk, a creature as yellowing
and wizened as an old piece of curling parchment.

"I'm hardly the one to ask," he said, as though glad of the
chance to see me squirm.

I knew Croÿ would seize on any chance to discredit me before
the king, and feeling that forewarned would be forearmed, I pulled
a crown from a pocket and flicked it at the fellow, who caught it
with practiced ease.

"You attended a drunken brawl in the officers' quarters last
night?" he asked.

"There was no brawl," I replied, unable to contest the first part
of the statement.

"And you recited there a filthy parody that makes odious allegations about the marquise de Pompadour?"

So that was what, in my stupor, I had been handed and read. I
began to see the fine thread that held this matter together. "What
sort of allegations?" I asked.

"Things I would not dream of repeating," he said, stretching his
neck in several directions as if his collar was too tight. "Something
to do with an alleged disease in her private parts. Now that it has
been publicly read, it is circulating at court."

I was appalled. Someone, taking advantage of my condition,
had prevailed upon me to read a scabrous attack on the marquise,

my benefactress. How could I ever convince her that I was not the ungrateful scoundrel she must think me? I followed the clerk across the palace into the secretaries' wing and was led into the prince de Croÿ's office.

"So it's you again," he said, without looking up from his work.

I decided that the way out of this mess lay on the road of flattery and respect. "Sir," I said, "I have done nothing to deserve such a chilly welcome from a man who has never taken pleasure in humiliating the unfortunate."

He raised two cold green-gray eyes so closely set to his beakish nose that they were like the finger holes in a pair of scissors, and asked: "And what of this filthy parody you have penned?"

"I am not its author," I said. "I can assure you of that as a gentleman."

A cackle that was meant to be a laugh strained in his throat, and he wagged a bony finger in my direction. "Nonetheless, you recited it," he said.

"Yes," I said, keeping my voice even and reasonable, "what I was given of it, during an evening of drinking with a group of friends. But I had nothing to do with the writing of it."

"And yet one sees it," Croÿ said, sounding more and more like a judge about to pass sentence.

"Written by another," I maintained.

"By whom, would you say?" he asked.

I had a good idea of the answer, but merely shrugged.

"You recited it in such a way as to appear its author," he insisted.

I laughed and said: "As for my manner of reciting, you might as well say that I am the author of *Phèdre, Cinna*, and the *Fables* of La Fontaine, for I flatter myself that I read all of them as if I were their author."

"Look here," Croÿ said. "Who wrote this parody? That is what you must tell me."

I raised my arms in a gesture of helplessness. "With all the good will in the world, I cannot. My senses were blurred by wine, and I cannot even say who handed me the verses and asked me to read them."

"Do you really expect the king to believe that?" he asked, with a smile that answered his own question.

My body temperature dropped several degrees when I heard the king mentioned. Was it any use to argue with this man? "Do you really think that whoever wrote the parody would be foolish enough to recite it himself?" I asked. "No, the author disguised his handwriting and probably had several copies made to spread through court. My mistakes were two, to have accepted the verses without noticing who they came from, and to have recited them."

"My dear fellow," Croÿ said, suddenly turning into a friendly witness, "I believe you, for you are speaking like a gentleman, but will the king? I see no way out of this that does not lead to the Bastille."

"I will go gladly," I replied, "if I can be sure that I do not count you among my enemies."

"You can still avoid going if you make a clean breast of the whole matter. A moment of folly, the effects of wine, these things are not beyond the king's understanding. And before this incident, the marquise always spoke of you favorably."

That particular snare was not covered with sufficient foliage. "I would rather go to the Bastille," I said, "and not lose your respect."

"You see me abashed at having to write this," Croÿ said, as wasting no time, he prepared the sealed letter ordering my confinement. "I will insist that you receive the best of treatment. You will have every freedom except that of leaving, and you can take with you those servants you need. When will you be ready? There is no hurry."

There was no way out. I decided that the sooner I began this cure the sooner I would end it. I wanted only to see Elizabeth first to tell her my version and have her repeat it in the right ears. I told Croÿ I would be ready the following morning, gave him a deep bow, and exited backward, an added sign of deference.

The next morning, a commissioner came for me. When he saw me in my guards uniform, he said: "I am in despair, sir, but I have an order, sir, ordering your arrest by the king, sir." I returned his bow, and there was established between us a climate of honest courtesy as he accompanied me to the prison.

We rumbled through the Faubourg Saint-Antoine to the Bastille gate, where a sentry cried: "Who goes there?"

"King's orders," the commissioner replied.

The drawbridge was lowered and the carriage bounced over thick, iron-laminated planks. The commissioner handed the sealed letter to the Bastille governor's assistant, who read it aloud: "In the name of the king: My intention is that you render yourself forthwith to my castle of the Bastille." It was an invitation that one could not turn down on the grounds of a previous engagement. I was asked to deposit my valuables and weapons in the guardroom and seal the package.

When these formalities were done, I was taken to meet the governor, the comte de Lastours. He had held the office for twelve years, and thus had been confined in the prison longer than any of the inmates. Its damp walls had stooped him and made his blue eyes listless, and his hair matched the color of the gray stone. He did his best to remain a gentleman. "I cannot tell you how sorry I am to see you here, my dear fellow," he said. "We will try to make your stay as pleasant as possible. You will find a great deal to occupy you. You may borrow books from the library, as many as you like, write letters—we will supply you with pen and paper—receive visits from friends, send out for food, keep pets, chart the heavens, study the violin or the flute. You will always be welcome at my table."

He took my arm in the friendliest fashion, and said, more in the manner of an innkeeper than a warden, that he would show me my room. "The best rooms are on the upper floors," he said, "less damp, better view. But not the ones on the top floor, hot in summer, cold in winter, vaulted. A man can only stand up straight in the center. You're in luck, one of our best apartments, with a tower view, just vacated. After you."

I passed before him into a spacious two-windowed chamber, containing a bed covered with green serge, matching curtains, a table, and several chairs. "But where is the damp straw?" I asked. "Where are the chains, the armies of rats?"

Lastours waved his hand, dismissing the calumnies. "Sorry about the bars on the windows," he said. "The furnishings are simple, but nothing prevents you from having your own things brought in, family portraits if you're lonely. Things advance slowly here. You might not be questioned for two or three weeks. We don't have the same sense of time, no one is in a hurry."

I said it was no reflection on his hospitality, but I hoped my stay would be brief. For better or for worse, I settled into Bastille life. I slept well despite the sound of keys turning in locks and the calls of the guards on their rounds. The food was good and plentiful; few taverns in the capital could have done better. Two jailers arrived punctually bent under pyramids of steaming dishes, fine porcelain, silver, and the best linen. My only objection to the menu was that the king wanted his guests to refrain from eating meat on Friday. On those days we had sole, perch, or crayfish. I am not partial to fish, and on the first Friday, I said: "Bring me a chicken from the caterer next door."

"A chicken, sir," the jailer said. "Don't you know it's Friday?"

"You are charged with the guard of my body, not of my soul," I said. "I am ill, for the Bastille is an illness." An hour later, the chicken was on my table. Meals were events that interrupted the day's boredom.

The rest of the time, I read, I, who, picking up a book, would drop it with a yawn after a quarter of an hour. I even made a stab at translating a Latin author, but decided that the boredom of the Bastille was preferable to the tongue of Horace. Lastours liked to mention the famous writers who had stayed there—Voltaire, Marmontel, Diderot, many others whose names I forget—and I could see that it must be a splendid place for a writer, for he could work uninterrupted, and the very fact of his having been interned there would further his literary career.

I was grateful to the governor for his visits. The day was probably as long for him as it was for me, for the prison ran itself. We often had dinner together, splitting a good bottle of Burgundy, and he would regale me with reports about the other inmates, of which there were at that time some thirty.

"I have just received a woman of gentle birth who is being punished for an extreme desire to become a widow," he said, on one of our evenings.

"You mean she killed her husband."

"Correct. Poisoned his wine."

I choked on mine.

"Also a Hollander who claims to be a doctor in the transmutation of metals," Lastours said.

"You mean he turns mercury into gold."

"Would that he did, he would not be here but with the king."

"I thought I saw a nun, yesterday, when I was strolling on the tower," I said.

"A nun whose behavior does not match her calling," Lastours said. "She received masked men in her rooms. When she first was sent to us, she asked the turnkey for scissors. He told her that was against regulations, and offered to cut her nails himself, and said that if she wanted her hair cut, that was the business of the surgeon major. She replied that it was not for her nails or for the hair on her head, but for that of her lowlands, which incommoded her most awfully, and that was not a man's job. We undressed her and found sixty-two gold louis cleverly stitched inside her belt."

"A prison is not unlike a nunnery," I said.

"The Bastille is far more lenient," Lastours said. "We enforce no rule of silence. The sexes are mixed. There is no fasting. And I sometimes allow my guests to pursue the very occupations for which they were sent here. Not only writers. Right now, I have here Clinchetet, the Raphaël of snuffboxes, who made the mistake of selling an example of his handicraft showing the marquise de Pompadour naked, throwing water into lime, with the caption: 'The more I am sprinkled, the more I burn.' He is making me one, showing two little girls caressing each other. His repertoire is limited, but his craftsmanship is exquisite."

"I believe I have an example of it myself," I said, thinking that this must be the maker of the box I had inherited from the Countess of Lawner.

Lastours' duties had made him more tolerant of human failings than most men. He was in constant touch with the flaws of life, like a doctor who sees of humanity only its illnesses. Instead of building up an immunity, he had developed an understanding of erratic behavior. He often said: "The people I get here are no worse than the people I do not get."

I Meet an Old Friend

Several days later, I was crossing the castle courtyard when my attention was caught by a knot of men at one end, who were listening to some sort of orator. I drew closer, and saw the green cape and braided hat of my old acquaintance Roger la Trompette. Even inside the Bastille, he could not resist an audience. He was informing his fellow inmates that "a prize of two thousand pounds has been offered by the king to whoever finds a way of lighting the streets of Paris. Apply yourselves, gentlemen, during these hours of enforced leisure, and one of you may leave the Bastille richer than he entered it. Existing methods have failed; the wind blows out the lanterns suspended over the middle of the street. I hereby announce that the competition is open."

"Let each man carry his own lantern, like Diogenes," I said.

"Impractical, young fellow," Roger la Trompette said, and then recognizing me: "By my faith it's my old friend Gramont." He broke through the circle of his listeners and clapped me on the back. "Whatever are you doing here?"

"I might ask you the same question. How have you been?"

"Not so good," Roger said.

"I'm sorry to hear that. What have you been up to since I saw you last?"

"I got married."

"That's good."

"No, that's bad, I married a shrew."

"That's too bad."

"No, that's good, she had a dowry of five thousand pounds."

"That's good."

"No, that's bad, because I invested it in a sheep farm, and the sheep died of smallpox."

"Too bad."

"No, that's good, because the sale of their skins brought in more than the cost of the farm."

"That's good."

"No, that's bad, because the house where the skins were stored burned down."

"Too bad."

"No, that's good, because my wife was in the house and burned with it."

Despite his mishaps, Roger was in fine spirits. He was the sort who floats on life's waters like a cork, light and buoyant. He always found some advantage to compensate for his misfortune. "This is not such a bad place," he said. "They feed you, they look after your health, and if you should happen to die, they bury you at the state's expense in the Saint-Paul cemetery. And as for the company"—shaking my spine again with his hamlike hand—"I could not have chosen better myself." He said he had heard echoes of my adventures at court, and had more than once planned to come and see me, but urgent business had prevented him from leaving the capital.

He was in the Bastille, he explained, because a police informer had heard him berate the army recruiters who ply their trade on the Pont-Neuf and in the Tuileries. Roger had called them "sellers of human flesh," and added, "Thanks to whores and drunken nights, an army of heroes is made, with each and every hero bringing thirty pounds to the recruiter." "Informers are everywhere," he told me. "The very next day I was sent here. Better than Bicêtre.

You don't find many commoners, only the top of the basket, the finest of the fine, the flower of the pea." Roger seemed genuinely pleased to be in prison.

I cannot say that I shared his glee. I had been there a month, and was beginning to find the days long, and to grow weary of the governor's company, with his eternal gossip about the inmates and his fussy, old-maidish manners. I had received no visits and no letters, and felt hopelessly cut off from the rest of the world. Thanks to Roger, however, who knew one of the guards, I was able to get a message out to Elizabeth. Three days later, a guard came to fetch me in my room and said: "You have a visitor," adding with a lewd wink, "too bad she can't stay the night." I went down to the reception room, where Elizabeth flew into my arms, covering my face with quick kisses as though I had returned from the grave. She had been told at court that I had left France, and thought I had abandoned her. When she had received my message, she had gone to the marquise, who told her that she did not want to hear my name mentioned again.

I asked Elizabeth to find out from Lauzun whether he could remember who had handed me the parody on the night of the regimental party, for there lay the key to the mystery. She said she would write me as soon as she had news, and left me in despair, covering me with kisses and tears. A week later, I received from her a letter worth quoting verbatim, for it shows the extent of a woman's devotion:

"Dearest heart," she wrote, "they say that sadness takes flight on the wings of time, but the longer we are apart the more despondent I become. Everything here echoes your absence. I gaze out my window at the slender poplars, which, like courtiers, bend at the slightest breeze, and am reminded of the injustice of our separation. I see the king a dozen times a day, and wonder whether he knows that my eyes implore for your release. It will come soon, my love, for we have made great advances.

"As soon as I returned to the palace, I sought out Lauzun and asked him who had given you the paper. He could not remember, being, as he said, 'as pickled as a pig's foot,' but promised to make inquiries. He talked to those officers who were sitting on your left and right that night, and both recalled that a Bulgarian officer named Panitza approached you and pressed a slip of paper into your hand, which you then proceeded to read.

"The man does not regularly attend court, and I was wondering how I could meet him when Lauzun said he would bring him to the Thursday ball. It was only by thinking of you, dear heart, that I was able to be civil to the man, for everything about him displeased me, his swarthy Balkan looks, his loud laugh, his insinuating manner of speaking. I led him on, and let him dance with me, although his touch made my flesh crawl. He was vain enough to believe that he deserved his good fortune, and began to press my hand, and whisper in my ear, and give other demonstrations of his ardor. I played the young innocent who has been swept off her feet by the dashing horse guard, and when he offered to see me to my door, I accepted, and after some mock resistance, allowed him to come in. Forgive my treachery, my love, it was all for you.

"Once I had let him in the door, it was all I could do to contain him. With his crude foreign ways, he seemed to make no distinction between a lady at court and the lowest tavern maid. The only way to deter him from chasing me around the room was to keep his brandy glass always filled. When he had drunk more than most men can endure, he fell to his knees and made a preposterous declaration of love which I received with shy blushes. I replied that I was not insensitive to his charm but wanted to test the sincerity of his feeling. He immediately shouted that he would swim the Bosporus for me. I said I did not intend so athletic a test, but only wanted to satisfy my curiosity on a minor matter, for I had heard he was friendly with the prince de Croÿ. 'He is my best friend,' he said, beating his chest as if commending himself for being on such good terms with a highly-placed personage. I said I had made a wager with a friend on the real author of the parody against madame de Pompadour. 'Only Panitza knows,' the fellow said, again beating his chest with self-satisfaction. I promised that if he told me, I would not repeat it, and it would count as proof of his feeling for me, and allow me to know whether I had won my bet.

"He replied that he would tell me if I first gave him a kiss. Shuddering, I surrendered to his uncouth embrace, nearly fainting from his brandy breath. Forgive me, my love, I would sooner have walked over burning coals. I made the kiss as convincing as I could, so that the promise of further pleasures would loosen his tongue. He made me swear to keep the secret, and proceeded to inform me that Croÿ himself had penned the parody, and given it to Panitza, who serves as his messenger for such ignoble tasks, in return for favors I did not take the trouble to have him describe, to give to you, in the hope that you would read it and draw the marquise's wrath. Is it possible that a man could be so malicious and ill-intentioned as the prince de Croÿ? Now that he has been found out, it will all fly back in his face, like a pail of slops thrown against the wind. Having answered my question, Panitza proceeded to claim his reward, throwing himself on me like a lion on a lamb. He seemed to have tentacles instead of hands, and they were everywhere at once, no sooner had I beaten one away from my bodice, than another appeared under my dress.

"I gave the prearranged signal, 'Ah, I am lost,' and Lauzun emerged from the next room where he had been waiting, his sword drawn. 'So this is how you abscond with the woman whose hand I have been promised,' Lauzun said, scowling fiercely, and waving his sword. Panitza was in a state of such confusion, mingling drunkenness with disappointed desire, that he forgot the French language, and could only babble in incoherent syllables which we took to be Bulgarian. His wig was askew, his coat was on the floor, his trousers were half open, and he did not know where to begin to pick up the pieces of his disarray. Lauzun pricked a bare triangle of bulging stomach between his shirt and trousers and said: 'You have ten seconds to evacuate this lady's apartment.' Grunting like a cornered boar, Panitza snatched up his garments and fled, while Lauzun and I fell into one another's arms, weak from laughter.

"The next day we informed the marquise about our discovery. She said she was relieved to learn that you were not the culprit, for she believed that your devotion to her was sincere, that she had in the past done what she could for you, and did not see you cast in the role of ingrate. She promised to take the matter up with the king, adding that she was satisfied you were guilty of nothing more than the excesses of your age. That is where things stand now, dear heart, and I have every reason to hope for your prompt release and your return to my arms and my bed, both of which have been forlorn and empty these past weeks. Your own, Elizabeth."

Every day after that, I waited for Lastours' liberation visit, but none came. I continued to hear from my loyal Elizabeth. The king had been informed; any day now; your pardon is imminent. I knew that release from the Bastille is a longer process than admission, but whereas previously I had been content to endure my imprisonment, now the smell of freedom made me impatient to leave. It made me chafe to depend on the whim of another man, to know that my fate hung on a word from him, and that the word did not come. A courtier was supposed to be grateful for any attention from the king. Once he told me: "You look terrible." I thanked him, for the remark was gracious, implying that he remembered me looking better at some previous time. But what one could tolerate at court became intolerable behind fortress walls. I resolved that if my release did not come within a week I would anticipate the king's decision. I was not born for confinement. Walls are made to be breached, and moats to be crossed. They provoke any man attached to his freedom of movement.

I put the matter to Roger la Trompette, who could not understand my impatience. "It doesn't make sense," he said. "It's like setting out on foot because your carriage is late. You won't reach your destination any faster."

I replied that the king's intention was as good as his deed, and since I had been told that he intended my release, I need not wait for a formal notification. When I asked for his help, he shrugged and accepted the gold coins I pressed into his palm.

I was lodged in the fourth room of the Tower of Liberty, above the chapel, close to the triple-locked door leading to the terrace. Three days after our conversation, Roger handed me the keys to those locks, made outside the prison from wax imprints.

Two days later, having tried the keys and found that they worked, I was ready. After midnight, the guards made their rounds every hour, and spent the rest of the time in the guardroom sleeping, for the ones on night duty had other occupations during the day to supplement their meager wages. That left me an hour between rounds. My only regret was that Lastours, who had been more than decent during my stay, might be penalized for my brusque departure. That was in the nature of things, however. He was in the business of keeping prisoners locked up, while it was a prisoner's business to try to escape. Our roles were as clearly defined as those of players in a game of tennis, who were adversaries on either side of the net, and friends when the game was over. I left a note saying how desolate I was to leave without thanking him for the courtesy extended, and hoping we might meet again in better-ventilated surroundings. I had to leave my things behind, taking only the keys and a ball of twine also procured by the resourceful Roger.

It was two in the morning on a clear night. I left my room and opened the terrace door, which groaned on its seldom-used hinges. The air was cool, for it was September, and the sky was filled with acres of stars. Below, I could see the wide ditch of the fortress, the abutment, and the empty, glistening boulevard. From time to time a carriage passed, and the sky was so bright that it threw a wavy shadow over the coblestones. I cursed the brightness, for I might as well have been escaping in the full light of noon. When I heard the hoot-owl call, I threw my ball of twine out and watched it unravel and land beyond the ditch, where unseen hands retrieved it. I waited until I felt a tug, and drew it in, this time considerably heavier. I repeated the operation until I had the necessary equipment, consisting of a stout rope, several iron rings with pitons, and a hammer. I tied one end of the rope to an iron bar on one of the terrace windows, thereby using as a means of escape what had been intended to ensure my confinement. I put all my weight on the rope to make sure the rusty bar would hold; it creaked, but did not give. I threw the rope over the side and lowered myself slowly down the outside wall. Once a guard heard my boots kicking against the wall and peered over with a puzzled look, but I was saved by the shadow of a tower, which covered me like a dark protective blanket.

Once on the ground, I rubbed my aching arms, and waited for the next move from my helpers on the other side of the ditch. Another rope soon came whistling through the air. I tied it to one of the iron rings, which I had hammered into the crack between two square fortress stones, and making sure that the rope was secured at the other end, I wrapped my legs around it and crossed the ditch hand over hand.

On the other side a carriage and two men were waiting. Silent and efficient, they did not waste time on greetings. I doffed my hat to the great looming mass of stone, and they bundled me into the carriage. I had no idea where they were taking me, but trusting Roger, I let myself be taken.

I Am Held Captive in Another Prison

The carriage stopped in front of a small house with curtained windows on the rue d'Angleterre. One of the men knocked twice, then twice again, and the door was opened by a small blackamoor in blue livery, who carried on his shoulder a parrot that kept foolishly repeating *"Je t'aime, je t'aime."*

The black valet ushered me into a drawing room that was elegantly furnished in the style of the day, with curtains of striped taffeta, walls lined with Flemish tapestries, and rugs of flowered hammercloth, except that the chairs and sofas were upholstered in glaring scarlet. In one corner of the room two lightly clad ladies raised champagne glasses to toast a gentleman with whom they seemed on the best of terms, for they laughed appreciatively at the liberties he took. On the far side of the room, lined up like bottles of perfume on a lady's dressing table, sat three vacant-faced girls in similar states of *déshabillé*, leaving little of their charms to the imagination. When I came in they smiled invitingly. I collapsed in the first chair I saw, exhausted by my rope-climbing exercises, and wanting only an empty bed with white sheets to lose myself in for ten or twenty hours.

Alas, it was not to be, for the proprietress of the establishment made her entrance. I saw a suety face with a three-story chin that made her look like a running candle, topped by a thick rumpled wick of reddish hair. But the wax of the candle, instead of being white, was as pink as a bullfinch, and the candle itself, instead of tapering, spread out in the shape of a pear. I rose languidly to my feet, and she held out a dimpled hand in the manner of a lady at court who expects to have it kissed. I obliged, skimming her knuckles with my lips, and she said: "Enchanted to make your acquaintance, my dear count. I hope you will find my establishment to your liking. Only last week I had the visit of the prince d'Arenberg and the marquis de Crussol."

I said I was delighted to be in such distinguished company.

"You have probably heard it said at court yourself," she went on, balancing her bulk primly on the edge of a chair, "Madame de Rouxpoil seldom has commoners, and she keeps the cleanest girls in Paris, regularly visited by her Aesculapius."

I had never heard of the woman, but tactfully added that the king himself had spoken favorably of her discernment.

She gurgled with pleasure. "I am so glad Roger sent you to me," she said. "I hardly know him," she added, to indicate the unbridgeable difference in station between Roger and herself, "but sometimes he lets me know when a gentleman needs assistance, and of course I am glad to oblige. Where would we be if people of condition did not help one another?" I said I hoped I would not get in her way. "You are a great addition," she assured me. "The girls will be able to see how a gentleman behaves. They have so little chance to get out into the world."

I stifled a yawn and apologized for my weariness.

She said she quite understood and led me to my room, which boasted one singular feature, a full-length mirror on the underside of the bed's canopy.

I spent ten days in this academy of the daughters of love, where a *passe** cost one louis, including a restorative bouillon, and where married men came for the variety their wives did not give them, along with single men between mistresses, and others whose penchants or condition made them prefer a business arrangement to the uncertainties of love.

Madame de Rouxpoil, for all her coarse appearance, was a woman of gentle birth and refined tastes, as she lost no occasion to let one know. There was in her the upstairs woman, all decorum and fine manners, and the downstairs woman, animated by a strumpet's heart. In order to reconcile the two, she had opened an establishment where gentlemen might spend a pleasant hour or two with young ladies who were not unsociable. As she told me, "I decided to make variety my law, and to endeavor to organize my passions, since I could not control them. When I was too old to compete, I became a teacher. I told my captains and colonels that it required more skill to make love well than to command an army. Humans make love like animals, granted, but a bit better. Soldierly ardor does not invariably communicate to the bedchamber. Strong physiques often promise more than they deliver."

For all that went on behind the locked doors of her house, I never heard her say a coarse word. She kept an iron discipline among the girls, making sure they had their weekly visit from the doctor. Sometimes a young lady would be kept longer than the others, and the surgeon would whisper to Madame de Rouxpoil, who would take the young lady's hand and say: "I'm afraid, my dear, that you are going to have to leave us." On Sunday mornings she took them to mass, demurely dressed, like young ladies from an exclusive school. For she was pious, and read obscure theologians, and told her beads each night before retiring. Indeed, if she had not been the madam of a brothel, I could imagine her as a mother superior, a bit pompous, a bit sententious, rigidly enforcing appearances, more concerned about a rumpled *coiffe* than a rumpled soul. If a client was vulgar, or addressed her too familiarly, or took too many liberties with the girls in public, she gave orders that he was not to be let in again, and she never relented. The parrot

---

* A *passe*, in whorehouse slang, is a brief moment.

who croaked *"Je t'aime"* also greeted offenders with *"Sortez, sortez,"** which was usually enough to unsettle them.

I had to adjust to the hours of the house. No one was awake before noon, for there were customers who elected to stay all night and left only when the street scavengers' hoses awoke them from their slumber. Madame de Rouxpoil, who kept an all-night vigil over her daughters, was served a copious breakfast in bed toward one in the afternoon, at which hour she summoned me to discuss the latest news at court. She seemed as well informed as our mutual friend Roger la Trompette, and probably held briefings during which her girls gave her whatever information they had gleaned that night on the pillow. She was an endless chatterer, and I felt I was back in the Bastille with Lastours as I listened to her rattle on. But I had no choice. After my escape, I had to remain in this secondary confinement until some disposition was made about my case. She would be lying in bed, surrounded by white pillows, like a cream bun topped with whipped cream, her lips as red and glistening as a candied cherry, impatient to tell me what the night had brought in the way of court gossip.

I think the stories she liked best were the ones about kicks of Venus.† She informed me one morning that "Monsieur de Cossé-Brissac gave it to the comtesse de Gaigneron, who gave it to the vicomte de Noblet, who gave it to the comtesse de Miramont, who gave it to the marquis de Bartillat, who gave it to the actress Guimard."

"Thus ends this genealogical chart," I thought.

She seemed delighted at the thought of these titled gonorrheans. She was also interested in the reasons for which men professed to come to her, and told me about an awful little court prig, the vicomte de Charbonnel, who, before seeing a woman in society, spent an hour with one of her girls so that he would not be tempted to take advantage of the lady. "It is more like five minutes than an hour," she said. "Charbonnel wins the speed record with his automatic sprinkler."

On another occasion, she showed me a little ball, smooth and golden, about the size of a pigeon's egg, and asked me to guess what it was. I could not imagine its purpose. She explained that it was a gift from a sea captain who had traveled to India, called a love apple. Introduced in the proper orifice, the ball took on a sort

---

* Get out, get out.
† A euphemism for venereal disease (*le coup de pied de Vénus*).

of perpetual motion, and procured multiple ecstasies. Madame de
Rouxpoil had grandiose plans for the manufacture of this splendid
golden egg. "Its success is assured," she told me, "particularly in
convents."

In the afternoons, when customers were few, the girls whiled
away the hours playing cards and gossiping. Whores I found to be
the laziest creatures imaginable. Their real vice is sloth, not lust.
The girls who enter the calling are not devoured by the demons of
the flesh, quite the contrary; they are essentially bovine and sub-
missive, content to spread their legs a dozen times a night, but
deriving little pleasure from the act. Any other exertion they studi-
ously avoided, although to hear them tell it, their customers
worked them to the bone. With my ready wit and banter, I became
quite a favorite of theirs. One wanted to iron my shirt, another to
bring me breakfast, a third to make my bed. I was waited on like a
pasha, and could at any time have obtained without charge what
others paid for. I did not avail myself of the privilege, however, for
too many pens had been dipped in their inkwells, and I did not
want the point of my quill blunted. With the use of astringent
water, the girls were able to make their coves appear unexplored,
but I knew that they were harbors at which any ship could berth. It
should also be said in their favor that they were lacking in hypocrisy. All the whores are not in brothels, far from it, and these at
least had the merit of giving a man what he paid for in an honest
fashion, without demanding words of love or promises of fidelity.
To reduce fornicating to a transaction cleared the air of romantic
vapors.

My favorite among the girls was a buxom country lass they
called the Ace of Spades, because, although blond, her cypress
grove was black. She was always cheerful, and saw the droll side of
her trade. She gave hilarious descriptions of what some of her
customers required, and I was such a good audience that one day
she promised me a special treat. She led me by the hand into a
small room that was like a pantry and opened what looked like a
medicine cabinet. Inside this cabinet there was a small *oeil-de-
boeuf*, which allowed one to see through the back of a mirror on
the wall of the next room. "Wait there," the Ace of Spades said.
"The exhibition will begin in a few minutes."

I adjusted my right eye to the opening, wondering how many of
Madame de Rouxpoil's customers were thus observed in the midst
of their revels, and congratulated myself once again upon having

abstained. I was delighted to be watching, but had a strong aversion to being watched. Presently I saw the Ace of Spades incongruously dressed like a little girl, her ample bust squeezed into a short white piqué frock, her blond hair tied with a broad pink bow of ribbon, her feet in patent-leather booties. On her heels came a man in ecclesiastical garb, with a thatch of gray hair and a florid retroussé nose that made him look like a Burgundian vine-grower. The abbot, or priest, removed his round-crowned black felt hat and sat on the bed.

"Well, my dear," he said, in the unctuous voice of the catechist, "you're a pretty little thing. Come sit next to me on this couch. How old are you?"

"Fourteen, sir," the Ace of Spades said in a simpering, little-girl voice.

"And have you ever had anything to do with the opposite sex?" the abbot asked.

"Never, sir," the Ace of Spades said with a conviction that made me cover my mouth with my hand to stifle a loud guffaw.

"All well and good," the abbot said, "for the first time determines all the rest. It's lucky you didn't fall into the hands of one of those court lechers who think of nothing but corrupting young maids. They want to ravish your innocence and lead you into a life of iniquity. Modesty," he added, passing a chubby ringed hand over the Ace of Spades' knee, "is the virtue most necessary to persons of your sex. A pretty girl is prettier still when she takes no pride in the advantages nature has conferred upon her."

"Father," the Ace of Spades said, responding like a trained actress, "you seem to be saying that I am not pretty." Perhaps this was a scene they had played before, and she knew her lines by heart.

"Oh, but you are," said the priest. "How dare you say you aren't pretty? You are offending the works of God. You know what you deserve."

And he took her across his knees and lifted her white frock, and spanked her bare bottom until it was the color of strawberries. Her howling was not feigned, and I hoped she was getting paid a good price. Eventually the abbot's hand tired and he said, out of breath: "I hope that taught you something. Now tell me how many mortal sins there are. I'll teach you to know them, wicked little thing. On your knees."

The Ace of Spades fell to her knees and began to recite a list of sins. After each one, the abbot interrupted to ask her whether she had committed that particular sin. The Ace of Spades nodded, and the abbot shouted, "Oh, you naughty girl, if your parents only knew, the shame of it," and things of that sort. When she had finished, he took a short whip that was hanging on a hook and she bent over so that he could whip her backside, giving her a lash for every sin she had mentioned. After that, it was his turn to confess his sins and be whipped, and the Ace of Spades went at it with genuine enthusiasm. The liturgical portion of the scene ended with the whippings.

The abbot then removed his cassock, folding it carefully over the back of an armchair, and the rest of his clothing, and started walking across the room on all fours. The Ace of Spades imitated him, and they began circling each other like animals, the abbot sniffing her, and barking like a dog, and the Ace of Spades rubbing and tickling him from behind to get him in condition to perform. When the abbot was visibly in heat, he mounted her from behind, crying "Woof Woof" at the top of his lungs. When he had finished, the naked abbot crawled into a corner of the room, curled up on his side in the position of a baby inside the womb, and whimpered.

I did not know whether to laugh or cry at this pathetic behavior. And this is the sort of man to whom parents entrust their children for a Catholic upbringing, I thought, but a small voice told me I shouldn't generalize, and that there were many austere and virtuous men in the church, although the ones I met always seemed to have stepped alive from the pages of Boccaccio. Later, when the abbot had been seen out the door, carrying his breviary under his arm, and walking with little mincing steps like a constipated chicken, I asked the Ace of Spades why she submitted to such brutal farces. She said Madame de Rouxpoil insisted that her girls obey the customers' whims, and besides, there was more money in what she called "special" sessions. On Sundays she went to mass with the other girls, and saw the priest turn the host and wine into the body and blood of Christ, while on other days, she helped debauched abbots play out their sexual fantasies.

She told me things I could hardly believe, things I am reluctant to commit to these pages. The Ace of Spades said I could observe her frolics through the peephole at any time, and I confess that on several occasions curiosity got the best of me. I would see a gentleman arrive, wigged and powdered, the picture of distinction and elegance, and I would have an overpowering desire to see him

shed, along with his clothes, the signs of his class and rank, and
enter an arena where high birth, inherited wealth, vast property,
and influential friends are of no assistance: The bed. Here, as
everywhere else, appearances were deceiving. There were brawny
horse guards whose frivolity you would have needed a lens to see,
and diminutive powdered marquis who bored through the cabbage
and made the jumpers fly.

One afternoon I found Madame de Rouxpoil making elaborate
floral arrangements in the large drawing room, great bouquets of
gladioli, long-stemmed tulips, roses, and lilac branches. I asked her
what the occasion was, and she told me that an important court
personage was coming that evening, and had asked to see some of
the tableaux, performed by several girls, that were a house specialty. She invited me to join in one of the tableaux. I protested
that I was known at court, and that this important personage could
easily recognize me. She suggested I wear a mask, but I said I had
no talent for exhibitionism.

"It's so hard to find someone suitable," she said. "I can't bring
just anyone here. My house is like a club, courtiers know they will
not have to rub elbows with riffraff. I had a young Italian, but he
ran off with one of my girls."

I decided not to watch the tableaux, but the Ace of Spades
advised me to remain faithful to my post at the peephole, for
afterward she was to take this important personage into her room
for a private session. I waited for some time until the door opened,
and when candles were lit, I rubbed my eyes in disbelief. But there
could be no mistaking those close-set eyes, that nose like a parrot's
beak, and the disdainful manner of a man who knows he is beyond
the law's reach. It was the prince de Croÿ, and for a moment I
panicked, for I imagined he had come to find me. But I soon
realized that he was there for other reasons, as he began to indulge
in a particularly odious aberration, which made me realize that he
was not only unscrupulous, but a bit deranged. To sum up what he
was doing while remaining within the bounds of propriety, let me
say only that it is called the Golden Shower. The spectacle made
me sick to my stomach, and I could not imagine that anyone could
derive pleasure from it. When it was over, he resumed his arrogant
manner.

"How was it?" the Ace of Spades asked, concerned over the
effectiveness of her treatment.

"My dear," said Croÿ, "you are sublime, you piss rose water."

To think that it was because of this old sapajou that I had been sent to the Bastille and lost my credit at court. Now, at least, I had a weapon to use against him. I am not by nature vindictive, but certain deeds beg for vengeance.

I was growing restive in my role as harem eunuch, for I could not leave the house, and the days there resembled one another as closely as two drops of water. One morning, however, I received the hoped-for message from Elizabeth: The king, although angry at my escape, had decided to pardon everything, for there was a special mission he wanted to send me on. He was quoted as saying: "Let us put that young fellow's ingenuity to better use." The king was now convinced that I was not connected with the parody against the marquise. Suspicion centered on the prince de Croÿ, whose blood relationship to the monarch protected him from reprisal. I informed Madame de Rouxpoil that I was returning to court, thanked her for her hospitality, and swore that I was her servant. She was touched by my gratitude, and her triple chins trembled with pleasure as I kissed her hand with feeling.

"It was a pleasure to have you here, my dear count," she said. "Please be assured that you are always welcome. Consider this your home away from home."

Such was her sense of her own dignity that in Madame de Rouxpoil's presence I forgot I was talking to a whorehouse madam, and felt instead that I was with a dowager of advanced years and position who deserved my most attentive courtesy. I kissed each of the girls good-bye, and the Ace of Spades dabbed stray tears from her cheeks, saying that she had come to consider me as a younger brother. I had even developed a close rapport with the parrot, who sometimes perched on my shoulder and said *"Je t'aime, je t'aime."* My carriage was ready, and I rode off, looking back as it turned the corner to see a white blur of waving female arms.

I Am in Love with Elizabeth

I was grateful to find that my tiny apartment under the eaves had not been given to another in my absence, for the king was quick to take back those favors he granted. My first duty, more urgent even than falling into the arms of my darling Elizabeth, was to compose a letter to the marquise, which, through a subtle blend of flattery and repentance, would put me back in her good graces.

"Madam," I wrote, "my first gesture upon returning to court is to take my pen and vow my continued devotion to your service. I call service what is really the most intense of pleasures, for you are not like other women. You are kind, although few people know it. You are simple, although your wit shines. Only you know how to dazzle without tiring the eyes. You do not chase epigrams, they seem to come and find you. Because you are superior, you alarm only fools. You are elegant, without making a career of elegance. Your tastes are followed, your phrases are quoted. You have only to appear in a white sunbonnet for every woman at court to be wearing one the next day. Two or three professional liars cover you with compliments, which you shrug off as you would a heavy shawl in summer. A dozen hangers-on flatter themselves that they have enlisted your support in some of their dubious affairs, having mistaken your smile for approval. But there are a few here, and I count myself among them, who, seeking nothing from you, want only to admire you from whatever distance you deem proper." I thought that would soften up the old bitch, and I was right, for thereafter, she went out of her way to show me signs of her goodwill.

As for Elizabeth, I found that my feelings for her had increased during our separation. I, who had thus far loved inconstant women inconstantly, found in her loyalty and selflessness the substantial bread of true love. Love is never the same, it increases or decreases, it does not stagnate; just as there is no stagnation among nations, one rises and the other fades, and the nation that stands still diminishes by comparison to the nation that is rising. Thus it is with the heart's history. The chart rose and dipped in cycles, and we were now at a peak of mutual devotion which it would have been embarrassing to show publicly in a court where love affairs had the same life-span as cut flowers, nourished as they were by the waters of fashion. Elizabeth, truer to the conventions of the court, gently mocked my condition, and said I did not know what love was.

"Why," I said, "a strong inclination of the senses."

"Such a threadbare definition makes me weep," she said.

"A feeling of deep regard," I added.

"Such as you might have for your grandfather," she responded.

I groped for words that expressed my feelings. "Love is . . . what cannot be explained," I said.

"Like the cosmos," she replied. "Is that what is called *reductio ad absurdum*?"

I took another tack. "Love is what addles a man's brain and turns him to quivering jelly in the presence of a lady."

"In other words, a disease," she said, "for which medical treatment should be prescribed."

"It does not respond to treatment," I replied. "That is its mystery."

"And yet we know well enough when we are in that state," she said. "There is nothing mysterious about that."

Wanting to impress her, I took for my own a phrase coined by Voltaire: "Love is the cloth of nature woven by the imagination." That was not precise enough to suit her.

"We should establish," she said, "whether we are discussing the love one feels or the love one makes." The only possible reply was to kiss her, and to try to prove that the two were not exclusive.

Elizabeth was a manor where I kept discovering new rooms, each one differently furnished. Her conversation was like the brushstroke of a painter, who suggests without delineating. By comparison, the other court ladies were as empty-headed and feathery as birds; they flew from tree to tree, never lit on the same branch twice, and filled the air with meaningless chirping. There was the coot, who did not have the slightest trace of passion in her nature. Everything for her was dictated by society and fashion. She took a lover as she chose a dress, and to keep him interested she condescended to grant her favors. Her letters followed the same principle; they ended with tender words consecrated by usage. Supper only amused her if one talked of where one was dining on the morrow. Her life was a flight into the promise of the future, the present moment was never enough. Then there was the quail, absorbed by the tiny details of life, curlers, orange powder, jasmine pomade, the difficult choice between rose water and honey water. She would break off a conversation to say that taffeta this year is not being worn. She was unaware that her love of novelty made her always and tediously the same. And then there was the dove, whose pretended piety was a barricade easily breached by praising her for it. One had to admire her sacrifice to God, and ask for her assistance in becoming more virtuous. She would momentarily forget her pious dispositions, but afterward, she would remember them, and it would be the same struggle repeated, like some tiresome formality in an official application.

Elizabeth had no place in this aviary. The iron rigidity of a convent education had given her, quite against its acknowledged intentions, an independent mind. Any hint of constraint simply fueled her stubbornness. I realized when she described her childhood how much harder it is for women than for men to challenge the pressures that make them conform to a model of empty-headed vacuity. They are bent and molded and trimmed into a prearranged shape, and few are strong-willed enough to escape their assigned roles. Elizabeth's struggle began at the age of seven, when she was received into the convent as a canoness. A priest slipped a gold ring on her finger, and tied a little piece of black and white cloth to her head. This was called a husband, and thereafter she was called Madame. She was so sad that her mother, to stop her crying, lied to her that the nuns would give her candy every day. Blessed with an invincibly cheerful disposition, she soon bartered her sadness for a sense of mischief.

One evening she poured a bottle of ink in the chapel's baptismal font. The nuns went to matins after midnight, when there was no other light than altar candles. They dipped their fingers into the font, crossed themselves, and came out looking like chimney sweepers. She was caught the next day because an ink-stained handkerchief with her initials on it was found in a side altar. Had it not been for the position of her family (she was born de Riant), she would have been expelled.

As it was, she was confined for a month to what was called her room: A bed covered with white in the winter and blue in the summer, a faldstool rubbed smooth by countless pairs of young knees, a chest of drawers, two chairs, a tiled floor, a shelf for books, and felt pads she had to walk on so as not to get the floor dirty. Thereafter, she did everything *a contrario*, and spent her days going without dessert, or having dry bread for dinner, or kneeling in the middle of the choir during services.

She did not learn her lessons because she could not take them seriously. The nuns taught that heaven is a large room full of diamonds, rubies and emeralds, and that sort of thing. She got another girl to do her homework.

"Was it you who wrote that?" the nun asked her.

"Yes, sister, it was," she lied.

"If it was you, write another page like it in front of me."

The sentence was "Masinissa, king of Numidia," and the letters she knew least well were *n*'s and *m*'s, because she made the downstroke crooked. It did no good to say the table shook; she was punished again, and punished so often that the good nuns, realizing they had a subversive in their midst, finally did expel her, on the grounds that she had been caught reading by candlelight books that were not in the curriculum. But the real reason was that she had complained to a visiting cardinal, a friend of her parents, that the convent food was inedible.

"One went to the convent in order to lose one's faith," Elizabeth said. This was untrue of most girls, who were cowed into submission, and learned never to raise their eyes or separate their hands from being joined in prayer, but in Elizabeth the mixture of mindless discipline and catechizing foolishness brought out a rebellious streak. Only now that I knew the story of her childhood did I understand how she had been capable of fighting a duel.

Her father, furious at her expulsion, immediately found another convent belonging to a different, but equally stern, order. He told her that the only escape would be on the arm of her husband. Effectively, four days after her eleventh birthday, Elizabeth received an enormous bouquet of flowers in the morning, with a note announcing the visit that same afternoon of the vicomte de la Morue, a short, fat Parisian in his late thirties, as round and bald as a croquet ball, who solemnly discussed the clauses in their marriage contract. "How ugly your husband is," her schoolmates said, and began calling her Madame Morue and *huile de foie de morue*.* Elizabeth's eyes did not dry for weeks, and when the vicomte de la Morue came on his second visit, she told the sister who came to fetch her that she had twisted her ankle running in the garden and could not see him, absolutely. He left, and she was told by the wise recruiting nuns that her only choice, made quite clear by her father, was to marry him or become a novice, a bride of Christ.

Elizabeth had this admirable phrase: "I chose Christ, because I did not know what He looked like."

A year later, the doors of the chapel opened before Elizabeth in a white crepe dress and she listened to a sermon informing her that it was a great merit in the eyes of God to renounce the world when one was made to be adored and to constitute one of its charms and ornaments. She was then led to the cloister, and the lock turned noisily behind her as the door slammed. The other novices looked

---

* *Morue* means cod, and she was called Mrs. Cod and Cod-liver Oil.

on as two sisters removed the pins from her long blond hair and it came cascading down her back. "What a shame," they said, and Elizabeth trembled when she saw the shears. A nun stood holding a silver tray to receive her shorn tresses, and the snipping sound the shears made reminded her of her father's tone of command. She exchanged her white dress for the gray homespun habit of the order. Pale as death, she was taken to the sacristy, held under each arm by a novice, where she was allowed to rest for a minute before prostrating herself in the middle of the choir, as sisters covered her with a winding sheet and voices rose in the Miserere and the *Dies Irae*. She realized, as she heard those funereal hymns, that they announced her own death to the world. A garland of white roses was hung about her neck, and she knelt before a priest who blessed her.

The mother superior took both her hands and began to pronounce the vows, which she was to repeat: "Between your hands, madam, I vow to God to remain poor, humble, obedient, chaste, and to live perpetually cloistered, according to the rule of Saint Benedict." She stumbled over the words and when she came to "chaste" could not get it out. It had nothing to do with her will; it was as if she had been momentarily struck dumb, the way others experience a loss of memory. "Now, now, my child, courage, complete your sacrifice," the mother superior said. Elizabeth was secretly hoping for a sign from the Almighty, a clear signal that she was not meant for the nunnery. The roof would fall in, or a bolt of divine lightning would burn her habit from her body without harming her. But no sign came, and everyone was waiting, so the signal had to come from her.

She jumped up and cried, "I can't," and ran from the choir.

The nuns and novices, frozen in disbelief, stared at the small retreating figure. Finally, the mother superior said, with a trembling, turkeylike gobble, "This has never happened before."

The priest who was about to say the mass replied with a wave of his hand, "The Lord's ways are ever mysterious."

Of course, after that, Elizabeth had to leave. She was a bad example for the other girls, having actually done what the rest of them secretly wished they had had the courage to do when they were mumbling their vows. They did not even give her time for her hair to grow out. They sent her home, her head covered with blond chicken fuzz, so that for months she had to wear a sort of *coiffe*, as if she were still a member of the order. Her father was beyond anger, fallen into apathy. He told her that with her reputation, no husband would have her, and no convent would have her. Elizabeth said that with her short hair she could dress like a man and volunteer for the army. With each day, however, she became more beautiful, and it was soon apparent that a lack of suitors would not be her problem. She bypassed the awkward age, and at fifteen, she was a woman, tall for her age, poised, graceful, radiant, confident about her beauty in the manner that one becomes confident about an acquired skill, like riding, or dancing. She knew the range of effects she could provoke, and made discreet use of them. There was in her, if such a thing can be imagined, a functioning blend of the calculating and the natural, something like a *chaud-froid* in gastronomy, when the same dish conveys the opposite tastes of hot and cold.

When the duc de Villiers, a recently widowed courtier in his fifties who had a permanent crink in his back from bowing, and a permanent squint in his eye from trying to see down the bodices of pretty girls, came to visit Elizabeth's father, he had as much chance of resisting her as the French archers, their bows limp from the previous night's rain, had of resisting the English at Agincourt. For Elizabeth saw in him the price of her liberation from her family. He was more than three times her age, but he had what she called "good remains"; he stood straight, his eyes were still bright and his chin did not sag. Moreover, he was amusing, in the simpering way that courtiers affect, and he would remove her at once to Versailles, beyond the reach of her provincial tyrant of a father. In effect, she was exchanging a father for a grandfather whose bed she would have to share.

Without coyness, she let the old duc know that she had decided to be his wife. This was not difficult, for he was in a trance, following her to pick flowers in the garden, holding her wool on his two extended wrists as she prepared it for her petit point, and accompanying her on her morning rides, even though the exercise crucified his gouty foot (in younger days he had been a passionate hunter). When he proposed, during a carriage ride through the great domainal forest of the Sologne where the Riants had their castle, she replied in her best convent manner, as though she were being asked if she wanted a piece of chocolate: "Oh, yes, sir, thank you very much." The old courtier, whose affairs had been so numerous that he could no longer remember the names of his mistresses, for the nights of conscientious lovemaking had blurred into a tangle of animated but anonymous bodies, kissed the blue vein on the inside of a wrist that led to a heart he knew was pure.

On their wedding night, he drank too much champagne, and fell asleep at the dinner table in the small country house outside Paris where he had taken her. His head dropped onto the white linen tablecloth as he held her hand, and he did not relinquish it once he was asleep and snoring. "And I am supposed to remember this as the most romantic night of my life," Elizabeth thought, wondering whether to pull her hand away and risk waking him, or keep it in his slumbering grasp. She suddenly feared that the day's excitement had been too much, and that his fingers were tightening around her hand with the stiffness that follows death. Not yet a bride and already a widow, she thought as she pulled it away. His head bobbed from the table, and he said: "Damned servants, always forget to clear the table." He had quite forgotten she was there, and when he saw her, he said, as if suddenly remembering that he had married her on that same day: "Oh, it's you, my dear."

It was not until a week later that the marriage was consummated. She was so innocent of the act involved that in the midst of it, impatient at her husband's prolonged efforts, she told him: "Either come in or stay out, but stop this eternal coming and going." There was no pain, and not much pleasure, and afterward she said: "I don't see what all the fuss is about."

They moved to the duc's apartment in Versailles, and Elizabeth applied herself to the duties of court life. This too was a novitiate, although the vows one made were not the same—the vow of chatter instead of silence, of promiscuity instead of chastity. Elizabeth was adopted by one of her husband's former mistresses, who, after taking stock of her beauty and natural elegance, told her: "Don't stand in the light of windows, the queen is jealous of youthful complexions. And don't try to be fashionable. Fashion means dressing like tomorrow instead of yesterday. Leave that to the queen and the royal mistresses."

Instead of freedom, she found a life as regulated as the nunnery. She had to learn the art of walking without tripping over the long train of the lady in front of her, which meant sliding over the floor without lifting her feet, and that of course reminded her of the felt pads in her convent cell. She had to follow the king and queen to the daily religious services she detested, clutching a six-franc piece, for the queen took up the collection, moving from pew to pew, shaking a little velvet bag and saying: "For the poor, please." Dancing was turned into torture by three-inch heels, headdresses a foot high, and a kilo of powder and pomade. It seemed to her that the court converted every pleasure into a dreary ceremony.

Between ceremonies, there was the idle talk of other women and the approaches of other men. For every gallant saw in her winter-spring marriage an opportunity, and the cynics made bets as to who would be first to claim what was vulgarly called her "married cherry." At first, she resolved not to listen to the compliments. To those who insisted, she said: "Sir, I love my husband passionately, and I have vowed never to listen to a young man's conversation if I find it improper." But when waves beat against a thin seawall, the thousands of waves the sea resists prepare the way for the one that eventually breaks through. The same process of erosion oper-ated at court against women with virtuous intentions. Add to that the persistence of the tide: It becomes embarrassing to say no when everyone else is saying yes. Add also the vagrant heart of Elizabeth's husband, who, to keep up appearances, felt obliged to have mistresses.

Elizabeth did not understand how a man she found barely toler-able could interest other women. She did not realize that to interest women it is enough to be interested in them. They sensed in the duc de Villiers someone who would always be attentive to their most trivial observations. His infatuation with his wife was not strong enough to withstand the conventions of court life. It was more important for him to be seen in a tête-à-tête with another woman, so that the court might know that he was still in circula-tion. He was delighted with his young bride, but afraid that some-one would notice it. He had no real desire to be unfaithful, but decided he should because it was expected of him. In so doing, he gave Elizabeth the best of reasons to pursue her romantic educa-tion. "My wife is as impregnable as the Bastille," the old fool boasted, not realizing that his behavior was contagious.

Infidelity was not enough, it had to be displayed. Elizabeth had to become an accomplice, in order to convince her that their situa-tion was the norm among court marriages. One day, he showed her a piece of English lace and said: "Madam, do me the pleasure of evaluating that. You know about such things. There is a gift I must make to a lady, and this lace, if it is not too dear, will be just the thing."

"Oh, well," Elizabeth said, "I think one hundred francs the ell would not be exorbitant."

"Ha," the old duc said, beaming, "I got it for eighty. Her birthday is in ten days, I can't overlook it, and this will do without ruining me." Elizabeth said nothing. "Don't you find it an honest gift?" her husband asked.

"That is a sort of honesty I know nothing about," she replied.

She grew less fierce with the young men who courted her. She let them sit at her feet, and walk with her, and compete for her hand at balls. She saw less of her husband, who had obtained a sinecure as inspector of the salt tax in the Guyenne, requiring him to make frequent trips to that province, and during one of his absences, she moved into a separate apartment. The old duc returned, and far from protesting the new arrangement, congratulated her on the taste with which she had furnished her rooms. He paid her visits every two or three days, and when they met in the palace, he was as courteous to her as he was toward other ladies. Over a two-year period, their marriage had developed into a polite acquaintance. There was no jealousy on either side, because there was no feeling.

Elizabeth had still not taken a lover. Her heart was available, but she knew its value and did not want to give it up to the first bidder. As a defense, she continued to pretend an interest in her husband, and made a list of her refusals, which she once showed me as a negative compliment. She had written out, in her small, neat, upright convent hand, with the *m*'s and *n*'s upside down like *w*'s and *u*'s, "the sort of men I dislike":

Those who say I love you because.
Those who are so self-assured that they seem to be saying:
"I strongly advise you to fall in love with me."
Those who take without asking, and those who ask without taking.
Those who pay more attention to the scaffolding than to the building.
Those who wish to give an impression of strength by speaking little.
Those who try to drown their foolishness in verbiage.
Those who complain about the price of things.
Those who order me about like a soldier and those who leave every decision up to me.

Those who fall to their knees too often.

Those who ask you whom you have been seeing, and those who don't care whom you have been seeing.

Those who kiss and tell. Those who don't kiss and tell. Those who don't kiss and don't tell.

The very young men who compose circular letters of the sort, "I am mad for you and will be at your feet tonight between eleven and midnight." The very old men who write similar letters.

Those who want you only because they have not had you.

Those who are so pleased with themselves that they interpret indifference as a lure.

Those who sell the bearskin before the bear is killed.

It was on the second anniversary of her arrival at court, almost to the day, that, having decided I did not correspond to any of the categories on her list, she chose me to practice the marital infidelity her husband so assiduously recommended. What had begun between us as an affair that, with luck, might last a month, each leaving the other without regret, like passengers in a carriage after a pleasant ride through a fragrant spring landscape, had now become an understanding to pursue the journey together, even though the seasons and the landscapes would change. I knew that the court was a forest filled with snares for lovers, but I believed, with the faith of my young heart, that we were destined to pass through it uninjured. At this moment in my life, I had no greater ambition than to awaken in the morning with the soft cadences of Elizabeth's breath announcing, like a messenger delivering a long-desired invitation, an intense pleasure that lay ahead.

I Am Sent on a Mission to Rome and Meet the Famous Casanova

Alas, I had not been back at court three days when Lauzun found me passing a saddle and harness inspection in the stables and took me aside to tell me about the mission I had agreed to undertake for the king.

"Have you heard about the pamphleteer Revel?" he asked.

"The one who said the king's ministers are like nuns, who recite Latin without understanding it?"

"The very one," he said. "The fellow has no sense of proportion.

The more offensive his words, the more pleased with himself he is. He is openly calling for an overthrow of the monarchy. And since a fool always finds another fool to read what he writes, the king ordered his arrest, but he has fled to Rome."

"Can't the king ask his good friend the Pope to extradite him?" I asked.

"Apparently," Lauzun said, "he is under the protection of the Sforza family. You know Italians, they'll befriend anyone who amuses them. They'd have the devil to dinner if he made them laugh." I nodded. "The king wants you to fetch him," Lauzun said.

"I don't even know what the fellow looks like," I protested.

"That's just it," Lauzun said, "he won't suspect you. You're to find a way to bring him back to France."

"In other words," I said, "I'm to worm my way into his confidence, and lure him into a trap."

"Not at all, my dear fellow," Lauzun said. "You are to perform a patriotic act in the highest interests of your king and country."

"I won't do it," I said.

"You have already said you would," Lauzun said. "Your cell in the Bastille is still vacant, and this time the governor will keep you under closer watch."

"I'll do it," I said. I could not face Lastours, who had befriended me and then been reprimanded because of my escape.

"It shouldn't take you longer than a month," Lauzun said. "Elizabeth will survive. She can work on her embroidery, like Penelope." He took me by the arm and led me out of the stables. "And now," he said, "you must share a bottle of champagne with me. I am celebrating the burning of two thousand love letters, one of my few virtuous acts. The first one was written to me when I was twelve. I threw them in the fire in batches of fifty and watched the words of love burn, darken, and curl into smoke. You would be astonished at some of the reputations I am protecting. I apprehended that if my house was ever searched, they would cause me no end of trouble. Ah, what a loss to history!"

It seemed that no sooner had I been reunited with Elizabeth than we were once again exchanging tearful farewells. She asked to come with me, dressed as my page, but I did not want her involved in this unsavory expedition. I told her I was going to Rome to deliver secret documents to one of the king's agents, so that she would not think of me as a Judas goat. She told me not to spend too much time courting the ladies of Rome. I said I would be in too great a hurry to return to her. As we parted, she slipped an envelope into my pocket. I waited until I was on my way before opening it, expecting to linger over her tender words. But instead of a letter, the envelope contained an English riding coat. The message was clear, and only Elizabeth would have thought of it.

The trip was uneventful. A three-master carrying sugar from the West Indies took me from Marseille to Genoa, where I bought a horse, preferring to ride to Rome and have my luggage follow me. The Italian language seemed as soft and pliant as the pasta they consume. Whatever I heard, even the imprecations of the long-shoremen on the docks, sounded musical and pleasant. On my way to Rome, I reached a fishing village on the Adriatic that looked as though it might provide a decent night's lodgings. I stepped into the church, for village priests often know where the best table is set, and at the right price. A candle was lit on the first step leading to the altar, an enormous candle with a bronze candlestick, nearly as high as I was. About twenty persons, mainly old women, knelt in front of this candle mumbling their prayers, as if it were Baal or Mammon himself.

"What's all this?" I asked the priest, who seemed a jolly, level-headed fellow.

"The villagers," he replied, "believe that if the candle goes out, the village will be flooded. There is always someone in attendance to make sure the wick stays lit, and to light another candle from the stub."

"You don't say," I said, and easing my way past the mumblers, I took a deep breath and blew it out like a birthday candle, plunging the tiny church into darkness, for the candle provided its only light.

"*Porca Madonna,*" the good father exclaimed, forgetting where he was, while the mumblers crossed themselves and pleaded with their favorite saints to spare them from a watery holocaust. I decided to leave them to their fantasies of doom, and was crossing the threshold when the priest shouted, "*Stai qui, eretico,*" and a dark shapeless mass of outraged true believers converged on me from between the pews.

I jumped down the perron to my horse, which was tied to a tree under a stained-glass window representing, I think, Noah's embarkation, and before taking my leave, I waved my hat and shouted at the superstitious *contadini*: "*Fra poco, l'inondazione,*" and rode away. I had to keep riding for three hours before I reached the next village, but the look on the priest's face when the candle went out was worth it.

In Rome, I took rooms on the Via Julia, where the famous jeweler Cellini once had his shop, and went to call on the various notables for whom I had been given letters of introduction. I knew that Revel was popular, in spite of his views, among certain families of the black nobility, and I planned to meet him by frequenting their circle. I flatter myself that my manner made a good impression, for I was soon invited to various suppers and receptions. When one comes from Versailles, the rest of the world has a rustic tinge. One moves from the center to the periphery, and one is received with consideration. The court's principal advantage lies, ironically enough, in being away from it.

My first *dîner prié* was at Prince Ruffo's. The Ruffo palazzo is on the Corso, the central thoroughfare of Rome, through which, in medieval times, once a year, Jews were chased naked by horse-drawn carriages as a form of civic amusement. The building was of noble proportions, to my taste somewhat massive and lacking in decoration, although it should not be forgotten that Italian workers were imported by François Premier to build the Loire castles. I was impressed by the Prince's collection of paintings, particularly by a charming Botticelli representing Venus rising from the waters, and several works by a Venetian named Carpaccio, who paints canal scenes of his native city that seem more real than the real. These Romans have a mania for enormous rooms with high ceilings and painted cherubs copulating in the cupolas. Every room is like an assembly hall, and one expects that a meeting is about to be called to order. Comfort is sacrificed to their love of the grandiose, for these barrackslike chambers are impossible to heat, despite the great stone fireplaces, and the Flemish tapestries that cover the walls. The scale is not right, a man feels lost in such vast caverns, and I found myself longing for the intimacy of the little apartments of Versailles.

We were herded into a room that seemed the size of the Palais-Royal, for warmth I at first supposed, to listen to a quatuor which had recently had the honor of playing before the Pope, and before long I was stifling yawns with my handerchief, for that sort of music always reminds me of a dog chewing its own tail, it never gets anywhere. On my left stood a man, who, with his sleeve over his mouth, said in French, for my costume betrayed my origins: "I would almost rather listen to a regimental march." Waving his handkerchief like a flag in front of my face, he introduced himself: "Your servant, sir, Giovanni Giacomo Casanova de Seingalt."

"Or to a wedding march," I replied, for I had heard of the fellow's reputation, and was astounded to see him in the flesh, having imagined a handsome, bright-eyed, clear-skinned, appetizing fellow.

He would in fact have been handsome had he not been ugly: Small darting eyes in a pudding face of Ethiopian complexion, and gross liverish lips that seldom parted in a smile, for that would have revealed teeth as rotten as a year-old *camembert*. Of average height, but pudgy, rotund, small-boned, the sort of fellow who is hopeless before midday, would rather ride a couch than a horse, and have his manservant do his walking for him. He gave an impression of indolence, of being slow to move and slow to act, and abandoned it only when food was served. I did not know whether he was a satyr in the woods, but I can vouch that he was a wolf at the table. It was, as I learned, not his appearance that charmed, but his conversation, which made one forget his appearance. His sallies were a sprinkling of Attic salt. Homer appeared often on his lips, and was made to endorse axioms of Casanova's own minting. He was a well of knowledge, a bottomless well, for the only things he did not know were those he pretended to know. One would mention Frederick II; he was with him in Silesia, and learned the secrets of victory and empire. One would mention Russia; he has drunk with Peter III and advised the great Catherine on how to dress. I hesitated to mention God, for I was sure he would pass on his private conversations with the All-High.

"I have a peculiarity of hearing," Casanova said in response to my question. "I am deaf to wedding marches. Why turn a pleasure into a sacrament?"

"Wives are not for pleasure," I said. "They are for convenience. What is the point of having a mistress if one has no wife?"

"People think you French are frivolous," Casanova said. "What a mistake. Your pleasures, like your labors, are organized like a bureaucracy, without whimsical variations."

"There is little whimsy in being here," I said. "You look as bored as I am."

"When someone tells me I look sad, I become sad, and when someone tells me I look bored, I become bored. You must be right. There are less boring places."

Taking me by the arm, he led me down the marble staircase and we took English leave.* Outside, in the courtyard, he whistled once and a carriage driven by a desiccated, toothless old reprobate rattled over the cobblestones and stopped in front of us. Casanova bade me get in, and told the coachman: Teatro Marcello. "We will visit there two lady friends of mine, who will kiss away from our ears the shrill sounds we have just heard. They're as common as barber's chairs, but they'll do for an evening."

I congratulated him on having always at hand a supply of compliant ladies for the entertainment of visiting foreigners, and he waved his hand wearily, as if to say: "There is no use congratulating a cow for giving milk."

"What is the merit in obtaining the favors of women?" he said. "All one has to do is listen to their little problems, their endless stories about nothing, about buying a pound of butter, or meeting someone in the street, or losing a hairpin. One must use flattery as one uses sugar in making candy, that is to say, liberally. A compliment is never out of season, and no matter how outrageous, will always be believed, for women eagerly accept from a man's lips what their mirrors forget to tell them. Everyone asks me the secret of seduction. I hesitate to reveal it because it is so simple: It is the patience to put up with their prattle, their migraines, and their slight indispositions. If I were handsome, I would let them come to me. Physical beauty is the greatest gift, because it is truly given; one can do nothing to acquire it. It is precisely because I am not handsome that I decided on the pursuit of women as a career. The greatest compliment that can be paid me is: What, is that fat, dwarfish blackamoor the great Casanova, whom no woman can resist? It baffles them because they have not understood that a woman is less interested in her lover than in his idea of her."

I asked whether our destination was still far and stifled a yawn.

"We are here, my friend. Blessed be the patient, for they shall be fulfilled. You will soon have occasion to notice that the women of our day give themselves with their eyes open, so as to lose nothing of the spectacle, and with an immodesty that announces an exquisite but dying society."

He took me up a flight of dark stairs and knocked on a door with his cane. It was presently opened by a rather swarthy girl with short curly hair, small eyes, and a full mouth, pulpous and granular like a tropical fruit. She asked who was there, but as soon as the

---

* A literal translation of the French colloquialism *filer à l'anglaise*.

light from within lit half of Casanova's face, she let out a short peal
of delight and threw her arms around him.

"Luisa, it's our little doge," she called, and Luisa, taller, thinner, fairer, bravely trying to look dignified, a shopgirl playing the
lady, appeared behind her and said: "Everything is in such a mess.
If only we had known you were coming, I'm really ashamed to
receive you like this."

"We didn't come to look at the furniture," Casanova said. Turning to me, he added: "Look at these two wenches, the finest
women Italy produces, Gina from Naples, sultry as a muscat
grape, and Luisa from the North, near Milan to be exact. She
would not disgrace your own court, my dear friend, but make no
mistake about it. Despite her airs, she can fuck you dry."

I am always embarrassed by coarse talk in the presence of
ladies, and I must have blushed, for both girls' cheeks inflated as
they suppressed gales of laughter. I suppose Casanova wanted to
show me the intimate footing he was on with them. It was not in
my nature, however well I might know a lady, to openly discuss
my intimacies in front of near strangers. Such was not his way. He
seemed to be telling me that, just as an athlete likes to be complimented on his prowess, women enjoy being praised for their romantic accomplishments.

"Come now, my darlings," Casanova continued, "I have praised
your charms all evening long to a man accustomed to the greatest
beauties in Europe, the ladies of Versailles. Don't let me down. I
told him you had the finest breasts in Rome, and now I want him
to make the judgment of Paris, for he is a connoisseur."

Casanova proceeded to seat me on a canapé in a corner of the
room and helped the girls remove their blouses. Far from protesting, they met his proposal with good humor. As Casanova unbuttoned Gina, Gina unbuttoned Luisa, and soon I saw them before
me, as nature made them.

"And first the test, my darlings," Casanova said, taking a small
wooden rule from his pocket and placing it under one and then the
other of Gina's breasts. "If the rule is caught in the crease, you will
have to pay the forfeit." Gina said it tickled, and Luisa held herself
very straight, for her breasts did sag a bit, but the rule dropped
and she was safe.

"Now what would you say, my friend?" Casanova asked, like a
peddler showing off his wares. "Gina's breasts are soldierly, they
stand at attention, they are the round sentinels of her body, these

large brown nipples look soft, but they become bayonets at the touch. These are mineral breasts, made to endure time and weather, breasts to be copied by a sculptor for his Aphrodite, breasts that adolescents dream of as they clutch their pillows in the moist morning hours, breasts a man wants to kneel before as before an altar and take communion in both species. Luisa's breasts are Fragonard breasts, pink and delicate, with long pale nipples, they are indoor breasts that need shielding from the sun, and while not as full as Gina's they are so deliciously arched that they seem made to be cupped in a man's hand. They evoke rose petals, satin pillows, rumpled sheets, a Scarlatti *aria da capo*, can you see, the nipples actually lift like the stamens of flowers, and these flowers, my dear count, are always in bloom."

Entering into the game, for it was pointless to maintain my air of embarrassment when these two nymphs stood half-naked before me, without a trace of shyness, I said: "You make it hard for me to choose."

"Don't choose by looking," Casanova said. "A man who buys a melon in the market without feeling it first is a poor shopper."

I was only too ready, and I cupped both Gina's breasts, lifting them and pinching the nipples and making appropriate approving remarks. Then it was Luisa's turn and her breasts, higher than Gina's and more closely set together, seemed to respond to my touch with movements of their own, like a pair of doves about to take flight. "As the guide who brought me to these monuments of Rome," I told Casanova, "and as the guardian of these ladies' virtue, first choice must be yours."

"I can never choose," Casanova said. "I can't even order a meal, and when I watch a game of chess I like to advise both players. But in order to make the game complete, and to avoid any disappointments, we'll each start with one and finish with the other, if your appetite is up to two courses."

"Excellent," I said, and in the same breath, I found Gina in my lap, her arms around me, her mouth nibbling at my ear. Casanova vanished into the next room with Luisa, and I spent a busy hour with Gina, whose lovemaking was unusually energetic. It was her conceit to encourage my advances and then fight me off, and we ended up on the floor like two Greco-Roman wrestlers until, through repeated holds and pinions, I straddled her naked, my knees holding down her outstretched arms, and my rump on her belly. She went limp, I released my hold, she squirmed under me until she had freed her legs, which she bent and opened like the covers of a book, wrenching at my hair to pull me on top of her. The pain made me drive into her with fury, and I pushed and pulled with a will to punish, as though thrusting a saber into an enemy. This seemed to be exactly what she wanted, for she began to shake, and dug her nails into my back, and shouted *"Madonna Mia."*

Some women, when they have arrived, shout, "Alas, I am dead," but Gina kept invoking the Mother of Christ. This confirmed an interesting linguistic point I have made in my travels, to wit, that one can tell a woman's national origin by her cries of pleasure. Italian women, because of their strong religious upbringing, shake the rafters with shouts of *"Madonna Mia."* Spanish women express themselves in terms of locomotion, and say *"Anda, anda,"* as if they were spurring on a horse. French women prefer to use gastronomic terms, calling out *"C'est bon, c'est bon."* Slavic women, whom I have never professed to understand, shout mysterious polysyllabic imprecations ending in "sky," while English women content themselves with emitting tiny squeals, as if the soles of their feet were being tickled with a feather. A specialist could draw conclusions from these observations, for I have never found them to fail.

Gina had now subsided, and I withdrew to lick my wounds, wondering whether, in my battered state, I would be up to another bout with the charming rosy-nippled Luisa. My back was bleeding, and the floor was littered with tufts of my hair. I kept discovering new bruised areas. Casanova appeared, dressed, and powdered, with not a hair of his wig out of place, and laughed when he saw us. Inhaling a pinch of snuff from the space between his thumb and forefinger, he pointed to the other room and said: "She is waiting."

Dragging my feet, and looking, I thought, like Struwelpeter, the German figure used to frighten children, I went in, not wanting to make *bruta figura* before the renowned Italian lover, but singularly lacking in any desire. Luisa was waiting demurely under silken sheets in the large canopied bed. She was as tender as Gina had been athletic. My storm-tossed ship found a calm and fragrant harbor. Her hands were balm, her lips kissed my bruises and awakened my desire, and we made a gentle, noncombative, soundless sort of love. She did not shout, she did not scratch, but she knew the body's secret rhythms.

In a moment of postcoital intimacy, as we sat on the downy field of amorous pursuit (as some of our eminent academicians designate the bed), buttoning and corseting and breeching and shodding, Luisa paid me the compliment of saying that I had been every inch the Frenchman.

"Surely I was no match for my guide and predecessor," I replied, "whose exploits are the talk of all the courts in Europe."

"Sometimes the most delicious-looking cakes in the windows of pastry shops are made of plaster," she said.

"And what does that mean?" I asked.

"It means that the little doge and I did nothing more scandalous than play a hand of trictrac."

"You mean . . ."

"That my virtue with him is always intact. He is a gardener who never uses his hoe."

Inwardly laughing over this revelation, we returned to the other room, where Casanova chided me for taking so long, and allowed that he had enjoyed Gina twice in my absence. I complimented him on his vigor, and he said: "Just show me a pair of bare buttocks, and I will always rise to the occasion. But tell me, Count, did my two lovelies live up to your expectations?"

I assured him that I was the most sated man in Rome. He offered me a pinch of his eucalyptus-scented snuff, the restorative powers of which he heartily recommended, and said: "Quite a change of diet after your bland French women, my friend. They are all alike. How could they be otherwise? They have been to the same convent, they have the same hairdresser, the same dancing master, the same dressmaker, and often, the same lover. They are pretty in the same way, like porcelain dolls, with painted features and glazed eyes. They enter a room in the same way, their handwriting is the same, small and guarded and more pointed than round. They make love the same way, one reaches the goal over a raked path in a garden where all the flowers are clipped, and they even break off in the same way, by pretending overnight that they hardly know you. No matter how often you change, you have the impression of being always with the same one."

I am no chauvinist, but I could not help being stung by this broadside against French womanhood. I was all the more annoyed for knowing how false the charge was, having myself plucked a bouquet of charming variety from the garden of Versailles ladies.

Gina by this time had brought a tray with a roast chicken, a bottle of good red wine, and four glasses, and was accompanying our midnight snack with ditties of her own composition, of which I recall several snatches:

> How do you think
> I made him comply?
> With a wink
> Of my third eye.

And this one of classical mien:

> Do you know why Ovid
> Wrote of love so often?
> I served as his guide
> And he dipped his pen
> In my well.

Upon hearing the last two verses, I could not help laughing, nearly choking on a piece of chicken commonly known as *le morceau du cardinal*,* and could not resist saying: "I understand that some of the pens in this immediate neighborhood have gone quite dry."

"And what do you mean by that, sir?" Casanova inquired.

"Nothing at all, sir, except that one cannot always be a peacock in a tree and a bull in the pasture."

"Is that remark addressed to me, sir?"

"It is addressed to anyone who promises more than he can deliver."

"Speak more plainly, sir."

"I will, sir. I have it from an unimpeachable authority that your idea of spending half an hour with a lady in her bedroom is to play a game of cards. And I suspect that if I asked Gina, she would have the same all quiet to report."

Gina laughed as she chewed on the wing of a chicken, and nodded in assent. "Oh, my little doge, no use pretending, you've been found out," Luisa said. "Come now, we don't love you any the less."

Casanova was crestfallen. His head dropped, he pulled a handkerchief from his sleeve, and looked for a moment as though he might use it to wipe tears from his eyes. He was as contrite and melancholy as a defrocked priest whose bishop has refused him the right to perform the sacraments.

* A colloquial name for the chicken's triangular rear end.

"You don't understand what I have to go through," he said, "with my reputation to keep up. It's not a life to be envied, I can assure you. I spend entire nights waiting under a window, trying to keep warm by beating my rib cage with my hands. I climb over a grille and rip my trousers, dogs chase me and bite at my ankles. I am taken for a thief by honest men and for an honest man by thieves. I am drenched by a thunderstorm, I lose weight from loss of sleep, and once I arrive, tired and chilled and wet as an alley cat, I am expected to play the great lover. It's more than a man can do. And if I do it, it only takes a moment and I hardly enjoy it, for in the dark all cats are gray, it only becomes enjoyable in the telling, and then I become known as a braggart, for women with nothing more to expect from men become unrelenting in their attacks on them. So you see, in order to maintain myself in the condition that my reputation requires I must abstain from the actual act. I would be a complete wreck otherwise. Now you know. *Guai e maccheroni si màngiano caldi.*"

I felt truly sorry for the poor fellow, prisoner of his legend, a lion who had lost his roar from being constantly asked to demonstrate it. Not wanting to prolong his humiliation, I left as discreetly as possible, after kissing my two charming hostesses *au revoir* and promising to renew my acquaintance with them.

I Fulfill My Mission and Find an Unpleasant Surprise Awaiting Me at Court

It was only when I undressed in my lodgings that I noticed the two gold pieces I had sewn into the lining of my jerkin were missing. I had left it in the room with Gina and Casanova when I was ushered into Luisa's bed. Naïve Béarnais dolt that I am, I told myself, to let myself forget that wherever he is, in Rome or in Paris, a Venetian remains a Venetian, that is to say, as deft as a puppeteer, as devious as a canal, as secretive as a hidden door, as false as a painted window, and as treacherous as a denunciation. I wrote off the two louis as a justified expense for the evening's amusement, and decided that Casanova, with his flexible moral standards, would be a useful collaborator in my quest for the pamphleteer Revel.

I obtained his whereabouts from Luisa and found the great lover in bed in his room on the Piazza di Spagna, recovering from a strenuous night. I told him how delighted I had been to meet him, lest he think that I had sought him out to recover my two louis, and explained my interest in Revel. Casanova had met the fellow on several occasions, and told me he was not well. He was suffering from a rectal abscess, and his condition was so painful that he seldom went out. I hit upon the scheme of pretending to be a doctor. We would find a way to attend a soirée where we knew he would be present, and Casanova would introduce me as Doctor Gramont, the renowned specialist whose skill had brought him wealth, fame, and familiarity with several royal rectums. Two days later, Casanova informed me that Revel would that evening attend a reception given by a dowager with literary pretensions, the Countess Spaziani. He also found a friend who was invited and would take us along.

We arrived that evening to find Revel, who was round as a cask, and could hardly see his feet for his belly, and had a red, congested Dutch tavern keeper's face, with the dour expression of a man who, when he is shown iron, sees only the rust, holding forth before an elegant assembly. "He is demonstrating his talent for composing verses on any subject," someone whispered to Casanova as we took seats.

Countess Spaziani, a thin, dry-skinned woman with a face like a camel, who sat so stiffly on the edge of her chair that she looked as if she had soaked all day in a tub of starch, said: "What would you say of the d'Orsini brothers, one married a widow, the other her daughter?"

Revel furrowed his glaring red brow, and after twenty or thirty seconds, said:

> If you want an opinion that is candid,
> One likes his bacon fresh, the other rancid.

"The rhyme limps," Casanova said.

"So does the widow, I am told," Revel replied.

"Excellent, my dear fellow," said a tall man with a long equine face, whom Casanova identified as prince Marescotti, who had a scientific turn of mind, "and now to more serious subjects. Is electricity useful or damaging?"

Revel covered his eyes with his right hand, and after a long moment, declared:

> The bolt that comes from the sky
> With shattering force
> Can splinter a tree in the wink of an eye

Or frighten a horse.
But harness the bolt for mankind
And it will move ships, like the wind.

"How true," Countess Spaziani said, "in nature it is destructive, but man can put it to good use. I believe that is the moral behind the verse. Now, dear friend, let me ask you, my daughter recently had twins. Was that a good thing?"

The veins on Revel's forehead bulged, his eyes closed as if in prayer, and he said:

> A double blessing, madam, is her lot,
> Upon finding that she has twins begot.
> An extra dividend did she receive,
> Since she did but one conceive.

A peal of delighted laughter rippled across the room, and prince Marescotti, who spent hours in his scientific cabinet, and who had a tendency to lisp, added: "There are false twins, who have issued from two separate eggs, and real twins, who are the result of a split in one egg. I believe that distinction is worth nothing, I mean worth noting. Do you know, madam, in which category your daughter's twins belong?"

"No, not really," Countess Spaziani said. "To tell the truth, I never noticed."

'One thing," prince Marescotti said, "has always puzzled me, and I look to you, my dear sir, for an explanation. What does God look like?"

"As for that," Revel said, "I have seen Him no more often than you, and yet, I have an idea that . . .

> When He smiles it is like spring
> And when He frowns like bitter cold.
> In all the world there is no thing
> He cannot turn from young to old.
> He alone has no age,
> He never turns the page.
> Not the years, but the world and its sights
> Have turned His beard white.

Murmurs of approval went around the room, and polite applause. I must say I was struck by the fellow's ability to turn a rhyme at the drop of a pin. It was unfortunate the king could not hire him as a speech writer. Casanova pulled my arm. "Come, let me introduce you," he said. "You are in marvelous form, my dear Revel," he told the rhymester.

"Ah," Revel said, raising his eyes toward the ceiling, "if you knew how I am suffering. The torture of the damned."

Casanova introduced me and I complimented him on his improvisations. Revel asked what I was doing in the Italian capital, and Casanova said: "Surely you have heard of Gramont, the famous doctor who cured George II's fistula. The English king refused to be treated by his own doctors. He summoned Gramont. It was a triumph of French medicine."

"Most doctors kill their patients more often than not," I said modestly, "because they ignore the nature of the disease. If a doctor knows the disease, the patient is half cured. And what is a patient? All men are patients, a healthy man is one who ignores the nature of his illness. Look at the language—we eat our hearts out, we have no stomach for this or that, we have or do not have the gall to do this or that, we go out of our minds. Laughter itself is a disease, for we can die laughing."

"How true," Casanova said solemnly, as though paying tribute to words of wisdom.

"If you could help a fellow countryman in his misery, Doctor," Revel said, "I would die not of laughter but of gratitude."

"I wish I could," I said, "but I am here on a holiday, not to practice. I promised myself a rest."

"I am not a rich man," Revel said, "but I would gladly give you all my savings to be relieved of this cursed abscess."

"Come, Gramont," Casanova said, "relent in the face of human suffering. It cannot take you long to pierce an abscess. I know you are unable to resist helping your fellow man."

"Ah," I said, "you have touched my weak spot, I cannot remain insensitive to the pain of others. I remember when I treated the poor duc de Noailles for the gout, each day I had to cut off one of his fingers. I could barely muster the courage to go through with it."

Revel shuddered and pleaded with me to examine him. "But there are many fine specialists in France," I said, "men as experienced as myself. Why don't you follow treatment there?"

"I am lost if I return to France," Revel said. "I have committed the one unpardonable crime, I have said what I think. No, you are the only one who can help me."

Grudgingly, after much coaxing, I agreed to operate on his abscess. To put him in good spirits, I promised to use a solid silver lancet which I said had been specially made for the anus of George II. He was so happy I thought he was going to throw his arms around me and kiss me. We agreed to meet the following day at Casanova's lodgings.

"Are you going through with it?" Casanova asked after we had parted company with Revel.

"I'll have to," I said, "for the abscess could kill him, and I have been instructed to return him alive. It's a simple matter, I saw it done to the dauphin."

As it turned out, we did not even have to use a sleeping potion. I asked Revel to lie facedown on Casanova's bed, with a bolster to raise his hairy buttocks, and Casanova holding down his legs. I washed my hands with alcohol and probed Revel with my finger, removing it covered with pus the color and texture of curdled mayonnaise. I probed again, deeper, and touched a hard lump where the abscess had formed. Revel screamed. The fellow obviously had a low resistance to pain. I gave him a gag soaked in brandy and told him to chew on it. I decided to remove the abscess without a lancet, for what did God give us fingers for, and I felt there was less risk of loss of blood. I introduced my middle finger forcefully into Revel's rectum, hooked it into the gut, and felt the abscess burst. A river of pus flowed out, and, slithering along on its current swam a live worm as large as a lizard. I picked it up by its tail and held it up, shaking and jumping, for Revel to see.

"Look what you have given birth to," I said.

He turned his head, spit out the gag, cried "My God," and fainted.

Casanova had taken care of the travel arrangements. A carriage was waiting to take Revel and me to Naples, where we would immediately board a French ship bound for Marseille. In Marseille, the king's police were waiting. We bound Revel's hands and had to carry him into the carriage, no easy feat, for he weighed well over a hundred kilos. I thanked Casanova, slipped some gold coins into a side pocket of his velvet coat, and promised someday to do him the honors of Paris as he had done me those of Rome. He gripped my hand in both of his and said: "My dear Ax, you are more than a friend. We are members of the same species. For us, the world is like the play of shadows in a Chinese puppet theater, blurred and shifting."

The trip from Naples to Marseille took ten days, and during that

time I became almost fond of Revel. It is dangerous to become an
intelligent man's guardian, for one becomes exposed to the contagion of his ideas. More than once, I wished I could tell the ship's
captain to turn back, for I did not look forward to turning over to
the police a man I had shared meals and conversations with as I
would with a friend. We usually spent the morning on deck, gazing
out at the glassy *mare nostrum*, discussing what for him was a
necessity, the replacement of a monarchy by a republic. As for me,
the quality of the monarchy depended on the quality of the king,
and I could not see that under a republic things would be any
different, for someone would always be at the helm. I replied to his
arguments about the monarchy's misdeeds with a quip: "Republics
are only tolerable if they are surrounded by water. Look at England, Holland, and Venice. Fortunately, freedom cannot swim,
and is prevented from finding other countries to contaminate. It is
suitable only for insular people. If the King of England were to
take what I am saying amiss, I would tell him, 'Sire, I know that
your people fall to their kneees and sing "God Save the King"
when you go to the theater, but if you are five minutes late, they
whistle.' "

Revel, himself the son of an Orléans cooper whose facility with
the pen had allowed him to join the republic of letters, charged me
with being a prisoner of my order.* "Would it sadden you never
again to hear the words 'majesty' and 'eminence' and 'grace' and
'lordship'?" he asked me.

I said I had my wits more than my title to thank for whatever I
had obtained, and that I believed in the right of every man to
outwit his fellow, as I had done with him.

He replied that because of my class origins, I could not see,
beyond my own ambition, the notion of general good. "This regime makes our century blush," he said. "We must clear the
ground to build something new."

"And the throne," I asked, "and the altar?"

"The throne and the altar, like two flying buttresses supporting
one another, will fall together," he said. "If one bends, the other
breaks. And when that is done, we will erect something less
Gothic." I had lured him into captivity, and yet he showed no
rancor toward me. In his eyes, my conduct was typical of my
background, and one more sign that "the house must be torn down

---

* Under the *ancien régime*, France was divided into three orders, the nobility,
the clergy, and the third estate.

from cellar to attic." He held to the novel theory that a country is not made up of a king and his subjects, but of classes, whose conflicting interests would inevitably lead to struggle. He predicted the eventual victory of the downtrodden masses, for they were more numerous, and as he put it, "They have nothing to lose but their chains." This would lead to a form of government he picturesquely described as a "dictatorship of the proletariat." He also believed that class loyalties were stronger than national ones, and that the downtrodden all over the world would rise up against their monarchs like one great smiting arm. With this particular notion I was in partial agreement, feeling far more compatible with someone of my station from Hungary or England than with a Paris fishmonger or chimney sweep. Despite his tavern-keeper appearance, Revel was a man of unshakeable conviction, and I was glad when the trip came to an end, for my own convictions went no further than my immediate needs, and I was beginning to see some logic in his arguments.

When our ship, the *Mistral*, came into sight of the island off Marseille where travelers from the East suspected of carrying the plague are kept in quarantine, I told Revel that to my sorrow I would have to bind him up again. He shrugged and put his hands behind his back, and I felt a flush of shame color my cheeks. "I will put in a good word for you when I am back at court," I said. "You will find the Bastille quite comfortable. Ask for the room I had in the Tower of Liberty. They will let you out in a month or two and you will be in the midst of writing something and you will curse them for having to leave on such short notice." The *Mistral* maneuvered slowly into Marseille harbor, and Revel and I, standing on the bow deck as sailors prepared to drop anchor, saw a detachment of soldiers standing at attention on the pier, the bayonets on their muskets glinting in the sunlight.

We came down the gangplank and he marched past the soldiers, his hands behind his back, as if passing them in review, and into the two-wheeled open cart that was then in use to transport prisoners. The coachman whipped the horses, and the cart rolled off, followed by the soldiers.

Alas, as I was soon to learn, Revel was not taken to the Bastille. A week later, I was informed that he was on public view in the Halles pillory. I went there at once. It was a six-sided structure with a pointed roof that looked like a gazebo one might build to enjoy the view in the middle of a garden. Its base was a platform six feet from the ground, and its sides from the base to the roof were open except for pillars. Near the top of the open sides, a wide rim of wood circled it, perforated between each pillar by one large hole flanked by two smaller ones. Revel stood on one side of the platform with his hands and head sticking through the holes, looking like an element of that peculiar structure's architecture. A small crowd ambled about the pillory, nurses with their wards, soldiers on leave, girls in search of company, the usual blend of Paris street life. I bought a bottle of wine, had it uncorked, and striding boldly up to the pillory, brought the bottle's neck to Revel's lips. He guzzled it greedily, and I again promised to intercede in his favor at court. "You can do nothing for me," he said.

He was right. After a week in the pillory, he was sent to the Mont-Saint-Michel, and was placed in a wooden cage in a dungeon so cold that his interrogators could not remain there more than half an hour at a time. At one point, he refused all food, and the monks who served as jailers had to feed him bouillon through a funnel. His great bulk wasted to skin and bones. At the end of three months, he died, completely mad.

I had won my freedom by turning in Revel. As far as I could see, he was inoffensive, but the king could not tolerate public protest. The king had not ordered him put to death. Things did not happen that way. The order was to have him interrogated. The fact that he did not survive his interrogation was incidental. There was no cruelty here, only a procedural flaw. I realized that powerful figures can have men killed without remorse because their orders are impersonal. But as the agent of Revel's capture, I brooded over the incident. I felt my conscience as I would a pebble in my shoe. For the first time in my life, I wished something I had done could be undone. Our deeds pursue us.

My first thought upon returning from my mission had been Elizabeth. In Rome I had found a lovely gold brooch, with a large Baroque pearl in the center, and had got a good price on it thanks to Casanova, who was a friend of the jeweler's, an Italian Jew. I was told by her maid that her ladyship was indisposed, a word vague enough to encompass every mishap from a cold heart to a fevered brow. I left the brooch, prettily wrapped in a piece of red Genoa velvet, and waited two days for an acknowledgment of my gift, which did not come. I kept up my spirits by reading the notes she had written not one month before. One said: "I have bought a tomb to be buried alive in if you ever leave me." I could see no reason why her feelings in the interval should have changed. And yet again I was put off when I tried to visit her, with excuses increasingly flimsy. I am not the man to pursue a woman when he is not wanted. But everything I knew of Elizabeth contradicted her present behavior. I believed in the strong, unerring current of her feelings for me. Patience, I told myself, and the mystery will solve itself. I had not, since my return, seen her in the palace, either at the queen's gaming table or at the afternoon concerts she normally attended, and yet I knew she was not absent.

It was fall, and the king, who hunted all summer in Saint-Germain, now moved his hounds and horses to Versailles. I decided to attend the first Versailles hunt, although I never shared the royal passion for running the stag. It is not a hunt for food; it is nothing more than the king affirming his ownership of the forests in the Île-de-France. A king is not a king, they say, unless he likes to hunt. Particularly the Bourbons. Running down stags is a sign as characteristic as the lines in their hands. Henri IV hunted every day even though he suffered atrociously from the gout and had to have his boots cut open. That's what princes call amusing themselves.

Paths wide enough for a carriage had been made in the forests of Versailles, without cutting down any of the trees, and the next morning I joined the hunters who advanced through the forest like the caravan of an Oriental potentate, hounds, huntsmen, whippers-in, pages, gentlemen, the captain of the hunt, and the king in a closed carriage because there was a cold wind. The coupled hounds sniffed branches, their heads low, their long floppy ears trailing the ground, their tails beating faster as they picked up a scent, and the whippers-in cracked long, bone-handled whips. Huntsmen had been reconnoitering the forest since dawn, and the caravan stopped at the crossroads known as the Croix de la Chère Reine to hear the head huntsman's report. The king stepped out of his curtained carriage and stood leaning on his cane as the captain of the hunt showed him a cap full of droppings and said he had seen a stag with two doe near the Javel mill. The king changed from his carriage to a horse, the hounds were uncoupled, and they were off, all tails and legs, followed by the horses. The next three hours were summed up by the coppery echoes of the horn, calling out its various messages: The stag's hoofprints have been seen, the hounds have caught the scent, the stag had been sighted, he's out of the woods, back in the forest, seeking water, facing up to the yelping pack.

This stag was very large, for in his race to flee the hounds his antlers were breaking branches six feet above the ground. I saw him twice, once leaping across a path in a blur of leaves and branches, legs stretched as taut as the string in a crossbow, antlers catching the sunlight that slanted through the foliage, and again, exhausted, surrounded by the pack, antlers lowered, breath coming in gasps, long graceful legs shaking, and eyes filled with the shadows of the forest. The courtiers had dismounted and assembled behind the hounds to attend the hunt's last scene. The hounds leaped at the stag, nipping his shanks. One hound rose several feet in the air, his jaws catching the stag in the side. The stag impaled the hound on the tip of an antler and sent it flying into the brambles. But there was not much fight left in him, and presently the huntsmen's whips flicked the hounds off, and the stag's legs buckled. The head huntsman approached holding his short knife and slit the jugular with a quick gesture. The stag's eyes clouded. Several courtiers leaned against carriages, bantering with the ladies inside. Huntsmen skinned the stag, emptied its entrails, and wrapped them in the skin. The horns sounded the quarry, and the hounds made for the warm entrails, their yelps rising to a higher pitch as they fought for the steaming skin.

In the meantime, a huntsman had detached and prepared one of the stag's feet, which he presented to the king on a green velvet cushion. The king took the foot, turned, opened the door of his carriage, and handed it to someone inside. I saw two alabaster arms take the cushion, and a woman's head lean forward, and in the instant before the carriage door closed, I recognized Elizabeth's Greek-coin profile. It seemed to me that her face was sad.

A Voyage

I Leave Court

VERSAILLES had become a prison more stifling than the Bastille. I could not remain in attendance to a king who, while I was absent on a mission in his service, had alienated the affection of the woman I loved. Unable to modify the situation, and incapable of accepting it, I resolved to throw myself into some far-flung activity, as I might have, were my temperament inclined toward the morose, thrown myself into the sea. I did not expect ever to return to court, and left word that my rooms should be allotted to some deserving young man who had yet to discover the traps and *trompe-l'oeil* that lurked in those marble halls. As for me, my last illusions had drowned in the pools of Elizabeth's violet eyes. For one brief and desperate moment, I thought of joining my wife near Bidache, of resuming my slight acquaintance with that lady, and of attempting the rustic existence of the provincial nobleman. But I realized that such a retreat into domesticity would lead to an early dotage. I was in need of foreign shores and open spaces. I felt that, like Bordeaux wine, I had only to cross the ocean to improve myself.

Two days later, I was in the noble Breton city of Nantes, admiring the substantial houses of cut stone giving on spacious squares, which would not have looked out of place in Paris. I was a guest of the owner of one of the finest of those houses, Monsieur Étienne Doucet, a prosperous merchant and director of the Royale Compagnie du Sénégal. My father, rest his soul, had invested in the company, and although I had never met Monsieur Doucet, when I made my presence known, he immediately sent a manservant to the harbor inn where I had left my bags, and would not have it any other way but that I would accept the hospitality of his own home.

Doucet was a mild scholarly man dressed in black broadcloth. His long pale face, the dominant feature of which was a nose that quivered with a life of its own when he grew excited, reminded

187

me of a sexton's, as did his tiny steps, as if he were walking across a main altar and making ready to genuflect. Shrewd blue eyes gave a weaselly rather than innocent cast to his face, however, and the way his mouth pursed indicated acquisitiveness. He was indefatigable in showing me his many fine paintings, his collection of Sèvres porcelain, and his furniture signed by the most famous cabinetmakers.

That same evening found us, along with Madame Doucet, a buxom, milk-skinned, fair-haired Flemish beauty some years younger than her husband, and to my mind the finest of his acquisitions, at the Nantes municipal theater, where an actor imported at considerable expense from the Comédie Française was due to perform in *Le Misanthrope*, not only to provide an evening's entertainment, but to help the good burghers of Nantes convince themselves that they had no lessons to learn from the capital where the pursuit of culture was concerned. The theater was full, but the spectators had none of the irreverent boisterousness of Paris theatergoers, for whom the spectacle is never on the stage. They sat in solemn silence, with hands folded in their laps, as if in church.

The curtain had not long been raised, however, when it became clear that the actor everyone had come to see had fortified himself with more than the mere knowledge of his lines. His speech was furry, his gestures wild, his eyes half-shut. The interventions from the prompter's box were frequently audible. Monsieur Doucet, who was a director of the theater (he seemed, in his thirst for self-importance, which he called civic-mindedness, to have made himself the sponsor of every activity that took place in Nantes), squirmed in his seat, and beads of perspiration formed on his pale narrow forehead. "Disgraceful, disgraceful," he kept repeating under his breath. Turning to me, he whispered: "If you only knew what we paid the man for one night's performance. For the same price, we could have hired an entire *corps de ballet*. And then to be forced to watch a drunkard rant."

In the second act, when the Misanthrope's great moment comes, his soliloquy on the mistrust of his fellow man ("to be a friend of humankind is not at all my style"), the actor raised his arm in a declamatory gesture, knocking over an end table that was part of the scenery, losing his balance, and following the table to the ground. This fallen Alceste, lying spread-eagled in stage center, as Oronte and Célimène looked on, with their hands over their mouths, was too much for the patient burghers of Nantes, who began to whistle and hiss and cry "Remove him." The noise seemed to revive the stricken Alceste, who managed to gather himself and rise to his full and imposing height. Taking in the entire audience in a slow sweep of his head, he quieted them, and said, in a voice that rang, for the first time that evening, with true emotion: "I have not come here to be insulted by a set of wretches, every brick in whose infernal town is cemented with an African's blood."

Monsieur Doucet leaped out of his seat as though activated by a hidden spring and shouted: "Liar!" The theater was a bedlam, with the proper townsfolk suddenly turning to roaring jungle beasts, climbing over one another in their eagerness to reach the stage and the blaspheming Thespian.

The curtain was dropped, and the actor spirited out a back entrance by his fellow troupers. I dare say he did not dally in Nantes, but took the first coach back to Paris. When the more irate members of the audience could not find him, they repaired to nearby taverns to quench their anger in carafes of Muscadet. Even as he sat drinking, Monsieur Doucet's frail body continued to be seized by spasms of rage, as if the actor's outburst had shaken the very foundations of his being. He shook his head, and, looking at me with trusting blue eyes, said: "We are the most misunderstood people on earth. The most scandalous accusations are leveled against us, when in fact we serve the cause of humanity and religion, for we relieve unfortunate blacks who are held in inhuman captivity by their own people, and we turn them over to Christian masters. What, may I ask, is the harm in that?"

I hastened to assure him that it sounded to me like a mightily good work, and omitted to mention something Revel had told me during a discourse on the slave trade, namely, that were the Atlantic to dry up tomorrow, one could trace the path from Africa to America along a trail of human bones.

Warming to his subject, Doucet went on: "They are barbarously treated by their black masters, who have kidnapped them or captured them in battle. The fate of those sold to Europeans is less deplorable than those who are doomed to end their days in their native land. For aboard ship, all possible care is taken to preserve them for their owners, who for the same motive use them well. Not to mention the inestimable advantage they may reap of becoming Christians and saving their souls."

I said it was a profession any good Christian could be proud of. In fact, I had no set views on the subject, having heard it called by some a Christian duty and by others the most monstrous of commerces, but I had no wish to vex my host, since my presence in Nantes was not totally independent of the subject under discussion. For there were only two professions, outside the military trade, that a courtier was allowed to undertake without derogation: Glassmaking and the slave trade. My lack of interest in the former outweighed my moral qualms about the latter. Doucet was intent on justifying the principal trade of the Royale Compagnie du Sénégal; indeed, he approached the subject with such passion that I found myself thinking: He doth protest too much.

He brought to bear so many arguments in defense of his case that it began to seem to me an overballasted vessel. He quoted the Old Testament, Genesis 9:25: Cursed be Canaan, a servant of servants shall he be unto his brethren. I allowed that my Biblical instruction had faded in the mists of time, so that the allusion was lost on me. Doucet explained, his lips moist from the pleasure of his discourse, that Canaan was the son of Ham, one of Noah's three sons, and that he had been cursed because Ham had caught his father naked, sleeping off a drinking bout. Now as it happened, when the sons of Noah divided the world among themselves, the part that Ham received is described as "all the countries from the mountains of Lebanon to the Western ocean," or, to call a spade a spade, Africa. In fact, the Ethiopians, descended from this very Canaan, have retained their Biblical name to this day. In plain language, it was a Christian duty to make sure that the curse on Canaan was carried out, and that his offspring, the natives of Africa, were sold into slavery. Not only that, Doucet said, the slave trade was also a patriotic duty, a way of fighting England and enriching our colonies. It was also, he said, the principal mainspring of our maritime commerce. And finally, the slave ships were models of hygiene and humane treatment that every ship in the king's fleet might envy. "We are proud of our reputation," he said, banging his fist on the tavern table in retroactive indignation over the incident at the theater. "Slavers are the cleanest and best-found merchantmen afloat."

In fact the only reason he did not give for the ebony trade was the one that jingled in my own mind, for as I knew from my father's participation in the company, this was the most lucrative commerce imaginable, three-cornered, selling cheap goods in Africa in exchange for slaves, selling the slaves in the West Indies for sugar, selling the sugar at home, and making a tidy profit on every transaction. An average expedition took a year, two or three months from Nantes to the Sénégal coast, five to buy the slaves, a month and a half to Santo Domingo, two months selling the slaves and readying the ship, and a month and a half back to Nantes. So that for the investment of a ship, a crew, and a year's time, and if no mishap occurs, a small fortune is made. The Compagnie du Sénégal had twenty ships plying the route. The incredible prosperity of the city of Nantes was due to its development as France's principal slave trade port.

To Doucet, it was all abstract, on the level of ideas. He had never seen a slave, since they were purchased in Africa and sold in the colonies. He knew from the register that on every trip some slaves died, but he was convinced that the cause of their deaths lay in their own carelessness and poor health, and not in the conditions of the voyage. These deaths affected him like an irrational, unpredictable element intruding in a perfectly well-laid plan, and they also cut into his profits. He sincerely believed that he was improving the lot of the slaves by removing them from their native land and their families. He and his partners built the ships, hired the crews, bought the supplies, and did not think themselves any different from merchants who sold goods rather than people, except that they lived in finer houses, were known to have bought the best farmland around Nantes, could be counted among the most assiduous churchgoers in the city, and held positions of importance in town councils and other public-spirited organizations. He must, however, have sensed the equivocal nature of his profession, since he was at such pains to defend it. Just causes need no advocates. His last words to me that night before retiring, uttered with the zeal of the crusader, were: "We must remove these pagan cannibals from their loathsome habits."

The beneficial sea air had me asleep as soon as my head hit the bolster, but I was awakened what seemed only minutes later by a soft knock on my door. I opened it a crack and saw the blond tresses of my host's wife, illuminated by a candle she was holding in the somber corridor. I had noticed earlier, thanks to a discreet pressure of her knee as I sat next to her in the theater, that she looked upon my arrival without distaste. She now complained that her husband's snoring prevented her from sleeping. The situation was delicate, for I intended to ask Doucet for a favor and could

not risk being caught in bed with his wife, even while his snores
signaled that we had nothing to fear.

On the other hand, I could no less risk offending his wife by
turning her away from my bedchamber, for she would then, out of
spite, conspire to turn her husband against me, perhaps accusing
me of the very sin I had refused to commit. As a man with court
experience, however, I did not propose to allow myself to be out-
maneuvered by a provincial Jezebel. I was extremely solicitous,
and made appropriate murmurs of commiseration concerning her
insomnia, opening the door to invite her in and taking her arm lest
she stumble. She leaned heavily on my shoulder, further persuad-
ing me that, far from seeking a night of slumber, she would not
have been displeased to engage with me in a bout of insomnia à
deux. This was precisely what my stratagem proposed to prevent,
or, in the most favorable of circumstances, to delay.

I led her to the edge of the bed, where she sat, breathing heavily.
I kissed one of her lily hands fervently, and said: "Ah, madam,
what goddess is this who has come to enhance my dreams?"

"No goddess," she replied, giving my hand a little squeeze, "But
a woman of flesh and blood who wishes you well."

"Compared to me, a goddess certainly," I said, "for I am a low
disgusting wretch unfit to touch the hem of your garment."

"You are too modest, sir," she said, "for I find your touch most
pleasing."

I dropped her hand as though it was an ember and said: "Ah,
madam, if you knew what propriety forbids my telling, you would
hide from my presence as from the plague. All the pleasures of
love are not worth the suffering its celebrants are sometimes, because of one moment of folly, made to endure."

"Sir," she said, sitting more stiffly on the edge of the bed and
gathering her nightgown about her, beginning to understand, "you
cannot mean . . ."

"I mean, madam," I continued, "that whatever physical pain I
am enduring is nothing compared to the anguish of Tantalus, who,
being so close to the edge of a lake of delights, finds himself unable
to drink. This, madam, is the worst punishment Venus can inflict
on a man, and I beg you to look upon me with compassion."

I took her hand again, but this time she withdrew it and wiped it
against the batiste of her nightgown. She rose and almost ran from
the room, as though unable to remain a moment longer in my
presence, mumbling irrelevant apologies: "Do excuse me for dis-

turbing you . . . I must have lost my way . . . and in my own home
. . . I am distracted." She was in such a hurry that she forgot to take
her candle.

The following morning at breakfast she was distant, but thank-
fully the vengeful gleam of the woman scorned was missing from
her eye, and I could tell from her husband's gregariousness that
she had not spoken of me unkindly. I explained to the good Monsieur Doucet that after spending some years at court planing the
rough bark of my natural disposition, I had felt an irresistible urge
to escape from the confinement of those silk-upholstered drawing
rooms and broaden my horizon. Like a drunkard forced to take
the cure, I was, I explained, in need of a totally opposite environment, and, remembering the warm words of praise my father had
always had for him, I had come to request engagement upon one
of his ships. Doucet snorted uncomfortably, annoyed that the
memory of a long-gone and largely fictitious friendship was
putting him at a disadvantage in any decision he would have to
make.

"Well, of course," he said, studying the cup of morning tea in
front of him as if in reading its leaves he would find the answer he
sought, "there are a number of factors involved in the matter
which you propose, not the least of which is your experience as a
seaman."

"That is quickly disposed of," I replied, "for until now I have
boarded ships only as a passenger."

"Aha," he said, as if that settled the matter.

"But where experience is lacking, willingness is not," I said. "A
seaman's lore I can learn, while there are other qualities which, in
all modesty, I believe myself to possess, that can never be acquired, a knowledge of human nature, an ability to rise to the level
of any crisis, a love of challenge and a natural adventurousness
suitable to this type of work. In addition, you and I share the same
social background [I said this to flatter him, for we were, in fact,
worlds apart]; you can trust me, having me aboard one of your
ships will be like having another pair of eyes. I may be able to find
ways to cut your costs, signs of waste, inefficiencies overlooked by
the captain. You know that from me you will get a completely
honest account of the trip, and that alone should be worth the cost
of signing me on."

Doucet turned a spoon in his nearly empty cup, as his thoughts
were turning in his ruminating mind, and said: "I can't pay you

much, you know, certainly not what you're worth. When you hear the wages, you may not want to sign on." He was not above turning a penny on the memory of a cherished friendship.

I said wages were secondary, I only wanted a rank commensurate with my army commission. He informed me that as it happened, one of his ships, the *Rôdeur*,* was due to leave Nantes in a few days, but was missing its first mate, who had come down with scurvy during the previous voyage and was not sufficiently recovered. The first mate's duties, Doucet explained, had little to do with the actual operation of the ship, but were concerned mainly with seeing to it that the slaves were kept clean and adequately fed, that the water supply was fairly rationed, that they got their turns on deck, and that those who rebelled against the humanitarian treatment of their captors were punished for their unenlightened behavior. "In other words," I said, in a rash moment of sincerity, "I am to be a slave overseer."

Doucet bristled. "Did nothing I said last night sink in?" he asked. "Have you not yet grasped the great favor we are doing them in providing them with passage to Western civilization? If you feel you are unsuited to this work, please say so at once, in order to avoid a change of heart when you are out at sea, and it will be too late."

"I was only joking," I said, "and stand ready to serve the cause of humanity."

"Well," Doucet said, opening a thick gold watch and holding its face under his nose, "that's settled, and just in time, too, for in an hour I'm to give his final instructions to Captain Shade, who despite his name—he comes from a Jacobite family—is as French as you or I. Not the subtlest of men, but he knows the coast of West Africa as few white men do, and he's never had a mutiny, of either crew or cargo."

We met the captain in one of the harbor taverns, at the end of a cobblestoned mall off the end of which I could see a forest of bobbing masts. The mall itself hummed with the thousand activities of a large port—men shouldered bales, mended sails, hoisted cargo in nets, and lined up to sign on in front of little booths. As I breathed the salt air and watched all these busy fellows going about their work, I felt almost giddy with pleasure at the thought that I would soon be a part of this great maritime life. Captain

* Prowler.

Shade was waiting for us, looking like an old corsair, with a patch over his left eye. I later learned that he had lost it in an early voyage, while trying to lower a sail in a storm, when the tip of a yard had struck him, and that he was known far and wide as Mind Your Eye Shade. His large moon face was flaccid, the skin hanging from it like folds in a curtain. He had a small bulbous nose, like the top of a champagne cork, and eyes that glinted a hard blue behind deep puffy pockets, giving his whole face a pugnacious, canine appearance. I was afraid he might protest my appointment as his first mate, but when Doucet made the introductions he clasped my hand in his great callused paw and said: "A gentleman, eh! Glad to have you aboard. If the climate don't get you the clap will, it's a short life but a merry one."

He ordered a carafe of white wine to toast my first voyage as Doucet buried his nose in a briefcase from which he extracted a pile of ledgers. Doucet's finger went down a column of figures until he found the one he wanted. "Now, Shade," he said, "on your last voyage, you had a cargo of six hundred and thirty-two slaves, and ninety-three of them died. That is too many."

"By my piles," said Shade, "you know as well as I do that was an epidemic of the white flux that carried 'em off that way. We were lucky to keep it from spreading any more than it did."

"That's all very well," Doucet said, slapping the ledger shut. "I have nonetheless been asked to instruct you that the normal margin of casualties the company will allow is ten percent. Anything over that the captain will be held to account for."

"Listen to that," Shade said, addressing me as a sympathetic witness. "You'd think I was God, with power over life and death. When one of these niggers takes it into his black head to die, there's nothing you nor I can do to stop him."

"Ten percent seems to us a very generous margin," Doucet said with finality. "Now, these other matters you are familiar with, I am repeating them mainly for Gramont's benefit. As the success of your trip depends on the Lord's blessing, the company recommends that you and your crew attend morning and evening prayers."

"And while we're praying," I heard Shade mutter under his breath, "who'll be minding ship and cargo?"

"Also," Doucet went on, "do your utmost to keep your crew from swearing. Take particular care that none of the ship's company"—and here, Doucet lifted his eyes from the ledger to look at Shade, as if this remark was addressed to him particularly—

"drinks palm wine or any other liquor, which is invariably the cause of disorders, and that none of the crew lies in the open air at night, a practice that has caused a great mortality and overthrown many voyages. Remember that on the health of the crew depends the briefness of the voyage, and on the briefness of the voyage depends the successful shipment of the slaves. Be diligent to prevent the debauchery of the Negresses with the Negroes. Cleanliness is essential. Wash your decks with vinegar twice a week and fumigate below decks with pitch and tar every other day. Bathe the slaves twice a week, and let them dance and beat their drums. Have your cooper inspect the water casks each week to prevent leaks. Always keep in mind that you are carrying a valuable merchandise and that your first responsibility is to prevent damage and deterioration. Well, gentlemen, I think that covers it. I must run. I have a meeting with the archbishop at ten to discuss the blueprints for our new foundling home. Gramont, perhaps you would like to stay with Captain Shade and get better acquainted."

I nodded in assent, and when Doucet had left and Captain Shade had ordered another carafe, I asked the latter how he had got mixed up in slaving.

"Supply and demand, my lad," he said, "these days there's very little else a Nantes sea captain can do. Slave labor's needed on the sugar islands to cut the cane and produce the muscovado* that's sent to the sugar boilers in Marseille. I'm just a link in the chain."

"How do you feel about it?" I asked, for I was looking for clues as to how I should feel about it myself, now that I was in it. Captain Shade raised his glass, winked his valid eye, and quoted what he said were "the words of a great poet":

> I own I am shocked at the purchase of slaves
> And fear those who buy them and sell them are knaves.
> What I hear of their hardship, their tortures and groans,
> Is almost enough to draw pity from stones.
> I pity them greatly, but I must remain mum,
> For how could I do without sugar or rum?

"Don't you feel sorry for the blacks?" I asked, wondering whether one should.

"Life was ever cheap in burning Africa," Shade said. "Reproduction is rapid and continuous, and the only law they know is eat and be eaten. They are so scorched by the heat of the sun that has

* Raw sugar.

blackened their skin and thickened their lips that they curse it when it rises. Human sacrifices are common. On my first trip the king fell sick and sacrificed a ten-month-old babe for his recovery. I saw the infant hanging from the bough of a tree, with a live rooster tied to it. The blighters don't even keep accounts of their dead, only of their livestock. In their view a cow is more valuable than a man. In our eyes, they are the livestock, and more precious than cows. That's all there is to it, my lad. Bit of a scandal, I suppose you'll think. To my way of looking, the worse that can be said of it is, that like all earthly endeavors, it's tempered with a mixture of good and bad. As for my own concern, and yours, the benefits far outweigh the pretended mischief."

"So that you would say," I persisted, "that trading slaves is like trading any sort of goods, wheat, or cotton, or salt and pepper?"

"Aye," said Shade, "I would indeed, were it not for the fact that you can't tell by looking at a merchantman what she's carrying, but you can always tell a slaver."

"How?" I asked.

"In harbor by the smell," Shade said. "You can wash a slaver down with vinegar and brine, and wash it down again, it will still stink of black bodies. At sea because we're followed by sharks, waiting for the dead ones we jettison and the ones who jump overboard."

"Jump overboard?" I cried. "Do you mean that they would rather drown than remain in captivity?"

"Don't seem possible, do it, lad?" Captain Shade said with a shake of his grizzled head. "And yet that's the long and the short of it. The savages believe that when they die they return to their own country."

"I suppose they do it because they know nothing of what lies in store for them," I said.

"They're loath to leave their shores," Shade said with a dreamy faraway look in his one good eye. "I tell you, lad, by signing on with me you'll be seeing some strange and wonderful sights. You'll see mermaids, that feed upon grass on the banks of rivers there, whose lower part is sealed like a fish and ends with a forked tail, but whose upper part is like a woman, with an oval head, and short arms and hands, and two strutting breasts. And you'll see sand so hot it burns the soles of your shoes when you walk on it, and herds of a hundred elephants crashing through the forest and making the noise of an army, and men who file their teeth as sharp as awls and load their bodies with iron rings like galley slaves, and ants' nests that rise above the ground like sugar loaves three feet high, and a tree they call the Crissia that gives milk, and bright-blue parrots that fly over the country in such numbers they seem to darken the air; oh, yes, my lad, you'll have some items to enter in your journal, in case you're keeping one."

I asked Shade when we were setting sail, and he said the very next day, for the winds were favorable. Did he have any advice for me before departing? I wondered. "Only this, lad," he said, "if you want to keep your health, stay away from wine and brandy in the morning, as most seafaring men guzzle from daybreak, which is highly offensive to an empty stomach, enfeebling its faculties by degree, and rendering it incapable of digestion."

I said it would be no hardship to avoid drinking in the morning. "There are two things you must learn to do without aboard ship," Shade said, "liquor in the morning and ladies in the evening. If you can keep the cork on the bottle and your cock in your breeches, you'll be all right. And when we arrive on the coast of Africa, you'll find plenty of palm wine; they have only to make an incision in the top of the tree in the evening, hang a calabash under it, and in the morning it's full. And the women are just as easy, fresh and lusty, with tawny complexions and uncommon large breasts. But beware, for their natural hot and lewd tempers waste a man's body."

I confessed that the thought of abstaining from the gentle sex for the long duration of the trip was a hard one, insofar as it was a habit I had regularly indulged since the age of thirteen, with interruptions of a week at most. It did not seem normal, I said, for vigorous men not in the least monkish to practice chastity.

"That's a mighty big word, my lad," Shade said. "Between you and me and the prow figure, most of the men, if they can't find wheat, try barley. Did you ever hear of a Cholon duck?" I confessed that the term meant nothing to me. "It's a duck they raise in South China, they keep it from infancy in a tub of oil. Its legs become so soft it can't walk. Sailors buy them plucked and vow their ass is as sweet as a woman's cleft. Arms they weren't born with, and legs they can't use, so these duck are bred to be, so to speak, all ass. Not everyone can afford a Cholon duck, mind you, they fetch a pretty penny, and them that can't go at themselves, or at each other, although you may be sure that buggery is not tolerated on my ship." With that, Captain Shade bade me farewell until the morrow, saying that he had to see to getting his ashes hauled before weighing anchor. That seemed to me an excellent idea, prior to two or three months of temperance at sea, not being provided with a Cholon duck, and I began to regret having scared off the lovely Madame Doucet.

I returned to the house and found her in a corner of the drawing room, looking mournfully out the window, her petit point abandoned in her lap. I took a look around to make sure her husband was absent, boldly entered, and knelt by the side of her chair, saying: "Madam, I lay myself at your feet."

"There is no need for that, sir," she replied.

"There is, madam," I said, "for kneeling is the proper position to adopt while making a confession."

"And you have something to confess?" she said, a slight smile lighting her face.

"Yes, madam," I said, "even though you think me a perfect fool and worse, I must confess that I lied to you last night."

The smile left her face, as if a cloud had blotted out the sun. "I would rather not discuss it," she said, "although I fail to see what reason you can possibly have had for lying."

"Your beauty, madam, was the cause, for I feared myself unable to resist the powerful attraction that drew me toward you, which would have led me to abuse the sacred laws of hospitality, and caused me to invent a stratagem designed to make me appear unworthy of you."

"And why are you now telling me this?" she asked, the cloud vanishing and the smile returning.

"Because, madam, I have just learned that my ship sails tomorrow, and the thought of leaving, perhaps forever, without having held you in my arms, has broken down all my reserves."

"It's a bit late for such admissions, don't you think?" she said, which I interpreted to mean: "You've had your chance."

"You see the lateness, madam," I replied, "while I see only that time has not yet run out. I want a memory to cherish during the lonely months under tropical skies."

She gave me a tender look, then checked herself, taking up her petit point and working at it furiously. "You are a confirmed liar, sir. How can I be sure you are not lying now and were not telling the truth yesterday?"

"Madam, I swear to you on everything that's holy that my only indisposition last night was in my mind, and that the lingering image of your loveliness has banished all traces of it. You hold my happiness in your grasp. Visit me tonight, and I will leave France with an inexhaustible provision of contentment. Refuse me, and I will sail defeated and forlorn."

"Ah, well," she said, "I can't have you going off discouraged. You would lower the morale of the entire crew." I took her hand and covered it with grateful kisses. "You are imprudent, sir," she said, withdrawing her hand, "be patient."

"Until tonight," I said, rising to leave. My left leg had fallen asleep in the kneeling position. It buckled under me as I rose, and I almost fell, grabbing a curtain to keep me steady.

Madame Doucet laughed and asked: "Are those what they call sea legs, sir?" But as I left the drawing room she threw me a kiss.

The hours that followed seemed endless. Doucet returned and insisted on showing me maps of the West Coast of Africa and pointing out the route I would take, while all I could see as I followed his finger down the indented coastline was the curve of his wife's shoulder. Dinner was interminable. The courses succeeded themselves like a glutton's dream of abundance, but I hardly touched my plate, and could not keep my mind on Doucet's discourse on the various kinds of chintz, taffeta, calico, madras, and painted India cotton that had been loaded onto the *Rôdeur* as goods with which to purchase slaves. I could think only of the white muslin dress his wife wore, and how, in a few hours, I would hear it rustle from her shoulders. Indeed, I was so locked in my thoughts that Doucet asked me whether I felt all right. I said I was affected by the excitement of the trip. "A young man like you must see all he can and do all he can," Doucet said. "Never forget that experience is the wealth of youth."

I heartily concurred, for I expected to enrich myself that very night at his expense, although strictly speaking, sleeping with another man's wife is no theft; one only borrows for a short time what her husband is not using, returning it in as good condition as before, sometimes better, for she may have learned something she can teach him. Better yet, in many cases, when husbands have stopped availing themselves of their conjugal rights, wives are of no more use to them than any curio gathering dust on a drawing-room table, so that in borrowing them one is borrowing a superfluous object, the absence of which is no more noticed than would be the temporary displacement of a pewter snuffbox.

I took advantage of Doucet's inquiry about my health to excuse myself early, saying that I had some last-minute packing to do and wanted to get a good night's sleep before starting out halfway across the world. He promised to take me to the boat the next morning and bade me good night.

I quickly climbed into bed. The full moon suffused my room with a soft blue glow that seemed to me the exact degree of light two lovers would require, bright enough to give their bodies the smooth milky texture of Greek marble, dark enough so that they could move in and out of pools of shadows, like anonymous swimmers diving and surfacing in the waters of each other. I lay there content, knowing that her husband's snores would soon herald the arrival of Madame Doucet, and thinking of the strange turns life takes. I had started with nothing, and still had nothing, save more memories than if I had already lived a thousand years. I had not accumulated wealth or gained fame, but I felt that my life had a quality of compression, which at the same time filled me to overflowing and propelled me in directions I did not always choose, but always met with eagerness. The sifter of my mind let pass only those moments that had contributed to my sense of haphazard but continuous advance, leaving blocked above the tiny selective openings the sediment of regret and ragged ends. It was not that I did not remember my failures and difficulties, my wrong decisions and poor judgment, but that in every instance I was able to retrieve from the very pit of despondency a gleam of light that allowed me to go on. In this sense, I thought, failure is as interesting as success, just as the greatest possible pleasure is reached from a threshold of pain. Indeed, I wanted above all not to arrive but to travel great distances, on the surface of the earth, in the private weightless sphere of the mind, and in the half-known, half-guessed, uncharted regions of the heart. Presently I heard snores echoing through walls, and that signal alone was enough to make my pulse quicken. I rose to open my door and peered down the corridor into a well of darkness. Give her time, I thought. An hour later, my door was still open, and in exhausting the list of reasons that could have prevented Madame Doucet from joining me, I had fallen asleep.

I Meet an Old Friend and Reach the African Shore

It was only when we were out to sea, and I filled my lungs with cold sea air, and watched the gulls circling slowly above the mainmast, that I felt the giddy liberating effect of departure, a

departure from the barren shores of my interrupted plans, toward
the promise that lay just beyond the flat, gray-green hemicycle of
the sea's horizon line. I have always felt a great surge of pleasure
at leaving, perhaps because every departure is an escape, from the
walls that we ourselves have built with others in our chosen forms
of confinement. No matter that we move from one confinement to
another, the moment of passage remains privileged. This departure
by sea, the passage from land to water, heightened the pleasure I felt.

The port of Nantes, which drew only twelve to fifteen feet of
water, made it impossible for heavily laden ships to sail out. Captain Shade used barges to carry our load of cheap cloths, kegs of
spirits, bars of iron, munitions and guns, and assorted gewgaws
much prized by the Africans, to the advanced harbor of Paim-
boeuf, on the Loire estuary. It was there, where the tide meets the
current, that the cargo was put aboard the *Rôdeur*, and when that
was done, we had only to weigh anchor, hoist the sails, and wait
for a favorable wind. Soon the sails were swollen, we sped past the
tip of the Carpenters' bar, Captain Shade set our course south-
ward, and the *Rôdeur*'s prow cut through the open sea. Every
thread of canvas she could carry had been spread, and she jumped
through the water like a racehorse.

Our timing, as he advised me, was excellent. We were leaving at
the end of September, and would arrive on the African coast in the
dry season, with time to carry on our trade and reach the Leeward
Islands by the following April, when the cane has been cut, allowing us to sail back to Europe before the hurricane season. The first
leg of our trip would take us to the Canary Islands. We would then
tack across the Atlantic in the direction of Brazil, so that the trade
winds could bring us back to the coast of Sénégal.

Captain Shade was proud of his crew, nearly all of whom had
sailed with him before; "You've got to be human," he said. "I
don't care if a man's dead drunk in his bunk as long as he's sober
to man his watch." He pointed out some of the men necessary to
the smooth operation of the ship, the armorer, the baker, the cook,
the caulker, the pilot, the carpenter, and the boatswain. There was
also a ship's surgeon, he said, whose real importance was not in
treating the crew but in detecting ill health among prospective
slaves. "He's in his cabin, sick as a dog," Shade said, adjusting his
eye patch, which had a tendency to slip away toward his ear. "This
is his first trip, he's like a whimpering babe."

It seemed to me that a sailor's lot was far from enviable. The

crew worked two twelve-hour shifts, and when they were not
working they were cramped in dark, foul-smelling, low-ceilinged
quarters, for every available inch of space had to be given over to
the slaves. In rough weather they had to clamber in the masts like
monkeys, and when the sea was calm they were put to work mend-
ing ropes and sails. Shirking was punished by public whippings.
Their food was a pound of biscuits and a pint of wine a day, salt
beef four times a week, salt cod three times a week, and rice or a
vegetable daily, while we at the captain's table partook of delicacies such as eggs, chickens, and fresh fruit. The sailors were themselves slaves, slaves to the sea, whose bidding was their hourly
concern. Crippled by scurvy, their backs scarred by the cat, there
was never a moment when the sea's comportment was not upper-
most in their minds. The sea might reward them by carrying them
to their destination, or it might punish them with a shipwreck. And
when one of them died, he was returned to the sea. On the third
day out, the wrinkled old wreck who waited on us at meals, and
whom Shade kept on out of good-heartedness despite his almost
total uselessness, complained of stomach trouble and died two
hours later. His body was sewn inside a hammock weighted by six
cannonballs and thrown overboard, and his pitiful belongings were
auctioned at the foot of the mast. There was too much to do
aboard ship to waste time over mourning. Death became a chore
one had to expedite, like washing down the decks or adjusting the
rigging.

The hold where the slaves were kept ran half the length of the
ship, with a ceiling six feet high. A sort of half deck had been built
along the side, extending perhaps ten feet out, like a broad rim or
a loggia, so that the slaves could sleep in two layers, one above the
other, as close together as they could be crowded. "See what I
mean about the smell," Shade remarked as he showed me this
gloomy pen for human livestock.

I put my handkerchief to my nose, for the slave deck reeked
with the sweat of captive thousands. They had sweated out their
anguish as they huddled there in the dark, like a species condemned forever to living in the abyss.

"The Portuguese cover the decks with straw mats for bedding,"
Shade said, "but Doucet screams about costs and says the niggers'
hides are tough as elephants and have worn the planking smooth."

I commented that Doucet, never having made the voyage, could
view the buying and selling of slaves exclusively in terms of the

figures in his ledger. The slaves for him did not take on human contours, but remained a merchandise.

"I consider the unfortunate buggers men like ourselves," Shade said, "though of a different color, and I try to humor them in every reasonable thing, but I must also consider the interests of the owners. It's a mistake to be too kind, for there are always stout stubborn niggers who are never to be made easy. Only last year, kindness killed one of my oldest mates, the well-known slaver captain Mad Monk Martel, so called because he had spent ten years in a Franciscan monastery before hearing the call of the sea. He must have thought he was Saint Francis himself, for he personally went below decks to mix the pepper and palm oil in the niggers' rice. I told him how damned imprudent it was to mingle with the savages, for when they rise up they always aim at the chief person on the ship, whom they can tell by the respect shown him by the rest of the crew. He replies to me: 'The Master's eye makes the horse fat.' Well, on his very next trip they beat out his brains with the tubs they eat off of. The chief mate in reprisal ordered the quarterdeck guns loaded with partridge shot and fired them into the lot, killing more than eighty. You can guess the reaction of the owners, bawling about the dead niggers with never a thought for Captain Martel."

I followed Shade back on deck, glad to be breathing clean air again, and he pointed to a heaving figure bent over the railing, whose groans became distinct as we approached him, and who seemed to be in such agony that he looked balanced between ship and sea, as though undecided whether to remain on board. "There's our surgeon," Shade said, "sicker than any of us, God curse his idle bones." The figure straightened up and turned to face us, and it was all I could do to stifle a cry of amazement, for it was Roger la Trompette, whose usually florid face was waxy white and whose great suety mass looked as if it had been whittled down by a soap carver. There was no sign of recognition from him when the captain introduced us, but I caught a flutter in his eyes indicating that he would bring me up to date once we were alone.

A seaman soon arrived to tell Shade that the pilot requested his presence, and no sooner was he gone than Roger, seeming to have regained his composure and some of the color in his cheeks, threw his arms around me and said: "One of us must be following the other. After the Bastille we now meet on this seagoing prison. As you can see, the ship's surgeon is in need of medication."

I congratulated Roger on his new identity and asked how he had come by it. He led me to his quarters, extracted a bottle of brandy from his locked medicine cabinet, filled two glasses, watched the amber liquid swill from side to side with the roll of the ship, and said: "After my release from the Bastille, I decided to exercise the means a clever man has of correcting fortune, and I took my Dutch dice to Blondeau's to get up a stake, but was caught by a reformed gambler he's hired who knows the ropes, and had to leave Paris. I have relatives in Nantes, and went up to take the air and see what was happening, for I knew there were great ill-gotten fortunes there, and does the Good Book not say: 'As the partridge sits on eggs and hatches them not, so he that gets riches and not by right shall leave them in the midst of his days.' I felt I could be of some assistance."

"I didn't get the impression that those partridges could be pried loose from their eggs," I said.

"As tight and well guarded as a virgin's flower," he agreed. "I had to think of something else. Fortunately my cousins are well connected, and were able to obtain for me a public appointment extremely well paid, with short hours and no paper work."

"What fortunate sinecure was that?" I asked.

Roger waved a hand, as if his tasks had been too momentous to describe. "I was connected with law enforcement," he said. "It was outdoor work."

"Were you a constable," I asked, "keeping a vigilant eye on the accumulated wealth of the Nantes bourgeoisie, or an informer, reporting the misdeeds of your fellow citizens?"

"No, no," Roger said, fidgeting on the edge of his bunk, "neither of those."

"Well, then, what?" I asked, perversely insistent when it was clear he wanted nothing better than to change the subject.

"If you must know," Roger said, opening his hands and staring at his palms, "I was public executioner. The salary is eighteen thousand pounds a year, not even the mayor is paid more to work less. Contrary to popular belief, the executioner is a much admired man. He officiates in a hood, but his identity soon becomes known, and when he walks into a café, invitations to buy him drinks echo from all sides. Executions are particularly well attended in Nantes, and I imagined my role as that of a great tragic actor. Also, the fringe benefits are not to be neglected: Collectors buy locks of hair and clothing, and the corpses are sold to the surgeon's college.

Once given tenure, I would have been in a favorable position to marry the daughter of a town notable. In short, for the first time in my life, I was respectable. I saw nothing wrong with the work, for I told myself that public executions are useful to the state in making justice seem more horrible than the crime. Did an assassin ever lay a man on a Saint Andrew's cross to break his bones with twelve blows? Did he ever bend his victim on the wheel, with a confessor at his side to listen to his delirium and exhort him to expiate his sins?"

"The theory behind that being, I suppose," I said, remembering the Paris crowds playing cards on the Place de Gréve while waiting for four horses to arrive and quarter the shackled criminal on public view, "that the more cruel the punishment, the less often it need be meted out."

"Exactly," Roger concurred. "As you can see, it was a position of some importance, with lifetime security. There was only one thing wrong with it . . ." I gave him a questioning look. "I couldn't stomach it. My first customer was a man who had murdered his wife. For that type of misdeed, it was my duty to chop off his head with an ax. The murderer was brought before me on the platform, he was a small meek gentle-looking fellow whom you couldn't imagine hurting a fly, and he was so helpful when I told him where to place his head, he answered, 'Yes, sir,' not like some of the others who struggle or want to make speeches, he just seemed to want to comply with whatever was asked of him. As I was sharpening the ax, I thought: If a man as mild and good-natured as that killed his wife he must have had good reasons. Who can know what sort of harridan she was, or what hell she made the poor fellow's life? When his head was on the block, placed sideways, he looked up at me with friendly eyes and a nice smile, as if to say, 'I know you've got a job to do, don't worry, everything will be all right,' and the sight of that gentle, trusting face so shook up my insides that I had a dizzy spell and was forced to sit down. The crowd began whistling and booing, and the police lieutenant, who always attends executions, afraid that things would get out of hand, had me replaced by one of his men, who with one clean stroke expedited the poor fellow into the next world. It was then I realized that I was temperamentally unsuited for the job, and resigned before they could discharge me."

"Poor Roger," I said, "your killer instinct failed you."

"My cousins were so humiliated they refused to have anything more to do with me," Roger went on. "I had to leave Nantes, but I couldn't go back to Paris. There was only one direction left, out to sea. I had a surgeon's certificate drawn up by a friend and signed on with the only sort of ship I knew would not check my credentials too thoroughly, a slaver. And now you see me, as ill suited to this sort of life as a cow in a tree."

The days passed quickly with Roger on board. I had little to do until the slaves were purchased, and his time was usually his own after sick call in the morning. The cure-all he prescribed was a ration of rum in the evening, bringing the unwell to his door in unprecedented numbers. The rest of the time we reminisced, or played chess. Two weeks out of Nantes we reached Madeira, and were going to put in for fresh water, but saw a Salé corsair in the harbor flying a black flag and decided to wait rather than risk a fight.

Some days later we were off the Canaries, and I was awakened from uneasy dawn slumber by the cry of "All hands on deck." Still yawning and stretching, I came upon a scene of frenzied activity, Captain Shade barking out orders in his gravelly voice, and sailors running under sprits and sails and rolling out cannon from concealed emplacements. Advancing toward us on our starboard side was a sleek frigate flying the Union Jack. I had been told that the British Navy's favorite sport was to intercept French slavers with their men-of-war, forcing them to fight or surrender, and towing them back to Jamaica, where the cargo was sold and the captain received prize money. For that reason, slavers were now heavily armed themselves, and when I saw that Captain Shade had no intention of surrendering, I asked for permission to command the starboard guns, for that was one thing I could acquit myself of honorably. "Go to it, lad," he said, and I had the men load with small shot and hold their fire until we could distinguish the frigate's name embossed on both sides of the bow, which was the *Pembroke*, and could perceive the resolute faces of our adversaries.

The next hours were chaos, for a sea battle has none of the order or prepared strategy of a land operation. There are no troops to deploy, no flanking actions or cavalry charges, only two floating gun emplacements bobbing uncertainly on the waves. We could do no more than fire as rapidly as possible and hope for the best, as Captain Shade tried to maneuver in such a way as to offer the narrowest target, while still keeping our guns within range. It reminded me of a combat between two fighting cocks, all spurs

and beaks and flying feathers, going at each other until one falls
exhausted.

The shot poured down like great black lumps of hail, my lungs
filled with sulfurous smoke, and I heard the crack of wood and
falling masts, but paid no heed, as I was too busy with my guns. I
told my men to fire low, thinking there was more damage to be
done below the waterline than above it. Seamen shouted and fell,
and I caught a glimpse of Roger behind a lifeboat, cleaning and
bandaging wounds, but through it all I had no idea whether we
were winning or losing. The *Rôdeur* might have been on the point
of sinking for all I knew, for I was obsessed with keeping our guns
firing, and when one man fell I had another brought up so that his
gun would not be silent. Finally, the clouds of smoke were so thick
we could no longer see our enemy, except for the flash of his guns,
and I felt I was taking part in an endless game of blindman's buff.
Suddenly the *Pembroke*'s guns stopped flashing through the
smoke. I still had no notion of the outcome of the battle, for when
I looked around me, I saw the smoking wreckage of a ship, and
broken men moaning in gutters and over scuttles. It was only when
I read Captain Shade's log that I discovered what had occurred,
and since I am woefully ignorant of nautical terms, I include it
here in the hope that it will bring as much enlightenment to the
reader as it did to me.

"*Le Rôdeur*, October the third, 1756. Leeward of the Canaries
at six bells, we saw a ship standing off to us with all sails set, so we
tacked to put ourselves in a posture to defend and with all expedition got our hatch ports off, our chests and hammocks up, our
cargo secured, our close quarters up and our guns ready, at which
time we furled our mainsail, clapped on our stoppers, our pud-
dings and plattings under our parrels, and lay by. It was a fine long
snug frigate. We let fly our colors and he hoisted the Union Jack.
We jogged easily under our fighting sails, and when he was within
carbine shot, he ran out his lower tier of guns, nine on each side,
which I was displeased to see, ordering that our eight wooden
cannon be positioned and manned to make it appear that we had
an eighteen-piece battery. I perceived he was resolved to pluck a
crow with us, and ordered the men to their guns, putting my first
mate, Count de Gramont, in charge of our real battery. Our foe gave
us his broadside and volley of small shot and we returned his civility
very heartily with ours. He shot ahead of us, brought to, fell along
our larboard side, and gave us his other broadside. Each of us fired

and loaded as fast as the shot could be rammed in the breeches. His shot passed with great fracas between our masts, and another volley took a six-inch chip out of our mizzenmast. He fired high into our masts and rigging, while we fired low into his hull. We must have killed a great many of his men.

"Finally, his fore-topmast came by the board and he fell astern of us and took his leave. We gave him a send-off with what guns we still had loaded. With God's assistance we had fought him off, despite the greater number of his guns. The *Rôdeur* was shattered and torn in her mast and rigging, having had eleven shot in our mainmast and our mizzenmast shot to pieces, our spritsail, topmast jack and jack staff shot away. We were as full of splinters as a carpenter's yard is full of chips. We had thirty shots in our hull, four below the watermark. It was a miracle we were still afloat. Our sails were shot through like strainers and we had five killed and thirty wounded. We would have had more killed had not our ship's surgeon risked life and limb to treat the wounded on deck. The fight lasted more than six hours. We gave them *vive le roi's* and they replied with huzzahs. The carpenter had an arm torn off and the cooper's skull was fractured by small shot, which was a most serious loss. We spent all night fixing our rigging, and gave the men as much punch as they could drink to keep their spirits up. We knotted our shrouds, secured our shattered mast, and kept our chain pump and our hand pumps going, for she was making a great deal of water through the four shots received underwater. We lived on bread and cheese and punch, for our furnaces were shot through.

"We had to put in at Tenerife for fresh water and provisions, and while there we fixed the mast with splices and iron hoops. Aside from the loss in men, for twelve of the wounded could not continue the voyage and had to be left off in Tenerife, we lost two weeks of good time, but were fortunate in view of the English frigate's superior strength that we were not forced to surrender to be towed to Kingston with all our goods and made to join Admiral Townson's fleet."

So we had won the battle, although no one would have known it from looking at us, and we put in at Tenerife to lick our wounds and bring ashore the worst of our wounded. Captain Shade was in high spirits, seeing our victory as a good omen. I only hoped our patched-up ship would not break apart at the seams before the voyage was through. We had less than half the distance to go now

before reaching the slave counter, a place called Momo Grande
between the Sénégal and Gambia rivers, whose king, a fellow
named Bangy Mambouc, was a friend of Shade's. The captain
preferred this station, where he had traded a number of times, to
the Gold Coast, which was twice as far, in the hollow of the great
hump Western Africa makes, and where one was likely to find
British, Dutch, or Portuguese slavers crowding one another in the
harbors and competing for the same slaves, which raised their
price.

We sailed along the coastline, pushed by favorable northern
winds, and one morning the men caught a porpoise with a cramp
iron, which they called a sea hog, and ate it. A multitude of birds
hovered over the ship, white under the belly, with long, sharp,
pointed wings and dark-brown backs, as big as pigeons. They did
not seem frightened and came so close that we could touch them.
The pilot sighted a palm tree floating in the sea, which created a
great stir, as it was felt we were approaching our destination, but
all I could observe along the coast were high cliffs, some gray and
others whitish, and a barren, dry, scorched country, red sandy
ground overgrown with shrubs, with neither man nor beast in all
that great tract of land.

Several days later, however, the water grew darker, and the
waves were full of roots and branches. Captain Shade announced
we were off Senegambia and would soon reach the harbor of
Momo Grande, which was distinguished by five high palms standing separately and forming a sort of grove. He ordered me to stand
by to have the gunners give notice of our approach. Great foaming
waves shook the sides of the ship. "It's dangerous surf," Shade
said. "The niggers have a saying, he who ventures into it ought to
have two lives. You'll soon see them coming out in canoes. If they
overturn, they either drown or are devoured by sharks."

"Then two lives are not enough," I remarked.

Borrowing the captain's spyglass, I saw the grove of five trees
overlooking a fine natural harbor, sandy and white, like a pearl
crescent. Beyond the harbor, cutting through the waves, a dozen
long narrow pirogues made from hollowed-out tree trunks were
moving toward us. I thought they were pilots come to guide us into
the harbor and was observing their advance when upon looking
with greater care I dropped the spyglass in horror. In every
pirogue, the sternpost was being used as a chopping block. One of
the natives held an ax as an unfortunate countryman bent his

docile head to the block. When he had finished, the nigger who had wielded the ax raised both arms to the heavens and chanted a prayer I could not hear. "Good God," I exclaimed, "they are murdering their own people, out there, just beyond the harbor."

"Don't let it bother you, lad," Shade said. "They're appeasing the god of the bay to permit our ship to enter safely. Bangy Mambouc doesn't want anything to happen to us. He gives the hungry gods as many heads as they can eat."

The spectacle of such naked barbarism turned my stomach, and I was grateful for the excitement of landing, as sails were furled and the anchor was dropped. Once inside the harbor the waters were calm, and more pirogues came toward us, laden this time with lemons, pineapples, coconuts and bananas, rather than human sacrifices. The natives came clambering up rope ladders, all smiles and quick chatter, to make their offerings, and wanting a bit of tobacco, which Shade was glad to give them. The headman, or *caboceiro* as he is called, carried a white staff, wore a cap of tiger skin, and necklaces of feathers, cowrie shells, sea horse's teeth, and monkey skulls that jangled when he walked. He presented Captain Shade with his staff, which, as it turned out, was made of ivory. Savages they might be, but I saw resemblances to our own customs, particularly that of distinguishing a person of rank by the way he is dressed, for with the exception of the *caboceiro*, they wore nothing more than loincloths. Some of their customs made no less sense than our own. They do not look upon it as good breeding to kiss or shake hands, but when they came aboard ship they dipped their hands in seawater and let some drops fall on their eyes, which signified that they would rather go blind than defraud us in their dealings.

I Meet King Bangy and Am Loaned a Wife

The natives who came on board were coal black, and I surmised that it must have taken several thousand years under the African sun to broil them to that charry hue. They seemed fit and sturdy, of average height, although Shade told me that they came in all sizes, depending on the region, from three to seven feet. Their faces were disfigured by rotten teeth, the canines being filed like those of a hound, and by long cuts in their cheeks and foreheads, which they purposely leave open, so that they raise thick welts. This is considered a sign of great elegance. Again, it seemed to me that elegance is whatever one wishes it to be, and that the ladies of Versailles who wear headdresses half as tall as they are themselves are in no position to call these natives ridiculous. The only difference being that the natives did not shrink, in the name of fashion, at permanent disfigurement. The women whom I saw later, when we had landed, are as vain as our own, and suffer for it, for they not only cut open their cheeks but imprint figures on their bodies as well with such art that at a distance they look like finely worked ebony carvings, for the figures rise above the skin like a bas-relief.

Some of the men aboard the *Rôdeur* were chewing betel nut, the bitter savor of which Shade told me was habit-forming, and they rolled it around their mouths with great gusto and let the red juice dribble down their chins. A few of them had nails growing half an inch from their little fingers, and hair plaited and twisted and dabbed with palm oil, which I took also to be signs of distinction. These men were members of a tribe called the Hausas, and the word that recurred most often in their unintelligible language of grunts was "hausa, hausa," which seemed to be a general sign of approval or pleasure. They spoke by fits and starts, without dividing their speech into words and sentences the way we do. It all came out in a torrent. During our stay in Momo Grande, I was able to pick up a few phrases, thanks to some of the niggers in Bangy Mambouc's entourage, who spoke a smattering of French. The little I learned I list here, for the instruction of any reader contemplating African travel:

How do you do	= Mamoune-ekiou-haine
Very early	= Cre-cre
I see you	= My-mon
Tomorrow	= Ezain
Thank you	= Aova-non
Hold your tongue	= Namoune-bazy
I would sleep with a girl	= Dun-hoinene-ova-domel-codemy
Give me some more drink	= Namy-a-haan
Put him in irons	= Mypoty-guenda-fogh

It goes without saying that the spelling can only approximate the strange sounds they make, for they have no alphabet, and some parts of their language seem imitated from the cries of forest creatures.

The *caboceiro*, having been regaled with a pouch of tobacco and a mug of our best brandy, made a sort of speech, which Captain Shade professed to understand, for he nodded and smiled and beamed approval. The speech, Shade told me, assured us that the niggers had much greater value and friendship for the French than for any other European nation, and that king Bangy Mambouc felt a special sympathy for our own king. Then the *caboceiro* got down to the nub of things, saying that they were ready for a brisk trade in slaves, having just fought and triumphed over a neighboring tribe, the Samory, and taken prisoners aplenty.

It must be said that these Africans are no different from ourselves, in that they are always warring, with the principal motives ambition and plunder. And as Doucet had been quick to tell me, they once offered their prisoners up as human sacrifices, whereas now, thanks to our beneficial influence, they sold them, alive and in prime condition. Another similarity with our own society is that individual disputes may be decided by duel, and each party chooses a second or two, who meet in an appropriate and secluded place, where they fight with javelins until one of the principals is killed or begs for mercy. Being so close in custom, I began to wonder: Are we all civilized, or all savages?

One thing they have over us is that they are very little concerned with misfortune, so that it is hard to perceive any change in them either in prosperity or adversity. This among Europeans is called magnanimity, but when we see it in the niggers we call it stupidity. When they have obtained a victory over their enemy, they return home dancing and singing, and if they have been routed, they still dance and make merry. They are insensible to grief and want, sing till they die, and dance in their graves. That behavior applies to their natural surroundings, for the most cheerful disposition turns to gall in the hold of a slave ship. I also noticed in many of them the instincts of courtiers, for they are arrogant with inferiors and obsequious with superiors. Indeed, they are bad paymasters, for if one raises himself to a considerable office, he never goes about the village without a slave to carry his wooden stool, to sit and rest wherever he stops, and he speaks to his fellows in a lofty disdainful way.

Unlike us, they do not believe in one Creator, but worship a great many gods, including the swordfish and the bonito, and birds, and four-footed beasts, and creeping things. They believe that man was made by a great spider, who created black as well as white. The deity offered them a choice between gold and arts and letters and the black man, who had first choice, took gold, leaving knowledge to the white man. The deity granted their choice, and, offended at their avarice, ruled that the whites would forever be their masters. This faith seems a curious attempt to bring their beliefs in line with events.

The *caboceiro* required another mug of brandy before taking us ashore in the pirogues tied to the side of our ship, and as he poured it out, Shade murmured in an aside: "If you are niggardly of your drams, Sambo is gone, he will never care to treat with dry lips." We finally got started, taking with us a party of ten, including Roger and the carpenter, who despite the arm lost in battle could still direct the construction of the *Quibanga** or negotiating counter, where purchased slaves were to be kept until they were taken aboard ship.

"We can only stay a day or two," Shade kept telling the *caboceiro* as he rubbed his salt-and-pepper chin with the back of his hand. And then to me: "Giving way to their humors is no article for success, for they would keep us all year if they could."

The pirogues came in on the surf, and the niggers promptly jumped out and pulled them up on the shore with easy practiced gestures, so that we would not get our feet wet in alighting. A manner of orchestra began to play when we landed, some with flutes, some with drums, and others with strings of bells, like sleigh bells, which they jingled to produce an undulating rhythm. The music had no regular beat that I could distinguish, but the musicians rocked as they played and shuffled their feet in a kind of dance. Shade nudged me and said: "You will see the real dancing later, that is fine lascivious sport."

Roger la Trompette's eyes were popping out of their orbits. "Imagine," he said, "imagine if I could bring some of these fellows back to Paris, what a success they would have in the Palais-Royal. I could end my days on it."

"The truth of the matter," Shade said as we walked nodding and smiling past the musicians and into a village of windowless mud huts with thatch roofs, "is that the blighters are happy here and miserable anywhere else, whatever we think of the way they live. It's perfect cant to say we're improving their lot and making Christians of them, for they are content to eat manioc and worship blue parrots."

We came to a square in the center of the village, where a palm-

---

* Also called barracoon, a fortified slave house that was built by the ship's crew.

wood hangar had been erected, with open sides and a raised floor.
It looked like the covered markets in the main squares of our own
French villages. On the platform sat the king, splendidly sprawled
on a throne made of precious wood and elephant tusks, under a
red velvet umbrella with immense brass-mounted handles, which
covered him like a canopy. Behind the king, on piles of cushions,
reclined a dozen cocoa beauties, naked to the waist, and behind
the women stood attendants wearing odds and ends of military
uniforms, one a three-cornered hat, another a shako, a third a pair
of high black boots, a fourth a gold-pommeled sword hanging
from a wide belt around his waist, a fifth a pair of white twill
cavalry breeches. Between them they might have been able to fit
out a full uniform. They stood behind king Bangy Mambouc as
solemn as chamberlains, holding various necessities he might request, palm-wine jugs, pipes, and silver and gold dishes. Like our
own Versailles courtiers, their demeanor seemed intended to show
that they were the objects of unusual distinction in being allowed
to serve their monarch. Two of them held large feather flappers,
which they waved over his majesty's head to keep flies off, for there
were flies in swarms, and I removed my own hat, partly in anticipation of saluting the king, and partly to defend myself against the
buzzing, stinging insects.

Looking down at the far end of the hangar, I perceived on a
wide ledge the origin of all these flies, for the heads of the natives I
had seen decapitated in the pirogues had been lined up there like
Toby mugs, and the flies were breeding inside their dead skulls.
Standing guard over these festering heads were two fetishists, or
juju men as they are called here, dressed all in feathers so that they
resembled, with their painted faces and feet, malevolent ostriches.
They glowered at us through the paint and made clucking sounds.
I understood from Shade that these juju men exercise as much
power as a minister in favor at court, and that the success of our
trade was dependent upon their goodwill, which could be obtained
with a liberal awarding of presents, or, as they are called here,
dashes. "If you don't dash the jujus, lad," Shade told me, "they put
a pox on you." The jujus are the high priests of everyday life, who
predicate upon the arrival of rain, favorable days to go to battle,
and the price of slaves. The natives, believing them to have magic
powers, pay them strict obedience.

When the king dies, the jujus dig a large pit and ask for volunteers to join him in his resting place. His favorite courtiers of both

sexes beg for the favor of attending their master in the other life. This honor is granted only to the best beloved and most qualified, which causes great dissension among the rest. The fortunate natives granted this great favor are let down into the pit, the mouth of which is shut with a large stone. Contrary to our own beliefs, the stone is not removed by angels on the third day. In spite of this elaborate burial ceremony, it is looked upon as a great crime to speak of death in the king's presence. None of his subjects dare say he is a mortal man.

King Bangy Mambouc was a great gorilla of a fellow, so large that he seemed to overflow his throne, for to these niggers size is a measure of importance. The king needs be the most voluminous and best fed of his tribe. And yet he never ate in public, so that his subjects would think he was of divine origin, accumulating layers of fat on the air he breathed. Nor is anyone meant to know the place where he lodges, and if anyone asks, he is answered: "Where does God lodge?" which signifies, "Is it possible for us to know the king's bedchamber?" Their deities are in their own image, black, with sausage lips and twisty black hemp hair. We are no less foolish in seeing God as a benign patriarch, snowy of skin and beard. In my eyes the king was a gross dingy lump of suet, but his people venerated him. His face was shrewd and porcine, the eyes tiny coals buried in shadowy pockets of flesh, and a bit of ivory split his upper lip like some extravagant additional tooth. He was got up in gaudy regalia, with a fine plumed green velvet hat, an old-fashioned scarlet coat, braided with gold and silver, which strained unsuccessfully to enclose his girth, and under it, a fine embroidered jerkin, not unlike the jerkin of the Saint-Esprit privileged courtiers wear at Versailles. From this jerkin dangled rows of military decorations, further emblems of his prestige that added a flash of color to the white of the cowrie shells hanging in multiple strands from a neck so thick it appeared goitered. These cowries are small milk-white shells as big as olives, gathered among the shoals and rocks of the East Indies and much prized by the niggers, who use them as coin of the realm. With all his finery, his wives sitting around him cross-legged, and his attendants fanning him, Bangy Mambouc was barefoot.

Shade and I and Roger la Trompette strode up to the platform, the rest of our party having remained on shore to see to the *Qui-banga*, and Shade removed his captain's hat with a great flourish and bent almost double, which was no easy feat, for he was both portly and rheumatic, saying: "Great king, we are your humble servants. We brought you plenty brandy, plenty cowrie shells, plenty tobacco."

"What you do here, no-good rogue?" king Bangy said in the ungrammatical but pungent French he had picked up in years of dealing with slavers. "Why your king don't come so we talk same-same?"

"He sent me to tell you that you are as great a king as he," Shade said.

"Your king big fella?" Bangy asked.

"Not quite so big as your majesty," Shade replied with unfailing tact.

"You talk true mouth, old friend," Bangy said with a cackle. "White men sick weak boys need strong black backs. How many wife your king got?"

"He has only got one queen, your majesty," Shade said.

"Haw-haw-haw." Bangy laughed, his rolls of fat quivering with delight. "Bangy he got twelve wife an' hump sweet ass all night. Bangy big mans let Cap'n Shade hump one too he good boy."

"The message I have from my king is that he is honored to trade with you and hopes you will be pleased with what we brought," Shade said, trying to steer the ship of commerce back on course.

"You king country bigger mine?" Bangy wanted to know.

"Alas, sire, I must confess that the least French province is twice as big as your country," Shade said, with a hint of chauvinism. This reply turned the king's joviality to a deep sulk at finding himself so little in the world. He sat on his throne silently glaring at us, as his attendants shuffled uneasily.

Captain Shade, seeing that he had committed a *faux pas*, handed Bangy a box full of brass rings called Bochies, which the native prize as currency. "Juju man he no lie, say Shade bring Bochies," Bangy shouted joyfully, extricating himself with difficulty from his throne, like a foot from a tight shoe, and playing on his hands and knees with the overturned box of Bochies, choosing the ones he wanted, as carefully as a child choosing marbles. Cowries and Bochies they are most fond of, while also partial to copper bars, iron bars, Guinea clouts, horse bells, hawk's bells, rangos, pewter tankards, beads and bracelets, and almost anything else so long as it is worthless and glitters.

Shade next had fetched an anchor of brandy and some hands of tobacco, which were offered to the black king, who rose, helped by two attendants who hoisted him under the shoulders, and announced that we would now retire to the palace. The palace turned out to be a group of connected clay huts surrounded by a bamboo enclosure, with two rusted iron guns flanking the gate, and guards armed with cutlasses. We followed him, with four or five of his wives, into a room where a meal had been prepared. Ever the courteous host, Bangy told us that had we given him firmer notice of our arrival he would have provided better entertainment. Special attendants for the king's dining chamber, deafmutes who could not betray the secret that he nourished himself like other mortals, filled polished oxhorns from an earthenware jug of palm wine, and passed them around.

Bangy raised his glass and proposed a toast: "To Captain Shade, he and me sabby each other long time, he don't act like white devils cheat poor Bangy, now we do sangaree." Before Shade realized what was happening, Bangy made a sign and two of the deaf-mute attendants held him pinioned as Bangy pulled a sharp knife from under his jerkin, slashed his forearm with it, then proceeded to roll up Shade's right sleeve and slash his.

"I've bought it, lads," Shade cried, certain that his head was about to join those lined up outside, but Bangy only wanted to be blood brothers with his old friend, and rubbed his cut arm vigorously against Shade's until their blood mingled.

We downed our palm wine, which tasted like sour milk spiked with a bit of rum, and the servants set before us trays laden with roast fish, yams, plantains, and cooked bananas. Bangy said he had ordered a young alligator killed in our honor, for us to eat as a delicate bit. It was brought in on a bed of palm fronds and tasted like veal, but more luscious, with a strong scent of musk. The greenish-brown scales the creature is covered with had been removed, and the natives make caps of them. These alligators have a great strength in their tails, with which they can overset a small canoe. Shade and Bangy kept exchanging toasts, and every time Bangy downed his oxhorn his wives clapped in token of respect and veneration.

After partaking of some local fruit, which seemed a cousin to the apricot, we returned to the hangar in the square, where cushions had been arranged so that we might sit close to the king. Musicians were playing, their instruments being a calabash that they shake and a strip of hollowed-out bamboo that they strike with a baguette.

At the sound of the music, the niggers began to emit strange shouts, unable to contain themselves, and after a few minutes of this one of the king's wives rose and was joined by a frisky young loinclothed buck. At first they were cold and impassive, each not even seeming to notice the other's presence, scarcely moving their bodies, and performing insignificant contortions. I admired the haughty expression on the woman's face, which was somewhat at variance with the shameless bobbing of her naked breasts. Soon, warmed by the music and the noisy encouragement of the onlookers, their movements became swifter and more conjugated. The woman held one hand at her neck and the other behind her waist, arching her back and undulating her buttocks, and then throwing out her belly in perfect time to the music, as the man, at a distance that kept narrowing, echoed her movements with his own. The tempo of the music increased, sweat made the dancers' bodies gleam like black marble, and soon they were rubbing breast to breast, and knocking bellies in a manner I had never before seen outside the bedchamber, as they uttered hoarse mysterious words in each other's ear. Rather than a dance, it seemed to me a public representation of the most private of acts, and just as the sight of someone drinking is enough to make me thirsty, the sight of the dancers aroused in me a sensation all too specific. After many strenuous minutes of this mating dance, the dancers, panting and exhausted, broke through the circle of spectators and ran into the bushes. The effect of their improvised ballet made me want to join them.

As if divining my secret desire, Bangy Mambouc motioned to one of his wives, who joined me on my cushion and began to nuzzle my neck with her rubbery nose. I noticed that two of his other wives had likewise joined Captain Shade and Roger, and decided that this was a routine aspect of his hospitality.

The girl led me by the hand into one of the rooms of the king's palace, which had a curtain of beads drawn across the entrance and, as sole furnishing, a straw mat and a few cushions. All the while she laughed and giggled, as if the sight of a European was the funniest thing she had ever seen, and I tried to forget the scars that covered her face and body, for without them she would have been quite pretty, with improbably high, long-nippled breasts like those on the prow figure of a ship, and high flouncy buttocks.

She motioned for me to lie down on the mat, and as soon as I was on my back, applied herself directly to my middle parts, undoing the buttons across my breeches and flicking away my cod-piece. She did not seem to expect anything from me, and I was so accustomed to proffering a thousand caresses before being granted a woman's favors that this was a welcome change. She did not want me to undress, being quite satisfied that the single object of her interest was exposed, and she hunched over me like a heifer at a salt lick. There was no question of my kissing or caressing her, so intent was she on our one point of contact, soon replacing her upper with her lower mouth, squatting down with her feet on either side of me and moving her pelvis with languorous rotating motions, and then, as she bit her pink tongue in concentration, with short, quick thrusts. I did my best to follow her rhythm, like the male dancer I had just watched, rising and falling with her through milky night skies and shadowy buoyant seas, until she reached a pitch of abandon I had never seen in a woman, rolling her head as though in a trance, with only the whites of her eyes showing, and shouting words I could not understand. A warm throb rippled through me that I was past restraining. I had reached the shore and left her behind. A moment later, she was again all diligence to hoist my half-masted flag, which she was able to do all the more easily for my enforced abstinence at sea, and this time I accompanied her to the end of the journey, until she fell panting beside me, and pulled on the hair at the back of my neck, which was quite painful, but which I took in good stride, as a mark of affection.

Afterward, I tried to converse with her but could get no further than to convey the impression that I was pleased, which I gathered was mutual, for she treated me like some rare new possession, touching my clothes and my hair in wonder, and frequently taking hold of that preferred part through my breeches, to confirm that it was still there. Her name, I discovered, was Tama, and her age, according to the count of her fingers, fifteen. Shade had told me that African girls from the age of twelve spare no pains to lure European gentlemen, thinking it an honor to be in their company, and that their nature is very fiery. He had also said that venereal disease is common among them, every man being extremely addicted to a multitude of women of all sorts, found or unfound, and that they commonly cure it with sarsaparilla boiled in brandy, but I wanted none of that, and sought the captain out to ask his advice. I found him in the room where we had earlier eaten, exchanging impressions with Roger.

"Well, lad," Shade called when he saw me, "I'll wager you got more than you bargained for."

"That's what I'm afraid of," I replied. "I don't want to export any African spirochetes."

"Don't worry," Shade said, "Bangy's wives are clean, or he would have caught it himself. As an added precaution, rinse your cock in your urine, it's the best disinfectant I know."

"I vow that black skin is softer than white," Roger said dreamily. "I would like to wrap myself daily in black satin."

"The women are hotter than the men," Shade said. "If they chance to get a young brisk fellow alone, they will tear the clout of stuff that covers his family jewels and throw themselves upon him, swearing that if he will not satisfy their desires they will accuse him to their husbands as having attempted their chastity."

"One need not come this far to see that sort of blackmail," I said. "Black or white, women everywhere use the same tricks to get what they want."

"These girls of Bangy's are by far the best," Shade said, "for they are reserved for him from the age of ten, while other girls of that age are circumcised by means of large yellow pismires fastened to a stick and applied to the part until it is bit to shreds and blood gushes out of it."

We were summoned from our discourse by the blast of elephant-tusk trumpets accompanied by the banging of many drums. "Bangy's signaling the opening of trade," Shade said. "Now that we've been wined and dined and fucked, he hopes he's softened us up for the palaver."

I Assist in the Purchase of Slaves

Bangy was back on his throne, belching noisily and picking his betel-blackened teeth with the point of a knife. Next to him stood the tiger-skin-capped *caboceiro* who had greeted us aboard the *Rôdeur*. His eyes were slightly slanted, giving his face a crafty look, so that he resembled a large and wily black cat, who would trail along behind whoever fed him. King Bangy felt that it was beneath his dignity to carry out the actual trading, which was to be directed by the *caboceiro*, who now went through a ritual of fidelity, rubbing his hand in the ground and carrying it to his forehead, after which he took one of Bangy's mud-crusted feet, spit on the sole, and licked it with his tongue. Again the elephant-tusk trumpets sounded. Bangy motioned us to a pile of cushions across from his throne and said: "Me win great battle, great god Jan-goema help Bangy take four, five hundred captives."

"You know what I want," Shade said, "muscled, white-toothed bucks, no old men with lined faces and hanging balls, lean-shanked and haggard-eyed. It's no use shaving them or waxing them with palm oil, I can tell the wheat from the tares."

"You and me sabby each other long time," Bangy said, "and you know me tell you true mouth. All captains come downriver tell me you king, you big mans, we trade and spose dat true wot we do? You sabby me have too much wife and too much child, some may turn big rogue, all same time we see some bad white man from some you ship. So I no trade, wait for old friend Shade, he give me forty iron bars, prime goods."

"Whoa there, old friend," Shade said, pulling nervously at his eye patch, "when I first traded with you it was eight or nine per man, last year it was twenty and now you're asking twice that. There's plenty of fish in the sea, and what's more, the market is glutted and prices are going down."

"God make you white, you baby dipped in milk, you sabby book and make big ship," Bangy replied. "God make me black and me no sabby book and me no have head for make big ship, spose some of we child go bad and we no can sell 'em, we forced to kill 'em. That no good for trade, for all we juju men tell me so, for dem say you country no can pass up niggers."

"Things ain't what they used to be," Captain Shade said with a mournful shake of his head. "The dashes increase each year, the prices go up, and the *caboceiros* rub the slaves down so you can't tell their age. You good friend, Bangy. I lose my shirt but give you thirty iron bars and extra anchor brandy."

Bangy went into a conference with his juju men, whom Shade had previously dashed with cowrie shells. They announced that the gods of sea and forest looked favorably upon the trade.

Having agreed on the price, Bangy repaired to his palace with two of his wives for an afternoon siesta, while Shade, Roger and myself accompanied the *caboceiro* to the shore to begin the long and painstaking business of actual purchase. The carpenter's men were putting the finishing touches to the *Quibanga*, a covered cor-ral where the slaves would be kept under twenty-four-hour guard until we were ready to set sail. A table sheltered from the sun by a blanket on poles had been made ready for Captain Shade, and close by stood a tent where Roger, in his capacity as surgeon, would inspect the slaves. It was so hot I could feel the sand burn through the soles of my feet and suffered from a constant thirst. The heat was made even more insupportable by a stench in the air, exhaled from a prodigious quantity of rotten small fish like pilchards, which were buried in the sand at the high-water mark. Shade told me the blacks love this putrefied fish, for the sand gives it a nitrous flavor they much admire. There is no disputing of tastes.

Shade sat at his table with knitted brow, a large ledger open before him at a blank page, and a quill pen already dipped in ink and ready to use. I stood beside him holding a slate and a piece of chalk to write the price down and show it to the *cabociero*, for the basic price varied with the age and physical condition of the slave, and when it was agreed, Shade would copy it in the ledger with a brief description of the purchased goods. No sooner were we installed than Bangy's men started leading slaves out of the forest to the *Quibanga*.

Each slave had his neck caught in a long wooden fork joined at the ends by an iron bolt that rested on his nape, while the fork pressed against his throat, so that at the slightest wrong move, he strangled. They call this device the Mayombé wood, and it is a sort of portable pillory, and proof of the natives' ingenuity in solving the problem of bringing the slaves out of the forest without losing them. One by one, they were released from the forks and brought before Shade, who grunted and called: "Surgeon." Roger then went over the slave from head to foot as he stood there, rubbing his sore neck. He measured his height, counted his fingers and toes, opened his mouth to inspect his teeth, and pinched his privates to make sure there was no suspect discharge. The slaves made no objection to this treatment, but submitted to it like the passive livestock they had become. Roger covered one eye and poked a finger at the other to make sure the slave could see. He made them jump and stretch their arms and bend over, and looked for signs of blood in the rectum. From time to time, they threw terrified glances at the sea, for they came from inland villages, and to them, the surf is the roaring of a great beast. Female slaves Roger took inside the tent so as to avoid a humiliating public (or rather pubic) inspection.

"You have got the best part," I told him.

"Do not think so, dear friend," he replied, "for there is nothing more repugnant to a delicate man than to oblige a woman, who may be of charming appearance, to take the posture proper to such an examination, and visit, with the *sang-froid* of medical speculation, parts intended to make the senses blaze."

Roger was like me. We were too accustomed to a more refined way of life to carry out our tasks with any enthusiasm. We had embarked upon the voyage with our eyes open, but our minds had been unwilling or unable to imagine what lay before us, and now I could not help thinking that I had become part of a brutal and inhuman enterprise, an open sore on the face of civilization, as I watched these men and women, who aside from the color of their skin were very like myself, being herded into a corral from which they would probably never escape.

The sickly ones were turned back, to a fate we could not or did not wish to imagine, for we had heard that king Bangy was fond of eating human flesh. Roger had to refuse quite a few because of worms, which are a terrible affliction in these parts. A man will sometimes have nine or ten worms at once, which rob him of his strength, some long, some short, some deeper in the flesh than others, some as thick as a raven's quill. You can see the swellings on their bodies where the worm has made its home. The only cure is to take the worm, very gingerly, as soon as the head has burrowed its way through the skin, and make it fast to a small piece of pasteboard, winding it up twice a day and softening the opening with poultices. Though the method is tedious, sometimes taking a month, it gets the worm out entire, for if it breaks, the part that remains in the body grows again. Roger became adept at telling those who had worms, even though they did not show, by feeling the lumps under the skin.

There was interminable haggling over every slave, for Shade seized on the slightest imperfection, a missing tooth or a wrinkled face, to bring the price down, while the *caboceiro* extravagantly praised each man's strength and willingness. An agreement being reached after arguments on both sides were exhausted, the price was set down in the ledger, and the goods Bangy was to receive in exchange was removed from crates. The *caboceiro* examined what we gave him as attentively as Roger had inspected the slaves, to see that the cloth was well sewn and the right length, that the knives were not rusty, and that the pewter was not cracked. He measured each iron bar with his feet and tasted the brandy for adulteration. The deal having been consigned, Roger branded the slave on the right shoulder with a silver seal bearing two crossed elephant tusks, the mark of Doucet's company, heating the seal over a coal fire and smearing grease on the slave's shoulder before applying it. The slaves screamed when the punched silver touched their shoulders, and were led into the corral. They now became our property. It was up to us to feed them and keep them secure, and Shade appointed various members of the crew to guard the *Quibanga*.

This trading went on for days and weeks, for the time we were forced to spend debating the merits and demerits of each slave made it impossible to process more than fifteen or twenty a day, and we went through our paces like puppets, Shade making the same objections a hundred times a day, wiping the beads of perspiration from his forehead and pulling on a jug of cool palm wine that he kept close by, Roger inspecting teeth and hindquarters until he said he was sure he had enough experience to apply for the position of veterinarian in the king's stables, and me marking down the changing prices on my slate like a broker in the rue Quincampoix. It was also my duty to keep order in the *Quibanga*, where fights broke out over the distribution of food and the presence of women. I had to build a dividing wall behind which the women could be kept separate, for the idle blacks filled their days with lascivious amusements. I did not object to what they did with each other, having done it often enough myself, but it was a bad example for the members of the crew who were guarding them, and were excited by the spectacle.

Toward the second week of these tedious transactions under a blistering sun, the *caboceiro* arrived one morning with a three-man guard pulling a slave whose wrists and ankles were in chains. "Tiptop boy," the *caboceiro* said, "Son of Samory chief." From what we could make out, it seemed that this slave, who was a good head taller than the others we had thus far purchased, and who, despite the grossness of his features, had a nobility of bearing undiminished by his present situation, was indeed the son of an important tribal chief, the sworn enemy of king Bangy, who had defeated him in battle and captured his son. This fine specimen, so lean and peremptory that he reminded me of an ebony letter opener, looked a natural leader of men, for the veil of defeat had not descended over his eyes, and was being offered at twice the normal price. The *caboceiro*, jumping up and down, his necklaces tossing noisily, made it clear that king Bangy would tolerate no dickering where this strong fellow, whose name was Lumamba, was concerned. He pointed out that he bore the mark of grandeur, one straight welt across the forehead. If he did not want him, Bangy would be very glad, for he would kill him and roast him on a spit and inherit his strength and noble qualities by eating his flesh. In other words, he was doing us a favor. I saw such defiance in Lumamba's face that it seemed to me that buying him would only add to our troubles.

But the gleam of profit shone in Shade's eye. "Aye, he makes these others seem scurvied goods," he said. "I know a party in Santo Domingo who'll not stint to have him for a *grometta*."* Taking a musket from a chest at his side, he handed it by the barrel to the *caboceiro* and said: "Give Bangy this gun for your Lumamba. Tell him big magic against enemies."

The *caboceiro* ran off to take the precious musket to Bangy. Roger heated the stamp to brand the chief's son, who neither cringed nor cried out when the red-hot metal bit his shoulder.

"All right," Shade said, "put him with the others. We've wasted enough time."

"Wait." The deep voice that rang out was Lumamba's. Staring directly at Shade, he said: "I am telling the red-faced men with long hair that the great spirit protects Lumamba. If you return me to my father, he will give you a mountain of gold. If you take me with you, you will be cursed by the gods of the sea."

Shade leaned over and whispered: "What do you think?"

"If we turn him over to his father behind Bangy's back," I said, "no matter how much gold he gives us, we'll be jeopardizing the whole expedition. As for the protection of the great spirit, look where it has got him."

"Quite right, my lad," Shade agreed, and addressing himself to Lumamba: "We'll soon see who puts a curse on who."

Despite Lumamba's arrogance, I could not help feeling a certain sympathy for the fellow, for he was, all proportions kept, one of my own kind, nobly born, the son of a chief, bred as a soldier and a leader. Within our distinct cultures, we came from the same class background, we had similar privileges and obligations. "I don't think he'll need those chains in the *Quibanga*," I told Shade. "They'll leave ugly marks when you want to sell him."

"You're right," Shade said. "Take the shackles off, lads, but mind you keep a close eye on him."

The shackles were removed, and Lumamba rubbed his aching wrists. Two of our men led him down the shore toward the *Qui-*

* Manservant.

banga, but as one of them busied himself pulling the long wooden bolts that locked its entrance, Lumamba made a dash toward the sea, apparently hoping to swim to a deserted stretch of beach and thence to safety. Bloody fool, I muttered to myself, the bay is full of sharks, he's determined to get himself eaten. A pirogue launched in his pursuit dipped in and out of the waves. From the knoll where I stood, I could see Lumamba fighting the breakers, disappearing in their deep hollows and surfacing on their foamy crests. The current was against him, so that for all the strength of his strokes, he seemed to be advancing hardly at all, and as the pirogue drew nearer, there came from another direction a triangular fin moving silently through the waves like a small gray sail. Lumamba saw it, and his direction changed. He now swam toward the pirogue, where waiting arms drew him in as two of the niggers slapped the sea with their paddles. He had abused my kindness, and I had no choice now but to treat him severely and order him committed to the dungeon I had fitted up in the *Quibanga,* as an example to would-be fugitives.

I kept him in the dungeon for two days and then had him join the other slaves in their bunks. That afternoon I went on my regular inspection tour of the *Quibanga* and found two of my men tying Lumamba to a post planted in the yard. "The captain has ordered him flogged in public for talking back to the guards," one of the men explained.

"Don't you understand that you are only making things more difficult for yourself?" I asked Lumumba, after ordering the men to untie him.

His expression revealed no sense of relief or gratitude at having escaped a flogging. "My father is a chief," he said. "They must treat me with respect."

I dismissed the guards and walked alongside him in the courtyard, as an equal. "I'm sorry for what's happened to you," I said, "but you must make the best of it. We are sailing tomorrow for the West Indies. You have the qualities and bearing to make something of yourself there. You can gain the confidence of your owner and eventually win back your freedom. Believe me, I know the price of freedom, but I also know the weight of circumstance."

Lumamba stopped and stared at me with intense coppery eyes. "You mean well," he told me, "but you don't understand. I can be no man's servant. I know only one thing and that is I must return to my people and take my rightful place among them."

Resolution of this sort borders on the fanatical, I thought, real-izing there was no way to make the fellow accept his new condi-tion with better grace, for he had never before experienced the vagaries of fortune, and saw only that, having for the first time fallen, he must right himself. "The fortunes of war have decided otherwise," I said. "You must learn the art of the possible."

"A sign will come to tell me what I must do," he replied.

Of course, I thought, when reason fails superstition must be invoked. The skies would open, and a godlike hand would reach down and pluck him from slavery. A belief in magic made any-thing possible. In their civilization, it was a way of subduing na-ture, as science is in ours. Lumamba knew he had been sold into slavery, but he could not believe it, for the powers he did believe in could not allow such a thing to happen. He was biding his time until they manifested themselves.

The following day was our last at Momo Grande. We had a full cargo of slaves and had unloaded nearly all our merchandise. The final afternoon, the slave trade being terminated, Shade had re-served for the trading of gold, for the niggers who find the precious stuff in mountains and rivers hold it to be of little value, and are only too content to trade it off against bright India cottons and clanging pewter. This gold trade brings out their worst instincts, however, and it appeared, as I helped Captain Shade weigh it, that an honest man was among them as rare as the Phoenix. They love to mix gold with copper and brass, or color ground coral and sell it as gold dust. Shade sat at his table with the scales before him, and I at another table. The niggers brought their gold first to me, and if it was a nugget I hammered it flat to make sure there was no lead core, and if it was a bigger lump I cut it through with a chisel to see if there was any cheat.

When the first cheat was found, Shade flew into a rage, and cocked an unloaded pistol at the man and pointed it at his breast, until he fell to his knees begging for mercy. This was intended to deter those others who might want to trick us, but seemed to have little effect. The next who brought us fool's gold Shade had drubbed with a knotted rope, laughing as he watched the sport and saying: "They are like spaniels, the more you beat them, the more they love you." I found that the best way to tell a cheat was to observe his behavior, for he was impatient and uneasy, and bid a higher price for goods than usual, and took the goods in a hurry without examination, which was a certain sign that his gold was tinged with brass. Whereas a black who knows his gold is good appears calm, stands hard about the price of goods, and examines every piece. All that hot afternoon I hammered and cut gold and inspected gold dust, heating it over a coal fire to detect copper filings until my eyes were flecked with it and I could smell it in my nostrils, like a savory dish cooking in someone else's kitchen, which I would never taste.

It was only when the gold buying was over and we were taking our ease in Bangy's palace over mugs of palm wine that Shade told me *sotto voce* that his scales were rigged. I remarked that if such was the case we had one less good reason to exclaim against the deceitfulness of the blacks. Shade shrugged and said: "You've got to take a broad, general view of things."

I Partake of a Farewell Feast I Find Difficult to Digest

For our last night, king Bangy had prepared a farewell feast. We had been his guests for nearly three months and could now take advantage of the good weather, when the winds abated and the sea was still, to set off for the West Indies with our black ivory. Great bonfires were lit, around which the natives danced, their skins oiled and gleaming in the firelight.

Between the two main fires lay the huge gray carcass of an elephant, which a hunting party had slain the previous day and brought back for the set piece of the celebration. They have a great hatred for this bulky creature, which does them much mischief, crashing through their villages and overturning houses and killing those inhabitants not nimble enough to get out of his way. They go out sixty in a company, each armed with six arrows and a javelin, and when they find his haunt they lie in wait for him, which they know by the loud rustling noise he makes, beating down whole trees if they stand in his way. They follow him, firing continually, until they have struck so many arrows in his thick hide that he looks like an outsize pin cushion. Dozens of niggers now crawled over the beast, like Lilliputians over Gulliver, carving hunks of meat from its generous flank, which they roasted on spits. The testicles, as large as melons, were brought freshly grilled to Bangy, who watched the celebration from his throne, but ate nothing, according to his conceit that he was not like mortal men. He cut them into slices with a gold-handled knife and had them passed on the tip of the blade to Roger, Shade and myself. The laws of hospitality required that we must taste this delicacy. It was surprisingly tender, reminding me somewhat of calves' brains.

"White man need that for little flabby dick," Bangy roared, for he was by this time in excellent spirits, as he kept a flask of brandy hidden under his jerkin and pulled on it when he thought no one was looking, ducking his head and shielding his slobbering chin with his free hand.

It so happened that his wife Tama, whom he had loaned me for the duration of our stay and whom I had made regular use of, was sitting beside me and could have borne witness at that very moment to the inaccuracy of Bangy's remark. She had grown attached to me, and called me her wallawalla, which is among them a term of great endearment. She had taught me a few words of her tongue, laughing at my efforts to pronounce them, and making me repeat them until she was satisfied, like a schoolmistress. We were thus able to converse, and I explained, or tried to, that I came from a great land over the sea, to which I must return. These women may be pagan, and walk around the village with nothing but a bit of cloth over their privates, but their emotions are like those of all the women I ever knew, and my talk of departure brought tears to her eyes. She wanted to come with me, and one night she brought me a bag of gold dust which she said I could offer Bangy as her purchase price. Where a woman of her condition had found such wealth I could not guess. Nor could I tell her that even were I able to buy her from Bangy, she would join the slaves in the hold of our ship and be sold upon arrival in Santo Domingo. I said instead that I would only be gone a short time and would soon return to see her. She insisted I keep the gold dust, as a sort of pledge insuring my return, and I did not have the heart to disappoint her.

Now she was sad, for she knew that tomorrow we must be gone, and she lay her head on my shoulder, and gave out long sighs, and kept her hand on that particular part of me, which she seemed to want me to leave behind. I told her to join the dancers if she wanted to, but she shook her head and said she would not leave my side during the brief hours we still had together. I had grown fond of her, even though I knew how hopeless it would be to remove her from her own setting. I had even begun to find her face attractive, in spite of the lattice of welts that covered it, and did not mind the slightly sour smell of her body, for it was like the smells that cling to certain rooms, and that one grows accustomed to from remaining in them. In transplanting, her bloom would fade and her petals would curl. It would be just as ridiculous as bringing a lady of the French court to Momo Grande for Bangy's entourage. Her refinements would be risible. Bangy would consider her perfumed and powdered pretentiousness unworthy of his attentions.

Bangy clapped his hands to silence the musicians and dancers and called out: "Got surprise for old friend Shade." His voice was more slurred than usual and his eyes were half shut, giving him a sly reptilian look. Thirty of the slaves we had rejected were brought before the throne. "Bangy sabby you got plenty brandy left," the king said. "Bangy do you one big favor. You take those sad niggers one bottle each."

Shade, wanting to remain on good terms with Bangy on our last night, rose heavily from the cushions, and motioned to Roger and myself, and we began to sort out those who looked as though they could do a day's work, eventually picking out about half the thirty. "All right, Bangy," Shade said, "I'm crowded as it is, but if it makes you happy we'll take this lot too."

Bangy was not as happy as we might have hoped. "You take rest for glass each," he ordered. His greedy mind swirled with brandy fumes, and he could think of nothing else.

Shade shook his head in dismay. His own patience was being tried, and he was working hard to control it. We took from the lot those least likely to die aboard ship, leaving half a dozen who were rotten with worms, half blind from ophthalmia, or scabby with syphilis. "That's the best I can do," Shade said, "for I've no more room and no more brandy."

Bangy grunted, heaved himself off his throne, and called for the tiger-capped *caboceiro*, who handed him the musket Shade had exchanged for Lumamba. He carried his great bulk over to the small huddle of rejected slaves, who had found a dark patch unilluminated by fires to stand in, as if hoping they might pass unnoticed, and picked out a wrinkled crone, weary bones in a worn skin bag, lifting the musket with one arm as though it were a pistol, and placing the barrel under her withered dug. "You buy," he said.

Shade had been pushed too far. Twice he had given in to the drunken king's whim. He was going to give in no more. Nor could he, or any of us, believe that Bangy was callous enough or soused enough to kill one of his prisoners for a glass of brandy. It would have been easy enough to give Bangy his brandy and let the old crone later disappear into the bush, but this had become a test of wills, in which Shade, and by extension everything that Shade stood for, by giving in again would lose his self-respect.

"No black bugger tells me what to do," Shade hoarsely whispered in my ear. Instead of answering Bangy, he shrugged, walked away from the group of slaves, and returned to the cushions where he had been sitting. Bangy fired, and the report of the musket drowned out the crackling noise of the bonfires and echoed in the forest like a distant salute. The old woman dropped as soundlessly as a wad of cotton. Bangy called for the *caboceiro* to load the musket again. He meant to make it clear that he was able to snuff out lives and dictate to the white man.

"There's no point in going on with this," I told Shade, "for he intends to kill the remaining five. Give him the brandy, and in the confusion of loading the slaves tomorrow, we'll let the sick ones go."

"I hate to see the bastard get away with it," Shade said, "but at least we'll show him we're not savages." Rising, he went over to Bangy and said, pointing at the musket: "All right, old friend, now that you've seen how it works, you can put it away. Don't waste your shot, you may need it. We'll take on the rest of your lot, crowded as I am."

The brandy was fetched, and Bangy at the sight of it seemed placated, and ordered it carried inside his palace. The old woman's body was thrown into the forest, for Bangy would not agree to a proper burial and said she was food for the ants.

I fell asleep that night reflecting on the abuses of power one comes across in every monarchy, where the peevish childishness of the king becomes a reason of state, men are undone on a whim, and wars are begun over a point of vanity. No one dared oppose this regal willfulness, or call it by its name, which was injustice. Bangy was reputed to be a deity, and you would have thought that his behavior had by now given the entire religion a bad name, while our own good king Louis XV was a monarch by divine right, ordained by God on high to mistreat his subjects as he saw fit. The difference was not of government or civilizing influence, or Christian principle, but merely of geography.

The next day the sea was calm, which everyone took as a good omen, and king Bangy, now in a fine and playful humor, came to watch the slaves carried in canoes to the *Rôdeur*. This was a service we paid for in addition to the slaves, and was under the direction of one of Bangy's men, called the master of the sand. He becomes during this operation the harbormaster, in charge of loading the seventy-foot-long pirogues that carry a crew of twenty and eighty slaves crowded together in their hollowed-out hulls. It is no mean task to get the slaves from the shore on board, for in addition to the breakers, it is when they are pushed into the canoes that they realize they are leaving their homeland forever. They have had all along a dim awareness that they were going to be taken away, but they could not be sure until this moment. It was now that their worst fears took shape, for they believed that the land beyond the water was a hell, and that the white men were taking them away to be eaten, since to them it followed that all captors were cannibals. In short, departure meant the most dreadful fate they were capable of imagining.

As I watched the operation, I was glad I was not taking part in it, for it made my heart sick to see their panic-stricken faces as they were pushed into the pirogues. Those who resisted felt the hippo-hide whips of the overseers, who lay about with a will, for their only interest was to keep the pirogues from overturning in the surf. But the slaves would not be quieted, and as they waited their turn on the sloping hard-packed beach, a mournful chant went up among them, in which they expressed the pain of leaving their homeland, and the fear of the unknown. They huddled together, finding comfort in one another's closeness, and their plaintive song, combined with the noise of the surf beating against the shore, reminded me of the chorus in a Greek play, announcing an inevitable tragedy, and made me feel more strongly than anything that had come before the mistake of this whole enterprise. However, I was in no position to back out, and could only carry out my commitment and profit from the lesson of it. I saw three of Bangy's men struggling with a slave who would not enter the pirogue. It was Lumamba, planted straight and firm as a palm tree on the edge of the water, until the whip lashed across his back and he was flung into the sloop. The big pirogues rose and fell with the waves, seeming at moments certain to overturn, only to be righted by the dexterous strokes of the oarsmen.

I Start on the Middle Passage

We had started at dawn, and it took most of the morning to transfer the slaves to the *Rôdeur*, after which we filled the pirogues with supplies: chickens, bananas, and a large quantity of yams, horsebeans and corn, for the slaves. We also took palm oil, which is useful as a pomade against gall, and enough water for five hundred persons during the eighty days of crossing from the coast of Senegambia to Santo Domingo.

My job was now starting in earnest, for I had been signed on to supervise the slaves during the crossing, and I boarded the *Rôdeur* with the first of them, seeing to it that they were made secure in the hold. Having noticed in the *Quibanga* how the men disported themselves with the women, I decided to keep the sexes separate by having a bulwark built across the ship, and I now allotted the waist to the men and the quarterdeck to the women. They filed passively into the hold, being handed on the way, as their only apparel, a narrow band of blue cloth to tie around their waist, which served the office of fig leaf worn by our first parents in the fruitful Garden of Eden. Once in the hold they were shackled in pairs, the right wrist and ankle of one to the left wrist and ankle of the other. Hard, unplaned boards formed a common bed, and they used their arms for pillows. The roof of the hold was so low that they could not stand without stooping, and they were so closely packed that when they lay down, it was impossible to set a foot between naked black bodies. Air arrived in the hold through hatches guarded by men armed with cutlasses. As soon as they were settled they took up their wailing again, their voices crying out the pain of their great loss, and the guards beat their cutlasses against the combings of the hatches to silence them, merely adding to the din. Doucet had assured me the slaves were treated humanely aboard ship, but would not have subjected his pet dog to what I was now seeing. Livestock was better treated, for it was not chained, and was given more room to breathe. All their visions of hell must have seemed to be coming true. Merely to be manacled to another slave made every movement a painful negotiation. And how they could be expected to sleep in such close promiscuity, with the manacles rubbing their wrists and ankles raw from the rolling of the ship, I could not guess. Never, I thought, could so much misery be condensed into so small a space as aboard a slaveship.

Shade came aboard, having bid farewell to king Bangy and been given an elaborately carved ivory necklace which hung from his neck, and told the crew to step lively, for the danger at this point was to remain too long in harbor. "They've been known to attack and kill the crew, cut the anchor cable, and drift ashore," he said.

"You can't expect them to like it down there," I said.

"Nothing we can do about it, lad," Shade said, with his usual quizzical air of a man asked to carry out unreasonable tasks and seeing no way out of it. "The builders designed this ship to carry four hundred slaves, and that's the number we've got to load. It's a bit like a tailor who gives a client ten fittings for a coat he can't get into, but he pretends it fits because of all the time and money spent. Now find me that damned ship's surgeon, the fellow's never around when you want him."

Roger was lying on his bunk. He said he was seasick, although we had not weighed anchor. He said he could feel the slaves squirming in the hold below him: "When I close my eyes I see the poor manacled devils like black worms swarming in a rotten tree trunk, indistinguishable one from the other, less than human, limbless creeping segmented creatures."

"We must do our best to make the crossing bearable," I said.

"Sealed into the hold like that, there's bound to be an epidemic," Roger said. "I may not be a real doctor, but I know enough about hygiene to know that. And then we'll catch it. No one will escape. We will become a ghost ship. Oh, how I wish I'd had the stomach to keep my job as executioner, at least on the gibbet we only killed men one at a time."

It seemed as if the slave's incoherent fears had contaminated Roger, who was letting his imagination run away with him. "Shade has been through this many times and has never lost a ship," I said to reassure him. "And he's clamoring for you on deck."

Roger groaned, and sat up on his bunk, holding his head in his hands, and finally stood, setting his face in a ready-for-duty expression, and said: "I suppose I'll have to go through with it."

"Ah, there you are at last," Shade said when he saw Roger's portly form approach. "When we set sail, you must expect trouble. Some of the slaves will try to do away with themselves. Their mouths must be rinsed out daily with vinegar and they will swallow the vinegar, thinking it's poison. It won't kill them, but it can make them sick, so you must report any slave that tries it and he will be flogged."

"I've heard they try to jump overboard," Roger said.

"Aye, they do that too," Shade said, "when they come on deck to be fed, and that's why we put them in leg irons. The tricky devils have to be watched every moment. I've seen them strangle themselves in the hold by pressing their necks against the back of the head of the man they're shackled to."

"Nothing I can do about that," Roger said.

"Flog the survivor as an accomplice," Shade told him. "But that's not the worst of it. Sometimes they die without cause, except fixed melancholia, an end of the will to live. And I know of one who held his breath until he smothered to death."

"But that's impossible," Roger exclaimed.

"These *bozals** can do it," Shade said.

"When you lose consciousness your lungs fill up with air," Roger said. "The body has its self-defense system."

"I tell you I have seen it," Shade said, adamant.

We weighed anchor at sunset, Shade not wanting to remain in Momo Grande bay a minute longer than was necessary, and set sail across the Middle Passage, as the Atlantic is called, having successfully completed the first leg of our triangular voyage. We could, with favorable winds, expect to reach Santo Domingo in between sixty and eighty days. There the slaves would quickly be sold in what was called a scramble, and we would load up with muscovado and return to Nantes. I vowed that this would be my first and last trip aboard a slaver.

Shade liked the adventurous life and the money, it was in his blood, he enjoyed skirmishing with old Bangy, and feeling the weight of gold or the black skin of a young girl under his palm. His general approach to life was to wink, rub the tips of his thumb and forefinger, and ask: "Did money change hands?" In his eyes, the answer to this question encompassed every known example of human behavior. He did not feel he was engaged in an immoral traffic, but that he was the agent of a system he had done nothing to create, an easily replaced cog in the works. "There's a score of captains waiting in line to take my place," he said. "If I didn't do it, somebody else would, who'd not be so understanding." Of course Doucet could say the same thing. If he hadn't formed the Royale Compagnie du Sénégal, someone else would have; there was never a want of volunteers to double their money in less than a year. You could follow that line of reasoning all the way up to the Maker of us all, whom believers held responsible for whatever took place on the planet, the old fellow with the glowing halo telling His assembled angels sitting on fluffy white clouds: "God of mercy or God of wrath, if I didn't do it somebody else would." So that it came down to whether you enjoyed what you were doing,

---

* *Bozal*: a black fresh from Africa.

which Shade and Doucet evidently did, losing no sleep over the purchase and sale of fellow humans, or over their treatment as less than animals.

I confess that I slept precious little that first night, for when the slaves felt the roll of the ship, they knew that the shore was receding, and they became desperate, beating their heads against the walls of the hold, and bellowing like the trapped stags I had seen on royal hunts. I went on deck and watched the African coastline drop slowly out of sight under the moonlit sky. The contrast between the silent immensity of the heavens, whose flickering stars signaled their mysterious messages from an emptiness beyond knowing, and the man-made tumult of our tiny ship, made our trip seem a vain and senseless undertaking.

I had no time in the days that followed for philosophical speculation, being caught up in a daily round of duties. The slaves were given their morning meal at eight, and were brought on deck by groups of fifty and attached by leg irons to a great chain that ran along the bulwarks on both sides of the ship. That meal consisted of Dabbadabb, corn ground as fine as oatmeal in iron mills and boiled until it had the consistency of pudding, which they ate with stewed yams and a pannikin of water. The pudding, served in small metal tubs, has a binding quality that prevents the flux. This was the best time of day for the slaves, after a night in the packed and manacled stench of the hold. They could breathe fresh air, massage their aching joints, and fill their empty stomachs. They were almost cheerful, ending their meal with cries of *"Pram, pram,"* which means "very good." After eating, they were told to sing and dance in their irons, this being a way of encouraging familiar activities to blunt the pain of departure. Musical instruments had been brought aboard, drums and flutes and calabashes, and were handed out to those who offered to play them, for in the most disconsolate groups, there are always a few who curry favor. But their songs were mightily sorrowful, even at that hour of the morning.

When they had finished their meal and their half hour of dancing, they were sent back to the hold, and the decks were washed down with vinegar, after red-hot bullets had been dropped into the pails, which somewhat prevented the smell in the hold from rising above decks.

Their second meal came at four in the afternoon, and this time they were given horsebeans and slabber sauce, a revolting concoc-

tion of palm oil, flour, water, and red pepper, to which was sometimes added chunks of the rotted fish they are so fond of, stewed
to rags. A pint of water came with this meal, which they swallowed
in one gulp. Roger then did the rounds with his vinegar bottle,
coaxing the slaves to open their mouths as if giving cod-liver oil to
children, and telling them to spit it out after gargling a bit, and not
to swallow it.

On the third day out, Roger came to tell me that one of the
slaves refused to eat. "Let it go for one meal," I said. "He'll eat
when he's hungry enough." But the second meal produced no
change, and Roger took me to see this strange phenomenon. It was
Lumamba, chained to the bulwark, with his plate of beans and
slabber sauce lying on the deck untouched. "I can appreciate that
the son of a chief is used to better fare," I said, trying to treat the
matter lightly, "but I'm afraid this is all we've got." He said nothing, but glowered at us with his strange, luminous eyes.

"You must eat," Roger said, "or I'll have to report you to the
captain. Does he understand?"

I assured Roger that he did, although he gave no indication of
it. Roger picked up the metal platter of food and pressed the edge
to Lumamba's closed lips. With a toss of his head, Lumamba sent
the platter flying overboard.

"That settles it," Roger said, and went off to find the captain.
Shade was concerned that as a chief's son, Lumamba would exert
enough influence over the other slaves to start them fasting as well,
and that soon we would have a hunger strike on our hands. The
solution was simple: Lumamba must be made to eat. If the captain
in a test of wills with a slave were to lose face, his authority would
be worth no more than coral dust colored to look like gold.

"So the bugger won't eat," Shade said, facing Lumamba, and
working himself up to a fine edge of anger. "So he doesn't like our
slabber sauce." He grabbed Lumamba by his woolly hair and
shook his head: "By God, I'd like to push your black head into a
vat of it and hold it there until you drown." Lumamba's look was
murderous. I knew Shade would not have touched him had he not
been in chains. "It just so happens I've got something here to pry
stubborn mouths loose," Shade said, pulling from his pocket a sort
of twin corkscrew. "It's called a speculum opis and I've never
known it to fail. Have a go there, Surgeon," handing it to Roger.

"I confess I am ignorant of the mechanism of it, sir," Roger
said, deferring to the captain's superior wisdom.

"All right then," Shade said with ill humor, "I'll do it myself. Hold his head."

He applied the instrument over Lumamba's mouth, holding it tight with one hand and turning the screws with the other. Lumamba abruptly opened his mouth wide, as if giving in, which made the instrument slip free. Shade lost his grip, and Lumamba sank his strong teeth into the side of the captain's hand. Shade let out a howl, pulled his hand free, and stared with astonishment at the jagged oval of broken skin turning a mottled red. The slaves on that side of the ship, who had finished their meal, watched with an amazement equal to the captain's, finding it hard to believe that one of their own would challenge the boss white man, who was protected by powerful spirits that propelled the ship in whatever direction he willed, who filled the big pieces of cloth with wind, and who could nail the ship to the sea to make it stop.

"Fine," Shade said, knotting a handkerchief around his bitten hand, "we'll do it his way." He strode off in the direction of the galley and returned carrying a lump of red-hot coal on the end of a pair of tongs in one hand, and a plate of food in the other. "Surgeon, hold the plate," Shade roared. Roger stood waiting with the plate in both hands, meekly, like a supplicant bringing a gift to a prince, as Shade slowly brought the coal under Lumamba's nose. "Open you mouth, nigger," he shouted, "if you don't want it burned off." There was no sign from Lumamba that he had heard. He looked disdainfully away from Shade and from the glowing lump inches from his face. "I'll give you one more chance," Shade said. And in a more conciliating tone: "You don't have to eat it all, just taste it."

I almost laughed aloud at this, for it sounded like all the nannies of my childhood, and their stratagems to make me down some hated vegetable, christening each forkful in honor of my father, mother, and other close relatives, hopeful that my plate would be empty before the list was exhausted. But however barbarous my nannies had been, they had never threatened me with hot coals. Lumamba would not comply, and Shade, having elected this method of public coercion, could not now retreat. He pushed the tong into Lumamba's face, whose flesh made a sizzling sound as the coal met the moist corner of his mouth. I was standing behind Shade and could smell burning skin. Lumamba let out a piercing cry that lasted no longer than the fleeting shrieks of the gulls that had circled over us in Nantes harbor, and fell to his knees, squeezing his temples between them like a bar of iron caught in a black-smith's vise.

Roger looked away. He could not stand the sight of pain. "Perhaps I'd better get some grease to put on his burn," he said.

Shade's punishment had been self-defeating, for Lumamba could eat nothing now that his mouth was burned. It was a stalemate. Shade had humiliated Lumamba and brought him to his knees. But on the principle of not eating Lumamba had not given in. "Fix up his mouth so we can get something down it," Shade said. "These prideful buggers will always want to do it the hard way. If he won't eat tomorrow, give him fifty lashes and swab his wounds with salt water."

I accompanied Shade back to his cabin for lunch. He shook his head, as if puzzled by the extent of human folly, rubbed his unshaved chin with the back of his hand, and said: "It would be so easy to have an orderly, peaceful voyage. Why can't they be reasonable?"

The following morning I had to see to the weekly fumigation of the hold. This meant that all the slaves would be brought on deck, but it had to be done, for the hold stank like the nest of a carrion bird, and the stench was wafting through the hatches and had begun to cling like an unhealthy patina to the entire ship. The main problem was that the offal pails were at one end of the hold, while the slaves at the other end had to climb over so many bodies, by twos, since each one was chained to a companion, that they found it more convenient to deposit their natural excretions upon the spot where they slept, soon turning their already airless and cramped quarters into a cesspool. On top of that, and despite my precautionary bulwark, we saw signs that the men and women were getting together. I could scarcely believe that the amorous instinct could arise in this pit of despair, considering the practical difficulties involved, for the bulkwark had to be breached, and each slave was joined to his Siamese twin; the act had therefore to be consummated in the presence of a third party, who in exchange for his cooperation was probably given his turn at the helm. This was true only of the men, for the women, being considered less dangerous, were not shackled. As a result of these couplings, many of the men were affected with a distemper they call the yaws, which added its own special odor of spent lust and diseased genitalia to the overall effluvium.

To fumigate the hold, I sent down a team of men armed with tin pots filled with tar and marlinspikes heated red-hot. They tied handkerchiefs soaked in vinegar across their faces and spread out through the hold, sticking the hot irons into the tar, until a thick cleansing smoke billowed up through the hatches, which were left open two hours. It was a dangerous method, for if the tar had ignited as it boiled over the tin pots and ran into the cracks in the deck, it could have set fire to the ship, but it was the method Shade prescribed, for it was effective and quickly done. Meanwhile, all the slaves had been brought on deck, out of their irons, and herded under heavy guard in the forecastle. They cast blank gazes at the rolling gray sea, probably wondering whether they would ever see land again, and huddled together for warmth, for a chill wind had risen.

I was directing my intrepid team of fumigators when I heard a commotion in the forecastle. I ran up to find out what was happening and saw a thin, slight slave, all bony joints and rib cage, bent over in pain as blood flowed from the back of his leg. It seemed he had rushed past the circle of guards and tried to jump overboard. One of the men lunged at him with cutlass swinging as he made for the rail and hamstrung him. The fellow hopped about on one leg and whimpered, then went for the rail and would have tried again had he not been held back. I saw for the first time that the will to die can be as powerful as the will to live.

Shade arrived, bursting with anger, directed not at the slave but at the sailor who had cut him. "Do you know what you have done?" he roared. "You have damaged my goods. This fellow is of no more use than a lame horse to a racing stable." The sailor protested that were it not for his quickness to react, the slave would have jumped into the sea. Shade's gruff voice dropped to a ferocious whisper: "Your quickness to react, sir, has cost me a thousand pounds. Are you going to pay it back out of your wages?" The sailor looked sheepish and hung his head. "Out of my sight," Shade roared, his one good eye as furious and unblinking as the eye of a vulture, "and pray that you don't come to my attention again for the rest of this voyage."

I tried to calm him, and said that perhaps the slave could be patched up.

"Naah," Shade said, "when they're hamstrung, they're crippled for life."

"Perhaps he could still be sold as a houseboy," I said.

"Who wants a gimpy houseboy?" Shade asked. "He's useless,

and there's no point wasting water and grub on him. He wanted to go overboard, see that he gets his wish."

Several members of the crew laughed at this sally, and one of them picked up the wounded slave by the waist, carrying him under one arm the way I'd seen farmers carry squealing piglets to market. He balanced the slave on the rail and lifted his legs to capsize him into the sea. The black body hitting the water made no more noise than the pails of slops we threw overboard each morning. The slave bobbed on the waves for a few minutes, then disappeared. But underwater he continued to swim, for I saw a red track slowly moving across the surface of the sea. By and by it widened and faded and I saw it no more.

I Make a Terrible Discovery

After the man-overboard incident there were signs that the mood of the slaves was shifting. Nothing overt, nothing one could put one's finger on, like Lumamba's refusal to eat, but an accumulation of clues, insignificant in themselves, but indicating when added that each slave had now become conscious that he was part of a common destiny. In other words, where they had before felt themselves lost and isolated, and their condition hopeless, a solidarity born of their common misery had now sprung up.

This was in some ways a great help to us, for now they passed the offal pails back to those who could not reach them, which kept the hold much cleaner. If a slave was punished, food was collected for him out of the rations of the others. At night, when before they had sung melancholy dirges, now their songs were less plaintive, more resolute, full of this newly discovered sense of unity. I could not of course tell what the words meant, but the cadence was energetic, like some of our own marching songs. And they began to accompany their songs with a rhythmical clanging of chains, using the symbols of their bondage like percussion instruments. To the attentive ear, the mixture of singing and banging of chains was an unmistakable call for freedom. On deck after meals, when Shade wanted them to sing, they refused, and those slaves who earlier had gladly agreed to play our instruments now shrank from them fearfully. It was clear that below decks, leaders were being obeyed, and were reprimanding those who cooperated with the white men. Personally, I had no doubts as to who the leader was, but since Shade seemed unaware of the changing mood of his cargo, I decided there was no point in worrying him with my observations.

However, the matter soon came to his attention in a more dramatic way. Water rations were barely adequate, a pint a day per slave, and as we neared the line that divides the hemispheres, we had several days of unusual heat. The hold was like an oven, and the slaves were a sorry sight, lying prostrate with their pink tongues hanging out over their thick blistered lips. On the third night of the heat wave, I was on the quarterdeck trying to find a breeze to stand in, when I heard a muffled banging sound that seemed to be coming from the fore hatch. Guided by my ears, I approached until the sounds became more distinct. A regular banging, like someone knocking on a door, and hoarse whispers. I fetched two men for assistance and to confirm that I was not hearing imaginary noises, for the open sea can play tricks on eyes and ears. The sounds clearly came from the fore hatch where the water casks were kept. My men quietly raised a hatch cover, and I peered through the grille into a confused mass of shadows and black bodies.

As my eyes became accustomed to the gloom, I could see flooring piled up in a corner. The slaves had apparently removed it to get from the hold to the fore hatch, and even as I watched, one of them lay beneath a water cask and banged on it with his fist to loosen the bung, as they had seen us do with a hammer or a marlinspike. Removing the bung with his fingers, he inserted a bamboo rod several feet long, which he used to drink from, taking long greedy drafts, and when he was slaked, he held the stick for the man he was chained to and got out of the way. At that rate, with every slave drinking his fill, our water supply would soon be exhausted. The slaves did not realize that by stealing water, they were doing injury mainly to themselves, for the loss was bound to be discovered, and their rations would then be proportionately diminished. I knew Shade would show them no mercy, for this was the gravest offense that could be committed aboard a slaver. I did not want to see them punished, and yet the incident could not be overlooked. Someone had to be caught as an example to the others.

I decided to feign surprise and cry out, which would give most of them time to get away by the time my two men had unfastened the hold. "Raise the hatch," I shouted, "they've gotten to the water." My men groped for the bolts in the dark as the slaves looked up in alarm, saw me watching them through the grating, and scurried away under the floorboards. The tunnel they had fashioned was only wide enough to take two of them at a time, but they retreated in an orderly manner, and by the time the hatch was up and my men had jumped down, only two of them remained among the water casks, in *flagrante delicto*.

The next morning Shade ordered all the slaves on deck in leg irons. The two water thieves were tied to ringbolts in the deck, on their stomachs, as the boatswain and one of the mates expectantly flicked two of the hippo-hide whips that Bangy had given Shade "to keep the flies off," as the captain put it. At a signal from Shade, the boatswain and the mate began lashing the backs of the two prostrate slaves, raising their arms with the same knitted-browed concentration as if they had been chopping wood. The whips whistled on the downward stroke and the slaves screamed as the leather bit into their skins, and their watching companions flinched with each stroke. After twenty-five or thirty lashes, the two slaves stopped screaming and seemed unconscious from pain, but the whips continued to flay, until it seemed they would be shredded into rat food. Finally Shade instructed them to cease, and the boatswain took a flat piece of wood like a ruler and beat gently all around the wounds to make them stand freely, this time resembling a mason smoothing over wet cement with a trowel. When that was done brine was poured over the bleeding crossed cuts, which woke the slaves up and led to renewed screaming. The intent of this treatment was to make sure the scars would always show to give away those two particular niggers as unruly. It would make their price go down, and showed me that there were after all occasions when Shade allowed himself to deviate from the profit motive. This deviation was, all things considered, his form of nobility. The two slaves, having been whipped and forever certified as whipped, were released from the ringbolts and placed in double irons.

The full portent of the water thieving was yet to come, when Shade the following day ordered Roger and myself to inspect the water casks, which were now under guard, and report the exact amount of water left. Each cask contained two hundred quarts of water, and the fore hatch held one hundred and twenty casks, on two levels of sixty each. This was considered water aplenty for four hundred slaves and a crew of one hundred during the crossing to the West Indies, which Shade calculated would take at most eighty days. For the slaves got a pint a day, which totaled four hundred pints,

or two hundred quarts, or one full cask a day, or eighty casks for
an eighty-day voyage, while the crew got a quart a day, or a total
of one hundred quarts, or half a cask a day, or forty casks for an
eighty-day voyage. Thus our supply of water was ample under
normal conditions for a trip that would in all likelihood last closer
to sixty days than eighty. Shade had even told me that if he saw we
were making good time, he meant to double the slaves' ration in
the last two weeks so that they would not look parched upon
arrival in Santo Domingo.

As we inspected the casks, Roger and I calculated the normal
water consumption during the thirty days we had already been at
sea, that is to say, thirty casks for the slaves and fifteen for the
crew, and then went about testing the remaining fifteen casks on
the upper level, where we had found the slaves sneaking water.
They had gone through nearly three additional casks in the three
days since the heat wave had started, which did not surprise me,
having seen the great greedy gulps they took. Each one who came
near a bunghole probably drank a gallon if he drank a pint. This
by itself was not serious, for even if the voyage took eighty days,
we could make up the three casks by putting the slaves on half
rations for a few days. We still had twelve full casks on the upper
level plus the sixty on the lower, which we decided to look at to
make our inspection tour complete. Climbing down a ladder, we
reached the gloomy partitioned lower half of the fore hatch and
Roger banged on the bolted oaken casks with a hammer to make
sure they were full and that the niggers had not got down there as
well. There was no reverberation, and Rober said: "The level's all
right, let's taste it to make sure it's not gone bad." I suspected he
merely wanted a drink, but at the same time I saw there was sense
in what he said, for our cooper had been killed in the encounter
with the British frigate *Pembroke*, and it's well known that water
kept in casks at sea and not looked after properly can go miry and
wormy.

Roger tapped his hammer above a bunghole until it loosened,
filling a tin mug with water, and swallowed it. "Baaaah," he
shouted, bending over and spitting it out, "it's bilge water." We
tried a second cask, and a third. They were all the same.

And then it came to me. On the first leg of our voyage, from
Nantes to Africa, the casks in the lower level had served as ballast
and been filled with seawater, for with no slaves aboard, and the
crew drinking wine, our fresh-water wants were far less. This sea-

water ought to have been replaced with fresh water in Momo Grande, but what with our cooper dead, and Shade obsessed with the price of slaves and gold, the roistering crew had neglected to change it, filling only the casks on the upper level. And now we were on the high seas, with our water casks full of the same briny undrinkable stuff that swirled all about us. We had, if the grim calculation was made, twelve casks of fresh water left, or enough for eight days at normal rations, whereas our trip was due to last another forty. What irony! Here was water everywhere, and hardly a drop to drink. It seemed almost as if Shade had expected bad news when he entrusted the water mission to Roger and myself, for had he asked any other member of the crew to check the casks, the news would have been all over the ship in less time than it takes to ring the all-hands bell, and who knows what dreadful panic might have ensued? As it was, the situation was disastrous, but we still had some control over it.

Shade did not even look surprised when we brought him the bad news. He took a nip at the brandy bottle he kept by his bed, rubbed his good eye as if awakening from a sound sleep, and said: "This voyage is cursed, lads, I've known it since Bangy killed the old crone with my musket. That was an omen of the worst kind. In all my years at sea I've never seen so many things go wrong, first the English frigate, then the business with Bangy, now the water. The only troubles we haven't had are an epidemic of the white flux and a mutiny, and we may get those as well."

"The problem is," Roger said, "that if we put the crew on half rations, they'll smell something rotten. But if we put the slaves on half rations we can say we're punishing them."

"But the slaves are already getting only half the crews' ration," I objected.

"That's their lot, lad," Shade said, "to be shorn lambs and whipping boys. The surgeon's right, if we let on to the crew we're going dry, we'll have a mutiny on our hands."

"What about rain?" I asked.

"Aye, there's a chance," Shade said, brightening a bit. "When the wind is light during the day we can stretch an awning over the main deck and leave the crowfoot halyards slack so that if rain it does, we can catch every drop."

Alas, in the following week, it rained not a drop. The sun shone steady, mocking us with its brightness. I even found myself abjuring my godlessness and praying on my knees for rain, devoutly, but the heavens remained closed despite my conversion. Shade had removed the entire store of wine and brandy to his quarters, where he kept it under lock, perhaps looking ahead to the time when, with everyone else dying of thirst, he would perish gloriously, drowning in spirits.

The slaves were now on half rations, getting a half a pint of water a day, barely enough to moisten their gullets in the morning. The precious stuff was carefully measured out in pannikins, and the slaves sipped it slowly and licked the damp sides of the cup. What with the heat and conditions in the hold, their health deteriorated fast. Many vomited up their food, and fifty or so were too sick to move. Among the women, several cases of scurvy had broken out, for the slaves got no fruit save bananas, which are floury and contain no juices, and no vegetables save yams. The only sound now heard aboard the *Rôdeur* was an endless chorus of groans, and the slow rattling of chains like the rattling of bones in a grave-yard.

After ten days it had still not rained and we had but two casks of fresh water left. I reported the situation to Shade, who now spent most of his time in his cabin, amid a litter of empty bottles. "How many do you say are too sick to come on deck?" he asked.

"Close on a hundred by now," I said, "and more than half of them women."

"There's only one thing to do, lad," he said, adjusting his eye patch and once again blustering with authority, "and that's jettison them."

"But you can't do that," I said, shocked at the very notion.

"Do you think I want to?" Shade roared, staring at me as if I were a certified cretin. "Think of the loss, one-fourth the cargo gone, Doucet will have my hide. But the only question now is who gets out of this alive, and I'd rather it was us than them. Wouldn't you?"

"There must be another way," I said.

"My dear fellow," Shade said, in a soft commiserating tone of voice, like a doctor explaining to a patient that a painful cure is for his own good, "I've got a heart too, although it ain't my job to show it, and my heart tells me that it would not be so cruel to throw the poor wretches into the sea as to suffer them to linger out a few days under the disorders to which they are afflicted."

I realized that for the general welfare of the ship, his was probably the only solution, but I was glad I did not have to make it. If it had been me, I would have continued to wait for rain until our water was exhausted. For after all, the blacks had not exactly volunteered to come with us, and it now occurred that they were no longer wanted, and had to be disposed of.

Now the crew had to be apprised of the water situation, and there was considerable grumbling, for even on half rations the four hundred slaves consumed as much water as the one hundred crewmen. They felt that Shade was risking their lives on the gamble that he could get his full load into port, and were only mollified when told that one-fourth the cargo would be jettisoned that night. For the simple seaman, badly paid, overworked, and prey to the same illnesses and disturbances that afflict the slaves, has no room in his heart for generous feelings. I had seen the crew catch fish during the voyage, eat their fill, and throw back into the sea what they did not eat, rather than give it to the slaves. Furthermore, being in some ways closer to the condition of the blacks, since he is himself indentured for the duration of the voyage, and seldom rises above his present station, the seaman is full of contempt for them, quick to call them animals, sneer at their customs, and swear that the lives of a thousand niggers are not worth that of one white man.

That night, seamen carrying oil lamps descended into the hold, their faces grotesquely illuminated in the half-light. Roger led them, and designated the sickest slaves. These were unshackled and half-carried, half-led to the quarterdeck, the deck farthest from the hold, in a naïve attempt to keep tha maneuver secret, for the other slaves would realize soon enough what was taking place. They lined up, thin shadowy figures on the quarterdeck, barely visible against the night sky, too weak to resist as crewmen hoisted them over the stern. This was their final cure and the end of their voyage. At least they would never again be sick, be thirsty, or be slaves.

On the following morning I awoke with an unpleasant taste in my mouth and a splitting headache. The hopelessness of our situation was undermining my health, even though I refused to believe that I had been put upon earth to die of thirst aboard a slave ship in the Middle Passage. The *Rôdeur* was rolling heavily and I heard great cracking sounds that I thought must be coming from inside my head, but when I went on deck I saw that we were under a storm.

The sky was a low, leaden gray, and from behind the clouds

claps of thunder burst. The *Rôdeur* pitched like a drunkard in the choppy sea, and on the horizon, flashes of lightning briefly lit the line that separates sea from sky. Captain Shade had the awning ready on the main deck, and all around it, men with buckets were posted like sentinels standing guard over a treasure. Soon the first scattered drops hit the deck beside me, and the rain began to fall like the Biblical manna that saved the Israelites in the wilderness. I felt it on my skin and in my face, and could not have been happier had I been showered with gold sovereigns. This seemed to be the general feeling, for cheers rang out among the crew, and old Shade stood at the center of the main deck, with his gray head thrown back, his arms outstretched and his mouth wide open to catch the drops that came his way. It was the first time I had ever seen him drink water. How odd, I thought, after the first moments of elation had passed, that it should rain so soon after the slaves had been jettisoned. It was as if, the angry gods having been appeased with a human sacrifice, our prayers were being answered. Most of the crew was busy collecting water, some filling buckets from the stretched canvas and carrying them to the casks, others filling whatever receptacles they could find with the heaven-sent liquid.

Shade emptied his hat over my head, like one of the disciples of old baptizing a Christian convert, and said: "What did I tell you, lad? You can't give up on old Shade, he always comes through," as if he was personally responsible for the rain, having ordered it as he might have ordered oil and vinegar from a ship's chandler.

It rained all that day and into the night, and Shade had the crew continue filling their buckets in the stormy darkness, by the light of oil lamps. The relief of having been saved did not last long with them, and they began to grumble at having to work the extra shift. I stayed up most of the night to give a good example and show that this sort of work, which ensured our survival, was more a matter of goodwill than of duty. The dawn came up as we emerged from the storm area, leaving the vast gray bowl of soup we'd been under for a sky mottled with fat dimpled clouds, and streaked with horizontal bands of purple and orange. The tabulation of our efforts showed that we had been able to fill five casks with water. This was hardly enough to guarantee our arrival in Santo Domingo, but if a man knows where his next meal is coming from, he worries less about the one after that.

I Escape from the Rôdeur

After so much misery, Shade felt the need for a celebration, and we had that very day an excellent reason for one, for it happened that we were passing the line, that is, the great circle that divides the hemispheres, which may have had something to do with our finding rain, for the area is known to navigators as the doldrums or belt of calms, because of its low pressure, light winds, squalls, and thunderstorms. In any case, the tradition aboard ships is that the passage of the line provides occasion for a celebration of sorts, with drinking and singing and dancing and carousing.

Those who have never been under the tropics are obliged to stand the crew a round of drinks or pay them off in coin. In that neophyte condition were Roger and myself. I was not in tune with the mood of gaiety, for, as I watched the men bump tankards and intone their chanteys, I could not help thinking that these jolly goings-on were taking place over the heads of chained men with less cause for good humor. I paid the crew my tithe and watched their merriment without taking part in it. Roger, however, became the center of their amusement, for he would not pay the tribute, saying that his earnings were too meager to squander, and that he saw no reason to share the slightest farthing with the rum-swilling scoundrels of the *Rôdeur*. In which attitude he reminded me of a condemned man who forgets that his head is soon to come off as he fusses over his wig, the buckles of his shoes, and whether his cuffs and jabot are spotless. For there seemed to be at this point, despite the general hilarity, precious little chance that he would ever spend his wages. I offered to pay the tribute in his stead, but he would not allow it.

Now, the tradition goes that if a man is miser enough to refuse the tribute, he must be bound and carried before a tribunal of crewmen, and Roger was grabbed and trussed like a Toulouse sausage as he protested vehemently that he was past the age for games. He was carried to the quarterdeck, where a tribunal of seamen waited to pass sentence. Three judges sat on piled-up biscuit cases, and the one in the center, the boatswain who had whipped the water thieves, a bulky florid man with a face like a boiled ham and small cunning blue eyes, was costumed like the god of the sea, wearing a crown made from a perforated pewter dish and holding a fishgig, a six-foot pole with strong barbed points at the end, as a scepter. In his other hand he held a tankard of

rum, which he lifted with liberality, each time toasting one or
another of the crew members in picturesque terms, and his corpulent frame was covered with a long robe of the sort worn by Bangy
Mambouc's attendants, from whom he had obviously bought or
filched it. In his guise as king of the sea, the costumed boatswain
went through an interrogation of Roger, who pleaded ignorance of
the customs of the ship.

"As ignorant as you are of the practice of medicine," the
boastswain said, taking advantage of his moment of triumph. "Ignorance is no excuse, men have walked the plank for less," and
more hectoring of that nature. He then announced that Roger, as
penance for his avarice and general lack of seaworthiness, would
be dunked in the sea three times, this ceremony constituting his sea
baptism.

Roger blanched at this, for the sea was filled with sharks, and
would have paid the fine twice over, but it was too late. He threw
me a piteous look, but I shook my head, indicating that I would
not interfere with the crew's amusement, idiotic though it might
be, and like all the amusements of schoolboys, soldiers, and sailors,
tinged with cruelty. He was tied fast with a rope, the other end of
which ran through a gully at the yardarm, and hoisted up like a
crate of goods, faint from fright, but instead of being dunked in the
sea, he was mercifully lowered into a large tub full of salt water,
once, twice, and a third time, until he looked like a floundering sea
mammal that had mistakenly jumped upon our decks.

The spectacle of Roger clumsily splashing about in the tub provoked great mirth among the crew, and the boatswain called for a
toast "in honor of our fat mermaid." The sky was a clear dusty
blue, the *Rôdeur* spanked prettily along on calm seas, and anyone
witnessing the scene would have thought it a happy ship, blessed
with a good-humored crew glad to be approaching the end of their
voyage.

Their mirth was contagious, for as I watched poor Roger spout-
ing water like one of the stone dolphins in the Petit Trianon fountain, I began to laugh myself, but my laughter caught in my throat
as I looked toward the end of the quarterdeck and saw a black
head bobbing at the top of the stairs leading from the main deck.
The head became a body and was followed by another and another. Instead of being bound by their chains, they carried them in
their hands like weapons. Roughly two-thirds of the crew was
massed on the quarterdeck, and when they saw the unmanacled

slaves coming at them, they shouted their astonishment and the few who had cutlasses drew them. A stream of slaves kept coming up the ladder, like nether creatures surfaced from the steaming bowels of the earth, and charged the merrymaking crewmen with savage tribal cries, flailing their chains, their eyes shining with the light of ancestral vengeance.

I ran to the other side of the quarterdeck and climbed down a halyard to the poop. I made for Shade's cabin and found him sound asleep, clutching an empty bottle of brandy in his arms. I shook him, shouting that the slaves had got loose. He opened his one good eye, blinked as he took in the information, and said: "What? Impossible." But at the same time he heard the tumult above, the sound of chains hitting bone and clanging against cutlasses, and knew that what I said was true. "The armorer," Shade said.

Guards aboard the *Rôdeur* did not carry firearms, it being felt that with the slaves in chains, cutlasses were enough. Accordingly, the guns were kept in the armorer's quarters, in heavy grease because the sea air made them rust, and chained by their triggers.

"One good volley will scare them into the sea," Shade said. "And good riddance to them."

We headed for the armorer's quarters and found them locked. Shade banged on the door, yelling "Armorer, armorer," but there was no reply. "I've got pistols in my cabin," Shade said. "We'll blow the lock off the door."

We went back to his cabin and he gave me a pistol to load as he prepared the powder and shot for his own. But when we tried to get back to the guns, we found the main deck blocked by twenty or thirty slaves in a state of frenzy, leaping about and waving hammers, marlinspikes, and fishgigs. Shade fired into the tangle of black bodies, and one of them dropped, hit the deck, and lay still. A thin trickle of blood leaked from the corner of his mouth. The others stopped their shouting and jumping to contemplate their fallen comrade, but they did not scatter as Shade had hoped. They squared off, no more than twenty feet from us, neither advancing nor retreating, as if serving notice that they knew white men had magic, but that no magic, not even the kind that made you fall and lie still and bleed, could be worse than what they had already undergone in the hole of the *Rôdeur*. I held my pistol trained on them without firing, for it took Shade a full minute to reload.

"The two of us can't do anything alone," I told him. "Let's find some of the crew."

"They're lost without me," Shade exclaimed, "not worth goat shit, not a one," and made for the quarterdeck.

A tall thin slave with rotten teeth blocked the stairs, brandishing a bloody cutlass he had taken from one of the crew. Shade dropped him at five feet and he tumbled down the ladder.

On the quarterdeck, the slaves seemed thick as monkeys in a rain forest, leaping through the shrouds, chasing crewmen up into the masts, three or four of them hovering over the body of a hapless seaman like hounds at the quarry. The crew's inferiority in numbers could only have been offset by firearms, and Shade was trying to round up half a dozen men to retrieve the guns, for the armorer was nowhere to be found. The black women had joined in the fray and were not the least ferocious, for I saw one leap naked from the quarterdeck rail onto a seaman's back and claw at his face until it looked like blood pudding, while other determined ladies had obtained knives and slunk in shadowy corners, waiting for the chance to sink them into white flesh. The din of battle was drowned out every so often by the scream of a man thrown overboard.

In the corner of my eye I saw the boatswain, still dressed in his long-robed Neptune costume, his back against the rail, the pewter crown fallen from his head, fighting off three chain-waving slaves with his cutlass, jabbing at one, slicing at the other, wheeling to block the blow of the third. He seemed to sum up what was becoming a hopeless defense, for there was no stopping the slaves, who fought with the desperate energy of doomed men, whereas the seamen, their senses blurred by drink and carousing, seemed to be in a bad dream, moving like somnambulists, not fully aware of what was taking place.

I had become separated from Shade, whom I now saw standing on a raised hatch, waving his pistol and shouting: "Rally round, lads, we'll give these niggers a taste of powder." Four seamen came to his side, drawn less by his appeal than by the promise of protection his pistol afforded, and they formed a tight little phalanx that started down toward the main deck again, but on the stairs the last one to go down was struck behind the ear by a bolt thrown with deadly accuracy. The three others followed Shade across the deck, and I thought I should probably join them, when I saw half a dozen slaves jump out from behind a lifeboat and engulf them. I heard Shade's pistol go off, and soon he emerged from the group, his left arm bleeding, running toward his cabin. What was he going to do, I wondered, lock himself in? Offer the slaves brandy?

The stairway to the main deck was now clear, and hopping over fallen bodies, I went after Shade to find out what plan he had, if any, for the ship was a bloody bedlam, and I could foresee no other outcome than the massacre of us all. Shade ran into the narrow passageway that led to his cabin and found himself nose to nose with the leader of the mutiny, Lumamba, who presented a frightening spectacle, having rubbed his face and arms with ash as a form of battle regalia. But Shade held his ground, seeing in this confrontation his last chance.

Raising the barrel of his pistol to the level of Lumamba's heart, Shade said: "Call your men off, or die."

"Your magic cannot touch me," Lumamba said, and he was right, for Shade had already fired the pistol and had not had time to reload.

Shade looked around and saw me behind him, with my still unfired pistol, and shouted: "What in God's name are you waiting for?"

Lumamba smiled and came closer to Shade, and raised his hand for Shade to give him the pistol. Shade drew back and flattened himself against the wooden partition to give me room to aim and screamed at me to fire.

I was at such close quarters that there was no chance I would miss. I would kill the leader of the mutiny, we would get the guns and distribute them to those members of the crew who were still alive, and order would be restored. All this was within my grasp, if I could only perform the simple gesture of pulling a pistol trigger, a slight pressure of the index finger so totally disproportionate to the gesture's results. I raised the pistol, my ears ringing with Shade's shouts, and my eyes met Lumamba's, which were like two hard and gleaming dark diamonds. A dizziness came over me, my whole body tingled with it, I felt as if my mind were being smothered in cotton. I do not know to this day whether it was from some buried instinct of my own, or from a spell that Lumamba was able to work on me, but I was unable to pull the trigger, and my hand suddenly became so numb that I let the pistol drop. At the same moment, I was struck a blow on the head from behind, and I lost consciousness. The last incongruous thought that passed across my muddled brain was of Roger, forgotten in the fray, still trussed and soaking in the tub.

I awoke in Shade's bunk, with my hands bound, and a staring slave hunched in a corner. When the slave saw I had come to, he ran into the passageway and chattered, and minutes later Lumamba came in, wearing Shade's uniform, his blue broadcloth frogged coat, black boots, and three cornered captain's hat. The two pistols were tucked in his belt, and what was most extraordinary, he wore over his right eye the captain's black eye patch.

"Now we talk as equals," Lumamba said.

"Not exactly," I replied, pointing my chin at my bound hands.

"They will come off soon enough," Lumamba said, adopting a hint of Shade's swagger. "Now come on deck so you can watch the victory celebration."

The slaves had taken Shade's brandy store, and those who were not drinking danced with triumphant leaps around the surviving crewmen, roped and squatting near the mainmast. Howling slaves waved cutlasses over the prisoners' heads or hacked at the deck beside them, inches from their feet. Shade himself was bound to the mast, clad only in a long wool undergarment, his bad eye staring blankly. When he saw me being led across the deck by Lumamba, he forgot the legitimate anger he must have felt for my not firing, and called out in the friendliest of voices: "Ax, my old friend, my comrade, tell that fellow he needs old Shade to run this tub."

Seeing the sense in this, I told Lumamba that it was not enough to take over a ship, he also had to navigate it.

"I have thought of that," Lumamba said.

"We're way off course," Shade shouted above the noise of the dancing slaves. "If he releases me, I'll see that he gets back to the shores of Africa."

I relayed this information to Lumamba, wondering whether Shade meant it and had really given up all hope of getting his cargo to the West Indies. "The gray-haired pig will never see shore again," Lumamba said, pulling Shade's well-worn three-horned hat low over his brow to give him a menacing air.

Shade called out, asking what Lumamba had said. "He's thinking it over," I told him.

The slaves had pulled the boatswain and the other man who had whipped the water thieves from the huddle of crewmen, and stripped them and tied them to ringbolts. The men who had been whipped, whom I identified thanks to the crisscross of welts that covered their backs, were now told to do the whipping. They did not have to be asked twice, and lay in with a will born of their firsthand knowledge of the experience. The two blacks lashed the white backs until the skin hung like strips of bacon and until they could no longer raise their own arms. Then the half-conscious boatswain and his mate were untied and each lacerated body was gathered up into a dozen eager black arms that joined under them like the netting of a hammock and bore them to the edge of the ship and heaved them over the side. They splashed about for a minute or so and then the waves closed over them. This was a signal for the rest of the slaves, who stopped dancing and drinking and closed in slowly on the remaining crewmen, who twitched and fidgeted in their ropes.

"Surely you're not going to throw them all overboard?" I asked Lumamba.

"All but you," he replied. "No water for them. I need you to run the ship."

I did not feel this was the moment to tell Lumamba that what I knew about navigation could be writ large on the head of a pin, for I could see that my survival depended upon his belief in my usefulness. At that moment I spied poor Roger, who had been until now concealed from my view behind other members of the crew, for he was lying down, still recovering from his enforced swim. The skin of his face and hands had the soft pink wrinkled look of someone who had been too long in his bath. "I can't run this ship alone," I said. "I need one other man. This man is very capable," I added, pointing out Roger. "He is also a medicine man in case there is sickness aboard."

Lumamba asked that Roger be brought to him, and stared at him for a long time, as if divining his most secret thoughts and opinions, before saying: "He is not a medicine man, but he is not a bad man. We can keep him."

I was very glad that I had at least been able to save Roger. He had always treated the slaves kindly and tried to relieve their suffering. On the other hand, it was he who had chosen the slaves to be jettisoned, but perhaps Lumamba did not know that. One could not tell what he knew, for he seemed to have sources of information not available to European minds. He had known from the start that slavery for him was inconceivable, and his gods in proving him right seemed more potent than our own.

I would have liked to intervene for other members of the crew who had not taken part in the various chastisements inflicted upon the slaves, but the splashing sounds I heard, coming from the rail of the main deck, told me it was too late. In a distressing reenactment of the jettisoning of the slaves, the remaining crewmen were now lined up, waiting to be lifted over the side by two brawny blacks. Some went without a murmur, while others cried for their mothers and clung with white-knuckled fingers to the rail, and had to be cut loose. The more a man resisted, the more the slaves laughed and chattered, as if it was all a highly enjoyable game, something like leapfrog, worked out in such a way that no real harm would come to anyone. How little time it took to kill a man, I thought, how quickly was unraveled the skein of efforts that go into the making of the most imperfect human creature. From the safest perch, the void beckons. It was now beckoning for Shade, for whom nothing could be done.

The notion of charity was foreign to Lumamba, whose credo seemed remarkably like the *lex talionis* of an eye for an eye, unless it was two eyes for an eye. He had a score to settle with the captain, and now, in another hallucinating reenactment, like a shortening shadow, which, at a certain hour of the day, retreats into the person who is throwing it, Lumamba had become Shade and Shade Lumamba. The captain, all spirit pricked from him, was tied to the mast, shabby and sagging, held up by the ropes, while the grotesquely costumed black advanced with stately step, carrying in his hand a pair of tongs tipped with a red-hot coal. Shade lifted his head and opened his good eye, and when he saw the coal glowing inches from his face, his head dropped again. Lumamba waved the coal in front of him so that its heat would revive him, but Shade did not move. Lumamba stamped his foot and flung the coal over the side, like a child whose puppet's strings have broken. He untied Shade and held brandy to his lips, reviving the ashen-faced captain.

In a friendly voice Lumamba asked: "Hungry?"

Shade nodded, probably not because he was hungry, but grateful for any respite.

A vat of steaming slabber sauce, the pungent mixture the slaves were given with their horsebeans, was set down on the deck about ten feet from Shade; Lumamba told Shade in a soft, caressing voice: "You tell Lumamba to drown in slabber sauce. Now you eat."

"All right," Shade said with the last shred of dignity he could muster, "fetch me a plate."

"Don't need plate," Lumamba said, pulling Shade by his grizzled bristly hair until he fell on his hands and knees, and leading him like a dog on a leash to the tub of slabber sauce. Still holding his hair, Lumamba pushed Shade's head into the viscous brown mess and said: "Eat."

Shade made appropriate noises to show that he was eating the stuff, and after a few minutes lifted his head and said: "There, that's plenty, thanks."

Those were his last words, for Lumamba pushed his head back into the tub and this time held it under, straddling his back to keep him from moving. All I could see now of Shade was his twitching feet, and after several minutes they too stopped moving. Lumamba rose, wiping the slabber sauce from his fingers onto his white cotton breeches, and Shade's head did not lift from the tub. Two blacks pulled him out. His head was covered with the stuff as though with a thick crust of lava, like those unfortunates found preserved in the ruins of Pompeii, and his arms and legs hung listlessly. They flung him overboard, the tattered remains of a man who had, only hours ago, been the only law aboard the Rôdeur. Slaving had been his trade, and he had died at it, like an actor collapsing on the stage or a whipper-in killed during a hunt. That was all I could think of, except that for all his blustering ways he hadn't been a bad sort. We'd had some pleasant moments together, and I hoped I would remember those longer than the others. At the moment I could think only of the poet's immortal line: "The woof of farce together bound by the warp of grimmest tragedy."

Now Roger and I were the only white men left on board. We decided to share a cabin for the sake of safety, although we realized we could at any moment become the victims of Lumamba's whims. Our only trump was that without us, he would drift aimlessly until his food and water ran out, and the Rôdeur would become a ghost ship, perhaps eventually spotted by a pirate or a merchantman who would board her to find only the decaying bodies of the dead. Lumamba wanted to go back to his own people, some fifty miles up the coast from Momo Grande. Roger knew a bit more about navigation than I did, for he at least could use a sextant and a compass, whereas the extent of my wisdom was that the sun rises in the east and sets in the west. We were close to the line, and knew that the Southern Cross that shone above us at night pointed in the direction of the African coast. I had heard poor Shade say it many a time, and could hear his gruff voice now: "Follow the cross and you can't go wrong, lad." Luck was with us, and we picked up trade winds that drove us along at a good speed. I told Lumamba we should put in at the Canaries, else we would want both food and water.

He was suspicious at first, fearing a trick on my part. "We go to white man's harbor and they shoot us with guns," he said.

I told him that we would drop anchor far from shore, and that I would take a sloop in and stay just long enough to load water and fresh fruit and vegetables. No one would come aboard. I described Tenerife, which I had briefly seen on our downward voyage, as a bustling, busy port where scant attention was paid to arriving ships except to attend to their needs and make a profit. "They don't care who you are," I said, "only whether you can pay." Lumamba remained uneasy about entering what he called "an enemy camp." I told him we were down to one cask of water and that he had no choice, unless he wanted to jettison some of his own men.

"Yes, I could do that," he said, considering the possibility with great seriousness.

Again I promised that I would not give him away, and that if anyone expressed surprise at seeing me with slaves, for the slave-carrying leg of the voyage to the West Indies did not stop over in the Canaries, I would say we had run short of water and doubled back, and that everything aboard ship was normal. Lumamba could keep Roger on board as a hostage to make sure I would not try to double-deal him. We would only have to stay there a day and a night, and the risk was far less than the risk of attempting to reach the coast of Africa without water. Lumamba finally agreed, for his credit with his own people and his father the chief would increase in proportion to the number of blacks he was able to bring home in sound condition. We set our course for the Canaries, which was so close to the African coast that the most fledgling navigator could have found it.

It now occurred to me that the gold Shade had traded in Momo Grande had been forgotten in all the hubbub. Lumamba had expressed no interest in it, and I set about trying to find it, on the principle that a bit of gold is as fortunate a thing to have as a bit of good health. I discussed the matter with Roger, since there was plenty for both of us, and he said that Shade was too suspicious to keep it anywhere but in his cabin. But the cabin, along with Shade's uniform and eye patch, had been taken over by Lumamba. He was in and out of it, for he liked to take his turn at the wheel and strut on deck, overseeing the blacks who worked in the rigging, but most of the time he was with either Roger or myself, and we could never in those moments count on having enough time to search his cabin thoroughly. Only at one time of the day was he sure to be out of it, and that was at twilight, when he went on the quarter-deck to pray to the great spirit, on his knees, wailing like someone who has lost father and mother. We decided that during these vespers of his, I would search the cabin, and Roger would stand sentry in the gangway, and sing if he saw Lumamba coming.

That evening, as the sun hovered over the waterline like a gas-filled orange balloon, we made sure Lumamba was communing with the great spirit, and I lit my oil lamp and crept into his cabin. There was, aside from the bunk, only a sea chest filled with dirty clothes and pieces of scrimshaw. I knocked on the walls, looking for concealed panels, but found none. There was nothing under the bunk. In my annoyance, for time was running short, I stamped the floor with my heel and noticed a hollow sound. I probed further, and with the aid of a hunting knife Lumamba had left on top of the sea chest, I was able to pry loose a floorboard. The gold was there, under the floor, in a recessed compartment, lying invitingly in canvas sacks. I was wearing a loose shirt like a nightshirt, and under it I had attached hooks to my belt. I hooked on bags of gold dust and filled my pockets with bars that glowed dully in the half-light, until I felt I could carry no more. I had removed less than half of Shade's store, and the sight of the gold lying there and begging to be taken was hard to resist, but I told myself that in greed lay discovery, and began replacing the floorboards.

Outside, Roger started singing "Auprès de ma Blonde" in a loud falsetto, and I wedged the last floorboard into place, put back the hunting knife, smoothed over the bunk, which I had rumpled in my impatience, and eased myself out of the cabin. At the end of the gangway I saw Roger in an animated conversation with Lu-mamba, pointing out to sea to distract his attention, and I slunk away in the opposite direction.

The next day small white birds like undersized gulls circled above our masts, and we knew we were close to shore. The blacks were excited and nervous, for they had been given little water and were sick of the yams and horsebeans in their montonous diet. For some reason they would not eat the salt beef that was the sailors' staple. That afternoon, as Roger was showing the niggers how to fix some shrouds, they began chattering and laughing and touching him, gently, as a shopper touches merchandise, softly pinching his arms and prodding his stomach. Roger pushed them away gruffly, and the blacks giggled, and kept throwing glances at him, as if they were trying to woo him.

When Roger complained to Lumamba about the incident, he laughed and said: "They think you are good to eat."

"Tell them I am rancid, moldy, and putrid," Roger said.

"That is what they like," Lumamba said.

Fortunately for Roger, we reached Tenerife the next day, and the blacks, absorbed by the promise of better food, no longer cast amorous glances at him. A fringe of palm trees lined the shore, and behind them stood a series of low ochre buildings. The weather was hot and muggy, and I looked forward to reaching shore and drinking a cool beer. There were half a dozen ships in the harbor, and I noticed among them a fine French frigate, all polished wood and shining brass. I told the five blacks I was taking with me to shore to lower the sloop. I calculated it would take four trips to bring the supplies we needed to the *Rôdeur*. I gave Roger his half of the gold and concealed mine in pouches inside my cape and breeches. Lumamba asked me suspiciously why I was wearing a cape in the heat, and I said I had a touch of fever. He grunted but made no attempt to inquire further. I asked Roger whether there was anything he wanted. He shook his head and looked at me in an odd forlorn way, and I clapped him on the back and told him to cheer up and that I would see him shortly.

Off we went in the sloop, the blacks paddling furiously, and when I set foot on shore it was all I could do to stop myself from falling to my knees and kissing the sand. I arranged for the purchase of water and supplies, and when the blacks had taken the first load out to the *Rôdeur* I went into a tavern called the India Rooster for a glass and there struck up a conversation with a mate from the French frigate. I told him I was a gentleman traveling for my pleasure, but that my ship had foundered in shoals and I had lost my luggage. I said I was eager for passage to France, and stood him another round. He said he would ask the captain, who was a friendly sort, ready to do a good turn for a compatriot, and that if I could pay something for my passage that would not hurt either. I assured him that I could, although I did not mention the gold, for that would only have served to excite general covetousness. To show I had money, I stood a round for four sailors who were singing an old chantey, the refrain of which still rings in my ears:

> So stand by your glasses steady,
> This world is a world full of lies,
> Here's a drink to the dead already,
> And here's to the next man who dies.

After that, I went back to the dock to meet the sloop from the *Rôdeur*, and this time, after it was loaded, one of the niggers pulled my sleeve to join them. I gestured that I had further business to transact, and he put his hand over his eye, to show that it was Lumamba who wanted me. I told him to wait, and returning to the tavern, I asked for a quill, paper, and ink, and penned the following note for Roger:

"*Adieu*, old friend, I saw no other way. Once, thanks to you, I escaped from the Bastille, and now I am escaping again. Will you believe that my heart is overflowing with gratitude? Remember that you have a debt to collect, and that you will live to collect it, for Lumamba needs you to run the ship. Bear me no grudge, for I would gladly have had you leave in my stead." This last was purely gratuitous, for I was in fact the one who was leaving, but I wanted Roger to feel that this was no trick on my part, but the result of circumstance, another turn blindly taken in the labyrinth of our lives, without foreknowledge of whether it would lead to an exit or a dead end.

I handed the note to the nigger, indicating that it should be given to Roger, but he kept pulling at my sleeve, sensing that if they returned without me they would be punished. I pulled a knife from my boot and held it at his throat and he retreated, mumbling under his breath, into the sloop.

When it was out of sight, I returned to the India Rooster, where the mate from the French frigate sat waiting. He said they were setting sail the next morning for La Rochelle. The captain, having been told who I was, would be delighted to have me come on board at once, for he had relatives in Bayonne who were friends of my late father, and looked forward to making my acquaintance. Thus, in this desolate spot, on the edge of barbaric Africa, and in this apparently hopeless situation, I learned the usefulness of having a family.

Return to Court

I Pay a Call on My Wife

WHEN we landed in the former Huguenot stronghold of La Rochelle, still bristling with turreted fortifications, I decided to take advantage of my relative proximity to my native Béarn to resume my acquaintance with my dear wife Thérèse, whom I had not seen for a number of years, and with the three children I had given her. It is so little trouble to make a brat that I made a point of it on each of my visits, for the hatching and raising of a brood is a fine thing to keep a woman occupied. Thérèse seemed able to bring only daughters into the world, like soil on which only one sort of flower will grow, and all of them the same insipid pink. I resolved on this visit to give her a son and heir, by planting my seed deeper, for I had learned that daughters are born when the seed falls shallow.

Thérèse's natural convent disposition had increased with the years, and when I crossed the threshold of our little Bigorre castle, I felt I was entering a nunnery, for everywhere there were candles, pictures of haloed saints, and baptismal fonts. Thérèse herself was dressed in a gray habit, her head encased in a wimple, and a heavy wood rosary hung from her neck. She showed no surprise at seeing me after lo these many years, for as she later told me, she prayed for me, as if this in itself was a guarantee of my continued good health. She did not return my greeting, for she had taken to observing the Cistercian rules of silence and austerity, and allowed herself to speak only an hour a day, every evening after confession. My daughters were dressed in the white robes of novices, even the three-year-old, who kept tripping on her train, and displayed none of the boisterous cheerfulness natural to their age. Piety carried to this extremity is a form of madness, and I hoped, as I looked at my three little nuns, with their folded hands and holier-than-thou expressions, that one at least had inherited her father's irreverence. It was clear that Thérèse was punishing them because she could not get at me.

The slightest infraction, a spot on a white dress or a forgotten prayer, meant a visit to the castle dungeon, which Thérèse had dubbed the Enfermerie,* and on a wall of which she had written in Latin: And the sun will not smite you during the day, nor the moon during the night. Thérèse's only pleasure was the collection of reliquaries, which seemed to me on the same level of religious observance as Bangy Mambouc's veneration of sacred animals. She kept several dozen in the castle chapel, where she spent many prostrate hours, doubtless sublimating urges I was not present to satisfy, and each one was more outrageous than the next—there was hair from a mangy dog that had been cured by Saint Francis of Assisi, a thread from a net Peter had caught fish in, a tiny vial of brown liquid that was said to be the blood of Saint Januarius, which never congealed, a small pile of damp sawdust said to be a piece of the true cross, and another vial containing the tears of Mary Magdalene. What I saw did not make me want to linger, for if Thérèse had been given the chance, she would have put me in the Enfermerie and thrown away the key. I wanted only to stay the night, conceive my son and heir, look over the accounts, and leave for Versailles, where the true religious temper can best be described as moderate agnosticism.

I had arrived in an amiable, kindly frame of mind, almost glad to see my sanctified bride and play father for a day, but her routine of prayer and penance soured my good will, and when she finally emerged from confession that afternoon, having regained the gift of speech, and turned a chaste cheek for me to kiss, I blurted out: "You must admit that confession is ridiculous."

She answered serenely, for it was part of her credo never to lose her composure: "Gladly, if you will admit that absolution is not."

"Watch a pretty woman kneeling in the box," I said, "her neck bent, her breath soft and pure, confessing her sins to a young vicar with soulful eyes, what limits can we set on the naïve trust of the one and the curiosity of the other?"

"You enjoy introducing the element of temptation," Thérèse said. "At worse, it will add one sin more to the list."

"Since we are all sinners," I said, "why keep accounts? Absolution is nothing more than a mandate to sin again with a clear conscience. I confess, and this is the only confession I intend to make, that whispering across a grating into a clerical ear all the

* From *enfermer*, to lock up.

things that make my life enjoyable is not only useless, it is unmanly."

Thérèse's laugh was dry and cheerless. "That hardly affects me," she said. "As for you, it can do you no harm, and might even relieve you."

"I relieve myself every morning," I said.

She wrinkled her nose in distaste. "What surprises me is how strongly you feel about it," she said. "I can understand why a Christian tries to make a Jew or a Turk think the way he does, for he wants their happiness. But why on earth should a nonbeliever proselytize?"

"I don't shout 'God is dead' in the street," I said, "I leave that to others. When I was last in Paris, a man snatched the host from the priest's hands one Sunday at Saint-Sulpice and shouted: 'What? Still the same madness?' "

"Poor misguided creature," Thérèse said, and excused herself for vespers.

I needed fresh air, and rode to the village two leagues away. It was six o'clock, the sepulchral hour when sinners repent, and I looked in on the parish church and dropped a coin in the poor box. I noticed several of the faithful waiting in a side pew to have their confessions heard, and among them a young lady whose veil did not conceal her loveliness. They waited in spite of a sign over the door of the confessional indicating the momentary absence of the curate. Temptation overcame me, the confessional was in a shadowy recess, and I was able to slip into it unobserved and hang the name-plate over the door to announce that someone was in attendance. After hearing a butcher who gave short weight and a pious grand-mother whom kidney stones had kept from mass two days running (the devout discover subtle sins the rest of us ignore), I heard the rustle of silk on the wooden seat. There was little I could distin-guish in the grated darkness, the oval outline of a face, blond ringlets falling into a bosom that gently heaved with the strain of having to disclose private acts. Women particularly like to tell their sins in gradation, as if climbing a mountain, from the easy incline to the steep. In a subdued but musical voice, she began with trivia, she had spoken roughly to a servant, lacked charity with the needy, lied to various relatives to avoid seeing them. She hesitated in her enumeration.

"Is that all, my child?" I asked.

"No, father," she replied, and her voice was like warm honey, "there is more, but I don't know . . ."

"Come, come, my child," I said in a comforting fatherly voice, "nothing that is human is foreign to us."

"Well, you see, I am married . . ."

"God blesses the sacramental union of a man and a woman."

"Yes, father, but I have been weak."

"In what way, my child?"

"I have given in to the desires of another man."

"You mean you have a lover?"

"Yes, father, I have."

"And do you see him often?"

"Quite often."

"How often?"

"Three or four times a week."

"Where do you meet?"

"He keeps rooms in Bayonne and I tell my husband I'm seeing my dressmaker and meet him in the afternoon."

"And do you commit the sin of adultery every time you see him?"

"Why, yes, father, of course."

"How many times, my child?"

Her voice became plaintive. "Is it necessary to go into so much detail, father?"

"Yes, it is, my child," I said sternly, "to determine the gravity of your sin."

"Well, sometimes only once, sometimes twice, on rare occasions three times."

"And is it always enjoyable, my child?"

"Sometimes more than others."

"Would you say it is more enjoyable the second time than the first, and the third time than the second?"

"Really, father," she said, and I could hear her gather her shawl about her shoulders in an involuntary gesture of indignation. "I don't see why that is pertinent."

"Because, my child," I said with the patience of one long accustomed to the ignorance of sinners, "the penance must be in proportion to the degree of pleasure you derived from your sin."

"In that case, father, my penance should be severe."

"One final point, my child, would you say that the degree of pleasure you derived depended to some extent on, how shall I put it, the robustness of your lover?"

"I'm not sure what you mean, father."

"I will try to be more precise, my child. What I mean is"—and here I raised my voice above the stage whisper I had adopted—"did he have a big prick?"

The girl muffled a cry of horror, and ran from the confessional as if fleeing a burning building. The other waiting penitents turned their heads to observe her in flight, which gave me the chance to slip away unnoticed and pretend to be lighting a candle in a side altar to the memory of a dear departed. The reader will think me a lewd rogue for what was, after all, a harmless jest, and I would not have mentioned it were it not my intention to paint myself unvarnished. Let each man be his own historian. At the same time, I beg the extenuating circumstances of my wife's fanatical piety, which had so stifled my mind that I needed the relief of irreverence, as someone in a stuffy room throws open all the windows, even though it is winter. Finally, I would like to say, as a point of historical fact, that more than one confessor has been condemned of the crime of *sollicitation*,* which implies, at the very least, an erroneous belief about the nature of penance.

I returned to the castle in time for dinner, in a far better frame of mind, and sat down before a bowl of barley soup and a pitcher of water, for Thérèse had forsaken all pleasures of the flesh and expected me to do likewise. Misery needs company. She did not ask about my life. Why should someone who communed with the angels be interested in the adventures of a mortal man? I announced my intention of begetting a son. She turned the color of her starched wimple and bowed her head. In a tiny voice, she said she was indisposed. I was glad I had made her break her rule of silence. I said I was only staying one night, that it had to be done, and besides I was no moon worshiper. She sighed and asked for time to prepare herself. I gave her an hour, and found her lying on her bed in a hair shirt, clutching her rosary. She would not remove the damn thing, and it scratched like the devil, and she told her beads aloud, in a singsong recitative, which I found so distracting that I had to conjure up a dozen other women before I was in a state proper to my task.

I left for Paris early the next morning, feeling as lighthearted as if I had escaped from prison, although sorry for my poor daughters who remained cloistered behind those gray walls. I could not forgive Thérèse her arrogance. She really believed that her life of

* *Sollicitation* was the seduction of women by their confessors.

mortification and penitence brought her closer to God. Saint Anthony said that no man who renounces the world should imagine that he has given up any great thing. But, my dear Anthony, it is all we have, and for all its faults, preferable to being flogged by imaginary demons. In asceticism there is a dryness that parches my gullet, and a thin skeletal quality that leaves me as hungry as if I had supped on fish bones that catch in one's throat and give no nourishment. Was the stomach made to remain empty, or eyes never to close? Those men of ancient times who were buried in snow or lived in rooms too low to stand upright, or who sat for years on the tips of Syrian pillars, were born mad. All extremists are brothers, the man who fasts and the glutton both seek to abuse the body. The man who washes his hands twenty times a day is a brother to the holy man who allows vermin to crawl over him because he refuses to destroy any living thing. Such men are uneasy inside their skins, they want to exorcise their bodies. As for me, I will always kneel at the altar of life, and be counted as one of its celebrants. My ambition? Not to see God but the nineteenth century, to live to the year 1800.

I Resume My Acquaintance with My Brother

Returning to Paris after more than a year's absence, I felt once again like a gawky provincial newcomer, overwhelmed by the sheer driving energy of the place. Cheer up, I told myself, I am not the smooth-cheeked babe I was when I first came here, I have been on the high seas and seen Africa, there is nothing so forbidding here. What is Paris after all but an overturned carriage, two quarreling pickpockets, an arrested swindler, a sad-faced thief in the pillory, a charlatan's tricks, a street hawker's cry, beggars, idlers, underpaid men's men, apprentices dismissed from their craft unions, unscrupulous jobbers, pensioned ruffians, shopping housemaids who know how to make the basket handle jump, the song of the day, the eternal spectacle that makes us forget the street's stink. I watched it go by as I sat in the café de la Régence in the Palais-Royal, surrounded by men playing checkers on marble-topped tables.

Across the street, under a leafy elm, a small crowd had gathered around a portly fellow standing on a crate, who held a black bottle in his outstretched hand. My heart jumped, for at that distance and in that light I thought for a moment it was Roger la Trompette, which set me wondering whether he had managed to survive the *Rôdeur*.

"Ladies and gentlemen," I could hear the fellow say, "I have before me in this tiny bottle the only indelible, incorruptible, full-strength ink that leaves no deposit or unseemly spots. I have seen deeds that were drawn up a hundred and fifty years ago with this ink; you would think it was not yet dry. Far from having suffered, time seems to have given it more luster and clarity. Every family has an obligation to draft its papers in such a way that they can be read centuries hence. Consequently, I flatter myself that I am rendering society an essential service. Beware of imitations."

What the fellow said about family papers made me reflect that this would be a good time to look in on my elder brother Antoine, whom I had neglected during my twelve years at court. He had become head of the family at my father's death, inheriting the title of duke and the castle of Bidache. He detested court life, saying he was only interested in "real" people, by which he meant drinking companions and obscure actresses who could be had for the price of a meal. I knew that he had married a woman of wealth, and that she had left him in less than a year, with what remained of her fortune. But more than that I did not know, and was curious to discover the extent of his dilapidations. It cost me bribes to three different concierges to track him down, for he never stayed long at the same address, and was now living in a garret near the Place Dauphine.

I also hoped to learn from him what had happened to my younger brother Alfred. I once heard a theory that a man's character was determined by the order of his birth. In a family of three brothers, like mine, the first was overbearing, the second aggressive and ambitious, and the third an idle dreamer. This was said to be due to uterine fatigue, the womb tiring with each successive child and bringing forth weaker products. In our case, uterine fatigue had worked in reverse, for the dreamer and idler was my older brother, whose head was full of unworkable schemes, and who despite his prestigious title, lived like a penniless vagabond. His greatest fault was that he promised more butter than bread, and what was basically misguided enthusiasm was sometimes mistaken for dishonesty.

The garret he lived in looked like a tavern on the morning after a busy night. The floor was strewn with bottles, plates caked with a layer of congealed fat were piled on a table, and the smell of stale smoke filled the air. Antoine was snoring on a couch in a corner, lying on his back with his mouth wide open. Three women were there like bitches in a kennel, slatternly, their eyes puffy with lack of sleep, their cheeks crimson from drink. Two of them were playing cards and the third one was petting a cat. This last one shook Antoine awake, mumbling: "Gentleman says he's your brother."

He shook his head, snorted, opened two red-rimmed, bleary eyes, and shouted: "Ax, you anointed rascal, look at him standing there, seventy kilos of insouciance." He got up, and smoothed his coat, which looked as if he had slept in it for a week. "A celebration," he shouted, "champagne. Ah, but there's no more champagne than there is butter up my ass. Hard times, Ax, hard times, I swim, I swim, and there is no bottom, my feet feel only water."

"What about Bidache?" I asked.

He pulled at the lapels of his frayed suit and said: "As you can see, I am wearing the ceremonial costume of a provincial nobleman whose feudal revenues from his vast properties are insufficient to allow him to mend his breeches." It developed that Bidache was mortgaged and was now being administered by the city of Bayonne. "They send me a pittance," he said, "they are devouring it acre by acre. Ah, well, it's in the nature of an inheritance to be squandered. Now tell me about you, you malingering layabout, I heard that two ladies fought a duel over you, like bitches over a bone."

I briefly told him about my departure from court and my year abroad the *Rôdeur*.

"And now you are back from the scrotum-tightening, wine-dark, Homeric sea," Antoine said. "Look here, we must drink a toast"—and looking about him dejectedly—"but all the bottles are empty."

"Let me get something," I offered.

"No, indeed," Antoine said, "can't allow that. Or wait. I'll tell you a riddle. If you don't guess it, you can stand the drinks. My first is the female organ, my second is a game of chance, and my all is a famous general."

I said I had no idea.

"Ha," Antoine snorted, wiping his nose on his sleeve, "Condé. Get it? Con-dé."* I threw him some coins and he called over one of the girls, saying: "Come here, my sweet, and let me sprinkle you with my aspergillum." He wrapped his arms about the wench in a bearish embrace, and said: "What a beauty. Those are not teeth in

* *Con* in French is the female organ, *dé* is a die and Condé is the famous general of the Thirty Years' War.

her mouth, but a row of pearls. My beautiful Colette. A former actress, particularly good in the venereal parts. She comes to me not for the singular but for the plural. I may not have the biggest pecker in the world, but good greyhounds come in all sizes, and, as they say, the tallest candlestick won't light without a wick."

Colette, a lumpy-faced harridan who would never see forty again and whose beauty was all in the eye of the beholder, wriggled away, laughing.

"If someone were to ask me the greatest discovery of our time," Antoine went on, "I would not say movable type, or the Copernican theory of the planets, or the two-seated chamber pot. I would say pleasure, we have discovered pleasure. You will never hear me say anything else, pleasure, my children. I see nothing else in the world worth seeking. And pleasure means change, I mean, pleasure itself doesn't change, it is always . . . pleasure, but the way of obtaining it changes. The pleasure of women is not only in their nature but in their diversity. Oh, they are a fine school, and I am always learning."

The two girls playing cards giggled.

Antoine bowed deeply, and said: "You, madam, are the jewel of this household, and you are its principal ornament. But now I'm going to ask you to excuse yourselves. I want to have a talk with my long-lost brother." They left, still giggling, and Antoine, pointing at the second one, a plump brunette with hair piled on top of her head like a plumed helmet, said: "That's Lili, she's just opened at the Opéra. All she does is lift her arms and drop them on her crumpet, like a good girl surprised to find herself in a place where it runs such grave risks. One day she said to me: 'Have you taken a good look at the object of your pleasure?' 'Well, I haven't really,' I said. 'You don't really know what you like, then, do you? You had better find out. Your pleasure is imperfect, you must have a good look.' I came behind her and threw her on the bed and held her down until I had looked and kissed and licked my fill, and I must say she was right, the eating of it is as good as the fucking."

Forced laughter concealed my disapproval. His coarseness, by which he meant to indicate that although nobly born and titled, he was a simple fellow lacking affectation, was itself a worse affectation that had become second nature. For him to talk like a cart driver was like a bourgeois affecting the refined airs of the court. Antoine seemed to revel in filth for its own sake, like certain animals that find their natural habitat in the mud.

"But you must have had a great deal of money," I said. "What happened to it?"

"Money, money," he replied, "I don't want to talk about it, any more than a man about to be hanged wants to talk about ropes. Look about you. I am a free man, for a free man is a man who owns no furniture. Where do you think it went?" And now, apparently still under the effect of the previous night's drinking, he grew maudlin, tears moistening his eyes. "Where do you think it went? To the hags and hoydens who are ruining my life, to the trulls, the whores, the drabs, the sluts who feed off me, who drink my life's blood like vampires. Every cunt is a bottomless pit. There is no end of it."

Colette returned with a basket full of wine bottles, and a cheerful flush of anticipation returned to Antoine's cheeks. "Ah, my precious," he said, and turning to me, as if to justify his fondness for her, he went on: "Women don't age below the waist, you know, for those nether parts are protected from the cruel erosion of climate. You may disdain a woman because of her face, and not realize that her other parts are as fetching as they were in her youth. Mature women, like racehorses past their prime, are so well practiced and so well trained that they go through their paces without having to be spurred or pulled on the reins."

The sound of corks popping brought Antoine's attention back to more immediate matters, but the more he drank, the more he wallowed in self-pity, not realizing that his heavy sighs and mournful face were out of tune with the principle of pleasure he pretended to serve. "What have I got left?" he moaned, his watery eyes squinting. "My wife couldn't take it, she ran off, not with a man, with a woman. What does that make me? Can I sue for adultery? Can I call myself a cuckold? I am not even allowed that. Ah, well, what have you, what is won with the fife is lost with the drum."

But was there no one who could help him? I asked. What had happened to our younger brother Alfred?

"Oh, he's one of your powdered court coatracks," Antoine said. "Before he can help me he had better help himself. Don't worry about me," he proclaimed in the tones of a brave soldier being sent on a dangerous mission and making light of the peril, "I'll get on. I'll sell my title and become a lowly mummer, shivering under windows, catching coins in my cap."

Indeed, I thought, it would be difficult to help Antoine, for he is so delighted with his role as the abused victim of fate that he would never want to abandon it. As long as he had enough to keep a few bawds and hangers-on, he would continue to enact his dismal charade of pleasure.

"Ah, God," he said, wiping a ruby stain from the corner of his mouth, "I wish I had a tree that grew gold apples."

This was the way he would always be, expecting roasted larks to fall from the sky into his mouth, cursing the world for his own idleness, and when the gold apples and roasted larks did not fall, retreating into squalor. I had more money than I needed, but giving him any would be like dropping it in the street. Although they were at opposite extremes, he reminded me of my wife, for they were both beyond help, beyond change, and beyond reason, the one claiming to have forsaken all pleasure and finding pleasure in mortification, the other claiming to believe only in pleasure, and finding mortification in its pursuit.

A knock on the door interrupted my train of thought. Colette admitted two clerical-looking men in black broadcloth suits and three-cornered hats. They were process-servers come to hand Antoine eviction papers, for the rent had gone unpaid for six months. They looked puzzled, for they found it hard to reconcile the surroundings with the prestigious name to whom the papers were addressed.

"You must let me pay this," I said, seeing a way to end my visit with a kindly flourish.

"What a day to visit the brother you once looked up to," Antoine said, referring to a past admiration that existed only in his own mind, "and see him thus caught between the tree and the bark. No, I can't let you do it. After all, it's I who should give the example. Do you remember when you were a small boy and I fought off that cadet who had insulted you?" His belief in his role as protector was playing tricks on his memory, for it was I who had fought the cadet as he looked on. "Here's what we can do," he said, suddenly brightening. "I'll tell you a riddle, and if you don't guess it you can pay the rent. My first is the female organ, my second is a game of chance, and my all is a famous admiral." I shook my head to indicate surrender. "Ha," Antoine said, "La Motte-Piquet. Get it?"* I smiled and gave him the money for the rent and some extra.

* *La motte* is slang for the female organ and *piquet* is a card game. La Motte-Piquet was a celebrated eighteenth-century admiral.

He offered the process-servers a drink, the two ladies who had gone out earlier returned with two chickens, and I could see the start of another revel in the making, and decided to excuse myself. Antoine, his natural ebullience restored now that the day's crisis was past, insisted on a toast, and said, nodding in the direction of the process-servers: "I don't mind saying it in front of these gentlemen, I am not proud of being a Frenchman because of our form of government or the quality of our kings, but because we are the only ones who can laugh at misfortune, while the Spanish waste away in dungeons, the Italians commit suicide, the English keep a stiff upper lip, and the Germans drown in their beer." I did not have the heart to point out that a moment ago he had been weeping at the clouds in his life and had only started laughing when I opened my purse and the sun of my sovereigns had begun to shine.

I bade them all farewell, and Antoine said: "Still the same impetuous young rascal, you must come and see me often, you jacket duster, you'll always find me at the sign of the frothing peter." I heard him as I shut the garret door behind me introducing the process-servers to his lady friends with mock formality: "Baron Risingcock, will you allow me the pleasure of introducing to you a very distinguished lady, Princess Moistmound?" and peals of laughter followed his sally.

I Am in Elizabeth's Arms Once Again and See My Brother

Upon arriving at Versailles, I took rooms in a discreet inn near the palace, not wanting to arrive there after a year's unaccounted absence without knowing how the land lay. I sent Elizabeth a note, not sure that she would reply, for the paths of our lives had diverged, perhaps too far apart to ever meet again. But in less than an hour there was a knock on my door, and she stood before me, abolishing time, abolishing distance. She threw herself in my arms with an eagerness that was not feigned.

I kissed her, and held her at arm's length, filling my eyes with the dear absent face as though quenching a great thirst. There was a change, not in her features, for her face was still radiant, her blue eyes large and trusting, her smile a balm, her skin alabaster. But in her expression there was a fixed sadness, even when it shone with happiness at seeing me again, the indelible mark of submission to a fate she had not sought, a melancholy resignation that would always be with her, like the wormholes in a fine piece of furniture, that are both the sign of its decay and the proof of its worth. We spent the next six hours bridging the distance that had separated us, telling one another all the letters we had not been able to write and had kept in our heads. I told her that after catching a glimpse of her face in the king's carriage at the Versailles hunt, I had left court and gone to sea. She told me that she had become the king's mistress under threats that he would banish me if she did not.

She said: "My loyalty to you was in finding only sorrows in the obligations I had undertaken." She had given the king a royal bastard, a son, who was being brought up in Paris by a governess, and whom she visited three times a week. "He is the only man in my life," she said.

I feigned jealousy and said that rather than share her we must separate and return what we had given each other.

She laughed and said: "Give me back my kisses and I will give you back yours."

She said the king was so callous that he had not joined her in Rambouillet when her labor started, but sent his surgeon instead, since no midwife was there, telling her it was a great honor. She had a difficult birth, because the surgeon had performed no deliveries since medical school. When Elizabeth protested that it was an exercise that called for practice, he said: "Madam, forget your anxieties, one no more forgets to take them out than one forgets to put them in." The principal advantage of her lying-in was that the king lost interest in her as a woman, while making her position in the palace more secure, since she was the mother of his son, and was no longer a threat to the court ladies who yapped at his heels.

A generous pension was settled on her, and she was sometimes consulted concerning minor appointments, although Madame de Pompadour still controlled most of the patronage, having made the transition from mistress to superintendent of pleasures. She now recruited unknown beauties who were housed in a seraglio near the palace called the Deer Park. Recruiters all over France kept an eye out for faces pretty enough to stir the languid blood of the sultan. Some stayed only a night, and were sent away with a coin bearing the effigy of the man whose bed they had shared, whom they were told was a Polish lord, an identity that ruled out conversation. Others, better able to kindle the sluggish passion in his veins, stayed for months, bore children, and were pensioned off. The house, run by a lady known as the Abbess, generally had between five and ten boarders, who in their spare time were taught catechism, history of the church, and sewing. This deer park, accounts of which have been magnified to sound like the orgies of Heliogabalus, whereas they were no more than the pathetic amusements of an aging monarch, continued in operation for ten years, and saw the passage of more than fifteen hundred nymphs, so that there is some basis in the popular song that says everyone in France is related to Louis XV.

It galled me to think of Elizabeth in the arms of the sultan. It gave her something in common with the inmates of the deer park, but she had only given in to save me from banishment, whereas I, no sooner had I seen her with the king, had preferred self-exile to that distressing spectacle. I knew that even when she had shared the monarch's bed she had been mine, and not his, and yet I also knew that women are astute politicians, adept at running with the hares and hunting with the hounds.

I recall a lady whose husband had bought her a finely tooled Venetian chastity belt, with metal barbs guarding the necessary orifices. She paid a locksmith to make her a key, and removed the grilles. But she would never let me kiss her on the mouth, explaining that her mouth had vowed fidelity, and that she could not soil it, whereas her second mouth had promised nothing, and had no such scruples, the upper mouth having no mandate to speak for the lower one without its consent. Which upon hearing, sounded to me like a point of argument worthy of the Scholastics. Another lady casuist of my acquaintance always chose to position herself astride me so that if her husband asked her if anyone had lain on her she could deny it with a clear conscience.

However, Elizabeth was not of that sort; she was a woman with strong feelings trying to survive in an artificial environment. She loved, in an era when love was out of fashion. And I was glad to return her love, for I had discovered through the disappointment of courting many women the joy of attaching myself to a single heart. And now we were more than lovers, we were allies, for she meant to prepare my return to court. The king had left for Flanders to attend the siege of a fortress which could determine the success of his campaign. My old enemy, the prince de Croÿ, had accompanied him as regimental commander, but my dear friend Lauzun was also at the siege. Elizabeth urged me to join them and by my valor restore myself to the king's good graces. I had no heart for anything to do with his service, having been ill-used too often, but resolved to go for the single purpose of furthering my own ambitions.

In the meantime, Elizabeth was on good terms with the marquise de Pompadour, and would see to it that lodgings were found for me at the palace. Finally, she told me that my brother Alfred had become the leader of a small circle at court, and that he too would be useful in my endeavors.

"When did you last see him?" she asked me.

"When he was a child," I said.

"You will not recognize him," she said. I closed her lips with my own and forgot everything that lay waiting outside the four walls of the room.

The next morning, I went straight to my brother Alfred's rooms, delighted to find another Gramont at court to share the burden of upholding the family name. His manservant informed me that he was dressing, and I put a finger to my lips, indicating that I did not wish to be announced, but would surprise him the way I used to do when we were boys. I crept into his dressing room and there, from behind a screen, saw a foppish bewigged fellow admiring in the mirror a coat of Persian cloth with a floral design, decorated with, instead of buttons, saucer-sized medallions containing bits of coral and tiny shells, trousers of pink silk, stockings of a mottled fabric and silver-buckled shoes with inch-high heels. He was fluffing out his wig and talking to himself, saying in two alternate voices, one high-pitched and feminine, the other a ringing schoolmasterish base: "Well, sir, and whose head grew your hair? All homemade, my dear, still in the first flush of youth, I have yet to sow my wild oats." He struck a pose with an arm outstretched and his head to one side, and said: "Now hold that for seven minutes while the greatest sculptor in France sketches you for a study of the 'Belvedere Apollo.' "

I coughed and he turned around, and said, without expressing the least surprise, in a drawl that blurred the final consonants of each word, after the fashion of the day, "Oh, there you are, Ax, I heard you were lurking about."

It was the same plump pink child's face I had known, glossy and cold-eyed, which had then seemed older than its years. Now the years had caught up with him. "Aren't you glad to see me?" I asked.

"Of course, dear boy, of course," he said, "it's only that I'm so *preoccupied*. I woke up this morning with my nostrils clogged, I pressed my index finger against one nostril and exhaled, but nothing happened, I just don't know what to *do*."

He strode across the room, balanced like a bird of exotic plumage on his high heels, and rummaged impatiently through a box filled with ribbons. "Where is my yellow ribbon?" he shouted, flinging the box on the floor. "I've got every color except the one I need today. I never get what I want. I'm the unhappiest man in the world. And of course, I've had no sleep. Ah, heavens, why don't they sell sleep in the marketplace the way they sell food and drink?" He pulled an interminable purple silk handkerchief from his sleeve and mopped imaginary beads of perspiration from his brow.

He made me feel that in some obscure way, I was responsible for his not finding the ribbon he wanted and for his lack of sleep. "I'm sorry if I've broken in on you," I said.

"Not at all," he said. "You stay right here and let me have a look at you. It's just that I'm giving a luncheon party for some dreary people and it's so hard to get anything done right. You must join us." He opened another box, this one was full of jewelry, and squeezed three large amethyst rings onto his pudgy fingers. "A friend brought these from Russia," he said. "Aren't they divine? I'm taking snuff again to show them off."

"I'm very happy to see you so well adjusted to court life," I said.

He sighed, picked up a fan, fluttered it nervously, and said: "It hasn't been easy. They whispered about me. They were cruel. I suffered direct affronts. The duc de Lauzun rubbed my cheek with a table napkin to see whether I was wearing rouge. Of course I *do* wear a little but it's imperceptible. And the questions about my wife!"

"I didn't know you were married," I said, for indeed, I knew nothing about this brother who had suddenly appeared before me in such an unexpected transformation. It was like finding that every page of a book one thinks one has read has been altered, so that it must be begun again.

"Oh, wasn't I," Alfred said, as he arranged a vase of flowers with little clucks of his tongue until he was satisfied with the effect and said, "There, they look almost real. Oh, yes, I was married, but my wife sued for nonconsummation. They called the poor girl the Virgin with the Chair, after that Flemish painter, you know the one. I did my best, but making love to a woman is like making love to a seal. Squish squish."

I laughed under my breath at this strange admission and gazed with increasing wonder at this bizarre, flamboyant creature who had come to inhabit my brother's body, slowly realizing that his attitudes were in a sense the logical outcome of the fastidiousness and precocious poise he had shown as a child.

"Of course the ladies here, eager to appropriate any newcomer, whispered how surprising it was that I had no liaisons. I told them straight out that on the article of my pleasures I consult only myself. Frankly, there is not a single woman in Versailles worthy of my attention. And yet, despite my reputation, several *threw* themselves at me."

"You could have pretended," I said.

"Pretended," he shrieked, snapping his fan shut with a clap. "My dear, one of them crept into my bed at night, I had to flee in my nightshirt. She offered me jewelry. She came to my rooms and had fits and broke vases. Her husband finally asked for an explanation. 'You must stop seeing my wife,' he said. 'My dear,' I told him, 'I do everything to *avoid* her.' He grew so distraught he challenged me to a duel. When he asked me my choice of weapons, I said roses, thinking of the thorns, you know. A charming young man who had overheard us, and whom I hardly knew, touched by my predicament, asked: 'Would you like me to be your second?' 'My dear,' I told him. 'I'd like you to be my *first*.' In any case the outraged husband, who could not be convinced that his wife's virtue was safer with me than with any other man, went ahead with the preparations for this absurd duel. I had forgotten all about it when my charming young second came to tell me the day was at hand. Well, it was much too cold and much too early, and besides the Grande Mademoiselle (my toy poodle) was having her enema that day, so I simply *couldn't* go. Duels are illegal, in any case."

"Had I been there," I said, "I would gladly have gone in your stead. After all, an affair of honor . . ."

"A fine honor to have grown men killing each other over a woman," he snorted.

"Tastes can be acquired," I said. "Even though you may not like figs, they are held by many to be delicious."

"I can't love anyone whose smell I don't like," Alfred said as he covered himself with a spray of perfume from a large gold atom-

izer. "I've sent lovers away after the first sniff. You can tell a lot by
kissing too. I don't mean sex kissing, just kissing. Also touch, that's
important—I don't like faces that feel like suet pudding. But smell
is everything to me. I have a nose like an airedale."

"Well," I said, for I did not know how to respond to his mixture
of candor and playacting, "as long as you're happy."

"Happy," he shouted, spraying the perfume inside two dove-
gray suede gloves, "I've just been jilted. I'm not made for one-
sided affections. I can't bear not to be wanted. How lucky you are
to love women, for they love you back. But in my case, the love
they picture as a cherub, an infant with a bow and arrow and a sly
smile, turns into a fool with cap and bells, singing nonsense songs,
his feet tangled in his own dance steps."

I was burning to ask my brother how the transformation I was
witnessing had come about. It did not lessen him in my eyes, for
many famous generals have had Italian tastes; the duc de Ven-
dôme liked both fur and feather, and the Sun King's own brother,
Monsieur, reared as a girl, remained one, although he was a vali-
ant captain in the field. In fact such people, whose natural inclinations are somehow deviated from the opposite sex and fixed onto
their own, are, in my experience, rarely cowards. They may affect
a woman's gestures and simpering attitudes, but they have none of
a woman's timorousness. As for Alfred, his evolution may have
had something to do with the fact that my mother had died in
giving birth to him. I had long resented him, holding him responsible for her death. I could see the confusion starting then, for he
did not know where to turn for affection, and with a loving model
of the fair sex absent, drew himself inward, and toward his own
kind.

"Well, go ahead," Alfred said, guessing my thoughts, as he carefully applied powder to his fleshy nose, "I can see you're dying to
ask, and there's no reason why you shouldn't know. I was seduced
in a mild way at age twelve by a cavalry officer, a friend of father's
who was visiting Bidache during a break in the Flemish campaign.
I felt it was the patriotic thing to do. He seemed so heroic, it was
my contribution to the war effort. I couldn't rat to the governess,
not knowing whether he'd be alive a week from then. A short time
later, the governess—it was that German lady, Miss Martha, do
you remember?—told me, 'Do you recall that nice Major de Mun
with the orange whiskers? He was killed at Dettingen.' I cried all
night. It was the first time I suffered for love.

"After that, there was a succession of village boys, but I was still quite naïve. The first time I went to confession, I said, 'Father, I've had relations with another boy.' 'In the mouth or in the rectum?' the priest asked. I was shocked. I had no idea it was done in the rectum. I learned more from that priest than I had from my lovers. Ah, well, and so it has gone. Mind you, I am not a lecher. I have had a great many friends who were not lovers. I have always been a gregarious person who enjoys the company of other people."

"Pleonasm," I said.

"What?" he asked.

"Never mind," I said, "I think I will go outside and kill time before lunch."

"*How* do you kill time?" he asked, dramatically raising his hand to his brow. "Men talk of killing time, while time is quietly killing *them*."

When I returned to Alfred's rooms, several guests had already arrived, and a table had been set in an alcove. Alfred introduced me to a pretty young man called Jerome, whispering, "He's a Capricorn, and Capricorns have *always* been my downfall." And leading me across the room where a heavily rouged, carrot-haired, puffy-faced woman sat, he said: "Try to be nice to comtesse de Merdon, with her necklace of warts, she makes no attempt to conceal them, I'm sure she thinks they're beauty spots, I feel like telling her to paint them. She's Swiss, which explains everything. You know the Swiss, cuckoo clocks, goiters, and people in tiny hats."

In the next few minutes, there arrived an Englishman with a long, motionless face, frozen in an expression of solemnity like an arthritic horse, whom Alfred introduced as Sir Richard Titwell, who sold Italian paintings at court ("Most of them clever fakes," Alfred told me in an aside), and a bulky lady, walking with a cane, her face as wrinkled as a crab apple, her low brow invaded by the gray patch of a widow's peak, whom Alfred introduced as Princess Lebensraum.

"Darling, you are forever young," he told her, and whispered to me: "She's five years older than God."

"Have you been busy, dear boy?" the princess asked, removing one of several cloaks she was wearing.

"Busy as a bride's ass, darling," Alfred said.

"I believe I noticed some of the third element descending as I came in," the princess announced, and pointing at the fire that roared cheerfully in the hearth, "I'm glad you have some of the combustible element."

Princess Lebensraum had moved to Versailles from one of those tiny German courts consisting of six courtiers and a jester. She had no permanent lodging, but stayed in the apartment of anyone who happened to be away. Determined to be fashionable, she had adopted the manner of speaking of the *précieuses*, which consists in never saying directly what can be said in a long and cryptic periphrase, so that the third element descending was rain, and the combustible element was fire. Alfred, who had helped her off with her cloak, came to my side, put his hand over his wrinkled nose, and said: "*Poisson, poisson,* I don't know whether it's her pits or her parts."

Comtesse de Merdon, in her singsong Swiss, as though her words had to carry up mountain and down valley, like yodels, complimented Alfred on his flower arrangement.

"Darling, you're *too* kind," Alfred said, then turning to me: "She likes simple things, and she should. You'll see, she'll open her mouth twice during lunch, once to say 'What a fine-looking fish,' and the other to say 'These cherries are good.' Well, don't stand there like a boiled owl, circulate."

In a few minutes, a footman announced that lunch was served, and the princess rose heavily on her cane, saying: "Ah, let us now take our midday necessities. I am greatly in need of an internal bath," by which I suppose she meant a glass of water.

The first course was soup, and Sir Richard Titwell, who had not yet unclamped his thin pale English lips, opened them to announce, and at the same time to reveal that he had not mastered the French language: "*J'ai un mouche dans ma soupe.*"

"No," the princess, who was on his right, corrected him, "*une mouche.*"

"*Une mouche,*" Sir Richard asked, his heavy-lidded eyes blinking, "are you quite sure?"

"Positive," the princess said.

"I say," Sir Richard exclaimed, "what remarkable eyesight."

The young man snickered, and Alfred, looking across at him adoringly, said: "I look into his eyes and I see the sky."

The princess, wanting to put the conversation on a more general topic, which she could control, said: "I have just received news that in Venice a lord of that city, convicted of the crime of sodomy, was put in a bag and thrown into the sea, at the very moment when he was about to leave for an important post in a foreign court." This announcement had the effect of a cold shower over the entire table, for alone among those assembled, the princess seemed to ignore my brother's penchants. Sensing that she had committed a *faux pas*, and seeing my brother blush, she turned to me and said: "Look, his thrones of modesty redden. Is he not partial to the sex of Diana?"

"No," I whispered, to forestall any further uncertainty, "he has inclinations of another nature."

Eager to change the subject, the princess said: "The king was recently shown some paintings by students of the academy, and one in particular stood out, a work entitled 'Christ Washing the Feet of His Apostles,' by a young man named Fragonard, only twenty-five. The king commissioned several paintings, one of Jupiter turned into a bull and carrying off Europa on his back, the other of Diogenes, who seeing a boy drinking out of his hand breaks his cup."

"How very interesting," Alfred said, then, half-covering his mouth with his napkin, he turned to me and said: "I hate intellectuals, they make me squeak."

The valet presented a cold fish in aspic, its mouth decorated with sprigs of parsley, and its glistening sides covered with a lattice of mayonnaise. "Oh, what a fine-looking fish," comtesse de Merdon said.

The princess, obtaining no response to her news about painting, turned to literature: "Fontenelle is nearly a hundred, and has written six new comedies," she said. "They were meant to be posthumous, but he says he grew tired of waiting. One, which I had the pleasure of reading, is entitled *The Price of Silence*. The plot has to do with a lady, who having declaimed against the strong sex and praising her own, writes each of her suitors that if he can keep a secret for twenty-hour hours he can marry her. All of them, out of indiscretion or vanity, betray her secret. I confess that I am full of admiration for the elevation of Fontenelle's mind."

"Plain women," Alfred said to me behind his napkin, "always praise the beauties of the mind."

At that moment, Sir Richard Titwell spoke up again, apparently feeling that at least one compliment should pass his lips as the price of his lunch. Seated as he was between Princess Lebensraum and the comtesse de Merdon, he gave each of them a little inclination of the head and said: *"Je suis une pine entre deux roses."**

Everyone burst out laughing and Sir Richard stared unhappily at his plate. Alfred told me *sotto voce*: "You would not think to look at him that he was dotty. Only the English can combine a dignified appearance with extreme eccentricity. He has just got over a long spell when he thought he was a carnation. He spent the entire winter in a hothouse, being sprinkled with water twice a day by footmen, and in the spring he had himself buried to the waist in a flower bed. Then he had his hair cropped and took to his bed."

The next course was pheasant on canapés, and the princess asked: "Will the little darling mind if I take him off his cushion?"

Alfred shook his head absently, for he was in the middle of a fascinating conversation with the pretty Jerome, who was an ardent bowler and was telling him about a game he had played the day before. Alfred cared nothing for bowls, and looked on all athletic activities as a waste of time, but his infatuation with the young man turned everything that came from his lips into pearls. He could have been speaking a foreign language and Alfred would have listened with the same rapt attention, which had nothing to do with what was being said.

After the sweet, fruit was served, a mixture of peaches and cherries. Comtesse de Merdon piled her plate high with cherries and said, "Oh, these cherries look good."

Jerome daintily peeled, quartered, and ate a peach. Alfred fluttered his lashes and said: "You look like a peach eating a peach."

Comtesse de Merdon was mutton trying to pass for lamb. Despite being in her late sixties, she used every weapon in the arsenal of cosmetics to make herself look young, so that she seemed to be wearing a brittle painted mask over her real face, and she now threw coquettish glances at Jerome, who, conscious of the older woman's attention, looked bashfully away. Alfred, who had also noticed her ogling, and who was aware of her reputation as a devourer of young men, in the satisfaction of which appetite she was known to spend considerable sums, said in an aside to me: "She receives every Wednesday, and will doubtless invite you to add luster to the company, for most of her guests one would not ask even were one thirteen at table, but I advise you not to accept,

---

* He had meant to say *"Je suis une épine entre deux roses,"* which means "I am a thorn between two roses," but garbled it and said instead: "I am a cock between two roses."

for the only difference between her cook and the celebrated poi-
soner Brinvilliers is their motive."

Comtesse de Merdon must have realized that she had been observed committing what to Alfred was the one unpardonable
offense, trying to take one man away from another, and she turned
her attention toward the princess and said, in a loud and unnatural
voice: "Have you been to the theater lately?"

"Indeed, yes," said the princess, to whom a question addressed
was a pretext for making a speech. "I did but recently attend the
paradise of the eyes and ears, and saw a tragedy by the Englishman Shaxpeer. The only way he can end a play is by killing off all
the characters." And quite forgetting that there was an Englishman among Alfred's guests, she went on: "The English theater is
so unregulated and indecent, these gloomy islanders know no
bounds, the most brazen scenes are not too much to divert them.
Do you want to know my definition of good writing?" No one said
they did, but the question was rhetorical, and the princess meant to
give us the answer. "It is the art of saying things without being sent
to the Bastille. The freedom to say anything makes a nation vulgar. You will have, instead of the subtlety of an oblique expression, a play in which a lover will say to his mistress, 'Madam, I
wish to bed you down,' or some such Anglo-Saxon enormity. The
main cause of the perfection of our wit is restraint, knowing how
to say anything within the limits of decency."

Alfred, either to take the defense of Sir Richard Titwell, who,
having understood only a part of what the princess had said, was
not sure of the attitude he should take, or because he was annoyed
with her pronouncements, exclaimed: "Our blood is thin from
being restrained. We cannot *bear* a strong idea. Everything is
watered down; the work of our painters and poets is full of cherubs
and pink mists. What must we do? Accuse Homer of vulgarity for
describing the blood of Ulysses' companions trickling down Poly-
phemus' beard? In Greece, men were naked in gymnasiums and
public baths, and statues of goddesses were modeled on the bodies
of courtesans. The same breasts one caressed during a night of
pleasure one admired on the altars of temples. The ease of morals
made one free. Religion was full of voluptuous ceremonies, one
did not yawn in church, one got an erection."

"Really," said the princess, shocked, "I think you have gone
beyond the bounds of propriety."

Alfred laughed, delighted at having shut the princess up, and also at having been able to combine his appeal for unrestrained art with the homophylic ideal of the Greeks.

The lunch came to an end, and the guests departed in various states of confusion. Only Jerome and I remained, Jerome sneaking furtive looks at himself in the mirror. Alfred gazed at him tenderly. "I had his measurements taken and found them to be in accordance with the classic golden rule," he told me.

I thanked him and said I would leave him alone with Jerome.

"Isn't he beautiful?" Alfred said. "He has lashes from here to the wall."

I told Alfred I was glad to see him again, meaning by that that it did not matter to me what he had become, he was still my brother, and we could help each other in the shifting currents of the court. I complimented him on the lunch, and he said, in the social equivalent of postcoital sadness when the guests have gone and the dirty plates and glasses are stacked in a dumbwaiter: "Aren't they pathetic? It's just *too* depressing."

I Leave for the Siege of Tournai

The court had not changed, it was still concerned with the passionate pursuit of futility. If those who hungered to be part of it had known that its essence was wind, they would have shifted their desires to worthier goals. And yet, as an astute Italian visitor once said, "To be a part of it was a bore, and not to be a part of it was a worse bore." For of course, you could only know that it was a bore if you were a part of it, and if you were not, you were free to imagine that you were being excluded from a garden of earthly delights. Also, a man who has lived at the heart of intrigue for a certain time can no longer give it up. He will languish in a more placid environment. Like the marble palace they lived in, the court was composed of very hard, very polished, and very cold men.

Crossing the Galerie des Glaces, I saw the same courtiers standing in the same positions, as if they had been planted there alongside the orange trees in their massive silver pots, and I heard them discussing the current campaign. One could leave the court for years and return to find it exactly as one had left it, preserved in amber, or like those imaginary landscapes made of feathers and bits of lace that fashionable women keep on their mantelpieces under glass. There was the tiny, ferret-faced duc de Gesvres, gesticulating like a windmill, and the pinhead prince de Conti, his head emerging like a bubble squeezed from the rubber bulb of his body, and the molelike La Trémoïlle, whose tiny eyes looked as though they rarely saw light, and the strutting duc d'Aumont, who turned a simple gesture like taking snuff into a complicated choreography.

I approached their little knot and they greeted me courteously, without effusion, as if they had seen me the day before and the day before that. One advantage of the court was that everyone was so concerned with advancing his own affairs that he paid no attention to anyone else. One could disappear for a year, and after the initial curiosity had vented itself, it would be forgotten that one had gone.

"I'd like to see how Richelieu would get out of it," the duc d'Aumont said, shaking with indignation all the way down to his two-inch heels.

"Richelieu would not have got into it," the prince de Conti replied.

"Our armies could be destroyed and our borders invaded," the duc d'Aumont went on, "before one trip to Marly would be canceled."

"That's unfair," said La Trémoïlle, who had reaped three thousand acres of Beauce farmland as a result of his wife's having been the king's mistress for a week. "The king left three days ago for the siege."

"Oh, yes," said the duc de Gesvres, pushing with his elbow at the others in his impatience to deliver his bit of news, "I saw him go. What a monstrosity that was; all the usages were forgotten. I don't know what the court is coming to, we might as well be living in a cave with cavemen for all the attention that is paid important matters. When he mounted his horse, an equerry held his stirrup, whereas everyone knows that the first footman should hold the stirrup. It's only during a relay that the equerry holds the stirrup; that is just common sense."

"All well and good," said the duc d'Aumont, "but hardly as ridiculous as Madame de Pompadour pledging to melt down her silver plate to support the campaign. Of course, we are meant to imitate her good example. All well and good, except that la Poisson has no silver plate to speak of, but I, gentlemen, I have silver plate."

"Did you hear," asked the prince de Conti, "about the memoir she requested on the campaign? The king said: 'I'll give it to your hairdresser so he can make curlers out of it. That's the only way to get anything into your head.' "

"Sublime," La Trémoïlle said. "You must admit that the king's spirit of apropos has not dulled. To add to that, I can give you news of the siege—" La Trémoïlle stopped, to measure the full effect of his announcement, as if waiting for drums to roll, and the others pressed closer to hear his report. "The king was bitten by a louse, severely, on the neck. He took the molesting beast between his fingers and said: 'This animal has just reminded me that I am a man among men.' "

There were murmurs of approval, except from the duc d'Aumont, who said: "He is no Frederick II, of that you can be sure. Frederick II knew that columns were meant to be deployed in the field, not to prop up useless buildings."

"Of course," the prince de Conti said, "Croÿ has been made regimental commander."

"Thanks to the influence of his mistress," La Trémoïlle pointed out.

"Yes," said the duc d'Aumont, "he went from the particular to the general."

I decided to put in a good word for the maréchal de Saxe, who was, I felt, our last great general, even though he was German and not French, and who had died seven years before. "Ah," I said, "now that we no longer have Saxe . . ."

"We may be better off," said the duc d'Aumont.

"Let us not speak ill of the dead," I said. "He did everything on a grand scale."

"You mean on an exaggerated scale."

"He was bold."

"You mean intemperate."

"His knowledge was vast."

"He had a talent for guessing what he did not know."

"He was easily enthusiastic."

"And easily disgusted."

"He repaired injustices."

"After committing them."

"He could converse on any subject with any man."

"He talked divinity to generals and tactics to bishops."

"He knew how to do without a great many things."

"But he wanted everything."

"At least grant him Fontenoy."

I had the last word, for no one could deny that Fontenoy had been the victory of a brilliant tactician against superior English and Flemish forces. Why, the Duke of Cumberland himself had praised Saxe. And now these flannel-mouthed tablecloth-hangers, who had never seen a shot fired except at royal hunts, and who pretended to be furious that physical complaints like the gout kept them from the battlefield, whereas in truth a team of horses could not have dragged them to the front, were indulging their favorite pastime of judging their betters. Their prattle made me want to be off as soon as possible, at the head of my old regiment, which in my absence had been entrusted to a junior officer, and was already at the siege.

Alas, after my reunion with Elizabeth, I had to leave her again. It seemed that my life was made up of farewells. I found her in the rose arbor, reading a book of love poems by Ronsard. The sun filtering through the rose-covered trellis bathed her in a soft dappled light and made her seem unreal, an apparition in a dream of longing. I passed my arm around her waist and kissed a spot at the side of her neck where alabaster turned to gold. She leaned her head on my shoulder and said: "I am coming with you." She felt my body stiffen and asked:

"Don't you think I would make a good soldier?"

"So good," I replied, "that I would put you under arrest and confine you to quarters—my quarters."

"And we would conduct our private battle."

"And I would raise the white flag of surrender."

"How can you be sure I would take prisoners?"

"I would throw myself on your mercy."

"And I would keep you captive until you were too old to be of use."

"And I would never try to escape."

"I will come as your aide-de-camp."

"Concern for your safety would make me forget my duties."

"Well, then I will be your camp follower, and wait in your tent until you return at the end of the day, and remove your boots, and rub your back, and bring life back to all your tired parts."

She saw the refusal in my eyes and added: "Why not?"

"A lady of the court following an officer to the siege," I exclaimed. "Only the king is allowed that privilege."

She took my hand and removed it from her waist, walking a step ahead of me. "Really," she said, "you are so conventional. You travel halfway around the world and your life is a series of adventures, but your mind is a tidy drawing room. And in that drawing room I am a chair, which should always remain in place."

"You must realize . . ." I said, but she would not let me finish, and ran off, saying: "I realize nothing of the kind."

I followed, but she lost me in the alleys of the bower, and I had no time to continue the game, for a sergeant major who had stayed behind with the rest of my regiment's horses had prepared mine, and I wanted to reach Soissons by nightfall, and, with hard riding, arrive at the siege of Tournai on the following day.

I found a comfortable inn in Soissons and was shown a spacious room where I had a roast capon and a bottle of Burgundy brought up. The wine made me drowsy, and I had kicked off my boots and thrown myself on the canopied bed, without bothering to remove my uniform, for I intended to be up at dawn, when there was a knock on the door. It was my hostess, a portly lady with a bun of gray hair piled on top of her head, who looked as if she appreciated her own cooking, and who came to tell me that a young officer bound for the siege as I was asked if he could share my room, for the inn was full, and I had a spare cot in the corner. I could not turn down a fellow officer, and paid scarce attention when I saw a slight figure in the candlelight turn down the blankets of the cot, without even a greeting.

I asked the lad if he wanted what was left of my bottle, and he grunted in reply. I asked him the name of his regiment, and was again repaid with a grunt. "Are you mute?" I asked. No reply. I sat up, annoyed, and peered through the half-light at the incommunicative sharer of my room. He was sitting on the edge of the cot, with his back to me, looking out the window, his musketeer's hat still perched on his head. "A gentleman removes his hat when he enters a room," I said. No reply. My patience was beginning to wear thin. "I invited you here, you know," I said. "You'd be sleeping with the horses if I hadn't. You could at least be civil." I thought I saw the fellow shrug his shoulders. "Did you hear me ask you to remove your hat?" Silence. "By God, sir, when I speak I want to be answered," I said, jumping from the bed. I snatched the hat from his head, and gold hair cascaded down the back of a leather jerkin. He turned around, and he was Elizabeth, who snuggled against my chest. "So that's why you wouldn't talk," I said.

She begged my forgiveness, which I readily granted, my anger at the young soldier giving way to the delight of seeing Elizabeth's beloved face. I asked how she had found me. She said she had dressed as a soldier and learned from the sergeant major who had prepared my horses where I planned to spend the night. She had persuaded him to accompany her to find me, telling him she had an urgent message from the king. He had not seen through her disguise, believing she was a young officer.

Two hours out of Versailles, the sergeant major had told her: "Sir, I must piss, but I know you are in a hurry and I don't want to slow you down. I can piss from the horse." He unbuttoned his trousers, while she did her best to look the other way, and went into a familiar monologue with the object of his concern, saying, "Alas, poor dwarf, you were once more fully grown. Believe me if you will, sir, I was once able to piss between the horse's ears. And what of you? Never miss a chance to pass water, I always say."

"I do not presently feel the need," Elizabeth told him.

"I see what it is," the sergeant major said. "You're shy about showing it, I understand."

Her account made me laugh until I was winded, and we had champagne brought up, and cakes, and turned her unexpected arrival into a celebration. What with one thing and another, I got almost no sleep. I was at her mercy during the night, and would have promised heaven and earth, and did in fact promise that when I left for Tournai I would take her with me. I rose at dawn, eased myself gently out of bed, kissed the tip of her lobeless ear, and took my clothing and boots in the corridor, so that the sounds of my dressing would not wake her. I went to the stable and shook the sergeant major awake, chiding him good-naturedly for having been taken in by a lady. He blushed to the roots of his grizzled hair, doubtless remembering the incident that had made us laugh so.

I gave him strict orders to take Elizabeth back to Paris and left a letter for her, which I dated: Every instant of my life. I told her that I had been too long deprived of her presence not to want her by my side, but that the purpose of my attending the siege was to obtain the king's favor, and that my purpose could hardly be served by taking her with me. These small separations, I said, are like the spaces that separate objects, which allow us better to perceive their form and outline. "Even though I am only gone a week," I said, "write me often, and let your letters be longer than Lent." With that, still warm from the night's long embrace, I was off.

I rode hard all that day and by midafternoon the landscape began to tell me I was in the war zone. I saw fields of wheat charred black, and smoke rising from the trunks of broken trees, and abandoned carts with bent wheels, above which vultures circled lazily. Amid such signs of recent battle, the present stillness announced that all life had been drained from the area. I passed by empty farmhouses with bolted gates and closed shutters. I saw a row of slight mounds on the edge of a field that could have been freshly dug graves. Crossing this no-man's-land gave me the eerie feeling that I had ridden off the face of the earth and entered the land of the dead.

I came to a crossroads only ten kilometers from Tournai and heard shouts coming from a large thatch-roofed farm partly concealed behind two smouldering haystacks. I spurred my horse between them and entered the muddy poultry yard. The air was thick with feathers. Two soldiers whom I identified by their blue jerkins as stragglers from our army were gutting mattresses. A third grimaced as he wrung a chicken's neck, dropping it into an empty mattress covering. A fourth was singing and dancing with what seemed to be a life-sized puppet, for its feet dragged and its head dropped, but when he turned around I saw it was the corpse of a young man. The dancer hummed a waltz, and circled slowly in measure to the music, wheeling the corpse whose head leaned on his shoulder, and occasionally pushing one of its legs back so that it kicked up its heels. A fifth had lined up the farmer, his wife, and their two children on the other side of the well, one behind the other, and was aiming at them with his musket. When I rode in, the one who was dancing dropped the corpse and the one with the musket lowered it. The others stared at me with sullen expressions, the same sort of expression an outsider would get from the habitués of a harbor tavern in Nantes.

"Where is your officer?" I asked.

The one with the musket, a swarthy, heavy-faced man, who had maintained a direct line of descendance with our common ancestors the apes, replied: "Back the road apiece, covered with dirt." The others laughed, as if to indicate that they were not foreign to the officer's demise.

"What are you doing with those civilians?" I asked.

"A scientific experiment," the swarthy man said. "I want to see how many of them one bullet will go through. Our officer told us not to waste ammunition."

"Quite right," I said, "but save it for the enemy, don't use it on these unarmed farmers." The terrified farmer in his shabby tabard was doing his best to shield the bodies of his wife and children with his own. They huddled behind him. The children, not fully realizing what was happening, peeked curiously out from behind their mother's skirts, and she scolded them, as if they had forgotten to feed the chickens, or wash their hands before mealtime.

"Well, you see, sir," the swarthy one said, leaning on the "sir" with heavy irony, "we've concluded a separate peace. We're going back to Paris, and we're living off the land."

The one who had been dancing with the corpse, tall and awkward, with bony wrists dangling from his sleeves, repeated foolishly: "That's it, we're living off the land."

"Look here," I said, "you can't do that. I'm on my way to Tournai to join my regiment, and I'll have to take you with me. Come quietly, and you have my word that no sanctions will be taken against you."

"We just come from there," the swarthy man said, "and we're not going back." The men with the mattress covers dropped them and picked up muskets that were leaning against a window.

"Your king himself is there," I said. "Since he is not afraid, why should you be?"

"He's there to watch us get killed," the swarthy man said.

"Yes," the tall one said, "you can be sure they keep him out of range."

"All right," I said, pulling my pistol from a saddlebag and leveling it in the direction of the man closest to me, "this is your last chance to come with me."

"Don't worry, lads," the swarthy one said, "there's five of us and one of him."

I could not dispute the fellow's arithmetic, and it occurred to me that if I tried to enforce my order, I would probably never reach Tournai myself. The essence of warfare is in knowing when to save one's life and when to sacrifice it, and I preferred to test my mettle against the enemy rather than against these scruffy malingerers. I fired at the tall one who had been dancing with the corpse, for he was only a few feet away from me, and as he stared stupidly at a poppy stain that spread at the crook of his right arm, I wheeled my horse about and spurred him to a gallop. They were slow to react, and did not even bother to fire after me. It crossed my mind that they had little or no ammunition, but there was only one way I could have found out. I was sorry for the farmer and his family, who would now pay the price of my intervention.

I did not, however, have the leisure to dwell on the incident, for as I drew closer to Tournai, several cannon shells landed quite close to me. Reaching a bridge, I dismounted and sought refuge behind its parapet. The firing continued in my direction and came closer to the bridge, and I began to hear cries coming from beneath it. I crawled to the end of the bridge and looked down. There must have been fifty women there doing their wash in the middle of the battle, soaping and rinsing as men fought and died. They shouted that I was interfering with their laundry, and to get off the bridge at once, for they said I was drawing the fire. I was so startled that I rode off to leave them in peace with their shirts and britches.

It is amazing how people are able to continue their normal lives while their countryside is being ravaged by warfare. It is as if two separate, unconnected events were going on in the same space simultaneously, isolated from one another by the very fact that they are not linked. There is a painting by Brueghel that shows Icarus falling as men continue to till their fields and discuss their crops, not even noticing the fabulous winged creature dropping into the sea. This is how the population feels about the war, if the war would let them. But unlike Icarus, sinking unseen out of sight, the war intrudes on the separateness of their lives. Their fields are destroyed and they are the victims of foragers or stray shells. Even allowing for the intrusion of the war, the degree of normalcy these people were able to achieve, as exemplified by the women washing their linen under the bridge, was a remarkable sign of their sturdy endurance, for their fields and valleys had served as Europe's battlefield for fifty years. Troops arrived like locusts, not every seven years, but every spring. And yet they did not leave their homes.

I Rescue the King and Am Rewarded

I reached the first trenches and my ears filled with the music of battle, the rattle of harnesses, the cries of soldiers, the sound of the fife and drums, the whistle of crossbows, the crash of pikes, the puffs of powder from muskets, the thud of horses falling on their riders, being borne by those they had been forced to bear. There had been furious fighting, for the earth, one of whose functions is to cover the dead, was now covered by them, by heads without bodies and bodies without heads, by arms, legs, torsos, and hands extended in one last grasp, the child's first gesture, and the warrior's last. Several thousand yards behind the trenches, the officers' tents had been pitched, in a semicircle, with the king's larger tent of fleur-de-lis cloth in the center, topped with his white banner, a waving target in the breeze.

The trenches had been opened and the front established as carefully as the seam in a tablecloth. Less than five hundred yards from this neat line dug in the earth stood the gray, crenellated walls of Tournai, and one could, with the naked eye, distinguish soldiers manning the towers, their helmets gleaming in the sunlight. The siege had lasted more than two weeks, and it was believed that, with most of the area's population having sought asylum behind the city walls, supplies were low. The Prince of Orange, who had been sent into the city as military governor, would either surrender or attempt one last desperate sortie.

How the splendor of our tents and officers contrasted with the horror I had seen approaching the siege. I left my horse with an equerry and joined a group of officers observing Tournai through their glasses. They wore white silk scarves and collars and furbelows of Malines lace spread over gorgets of gilded steel. The hilts of their rapiers, the tops of their knee-high jackboots, the housings of their holsters, were fringed and tasseled with gold and silver. It was a question of who could outdo the other, not only in bravery, but in elegance. They went into battle dressed as formally as for a royal audience, and made it a point of honor to return spotless. A regiment could be famous because of the battles it had taken part in, the names of which were stitched in gold letters on its flag, or because it had never lost a banner or a kettle drum, or because of the richly ornamented roweled silver spurs of its commander. Particularly with the king present, a siege tended to turn into a formal, ceremonious affair, where fashion became as important as strategy.

One of the officers, detaching himself from the group, ran toward me and clasped me in a hearty embrace. It was dear Lauzun, still youthful and ebullient, powdered and periwigged as if for a ball. He told me I had missed the fiercest battle of the siege by a day, for a cavalry regiment of Scottish mercenaries had left Tournai at night, hidden in a wood, and attacked our forward trenches at dawn, inflicting serious losses thanks to the element of surprise. I told Lauzun I had been struck by the signs of carnage, and asked him how things looked.

"The king's presence does not help," he said. "The maréchal

d'Ausseil is in official command, but the king thinks he's too old
and has brought your old friend the prince de Croÿ with him. He
has ordered Croÿ and d'Ausseil to command on alternate days,
like team captains in war games, with the result that each one
sabotages the other's efforts to make sure he will not carry Tournai
while he is in command."

I accompanied Lauzun on an inspection of the forward
trenches, where bored soldiers playing cards and drowsing rose
sluggishly to attention when they saw us. "The great trick,"
Lauzun said, "is to ride up as close as possible to the enemy when
the king is watching, and draw their fire. I can't tell you how
foolish we have become. Three days ago I bet the comte de Noblet
that I would stand in front of the forward trench for a full minute.
I threw myself back just in time, before the enemy could aim, and
he insisted on showing me he could do as much, but by that time
the enemy was ready, and when he stood up and shook his fist, he
received the volley intended for me. It caught him in the right
kidney and pierced his groin, and he died after three days of
agony."

Could it last much longer? I wondered.

"They must be reaching the end of their tether," Lauzun said,
"for the king only yesterday received a message from the Prince of
Orange asking him to abandon the siege because he wanted to
spare the lives of his subjects and his enemies."

"What did the king reply?"

"That he was neither one nor the other."

We returned to Lauzun's tent, which he asked me to share, and
he pointed to a knoll facing the one we were on, where he had
installed blunderbuses to support the defense of our farthest
trenches. A crown of heavy, earth-filled baskets had been piled to
serve as a screen against musket volleys. As we watched, three
horsemen sped past the knoll, riding like Tartars with their heads
low, and, waving long hooked poles, pulled down some of the
baskets and galloped out of range. "It's those damn marauding
Scots," Lauzun said. "They refuse to respect the rules of a siege
and cross the lines each day to harass our troops. I'm told that
plunder is their only pay. The Prince of Orange gives them five
liters of Dutch beer a day and their mouths are in a permanent
foam."

I stretched out on the camp bed Lauzun had graciously offered
me, and soon several servants were setting a table with clean linen,

Sèvres porcelain, the finest crystal, and Lauzun's family silver. "There is no reason why one should be uncomfortable on campaigns," Lauzun said when he saw my surprise. "If I risk my life, I can just as easily risk a few broken plates and glasses."

The king had come with a caravan full of delicacies, which the officers were invited to share, so that every meal was a banquet, and that evening we ate fresh sole from the North Sea, kept on ice at great expense, venison from the Ardennes, five different sorts of fruit, three kinds of sweet, and wines from the king's cellar. Lauzun opened a magnum of champagne to celebrate my arrival, and invited some of our fellow officers, and we were as gay and carefree as young cadets on their first campaign.

We drank toasts to every lady at court, which gave Lauzun the idea of visiting a nearby village behind the lines, where, in honor of our arrival, a house had been furnished with available ladies. The others seconded Lauzun's motion, but I begged off, pleading my long and arduous trip. They coaxed me and tried to pull me to my feet, and Lauzun, who was my senior in the rank of colonel, said he would order me to come, and playfully pointed a musket at me, as if placing me under arrest. Fortunately I jumped back on my bed, for the musket was loaded and went off, the bullet missing me by inches. Lauzun was so shaken by the thought of having almost killed me that he did not insist, and I was given some rest at last.

But I was awakened in the middle of the night by the same merry band, by now so drunk that they were drinking beer out of their boots, and singing barracks songs, and holding each other up. Lauzun sat on the edge of my bed and said in a slurred drunkard's voice: "My dear Ax, you'll never guess. There was a Flemish beauty who resembled Elizabeth de Villiers like two drops of water. We wanted no other. All four of us chose her, and as we fucked her we called out, 'Oh, Elizabeth, it's so good. Was it good for you too, darling?' " That was too much. First, Lauzun had almost shot me, and now he was mocking the woman I loved. I felt he had gone beyond the bounds of friendship, and I roughly pushed him off the bed and doused him with the bucket of water each tent kept filled in case of fire. That nailed his beak.* The next morning, his splitting head remembered nothing, and we remained the best of friends.

A message I had been expecting came before noon, summoning

* Literal translation of the French expression *clouer le bec*, to make someone shut up.

me to the prince de Croÿ's tent. I was sure he continued to nourish against me the same ill will that had made him send me to the Bastille on trumped-up charges. Now that he had me under his orders, he would be able to continue his vendetta. He was a cat on his back, showing only his claws, and I knew that I would receive from him nothing but scratches. His tent was lined with cloth of gold, and he sat at an ormolu desk, in the shadow of a bronze bust of the king, and scratched out letters, stopping when he finished one to warm the seal wax and bang the back of an envelope with his ring. He kept writing for several minutes as I stood waiting in front of the desk, shuffling my feet and coughing. Finally he looked up and his cold blue eyes met mine, and I saw in them great depths of unsatisfied vengeance.

"So you are among us again?" Croÿ said in a voice that made his every word sound as if it had been dipped in bile.

"Why, yes," I said, "I am a soldier. I came to give you whatever assistance I could."

He shuffled papers nervously and said: "We are not in need of assistance. I thought you had left court for good."

"No," I said, "I decided to come back."

"And what of your lady?" he asked. "Did you find her much changed?"

I had heard that Croÿ had prodded the king in Elizabeth's direction, as another way of spiting me. "Only by an attachment she was forced to form," I said.

Croÿ's mouth twitched. With advancing age, he was less capable of dominating his nerves, and was now given over to a series of tics that betrayed his internal agitation. His face was never still; it moved in constantly renewed patterns like a piece of modeling clay indented by a sculptor's thumbs. I had to look away, for I could not watch his contortions without laughing.

His face settled, and he asked: "And what of those where she did not have to be forced?"

"What do you mean by that, sir?" I asked.

"Only that a pretty woman at court does not long remain idle," he said, "particularly when she is known to have enjoyed the favor of her monarch."

"If you are referring to Elizabeth," I said, "I wish you would speak plainly."

"If I were any plainer, sir," he said, shaking his spine the way cats do when water has been thrown over them, "I would be coarse. But that's enough. I only summoned you to make sure you realize that you are under my orders."

"Yes," I said, "I have already been informed of that honor."

"I will keep my eye on you during this siege," Croÿ said, with a tone that meant my enemy would be on both sides of the trench.

I wanted to show him his threats did not impress me, and said: "And I will have mine on you, since you have never commanded troops in the field before, and seem capable only of making insinuations about ladies who have made the mistake of considering you a man of honor."

Croÿ banged his fist on a lump of warm sealing wax, which spread out like a red stain over the blotter. "I realize, sir, that you disapprove of my command," he said, "that you and Lauzun make remarks behind my back about the orders I give, and I will do my best to see to it that you leave the army, unless you are killed in battle before then, which I doubt, for you are the type who is sentenced to hang, and then the rope breaks."

At least we knew where we stood. I saluted, and—this will give an idea of the man's pettiness—he made me repeat the salute three times, claiming my fingers were not close enough together, or at the right angle. It was then that I vowed Croÿ would be taught a lesson.

That afternoon, Croÿ took the king to visit the advance trenches. The king made a fine figure on a big roan stallion, surrounded by his red-uniformed guards. A tent had been pitched where the royal party could watch at leisure, and be served refreshments. I was in the trenches with Lauzun, checking the range of our small cannon, and saw Croÿ take out rolled maps and spread them out for the king to see. Croÿ would point at the map, then designate some feature of the landscape with his hand, and the king would nod solemnly.

The royal party had attracted the enemy's attention, however, for shells from those small thick fortress mortars called Comminges, after a courtier who was prodigiously fat, began to burst around them, sending clods of earth against the sides and roof of the tent, under whose front flap the king sat. When I saw that the king was within range of the enemy guns, I jumped on my horse and rode up to the royal tent. "It is a gross imprudence to have brought the king here," I said, "but now that the wine is drawn it must be drunk." Leaping from my horse in front of the amazed courtiers, and the open-mouthed prince de Croÿ, I snatched the king's plumed and jeweled hat and exchanged it with my own, saying: "Sire, what do you need this bouquet of feathers for? For me it does not matter, whatever happens will soon be forgot." And with that, I mounted my horse and rode above the tent, brandishing the royal hat, and drawing the enemy fire.

When the shelling had abated, I returned to the royal tent to beg forgiveness for my impudence and give the king back his hat. Kneeling, I removed it from my head, and held it outstretched. The king smiled and said: "Although it seems a trifle large for you, keep it for the moment, and I will keep yours, and we will ride out together on a reconnaissance, for my generals do not let me see anything."

"But, sire," the prince de Croÿ said, "do you think that is wise? It is my duty to advise you not to take unnecessary risks."

"Bah," the king said, "look at the risks Gramont is taking, wearing my hat. You keep me bundled up like a grandmother, and I want to breathe the smells of battle."

With that, he called for his horse, by which in truth he could be readily identified, for it was richly caparisoned, and wore a royal cockade over its mane, and its coat was as glossy as a waxed parquet floor, and we were off, followed by six of his personal guards, and by the unhappy, envious glances of the prince de Croÿ.* The king, far from having been frightened by the shells landing almost at his feet, seemed to enjoy the risk, and was like a child seeing how far over a parapet he can lean without falling. There could have been no greater contrast to the calibrated court life than the surprises of a military campaign and the satisfaction of victory. It crossed my mind that the king was capable of declaring a war simply because of the pleasure he would derive from attending the campaign, and that one might need look no further for the cause of Europe's misery. Once again, we were the victims of his whims, as when, on a trip to Marly, the royal cortege had gone miles out of its way, and we only learned hours later that the reason for the detour had been the king's full bladder.

Now we galloped past our bivouacking soldiers to the forward trenches, and the king leaped over them as if running in a steeplechase. I followed as best I could, as the king sped across plowed fields littered with the bodies of the dead and wounded, apparently seeking to circle the entire perimeter of our defenses. The horse

---

* Gramont here is guilty of a zeugma, which I have maintained in the translation.

guards had been left behind, and I was having trouble myself keeping up with him, for his stallion, unexercised for days, was racing as if a firecracker had gone off under its tail. I spurred my mare on to catch up to the monarch and advise him that we were straying from our lines, when on the edge of a wood not fifty yards away, I saw three horsemen advancing toward us. As they drew closer, I identified them as Scots mercenaries, wearing over short doublets coats of mail rusted with winter storms and dented with saber cuts, and plaid stocking caps pulled low over their foreheads. They waved long matchlocks with one hand and held the reins with the other, and shouted fierce war cries as they descended upon us.

"Go back," I yelled at the king, who, I was sure, had never seen the enemy so close. His stallion reared and neighed, he pulled the reins hard to wheel it, and was off in the direction whence we had come.

I decided that with three horsemen coming at me, my best chance was to divert them from the king and pass between them to reach the shelter of the wood. I cocked my pistol and bent my head to the side of the mare's neck and rode between the first two Scots, hearing only the drumbeat of the hooves, the guttural cries of the horsemen, and the crack of shots from the matchlocks they were firing with one hand. I reached the wood and picked my way through the trees, and soon heard twigs breaking behind me. One of them, guessing my tactic, had doubled back, and now raised his matchlock and aimed it at my mare, apparently thinking that he would capture me on foot and obtain prize money for an important prisoner. I fired my pistol without aiming, from the hip, and caught him in the chest, piercing his mail as if it had been gossamer. His head fell forward against his horse's mane, but he did not fall off. The horse bucked, until his body lurched to one side and fell in the undergrowth, one foot still caught in a stirrup. I returned to the edge of the wood, where I saw red-coated horse guards firing in the direction of two fleeing Scots.

I returned to the man I had shot and disengaged his foot. He was young and fair, and his face wore the sleepy disappointed look of someone interrupted in the middle of a pleasant dream. He had none of the fierceness attributed to the Scots by Lauzun, but seemed remarkably like one of our own shy young conscripts, who were handed a uniform and a musket and hardly knew what to do with them. As a soldier, I did not relish the killing of others, for I felt that battles should be won by positional warfare and the intelligent use of firepower, resulting in minimal losses, rather than by butchery. If there was a military science, it lay in preserving that most precious resource, the lives of one's men, rather than in plugging enemy shell holes with live soldiers, which was the view some of our generals held of military strategy. And now this young Scot I had not known lay still at my feet, with his horse nudging his blond head as if trying to wake him. My only bond with him was that I had killed him, and yet I felt that in other circumstances we could have been friends. I went through his pockets, looking for the address of a close relative I could write to, and found these verses in his wallet:

> Oh, woe unto these cruel wars
> That ever they began.
> For they have reft my native isle
> Of many a pretty man.
> First they took my brethren twain
> Then wiled my love from me.
> Oh, woe unto the cruel wars
> In Low Germanie.

Who could know what circumstances had forced the young Scotsman to join a war in which he was not involved, or how many young women in his homeland would be widowed before they were wed?

Five hundred yards away, the king's stallion, surrounded by his guards, was impatiently pawing the ground. "Here is your hat, sire," I said. "You had better examine it to make sure there are no holes in it."

Danger had calmed the king, and his voice was subdued as he said, once more donning his wide-brimmed plumed hat and returning mine: "Do not imagine I will forget what you have done today. But pray, for the time being, mention the incident to no one."

I was in no mood to boast of my exploits, or to alarm the king's entourage with accounts of his near-capture, although I regretted those ancient Roman times when battles were decided by champions chosen by each of the warring sides, like the Horatii and the Curiatii.

The day after the king's sortie, the sky was a leaden gray, and toward noon the clouds broke and the rain poured down, disrupting our battle plans and dampening our spirit. Soon the hill where we had pitched our tents was rich, chocolate mud. The trenches lined with brushwood linking the king's tent with his captain's were washed out and had to be dug again. Cannon could not be moved, and cannonballs had to be carried by mule. The fodder rotted, and the cavalry was reduced to feeding even the king's horses with leaves gathered from nearby woods. After three days of incessant rain, with all the officers staying close to their tents except the ones on duty, who cursed their bad luck, someone announced that the downpour had started on Saint Médard's feast day, which traditionally means forty days of rain. The soldiers, upon hearing this news in the dank mud of their trenches, were so furious that they burned the good saint in effigy, hoping that wherever he was, the flames would reach him and prompt him to turn off the sky's faucets. Alas, the rain continued, until the king announced that pressing business at court required his return.

It has always been my turn of mind to convert liabilities into assets, and I saw a way to put the weather on our side and end the siege. I broached my plan to Lauzun, who was enthusiastic (as he is, I should say in all fairness, about almost everything), and together we went to see the monarch, who was glad that a way to end the siege could be found while he was still there to see it. Lauzun and I, certain that Tournai would be poorly guarded in the downpour, planned to set an explosive charge at one of the side gates an hour before dawn. Once the gate was open, our troops would pour in and extract a swift surrender from the Prince of Orange.

The regiments were alerted that night, and given double rations. The last of our dry firewood, preserved with great care under tents, was distributed so that the men would be warm when they set out. Wine that night was as plentiful as ditchwater, and as I strolled through the camp with Lauzun, stopping to warm my hands at each roaring fire, and watching the soldiers' heads nodding on their chests, I wondered how many were taking their last mortal sleep before going on to the one that knows no waking.

At four that morning, Lauzun and I crossed our front lines in a light drizzle, glad that the clouds blanked out the moon and made the night an ink bottle. Five kilos of cordite were strapped to a horse in saddlebags, and Lauzun had prepared several fuses, in case one should sputter out because of the rain. We had the day before reconnoitered a lateral wall of the fortress and found an out-of-the-way side door up a steep path. We took advantage of groves of trees, moving from one to the other until we could see the brass cannons in the fortress crenels gleaming in the light of the sentry's fire. We advanced to the base of the path leading to the gate. The horse carrying the cordite struck a rock with his hoof and the noise, to my ears, reverberated like the blast of fifty trumpets. A sleepy voice near the gate asked, in a tone less menacing than alarmed: *"Was vor Volks?"* We stripped the horse of the saddlebags and I whipped it hard with a branch. It bolted, running parallel to the fortress wall, and the sentinel left the protection of his half-moon lookout turret and went chasing after it.

Lauzun and I carried the cordite up the path, wedged it between the gate and a loose cobblestone, and Lauzun fastened the fuse to the saddlebag and took out his tinderbox.

I started back down the path, and Lauzun soon overtook me, saying: "Run for your life, the fuse has ignited and will have a terrible effect."

I did not have to be told twice. I ran sixty or seventy yards in what seemed less than a second, and crouched behind a large barrel that was lying in a field. The blast was even greater than I had expected, and blew everything in its vicinity into the air. My barrel exploded into splinters, and thousands of pounds of earth covered me. I dug myself out, and rumpled and dirt-covered, I staggered in the direction of our lines. Ten feet away, I saw Lauzun, on all fours, still winded by the blast. It was the first time I had ever seen him disheveled. I helped him to his feet and slung one of his arms across my shoulders. "Sweet music, sweet music," he murmured.

In the faint glimmer of dawn, like the uncertain white flame of a candle flickering above the horizon line, I saw in the distance what seemed an enormous gray centipede. As my eyes grew accustomed to the light I made out the long line of our foot soldiers advancing in formation, with their bayonets fixed to their muskets and held out horizontally, and behind them, the cavalry, its guidons bobbing and waving in a light morning breeze. I could also hear the pattering reports of the calivers fired by the Prince of Orange's men in the fortress walls. Lauzun, still semiconscious, weighed heavily on my back, and I decided to stop on the other side of a slight ridge and wait for our troops to reach us. They soon charged by and up the narrow path where the gate had been blown. After their first volley, the fortress muskets were silent for more than a minute, for after each shot, the soldiers had to put in fresh priming, shake out the old powder, smear the cover of the pan with tallow to guard the touchhole from the damp, and set fire to the fresh powder.

These operations gave our men enough time to approach the fortress walls, and soon they were clambering up the narrow path, which was so steep that, encumbered by their muskets and bandoliers, knapsacks and heavy jerkins, they moved from rock to rock like sailors climbing the shrouds of a ship. There was fierce fighting at the gate, sword clashed against sword and pike agaist pike, but soon our men poured into that opening like a surging ocean through a hole in a dike. As dirty and shaken as I was, I did not want to miss entering Tournai, and I followed them through the gate, leaving Lauzun sleeping safely behind the ridge. With victory in sight, our troops were irresistible. The streets of Tournai were littered with enemy dead.

I came upon a wounded Dutch officer, disarmed, on his knees, and pleading for mercy. I pulled him from harm's way into a courtyard and told him not to move until the noise of fighting had ceased.

Less than half an hour later, the *chamade* sounded, announcing the surrender of Tournai. At the same moment, it stopped raining, and the sun came out. Hostages were gathered to be taken to the king, who would decide the terms of an honorable capitulation. I asked the hostages where the Prince of Orange was. They pointed to a cart in the main square. His body had been thrown over a pile of empty charcoal bags, and was sprinkled with black dust. I looked into the vacant eyes of the man who had once commanded the most powerful army in Flanders with absolute authority, who from his horse had seemed an impregnable equestrian statue made of stone, around whom shells burst ineffectively, and who several hours earlier had been feared throughout the lowlands, whose very name made honest farmers scurry for their cellars. He now lay naked, with his belly to the sun, in a sutler's cart, his mouth gaping open, rolled in coal dust like a chimney sweep, with a pair of camp followers for attendants, who chattered away without paying him notice.

I went back to the courtyard where I had left my Dutch officer. "We were forced to surrender," he said, "we were out of powder." "The only reason we accepted your terms," I replied, "was that we were out of both powder and shot." With that, he admitted that their situation had been desperate.

No supplies of any importance had been able to reach Tournai since the beginning of the siege, and the city's population had swollen by several thousand. Food had run out, and people had at first eaten dead horses. They then began to eat the bodies of the human dead. They even ate the heads, like veals' heads, he said, with vinaigrette, after scalding and baking them. The principal activity of the townsfolk was to hunt rats, of which there were plenty, and eat those carriers of disease. In the last two days, however, the rats had grown scarce, as though they sensed the city would be taken. I took the officer back to the king, so that he could hear from the man's own lips to what extremes the people of Tournai had been led.

The terms of capitulation were quickly arranged, the enemy leader not being alive to dispute them, and not having been in a position to do so in any case. A small garrison was picked to keep the city under control, and the king announced that the rest of his force would leave once the troops "had thrown their bonnets over the windmills," a euphemism for the condoned day of looting.

All the next day, the reins of discipline were slackened, and our men were allowed to give bent to their natural rapacity. This was a practice I could not endorse, but it was the traditional reward of the victor, and penance of the vanquished. An endless file of drunken soldiers, bent double under the weight of their loot, lurched in and out of the camp, like columns of ants capable of carrying several times their own weight back to their own nests.

Lauzun, recovered and dapper once again, joined me for a ride in the now peaceful farmland around Tournai. We were stopped by an elderly woman gesticulating wildly in the middle of the path. "Your soldiers," she cried, "your soldiers . . ." She was too indignant to get the words out and put her hand to her chest, gulping air.

"Did they take everything?" Lauzun asked.

"No, your lordship," the woman answered, "they left me a few chickens."

"In that case," said Lauzun, "they are not my soldiers."

And we rode back to camp through adipocerous fields, that last being a word I learned from a scholar, designating the grayish-white soapish substance into which the flesh of dead bodies buried in moist places is converted.

That afternoon couriers arrived from court, having ridden all day and all night to bring news of our victory to Versailles and letters back to us. They brought me a letter from Elizabeth, who had learned that I had singled myself out, but did not know in what manner. "I am glad that you were heroic and are alive," she wrote, "for I want no dead hero and no live coward. Return quickly, I need you for my days and for my nights."

Lauzun, in a state of considerable agitation, interrupted my tenth reading of her letter, shaking my arm and saying the king wanted me in his tent. I ran to my own to put on my sword and a clean uniform, and presented myself minutes later.

The king sat at a desk, smiling benignly, flanked by an obsequious prince de Croÿ and a solemn Lord Privy Seal. "This gentleman has some news that may interest you," the king said, nodding toward the Lord Privy Seal, who cleared his throat and said: "Sir, I had intended to send you your letters by messenger, but the king insisted that I deliver them personally."

"What letters?" I asked in unfeigned and total surprise.

"The letters making you a maréchal of France, for which you will now give your oath."

I was struck speechless by this unexpected marvel, and could only stammer like an idiot.

"Sir," the king said, "it is my intention to recognize the great and good services you have rendered to me for many years, as well as your exemplary conduct during this siege, and to reward you with the office of maréchal of France, believing that you will serve me in that capacity with dignity."

I fell to my knees and gave the oath, and the Lord Privy Seal handed me the scrolled and gilded stick. At thirty-two, I was the youngest maréchal in the kingdom. Pleased as I was, I knew that this honor would arouse much envy at court. I was surprised, however, to see Croÿ advance toward me in the friendliest of manners, take hold of my shoulders, and kiss me on both cheeks, saying: "My dear cousin, you cannot know how pleased I am." It was the first indication he had ever given me that we were related, and it made me realize that I would now gain many such cousins, and as many new friends. The first law of the court being that when a man is in power, the others hold the chamber pot for him, and as soon as he slips, they cover his head with it. The king said that was all for now, but that he wanted to see me when we returned to Versailles.

I left the royal tent staggering under the weight of my new honor, and was glad to hear from Lauzun that he had not been forgotten, for the king had awarded him the order of Saint-Louis, and he would be one of the handful allowed to wear its diamond and ruby cross. I knew courtiers who would have given one or both testicles to obtain it.

As for me, my maréchal's office guaranteed me an annual pension of ten thousand pounds, a small castle near Paris, carriages and horses, and a larger and better situated apartment in the palace, close to the king's, and removed from the renovations of his architect Gabriel, who had turned the palace into a damned construction site, swarming with workers, and resounding all day with the banging of hammers and the whine of saws. It also meant that I would leave my regiment and be given some new post in the army. The only cloud in this bright sky was that my superior, as Inspector General of the Army, would continue to be the prince de Croÿ, whose kiss was the kiss of Judas. I knew the king encouraged rivalries among his collaborators, believing that the best way to keep their loyalty was to play them off one against the other, and I resolved to learn the tricks of this new game so that I would not be caught wearing the dunce's cap. As an ancient Chinese curse says: "May you live in interesting times."

As for the money that came with the office, I was glad to have it, for poverty is charming at twenty but unbecoming at thirty, and I had only been able to meet court expenses thanks to the gold I had prospected aboard the *Rôdeur*. And yet wealth as such did not interest me. It was too common at court, where one stepped over the rich, as in the rest of the country one stepped over the poor. The simple fact of being admitted at court was like receiving capital to invest. The palace was full of brokers and middlemen, marriage brokers, promotion brokers, change-of-garrison brokers, when-will-an-office-fall-vacant brokers. Everyone had his finger in the pie. I knew countesses who could obtain a naval commission for two thousand pounds, and a royal mistress who received a tidy sum from a doctor she had introduced to the king's service. I was glad my money did not come from this sort of influence peddling, for it is not true that money has no odor; it smells of damp palms, stale-breathed promises, and the sour sweat of greed. For such people, there was no such thing as a small profit. I knew ladies who took commissions for getting other ladies invited to Marly.

Scaramouche was once asked what he found most curious about the court and replied that in the palace one could always find *casa e bottega*. Money was only worth having if one had shown one could do without it, for it came between one and one's friends, and

I had never seen it change a man for the better. My only falling-
out with Lauzun came about when I lent him fifty louis. He felt
guilty that he did not pay me back, and avoided me, until one day
I approached him and said: "Give me back my money, or give me
back my friend."

And I had never forgotten the advice my father's banker had
given him, which I had overheard as a child. "Wealth is a matter of
mentality," he had said, warming his hands at the fire in my father's study. "During a sandstorm, stay in your tent. Avoid ship-
wrecks, and leave no flotsam lying about. Do not ride your horse
faster than it will go. Do not travel on unpaved roads. If a strong
wind comes up, go into harbor."

Whereas I hungered to ride my horse to exhaustion, to weather
storms, and to make new paths where there had been none. If the
wind does not find the sail, I say, make the sail find the wind. For
in truth, one can always draw back from the suffering of this
world. It may even be part of my nature to do so. But it may also
be that this holding back is the one evil I can avoid. And wealth is
a holding back. I kept always in mind the words of the Bible: "He
that loveth silver shall not be satisfied with silver. The abundance
of the rich man will not suffer him to sleep."

I have seen the gouty rich in their lonely palaces, taking constant inventory of their worldly goods, walled in by their gold,
made suspicious by it, their home in daylight hours besieged by an
army of petitioners, impecunious priests, pregnant scullery maids,
rheumatic old retainers, a provincial manufacturer of healing
water, a former mistress in need of a dowry, a ruined gentle-
woman, an acquaintance suffering from temporary embarrassment, the inventor of a new way to slice butter, a never-ending list
of disguised beggars. The rich are envied but not to be envied. I
remember my father's banker, who owned a property four times
the size of Bidache, kept immaculate by a platoon of gardeners,
asking him as they were walking through elms across our unkept
autumn lawn: "How do you manage to get dead leaves in your
park?"

I Am Rid of My Worst Enemy

We made a triumphant entry into Paris before returning to the
palace. The streets were lined with crowds cheering the king, who,
for reasons I could not fathom, had been dubbed the well beloved

—unless it was a sly allusion to the number of ladies who had shared his bed. Nothing impressed the Paris populace more than a military victory, although they knew as well as anyone that the king's campaigns were the principal cause of poverty. But the young men killed in foreign fields and the wheat famines did not stop their thin piping. Nothing else mattered as long as the glory of our arms remained shining. In this there was a genuine identity of views between the king and his people. The Parisians had even coined an expression: *Bête comme la paix.**

The contagion had spread to court, and to Elizabeth, whose eyes shone like a little girl's on Christmas Day when she saw me, for she was seeing the maréchal and not the man. Women are like those savages of distant Arabia who believe that if they touch a powerful man some of his magic will rub off on them. Elizabeth's good judgment was confirmed. She had not loved a loser. The delight of others in my good fortune has the result of robbing me of my own delight, as if there was a fixed quantity not to be shared, and Elizabeth's solicitude soured my good humor. I decided to bring up my meeting with Croÿ.

"The prince de Croÿ made some unpleasant insinuations about you," I said. "I had to put him in his place."

She was sitting in a straight-backed chair in front of her dressing table, at the same time looking at herself and at me reclining behind her on a divan, and she placed her arm across the top of the chair and turned her head, so that I saw her in profile, which gave her the hieratic stateliness of one of the Egyptian profiles I had seen on the obelisk an Arabian sultan had given the king. Whenever I want to conjure Elizabeth in my mind, I see her in profile, with her bust drawn back, her shoulders straight, and her arm folded at the elbow across the top of a chair—in that vision woman's grace is concentrated, and woman's unreleased force, like that of a crouching cat.

"He made advances," she said, "and I pretended not to understand."

"I am not playing the jealous lover," I said, "and cannot blame you for whatever you did while I was gone, since you could not know whether I would ever return. It annoyed me to hear your virtue questioned, not because I require you to be virtuous, but because it pains me to hear your name connected with rumors. In

* As stupid as peace.

Spain, a man killed his wife because he had heard she was suspected of adultery. She convinced him she was innocent, but he killed her nonetheless, because where she walked, the cloud of suspected adultery accompanied her."

"Well, then," Elizabeth said, bringing a hand to her throat, "have I met my executioner?"

"I am no Spaniard," I said. "I simply want to know what attitude to take should Croÿ ever bring up the matter again."

"And if I told you that aside from the king there had been no one," Elizabeth said, "would you believe me?"

"That's an odd way of putting it," I said. "It is a way of saying that you might as well lie, since I won't accept the truth."

Elizabeth rose from her chair and sat next to me, taking my hand. "Men always want to know what will make them unhappy," she said.

"And can you say that you have never lied to me?" I asked.

"I have lied the way I put perfumed oil on my skin to smooth it," she said. "I have lied about being busy when I knew you did not really want to see me, or to explain absences you would not have understood, or to make me more desirable in your eyes, or to keep from you unkind things people said. You can see that I am an accomplished liar."

"He (or she) that steals an egg will also steal an ox," I said.*

"My darling," Elizabeth said, kissing me lightly on the cheek, "you must trust me. You are a soldier. Think of me as an ally, who will bring reinforcements when you are outnumbered, offer asylum if you are defeated, and nurse you when you are wounded."

"What if I win?" I asked.

"I will applaud your victory, disclaiming any part in it."

And it was true, we had gone beyond the stage of courtship and passion. Elizabeth protected me, like a coat of silk brocade lined with substantial fur. Only an alliance of this sort made life at court possible, and it also gave us opportunities to demonstrate our mutual affection. She became an extra pair of eyes and ears for me.

Several days after our return from Tournai, the king summoned me, and said he was making me Secretary of the Army. He wanted me to enact important reforms, such as opening the officer corps to those who were not of noble birth. I endorsed the plan wholeheart-

---

* The French maxim being *qui vole un oeuf vole un boeuf.*

edly, for the abuses of the present system were too numerous to mention—regiments bought and sold like dry goods, officers who spent the year at court while their regiment was garrisoned on a distant border, and who were more often seen in salons than on the battlefield, an army top-heavy with generals because the government created unnecessary commissions to raise money, and regiments sold to bib colonels who had not yet reached the age of puberty. What the king took in with one hand from the sale of regiments he gave out with the other in the form of pensions. At the time I was named maréchal, for example, there were eighteen of us, whose annual pensions totaled four million pounds. Under the new system, officers would not have to pay for regiments, but would be expected to maintain them at their expense, except in the case of men of merit from modest families, when the cost would be paid from a royal fund. The king warned me that the prince de Croÿ opposed these reforms, but promised to support me should any conflict arise.

The king was right. Croÿ made my work impossible. He assigned me a staff of incompetents, whose main duty was to keep him informed of how I spent my waking hours. The military archives and officers' dossiers were in his care, and when I needed to consult them he kept me waiting for weeks. He sent a never-ending stream of officers, some of them friends and nearly all of them acquaintances, to petition me against changing the system. Whatever measure I took, he found one to counter it. The king had asked me for a list of regiments, with the purchase price and cost of upkeep of each. Croÿ had the necessary information and would not give it up. He wanted to undermine the king's confidence in me, and he would succeed, for complaining would only give the impression that I was unable to cope with my new position.

One afternoon Elizabeth came to my office near the Hercules Salon to report a conversation she had overheard. She had been arranging flowers behind a screen in the queen's drawing room, and Croÿ, having been to see the queen, was coming out of her study with one of his secretaries.

They stopped in front of the drawing-room fireplace, thinking they were alone: "There is nothing easier than getting rid of someone who displeases you," Elizabeth heard Croÿ say. "I have learned the technique by observing my servants. If a servant wants to get rid of a new footman, he hides what he is supposed to bring.

Say the master has asked for a handkerchief, he hides the handker-chiefs. When the impatient master rings again, the footman loses his head, keeps looking for the handkerchiefs, and arrives before the master empty-handed, and late. After four or five times you can be sure that he will be dismissed, particularly if you soil what he is supposed to bring. There are a thousand devices. Don't leave him a moment of rest. Pour ink on his livery minutes before he is supposed to serve a formal dinner. Finally, he won't even have to be dismissed, he will prefer to go." The secretary laughed appre-ciatively and Croÿ gave him a friendly tap on the shoulder. The identity of the hapless footman was not hard to pierce. I had to discredit Croÿ before he could discredit me. I considered the ways. After escaping from the Bastille I had stayed in Madame de Rouxpoil's brothel and observed Croÿ one evening indulging his perversions. I could see to it that the king received a report describing them. In a few days, the whole court would know it, and at court, ridicule kills. But would that be enough? They would make fun of him for a few days and then forget it. And the king, on the chapter of private pleasures, was in no position to preach virtue. It was the sort of disclosure that might work against me. The king would be amused, he would see in Croÿ a fellow lecher, it might create a rapprochement. The king would look at Croÿ's frosty-eyed, arrogant face, and no longer be intimidated, for he could balance his official hauteur against the vision of Croÿ at Madame de Rouxpoil's. No, it was dangerous to use a man's vices against him at court, where vice was s common as candle wax.

I had something else to use against Croÿ, the verses concerning Madame de Pompadour which had been planted on me when I was drunk, and which he had penned himself. It would be easy to prove to Madame de Pompadour that Croÿ was the true author of those lines, and easier still for her to bring the matter up before the king. But that was an old story, and the court does not like warmed-up dishes. Yesterday's scandal will not serve. Moreover, the marquise would not want to be reminded of the lampoon against her. As she grew older, she grew more pious, despite her pimping for the king, and she would not look kindly on whoever resurrected her youthful errors. This, too, could turn against me and leave Croÿ unscathed.

Alas, the truth was not good enough, something had to be man-ufactured. Elizabeth was right. Men will often more readily believe lies. Again she came to my rescue. It happened that one of her second cousins was a police inspector whose job it was to control the activities of foreigners in Paris. This inspector, like a great many others, had an old score to settle with the prince de Croÿ, who had had his son whipped for not doffing his hat to him in the street. Like most members of his profession, the man was venal, and the combined lure of gold and revenge brought him most solidly into our camp. One of the inspector's duties was to forward intercepted mail to the king's cabinet. The letters of foreigners were opened, and if there was anything seditious or informative in them, the head of the black cabinet showed it to the king, who took a voyeur's delight in reading other people's mail, that of distinguished visitors as well as that of his subjects. It was his way of keeping his finger on the pulse of the nation.

Our inspector had been keeping under surveillance a certain Lord Nutting, a free-spending Englishman ostensibly in Paris for his pleasure, who had been able to form important contacts at court and collect snatches of gossip. This Lord Nutting had been in Paris six months, spending lavishly on entertainment, and was now returning to London. Some of his letters had already been intercepted and forwarded to the black cabinet. It was child's play for our inspector to duplicate Lord Nutting's handwriting and pen an intercepted letter intended for the prince de Croÿ. Elizabeth and I composed the letter together.

"My dear prince," it said, "your information concerning the nymphets in the king's daisy chain will make him the laughing-stock of the Court of Saint James's, and I am deeply in your debt, as I am for the notes of the last cabinet meeting. It would seem that England has nothing to fear from France for the moment, since the king, having recently returned from a campaign, will not, you say, launch another until spring. We can thus count on seasonal peace. I am glad to have your opinion that the projected army reforms are bound to fail, for they would indeed strengthen the French cock at our expense. Again I thank you for your precious counsel, and advise you that the sum of ten thousand pounds is at your disposal in my offices upon your next trip to London. Yours faithfully, etc., Lord Nutting."

In drafting this letter, I considered the fact that the king did not like to confront those who incurred his displeasure. They were usually dismissed without knowing why, and without the chance to explain themselves. A short note would inform them that their time in office was up, that they were expected to leave the court by such and such a day, and return to their provincial residence, when they were not told to go forthwith to the Bastille.

I was thus fairly certain that there would be no confrontation between the king and Croÿ, giving the latter the chance to deny any connection with Lord Nutting. The king was secretive; once he made up his mind, he wanted no contrary views to disrupt his decision. I was sure that when he had seen the letter, he would not want to lay eyes on the prince de Croÿ again. Nor would he, despite the seriousness of the charge implied, wish to put him on trial, for he would not want the court and the Paris Parliament to know that one of his close collaborators was guilty of treason. Everything with the king had to be done *in petto*. He believed that everyone was better off for what they did not know.

We also had to make up a story explaining how the letter had been intercepted, for no missive with such contents would be sent through the ordinary mails, but would be given to a private messenger. The solution was simple. Our inspector knew several young delinquents whom he used for odd tasks, for it is in the nature of police inspectors to be on close terms with the criminal element, and he would simply hire one of these to pose as messenger. He could vouch for the youth, for he had information that could send him to prison. The youth could be shown to the king, if any need arose to confirm the interception of the letter. The inspector would say that one of his men, posted outside Lord Nutting's lodgings, had noticed the youth making frequent visits there, had decided to arrest him, and had found the letter on him.

We went to the trouble of forging a seal with Lord Nutting's coat of arms, a rampant lion gules on a field sable, with the motto *faire sans dire*, with which we stamped the letter. The handwriting was imitated to perfection, in case the king should ask to see other, authentic letters of Lord Nutting's. But the reverse of secretiveness is gullibility, for a man who never seeks counsel and relies only on his own judgment is all too easily fooled by appearances. The letter was forwarded to the black cabinet, and must have been brought immediately to the king's attention, for one morning when I arrived for my daily conference with Croÿ, I found him cleaning out his desk.

"Going on holiday?" I asked. "You deserve it, the way you've been working." Croÿ was so distraught, so numbed by the shock of his disgrace, that he seemed to forget his aversion toward me, and welcomed me as someone bound to be sympathetic to his plight.

"Would it were so," he said. "The king has ordered me to leave for my country estate in the Rouergue."

"He probably wants you to have a well-earned rest, and knows that you are too conscientious to take it unless you are ordered to."

"Do you really think that's it?" Croÿ asked, clutching at straws.

"I'm sure of it," I said. "In a month or two, he will order you back."

"Then why was I told to take all my personal papers with me?"

"So that if you have a spare moment you can work on the reforms," I said.

Croÿ shook his head and slumped into a chair. "I've been in *ce pays-ci* too long to believe that. I can sniff the direction of the wind. Mark my words, when I leave this office, someone else will occupy it."

"If that is the case," I said, "the king will soon realize that you are indispensable, and ask you to return."

"Yes," Croÿ said, brightening for a moment, "that is what I am hoping too. For I do not think I have acquitted myself badly of my office. I have nothing to reproach myself for. My loyalty to the king is absolute. Try as I may, I can think of nothing I have said or done that could have displeased him."

It was done for you, my friend, I thought, but said: "I will keep my ears open and let you know anything I hear. If there is a reason, I may be able to ferret it out."

Croÿ was overwhelmed with gratitude. He took my hand and said: "That is good of you, Gramont. We have had our little differences in the past, but I see that I misjudged you, you have a kind heart."

"Think nothing of it," I said. "I would expect you to do the same for me."

"Now that I am going," Croÿ said, shoveling folders into a leather bag, "you will have more chances to see the king. Perhaps his plans concerning me will come out in your conversation."

"Whatever he tells me, I will pass on at once, and I advise you to keep your bags packed for a quick return."

"I feel much better after having talked to you," Croÿ said. "All morning I have felt like a discarded old shoe, but now you make me see that the king may be saving me for more important things."

"I'm sure that's it," I said, clasping his hand warmly and bidding him *au revoir*.

It was the last time I saw him. Three days later, the king summoned me. He was standing by the window near his desk, looking out at the sculpted hedges of his garden, and toying with a gold letter opener. I came forward, knelt, and kissed his hand. He continued staring out the window, lost in his thoughts. I waited, and after a long silence, he said:

"I have just heard some very sad news of which I must inform you."

"Yes, sire," I said, giving my face the proper mournful cast.

"The prince de Croÿ's carriage overturned as he was returning to his country estate, and he was killed. His coachman was killed too."

"I am sorry to hear it, sire," I said.

"It is a great blow to me," the king said. "It is like losing a member of my own family. I trusted him and I loved him, and now, fate has snatched him from us."

"He will be hard to replace," I said.

"Indeed," the king said, "indeed. The death of an old collaborator is painful. It means having to change one's working habits, it means not being able to count on a mind whose every corner one thought one knew. And yet every mind contains dark recesses."

"What a shame," I said. "He was looking forward to a bit of rest."

"Yes," the king said, "I wanted to free him from the cares of office for a time, for it seemed to me that the weight of his duties was making him . . . careless. And now. . . ." The king's phrase trailed off, acknowledging the finality of the prince de Croÿ's fate. Suddenly, his tone became more businesslike. "We will give him a state funeral and a solemn high mass at Notre Dame," he said. "It's the least we can do. Will you see to the arrangements?"

"Gladly, sire," I said. I bowed to excuse myself, but the king motioned for me to stay.

"Now that poor Croÿ is gone," he said, "he will have to be replaced. Who do you see?"

"There are several qualified persons," I said, with a modest expression intended to convey that I excluded myself. "I think it should be a military man, one who knows the inner workings of the army and has had some administrative experience. What about Cossé-Brissac?"

"A mealymouthed hairsplitter," the king said.

"And Lastours, that stalwart soldier who has served so long as governor of the Bastille?"

"He is made to take orders, not to give them," the king said.

"What about the marquis de Beaufre?" I asked. "He has done a good job handling veterans' affairs."

"There is a scene," the king said, "where Harlequin is carrying a heavy trunk with his friend Scapin. Harlequin gradually drops his shoulders so that nearly all the weight of the trunk is being carried by Scapin. That is the marquis de Beaufre for you."

"I can recommend Lauzun as someone who pulls his own weight," I said.

"And he will pull us all down with him," the king said. "No, I have given the matter some thought, and I see only one man who can replace the prince de Croÿ as Inspector General of the Armed Forces."

"Do I know him, sire?" I asked.

"I hope you do," he said with a broad smile, "for it is you I am thinking of."

I fell to my knees, genuinely startled, and said: "Your Majesty is heaping kindnesses on me. I only hope that I am worthy of them."

"If I did not consider myself an astute judge of men," the king said, "I would give up my throne. A farmer who cannot tell a sound from a rotten apple has no business owning an orchard. Clever men, honest men, men of character, these one can find; what is rarest is loyalty. I have had some terrible disappointments on that score, and it is the one lapse I will not forgive. You have shown that you are attached to my service, and that I can count on you."

"I hope now to give you greater proof of my attachment," I said. I exited backward, in order not to turn my back on the king, all the while wondering what had really happened to Croÿ, and all the while certain that I would never know and would do better never to ask. How unfortunate that our happiness is so often gained at the expense of others. I had never wished Croÿ dead; I was only defending myself against his malice. He had brought it on himself, with his relentless animosity. His gift for making enemies had caught up with him. It made me shudder to think how easy it was to dispose of a rival, thanks to a king who fed on suspicion and was eager to believe the worst about his closest aides. From the day when our carriages had almost collided, Croÿ and I had been adversaries. I did not bear grudges, and would have been his friend if he had let me, but his vanity was pricked and he had me sent to the Bastille. After that, I knew him for the viper he was, and could not feel sorry that his fanged and hissing mouth was forever closed.

Having replaced him, however, it was the least I could do to see him to the door, and I arranged a funeral procession that rivaled in splendor those of the ancient Egyptians for their pharaohs. After a discreet period of mourning, lasting a week, I moved into his office. It was remarkable how old courtiers who had only recently favored me with curt nods now ran to warmly greet me, and how fashionable women whose eyes had once looked past me now fluttered them to catch my attention. I had in my early years at court felt like a piece of soap, diminishing with use. But now, with my new honors, I felt I had a greater density, that I displaced a greater volume of air, that when I entered a room I was immediately noticed, instead of blending with the walls, and that when I came up to two chatting courtiers, their conversation stopped, whereas before they had ignored me and kept on. I had been transmuted, turned into a more durable substance, and would never again be any man's scapegoat or whipping boy.

Instead of courting, I was courted. I saw womankind as an apple tree. Some men pick the apples, others knock them from the branches, still others climb the tree and shake it like very devils. In my new circumstances, I only had to wait for the apples to fall into my hand. Women sent me notes, and gifts, and the keys to their apartments. It would have been graceless to refuse them. I used them the way one uses a relay horse that one rides once and never sees again. From time to time I needed a change of skin, the way one needs a change of air. These diversions had no effect on my love for Elizabeth. On the contrary, by allowing me intermittent escapes from the conventions of a permanent attachment, they enhanced its value. Elizabeth profited from the comparison with women whom I could not tolerate for more than a night. When the heart is untouched, the pleasures of the flesh are urgent and quickly forgotten. If a woman grew insistent, and wrote that she had to see me again, I made an appointment with her, and asked Lauzun to keep it. In that manner, he was able to share my good fortune.

I Am Elected to the Académie

For that matter, Elizabeth was less interested in sharing my bed, although we continued to sleep together once or twice a week, than she was in plotting my career. My success had awakened in her the instincts of a strategist. She would not let me rest on my laurels; she said I must use my honors as leverage to win new ones, for money is loaned only to the rich. I was content with what I had, and was kept busy by my work on the army reforms, but I was Elizabeth's dray horse, continually spurred and prodded. One afternoon she came into my office and announced that Caron was dead. I had never heard of the fellow.

"He is dead, but he is immortal," she said.

"Oh, one of those," I replied, for I found the Académie, that collection of sallow bookworms, with their laborious hairsplitting over dictionary definitions, as tedious as the queen's sewing circle.

"Yes, and a new member will be elected three months from now," she said, "and that new member will be you."

"But I have written nothing," I protested.

"That will be an element in your favor," she said.

"I'm a soldier," I said. "I want nothing to do with these quill-drivers chained to their inkstands, these parchment-faced abusers of the language."

"Some of the greatest soldiers have been members," Elizabeth said, "Turenne for one. A maréchal of France is expected to become an Immortal."

"As long as I don't have to write anything," I said, for I saw she would not let the matter drop until I agreed.

"Not even your reception speech," she said. "The only thing you must do is attend the salon of the comtesse de Pastre, for the key that unlocks the door of the Académie is in her handbag."

"And mingle with the semi-authors and the quarter-authors, and the other fractional authors, who are like wasps buzzing around a beehive, talking of honey and never making honey?"

"Not at all," Elizabeth said. "She knows how to mix men of different and sometimes opposite turns of mind. Aphorisms fly, the conversation sparkles, new works are read. She always invites a few pretty women; she says they are the sugar in her coffee. Your friend Lauzun has gone several times."

"Then he's a bigger fool than I thought," I said, "to parade himself before a bunch of parlor mimics, grammar quibblers, and composers of medallion inscriptions. I would rather eat nettle soup than play the belle-lettrist in a salon."

On the following Wednesday, I accompanied Elizabeth to the comtesse de Pastre's salon. Wednesday was her night; it was on Wednesdays that the faithful came with their weekday wit. The comtesse de Pastre was not a bad old girl. She had a sense of humor. She called her salon her menagerie, and at Christmas she gave the faithful two ells of velvet to make a pair of breeches to replace the one they had worn out sitting in her chairs. Lauzun sent her a straw hat, with the note: "Madam, you cover my rear in the winter, let me cover your head in the summer." She was a small woman, with narrow slate eyes and a high brow, as smooth and yellow as wax. Her nose was an extraordinary organ, trained in exceptional mobility. One had the feeling that it was through her nose that she received her impressions of people. She looked like an elderly muskrat, sniffing and ferreting in the thicket of literature for the most tender leaves on the bushes. She was always worried about renewing her "inventory."

Her drawing room was hung in gold watered silk, over which hung paintings by court artists. It was of course more than a drawing room; it was an enclave where, unlike the rest of the kingdom, intelligence was supposed to reign. She had devoted her life to her salon, hardly ever went out, and was not known to have had any adventures save those of the mind.

She never took sides, and scarcely ever expressed an opinion, considering her role as that of arbiter. She was like that Englishman whose delusion was that he was made of glass, and who was terrified that he might bump into a piece of furniture and shatter. In the same way, she avoided any involvement in human passions. She liked people who did not ruffle the waters. Her highest compliment was: "I like him, no one complains about him and I never have to defend him." She once surprised me by saying that one should praise one's friends for their qualities rather than for their deeds, for if one was told that someone was sincere, one could tell oneself, I am sincere too, while if one was told that someone had rescued a drowning child, one might not be able to say that one had done as much, which turned the praise of the other person into an involuntary reproach. This is the way she was, always looking for subtle arguments. The success of her salon was mysterious. Several other women, better born, wealthier, wittier, had evenings that no one attended. It was like mayonnaise; sometimes it takes, sometimes not.

She hired an upholsterer and a cook, so that her guests would be comfortably seated and reasonably well fed, and announced that she was at home on Wednesdays. Soon, people at court began to say, "Will we see you this evening at the comtesse de Pastre's?" Partly, it was a relief from the monotony of Versailles, partly the snobbery of being among the chosen, partly the pleasure of meeting people one did not see at court, and partly a matter of sheer momentum.

The room was crowded when Elizabeth and I arrived, guests had not yet taken their seats, and we pushed past them so that I could be introduced to the ruler of the enclave, overhearing snatches of conversation as we forded the human stream:

"British America is forever lost."

"And so I said, Grétry is the French Pergolesi."

"I recited some verses, and she said, 'But they are totally unsuitable,' and I said: 'But, madam, they are all in Racine.' "

"Of course I have atheist friends. Why not? They are so unhappy."

"Let us admire the ancients, but not blindly—we moderns stand on the shoulders of the ancients in order to see further."

"The country doesn't know what it owes to men of letters, they are our streetlights, and brigands fear streetlights."

"Diderot, my dear, tried to swim across the sea of metaphysical darkness, but drowned in it."

"Alas, Paris is full of shop assistants who want to be authors."

One might as well have remained at court, I thought, to hear equally futile remarks.

The comtesse de Pastre's nose became quite animated when I presented myself, and she clapped her little hands and chippered: "New blood, new blood, how exciting! I hope you will be one of my rainy-day people, I mean, that I'll be able to count on you."

"I am a plain-spoken man, madam," I said, "and here I will be happy to bask in the light of others."

"Splendid." The comtesse beamed, pushing me in the direction of a gaunt, hollow-cheeked fellow. "You must meet our Swedish poet, Mr. Berglund. He is terribly interested in our grammar. He wants to know, not only where a word comes from, but where it is going."

I was eventually able to disengage myself from the Swedish poet's unintelligible mumbling, but fell straight into the path of a notorious bore, the marquis de Droit, which was like falling from Charybdis into Scylla. Droit was silky and unctuous with important people, and full of false erudition. He had become a member of literary academies on the strength of two or three Latin phrases he had learned by heart. I felt for him the natural antipathy that a simple, truthful man has for a charlatan.

"Shall I tell you, sir, about my new play?" he asked. The offer seemed impossible to refuse. "It is about a father betrayed by a daughter who idolizes him," he went on. "The unfortunate creature sacrifices everything to an unbridled passion, leaving everything for her lover, and finally being abandoned by him. It is a struggle between insurmountable passions. As for the heroine, imagine a creature half Héloïse, half Isolde, and half Juliet, with a dash of the princesse de Clèves, a sprinkling of Chimène, and a great deal of a lady too dear to me to name. I will say no more, except that I have an immoderate urge to make you cry."

I drew my handkerchief from my cuff and said: "Sir, you have succeeded," for it was the only way to get rid of him, and indeed tears had come to my eyes from trying to stifle a yawn.

"As for depth of judgment," the inexhaustible marquis de Droit went on, "I think it is fair to say that few persons can match me in that department. Many are the times I have thought that of all the duties in the kingdom, that of king would suit me best."

"I would like to pay you the compliment you deserve," I said, "but I would need the keenness of your own mind."

"That's quite all right," he said, "go right ahead."

I was rescued by Elizabeth, who wanted to introduce me to a Monsieur de Bernier, a smooth-faced, porcine man with wattles, whom she whispered was the comtesse de Pastre's confidant and a power in his own right in the salon, and who was, she informed me, susceptible to flattery.

"My dear count," de Bernier said, taking my hands in his two pale pudgy ones, "your reputation precedes you."

"Then I had best leave at once," I said.

"I see you are a man of wit," de Bernier said, "and I would like to ask your advice on a madrigal of seven hundred verses I have just composed."

"What is the subject?" I asked, as I searched for an escape route.

"Well, you see," he said, "my footman made the mistake of getting one of the downstairs maids with child, which gave me the basis for the plot." He pulled a thick notebook from his pocket, cleared his throat, and turned the cover.

"But, my dear fellow," I said in desperation, "when one is gifted with a talent as certain as yours, one must write tragedies and not waste time on trifles like madrigals. You remind me of a man of great strength lifting feathers. Allow me to say that I will not read a single verse until you have shown me a tragedy in five acts."

"You're absolutely right," de Bernier said, his face beaming. "If only I weren't so horribly shy . . . but let me read you two verses at random:

> The prince who a thousand of the uncircumcised defeated,
> Trembled at the thought that David might suffer ten
> thousand executed.

"Excellent," I said, "but why executed rather than killed?"

"I could tell you that the rhyme requires it," he replied, "but you have imagined that executed and killed are synonymous. I must insist that they are not. One says customarily, this man kills me with his conversation, but one is not executed. It is terrible to be executed, but I am not afraid of being killed."

"Yes, of course," I said. "It was stupid of me to think they were alike."

"Here are two more," de Bernier said:

> The might of David's armies was superfluous,
> Thanks to a series of events most curious.

"But that rhyme limps, sir," I observed.

"Well, sir," de Bernier said, ruffling the pages of his notebook, "I do what I can, I have tried to please the greatest number. I am beginning to think that you find my verses uninteresting, and yet I am sure of the opposite."

"And you are right, sir," I said.

De Bernier went on reading, in a loud declamatory voice. The contrast between the nonsense he was reading and the seriousness with which he read it made me cover my mouth with a handkerchief to stifle a laugh. De Bernier frowned and looked up from his notebook. "You are laughing, sir," he said.

"I, sir," I said, "I have never laughed in my life."

"I see," de Bernier said, "you envy work of a certain stamp, which could absorb the public's interest. Perhaps you have tried to write yourself, without success. I say, let the public judge."

"I did not mean to offend you, sir," I said. "Pray read on."

> Like Icarus reaching the heights
> And across the heavens seeing the sights . . .

"Ah," I said, "that verse is admirable. How beautifully you express lofty sentiments. It must be damned difficult to find the word that suits the thought."

"That's true," de Bernier said, flushing with pleasure, "but how happy one is when one stumbles on it."

Elizabeth said we should find chairs, for the formal part of the salon was about to begin, and we joined the large oval, at one end of which the comtesse de Pastre sat on a chair that stood above the others, on a low platform. At first, there was general conversation, and everyone was supposed to make bright sallies. I found the whole thing so confoundly boring that I did not open my mouth. The trick was to hold the floor, to seize a moment of silence and make it your own, to have the knack of being to the point, even if the point was brought in from a considerable distance. When everyone had been given his chance to shine, several men of letters read from their latest work.

First, there was a historian who had made his reputation by proving that the Chinese are of Egyptian origin, and that their eyes became slanted because they had to protect them from sandstorms during their long peregrination Eastward.

Then came the turn of a fellow named d'Alembert, one of the authors of a fat tome called the *Encyclopédie*, which purports to give information on every subject from rouge to revolution. He read a treatise on the senses, of which I still recall several phrases: "The advantage of the eyes is that they have their curtains, and can see only what they wish to see. Would that ears might hear only what they want to hear! Should nature be accused of negligence? Particularly when one sees that the tongue is locked between two walls like a madman, with only a tiny and limited passageway through the grille of the teeth."

This last, in an assembly where everyone's tongue was not only unlocked but running wild, seemed to me to defy common sense, and I said: "Your tongue, sir, has escaped from its prison." Necks craned to catch a glimpse of the author of this impudent remark, a buzz went around the room, the comtesse de Pastre looked as if she had swallowed a live frog, and d'Alembert was, for the moment, silenced.

"The idea is to praise their work," Elizabeth whispered.

"This is more than I can endure," I replied.

On d'Alembert's heels came a lisping poet named Posner who said he would read a scene from his tragedy *Pharamond*, and who explained: "I have tried to avoid what I might call the gigantism of Corneille and the flatness of Racine."

To listen to this self-inflating balloon compare himself favorably to the greatest tragedians in the French language was too much for me. The words escaped between the grille of my teeth before I could stop them. "You mean, sir, that you have fallen between two stools." The poet chose to ignore my remark, but several persons chuckled behind their handkerchiefs, showing me that I had not been far off the mark.

Elizabeth tugged at my sleeve, and I promised that I would interrupt no more. I placed my hand on my brow as if in deep concentration and dozed off until the iron-edged voice of the comtesse de Pastre brought me to attention. She was giving the faithful a glimpse of the following week's festivities. "I have invited a young author," she said, "who has written a fascinating book called: *Paradox*—that adversity is preferable to prosperity, and more necessary, and that of all conditions prison is the most advantageous."

"I wish I had thought of that when I was in the Bastille," I said. "It would have made the time seem shorter." Several persons laughed, and the comtesse de Pastre smiled, as if to show me that she too realized the absurdity of the fellow's contention.

"And," she went on, "we are particularly fortunate next week to be the first to hear a chapter from a novel by our dear friend d'Alembert, whose versatile talent we have come to appreciate. Can you give us an idea of the subject, my dear friend?"

D'Alembert, who looked like a plucked chicken, spindly and undernourished, sat up in his chair, straightened a sort of ridiculous turban he wore, and said: "It is a philosophical novel, madam, which presents a fertile field to eloquence, and in which I modulate my effects from the stoic to the cynical. I promise, in this work, to give the reader more fruit than flowers."

"Admirable," comtesse de Pastre said, with a little tremor of pleasure at the prospect of d'Alembert's new work. "And what do you think of that, Count Gramont?" she asked me, apparently offering me a chance to redeem myself.

"A novel, madam," I said, "I will give you a novel: I was strolling down the rue Montorgueil when I saw a pretty girl wearing silk stockings and pink shoes and a white muslin dress. There is my novel." And turning to d'Alembert, I added: "Can you improve on it, sir?"

He twisted in his seat as if he had been speared to be roasted on a spit, and said: "I could write you one, sir, about mistaking the privilege of birth for wit."

That touched me to the quick, and made the mustard rise to my brain. "Whereas you, sir," I shot back, "having no birth to speak of, are the son of your works." I had no sooner got the words out than I regretted them, for d'Alembert was in fact a foundling, the bastard son of the celebrated Madame de Tencin and an obscure officer called the chevalier Destouches. He had been named Jean le Rond after the church on whose steps he had been found, only adopting the name of d'Alembert once he was grown and educated.

A man of honor would have thrown down the glove, but d'Alembert fought with words, not swords, and said: "If I am the son of my works, then I at least am a man of honest blood. Have you ever heard of that book, sir?"

"Why, yes," I said, "I'm up on all good books. Isn't it a meager volume bound in calf, with a tiny preface and a long list of errata?"

D'Alembert's eyes blazed, and who knows what he would have said or done, if the comtesse de Pastre, accustomed to throwing oil on troubled waters, had not caught his attention? Elizabeth was furious.

"You will never be asked again," she told me.

"Nothing could please me more," I replied.

"You have forfeited your chances for the Académie."

"It was your idea, not mine," I reminded her.

"You turned the comtesse's salon into a barracks room."

"I said what I thought. Is that a crime?"

"Your only chance is to apologize."

"I have said nothing that requires apology."

At that moment the comtesse joined us, and I thanked her for a delightful evening.

"Yes, it was one of our more stimulating soirees," she said, "and your own contribution was not negligible."

"I hope d'Alembert is not the sort to bear grudges," I said, "for I have already forgotten what was said."

The comtesse's nose twitched and she put her withered hand on my sleeve: "Men of talent have always quarreled," she said. "Pythagoras threw his instrument case at Xenophanes, after removing the stylet, and engraving the formula for the square root on his cheek."

"At least tonight, nobody threw anything," I said.

"I hope you noticed," Elizabeth said as we left the comtesse's lodgings, "that you were not asked to come again."

"I am delighted of it," I told her.

"Ah, but you are not getting off so easily," she said. "You can offset tonight's fiasco by paying visits to the academicians and asking for their support."

"That I will never do," I said. "My desire to be one of them should suffice."

Several days later, I made my first visit, to a cardinal of recent vintage who had rooms at the palace. He was admiring his rochet and corn-poppy stockings in the mirror when I entered. I bowed, and he asked:

"Am I not well turned out?"

"Extremely well," I said. "Eminence suits you, you were born to wear the purple."

"And my servants outside, how do you find them?"

"I mistook them for the crowd of faithful come to pay their compliment."

"So you are presenting yourself for the vacant seat in the Académie?" I nodded. "When we are forty, everyone mocks us, but when we are thirty-nine, everyone flatters us."

"I'm hoping that your eminence will not look unfavorably upon my candidature."

The cardinal threw his cape over his shoulders, trying different poses, and said: "You have a rival, but he is not a threat, a bishop who wants to become a man of letters."

I left it at that, for I felt I could count on one ecclesiastic to vote against another. It was not always so easy, I sometimes had to swim against the current. Each day I reported my efforts to Elizabeth. One evening, she cut me off impatiently and said: "Darling, you spend your life making enemies, I have just spent the day trying to soften two members who are furious at you. Coislin claims you made fun of him, and Dugon that you recited some of his verses at a dinner and misquoted him."

"True in both cases," I said.

"They are very influential," Elizabeth said. "You had better go and see them."

I had to pocket my pride and play the penitent for those two fools. Coislin was a writer of fables more or less copied from La Fontaine, who had acquired the reputation of a refined wit. There was always some subtle distinction that only he had noticed. When I went to see him, he greeted me warmly. "Well, sir," he said, "I'm delighted to see you, you are presenting yourself, are you? What a good idea, I'm sure you have a great deal of support."

"I entertain the hope of having yours as well," I said, as meekly as I could.

"That reminds me," he said, "have you forgotten the evening at Madame de Choisy's when you were sitting next to a lady, and you never stopped looking at me and laughing and whispering in her ear? It was me you were laughing at, and yet I was no more ridiculous on that day than usual, than I am today, for instance, and today you are not laughing."

"But of course," I said, "I remember the evening perfectly, the lady had not met you and asked me who you were. I told her, and she said she knew someone with a similar name who was in the Horse Guards, and that started us laughing, that's all there was to it."

"Perhaps," Coislin said, "but you both had a malicious and mocking air that indicated more than mere banter."

"And yet it is the unvarnished truth, sir."

"I wish I could believe you, for it seemed clear to me that your laughter was at my expense."

He was like a dog who has sunk his teeth into the side of a stag and will not be shaken off. I had to profess my innocence for another twenty minutes before he grudgingly granted me his support.

Dugon was even worse, for he was the sort who always saw the small side of everything; he noticed the crumbs on the tablecloth rather than the meal set before him. His only ability was that of magnifying trivia. I came to Dugon beating my breast and proclaiming *mea culpa*:

"I understand, sir, that I have misquoted you, but I don't remember doing so, and if I did, it was unintentional."

"You did, sir," Dugon said. "The line was: 'What beauty, O Gods, what beauty.' Which you rendered as: 'What beauty, Gods, what beauty.' "

"Begging your pardon," I said, "but I fail to see the difference."
"You deleted the 'O,' " Dugon said.
"Oh," I said. "But the meaning is the same."
"Yes, but when one quotes, one must quote faithfully."
"But I quoted to praise."
"But since there was an 'O,' you had no right to remove it."

And again for twenty minutes I had to beg forgiveness for the omission of the all-important 'O,' and Dugon only yielded when I had sworn that in heroic verse, I considered him the equal of Voltaire.

Those academicians one had not offended, who were eager to give their support, were worse than the Coislins and the Dugons, for they felt that in exchange for their vote, they had the inalienable right to bore one to death. The Académie, I saw, was full of irreversible dotards, dukes so ancient they must have obtained their peerage from Hugues Capet himself, who kept me entire afternoons to discuss their weekly labors on the language in the office they called the bureau of doubts. This business was more of an effort than the siege of Tournai, and I deeply regretted having embarked on it. However, Elizabeth insisted that her greatest joy would be to hear me make my reception speech, and I persevered.

Finally, there was only one more visit to make. It was also the most difficult, for I had to go to Blois to see the old prince de Rohan, who had declared that he would vote for my adversary. I had never met the man, and so could not have offended him, but he either had listened to slander, or looked askance at my quick rise to fame, or numbered one of my enemies among his friends. He had in any case let it be known that if I presented myself at his door he would not receive me, but I had learned to spin around the balkiest of horses, and I arrived at his front gate one fine autumn morning, when the first golden leaves had begun to fall from the elms in his park. I announced my name to a footman, and after a long wait, I was led to a paneled study where the prince was sitting in a high-backed chair, in front of a crackling fire. He did not move from his chair, so that he remained concealed, but I heard a disembodied voice ask: "To what do I owe the honor, sir?"

"I hope, sir," I said, "that you will not be surprised if someone who frequents the court of Versailles wishes to bring back news of a man who is held there in the deepest respect and affection. They would never forgive me for passing through Blois without inquiring about your health."

"Sir, you are too kind," the prince said, "but is there not another reason for your visit?"

"Not a reason, sir," I said, "for my only reason is to pay you my compliment and convey the good wishes of your many friends, but an entreaty, for as you know, my name has been proposed for the Académie."

The prince, still invisible behind his chair, grunted and said: "In fact my health is terrible, I have vapors, my nerves get the best of me, and my internal organs are in a considerable state of weakness."

The old fool was as thick-skinned as a rhinoceros, I could see no way to dent his hide, and I was ready to admit the failure of my visit. "In that case," I said, "I will remain no longer."

At that he swerved around and fixed me with piercing gray eyes under bushy white eyebrows. "So you want my vote, do you?" he asked. "Don't you know I've promised it to your adversary?"

"I thought I might persuade you to change your mind," I said.

He rose, leaning on a cane, walking with the measured step of the aged, and muttered, loud enough so that I could hear: "Change my mind! Impudent young scamps. Think the earth turns for their pleasure." Then, addressing me: "Well, I don't want you to have made the trip for nothing. Come and look at my paintings. Do you like painting?"

"I don't know much about it," I said, "but I know what I like."

He shuffled out of the room motioning with his arthritic left hand for me to follow, and we entered a long corridor that was literally tapestried with paintings, hung so close together that one could not see the walls. "And what do you think of this?" he asked, as he stopped in front of a large dark landscape that seemed to me to have been painted with floor wax.

"Why, it's uncanny," I said. "I took the painting for a window through which I thought I saw these hills and fine flocks of sheep."

I knew that his art collection was his single passion. Instead of dreaming about people, he dreamed about his canvases. His animosity seemed to evaporate as I spoke, and I thought I saw a tear in his eye as he said: "That is the finest compliment I ever heard." I continued to find each painting more lifelike than life itself.

When we came to a self-portrait by a Dutchman named Harmenszoon van Rijn, so shadowy that the outline of the head was confused with the obscurity around it, I exclaimed: "Why, the fellow seems so real I would like to shake hands with him." Another portrait showed three rosy-cheeked, plump, half-clad women. Rohan said it was by another Dutchman, by the name of Rubens. I told him I could feel their warm shapes in my arms and their lips on my skin.

"You may not know about painting," he said, "but your instinct is a better judge than many of the so-called experts who examine a painting for hours with a magnifying glass without feeling anything." I told him the credit was all his, for he had assembled under one roof more beauty than I had seen in all my travels.

"Young man," he said, "I was misinformed about you. I was told you were a cad, totally lacking in sensitivity and culture. Whereas in my opinion you are a diamond in the rough, a bit crude, unpolished, but possessing, in their natural state, the necessary qualities to join our illustrious company. I promise you my first choice, despite the extraordinary eagerness your rival had demonstrated."

I was dumbfounded, and all I could say was: "Sir, you are most generous."

"I will even put it in writing, in a letter," he offered.

"Your word," I replied, "is worth every letter in the world."

And so it was that two weeks later I waited in my rooms for the outcome of the vote. I had invited friends and prepared refreshments, without knowing whether they were intended to drown my sorrow or celebrate my victory. Lauzun was with me, explaining the manner of voting. "There is a box," he said, "half black, half white, with no communication between the parts. Each academician is given a black ball and a white ball, and all the balls must be in the box of their own color. Since some of the members are very nearsighted, unfortunate mistakes can occur." In my case, there were no mistakes, however, and Elizabeth, who had an informant among the voters, ran breathlessly into my arms to tell me that I had been elected.

Alas, every success gives birth to a new problem, and I now had to attend to my reception speech. "The hardest part of that," Lauzun told me, "is to hire a scribbler to write it. Be sure to begin by saying that you do not know to what to attribute the honor you are being done. Maintain the tone of a sermon, unwind slowly like scripture. All you really have to say is that the Cardinal de Richelieu was a great man, that Louis XIV was a great man, that the present king is a great man, that the fellow you are succeeding was a great man, that all the present members of the academy are great men, and that you, merely by joining such an illustrious assembly, have the makings of a great man. You could do it in three words: 'Gentlemen, thank you.' And the chairman, to be equally concise, could say: 'You're welcome.' Unfortunately for those of us who have to attend, each of you is bound by tradition to speak for more than an hour."

The reception was a great bore and a great success. All of my new colleagues insisted they had voted for me, although Elizabeth learned that the vote was by no means unanimous. There was a good-sized crowd, including, what is unusual, quite a few ladies, and foreign ambassadors arriving at the last minute found that every seat was taken. I had my speech in my hand, and before climbing to the lectern, I told Elizabeth: "I must not forget to congratulate the industrious fellow who wrote this for me."

The prince de Rohan, the very man whom everyone had called my confirmed enemy, gave the welcoming speech, and saluted "not only the hero of Tournai, but the *connaisseur* of what is finest in all the arts."

At first, I attended the weekly meetings on the dictionary, for new members are expected to be assiduous and defer to their elders. In every group of men, from school to army to the Académie, there is an old-boy network one is expected to respect. However, I found these meetings a crashing bore, and I was not the only one who dozed through them. There was a group of five or six who attended regularly, for the pleasure of quarreling over word definitions. On one occasion, they discussed whether one should say "If I were you" or "If I were like you." The discussion grew heated, and the duc de Créquy, one of the most obstinate of these senile grammarians, told maréchal de Clérambault: "If I were like you, sir, I would go and hang myself as soon as this meeting is through." To which that old soldier replied: "By all means, sir, please be like me." I soon gave up attending such futile sessions.

I had a valid reason, for I had to go into mourning, my brother Antoine having died. He perished in the arms of a lady, who had considerable difficulty disentangling herself, for as his life ebbed, he held her more tightly. His last words, she told me, were the expression of an intense physical satisfaction. I could not think of a more fitting end for the poor fellow. He had lived for pleasure, and pleasure had killed him.

He had neglected his family duties, and caused our family

home, Bidache, to be placed in the hands of Bayonne bankers, but who was I to cast the first stone? I remembered him as a Falstaffian figure, lusty, droll, and always spending more than he had, as if that was the way to get the best of life. I could understand his scorn for court life, although his own did not seem to me superior. I had sent him small sums from time to time, but it was like trying to feed all the fish in the sea, he always needed more. He was as eager to disclose his vices as he was careful to conceal his virtues. That was my epitaph for him. I shed a tear or two, and arranged for the funeral in Paris. With Antoine dead, and leaving only natural children whose mothers would fight over an inexistent estate, I was now duke, which completed the panoply of my honors.

When I told Alfred, he shrugged and said: "Ah, well, life is a rondeau, it finishes much as it began, one stumbles in and stumbles out." I could not tell whether he was as unfeeling as he appeared. Perhaps his indifference was a way of concealing a genuine sadness he did not want to show. On the other hand, he had made no effort to see Antoine since coming to court.

He covered whatever he was feeling with gossip, as if saying that there was no point in lingering over memories of the dead, and that we had to get on with the business of living. "Poor comtesse de Merdon," he said. "She suffers from the illness known as military. Her skin is covered with an innumerable quantity of buttons. Her face looks as though it had been sprinkled with birdseed." I congratulated him on being so little upset. "On the contrary, my dear," he said, "I am terribly upset, and find it hard to control myself, for last night at a sit-down dinner given by the duc d'Aumont, he had the effrontery to seat me at the end of the table. Do you know what I did? No, I didn't turn my plate upside down, that's terribly *démodé*. I simply said to my neighbor in a loud voice, 'I'm not accustomed, do the dishes come this far?' That put him in his place."

"Are you coming with me to the funeral?" I asked.

Alfred sighed: "I suppose I'd better. When you're dead it's for a long time."

I Am Bored with Honors

My life grew settled after Antoine's death. There were no more sudden changes of fortune. My position at court was unassailable. I was a duke, a maréchal, a member of the Académie, Inspector

General of the Army, and a confidant of the king's. I had no taste for intrigue, and I served the king to the best of my ability. Now that I had scaled the heights, I realized that I was not on a summit, but on a high plain, where all the pettinesses and gluttonous ambitions were repeated on a different level. It was like traveling to a land described as exotic and finding that it is very much like the country one has left behind. The king remained capricious, moving in unpredictable directions, by fits and starts, like a rudderless ship. But I had learned to profit from his moods, and within several years, most of the army reforms I had planned were enacted. The waters of my personal life were equally becalmed, and most of the hours I could snatch from my duties I spent with Elizabeth, whose warmth and wise counsel sustained me through many difficult times.

Indeed, when I look back on those years from the gloom of my prison cell, I find it hard to recall anything worth setting down. Memory is a horse that needs the spurs of adversity. In placid times it grows loath to leave the stable. These memoirs are the child of adventure and desire, and I had reached a time in my life when my adventures seemed over and my desires were fulfilled. My days were crowded with matters that seemed important but are scarcely worth the ink to set them down: military inspections, trips to border posts, meetings with foreign delegations, consultations with the king. I balk at turning these pages into a court calendar. And yet there is a gap of eighteen years that must, like a tideless and glass-smooth lake, be crossed, in order to reach the final chapter of my life when I once again embraced uncertainty. During that time, starting with the year following Antoine's death, 1760, the barometer always read sunny. It was enough to make one long for clouds.

Rather than omit those years from these memoirs altogether, however, I have decided to jot down random items that enter my head, to mark their passage, and form a bridge to the chapter when the barometer once again begins to read variable. The reader will, I hope, pardon the tedium and irrelevance of these entries. They are signposts to guide me through years that were as alike as drops of water, and reminders that the real pleasure lies in the running of the race, not in the arrival.

1760—The comtesse de Pastre still held her salon, and I went once to please Elizabeth, but this time the blunder was not mine. The composer Rameau preceded us, bowed and kissed her hand,

and patted the Peking terrier nestling in her lap. The terrier barked, and Rameau picked him up and flung him from the third-floor window. The comtesse de Pastre let forth a short, shrill cry and asked: "But what are you doing, sir?" Rameau smiled and said, with perfect composure: "He barks off-key."

1761—Everyone that year was talking about the Marquis de Mirabeau, scion of a noble Provençal family, who had published a controversial book called *The Friend of Man*. Three considerable volumes on the oppressiveness of an unenlightened regime. It was easy to see that he had never had to cope with the problem of governing. The cook in the kitchen sees things differently from the guest fuming in the dining room because the service is slow. This Mirabeau became something of a public figure (read miscreant); he turned his back on the interests of his class to espouse the cause of the dispossessed. As to his personal life, his face looked like a map of those far-off lands strewn with volcanic craters. His every sin erupted on the surface of his skin, and though his appearance was monstrous, he still found women who considered him the flower of the race. He dissipated, he gambled, he drank, he whored, and to such gross misconduct he added a passion for the common man. I was brought up to believe that men should uphold the convictions of their class. Where would we be if priests attacked religion, if generals were pacifists, if whores were virgins and virgins whores? This Mirabeau was an apostate, and shouted it to the rooftops. I am not a believer myself, but I keep quiet about it, for religion is an affair of state. As for the book's style, it was like him, misshapen, ponderous, crude, festooned with running sores and strange lumps, and pretending to advance while standing still.

1762—The Jesuits were banned from France. This strange sect, with its Hispanic discipline, founded by a crippled soldier, set itself up on the lines of an army, and its director in Rome is a general. Its members dedicate their lives to the society's advancement and believe that all means are proper to attaining its ends. They are not above using deceit and hypocrisy, as when the Spanish king's Jesuit confessor told him he could have hot chocolate for breakfast during Lent without breaking his fast. They make a special vow of obedience to the Pope, and the question is: Can a Jesuit be a loyal subject? Louis XV, unlike his grandfather, rightly considered that a Jesuit confessor was a papal spy. The order formed a powerful camp inside the state and was believed responsible for the publication of a clandestine sheet criticizing the king's private life. Their schools were nests of sedition. They boasted that if they were given a child until the age of ten, he was theirs for the rest of his life.

1763—A Strasbourg chapelmaster named Mozart arrived at court with his two children, a twelve-year-old daughter who played the most difficult pieces on the harpsichord, and her brother, barely seven, who played with extraordinary precision with hands that scarcely reached the sixth. Many musicians heralded for their art have died without knowing a fraction of what this child knew. In London, Bach took him on his knees and they played alternately on the same keyboard for two solid hours in front of the king and queen. The queen kissed him and asked him what he wanted, and he said, "A piece of cake," for aside from his unique gift, he behaved according to his age, which reassured those who feared that such a precocious fruit would fall from the tree before it ripened.

1764—Was the year de Pompadour died, in her ground-floor apartment in the right wing of the palace, after a chest inflammation during a trip to Choisy. The king's eyes remained dry, but then apathy was his wont. Malicious tongues said that she took too many of the potions she needed to inflame her senses, for the king still used her from time to time. In her last years, she complained a great deal, saying that her life was a daily struggle. Her appearance was skeletal and she hid her wrinkles under a thick coat of rouge. Her glances had been more powerful than laws. She held no rank but regulated every rank, she wore no decorations but decorated whom she liked, she held no office but distributed all the important ones. All of those who were once at her feet lost no time whispering that she was a sorceress who beguiled the king, that she was in the pay of Austria, that she emptied the state's coffers, and other funeral wreaths of that sort. A number of scandalous epitaphs circulated at court. One of them was: She sucked too avidly on the royal lily. Her death was soon followed by that of Nattier, the celebrated portraitist, who killed himself at the age of forty. He was implicated in a ring of sodomites who preyed on schoolchildren.

1765—Lured by the promise that Diderot, recently returned from the court of Catherine the Great, would be there, I went to the comtesse de Pastre's to hear the report of this brilliant philosopher. Here is what he had to say: "What is she like?" "Like any woman." "What did you talk about?" "Nothing in particular."

"But what of her entourage?" "I did not notice anyone special." "And St. Petersburg?" "A large city, like any other. Cold." "You must remember what she said." "Nothing stood out. It was mainly small talk. Nice day, how do you like Russia, that sort of thing."

The dauphin died. He was a colorless fellow. His son, then a chubby eleven-year-old whom his teachers said had no disposition for learning, became first in line of succession.

1766—If I had a thousand pounds for every duel I have fought, I would be a rich man. That year the king, upset by casualties in one of his guards units, asked me to speak to the officer corps and denounce the practice, which is comparable to the king himself making a speech to denounce the cruelty of hunting stags. Nonetheless, I did my duty, although Lauzun said my voice lacked conviction. I thought my speech was rather good, for I have always been able, when circumstances demanded it, to argue either side of a question persuasively. "This barbarous, Gothic prejudice," I said, "child of ignorance and ferocity, which, ceaselessly pitting against one another friends, brothers, and fellow citizens, risks the most precious heads and exposes the best of men to the blows of a vile ruffian, is beneath you, gentlemen." I almost convinced myself.

1767—There was an execution in Saint-Jean cemetery that year, which was convenient because it is easy to guard and hidden from the eyes of the curious. The oilcloths strung above the tiny shops of the fishwives were removed, for they are suspended by four sticks, possible weapons in an uprising . . . as if every fishwife did not have a broomstick. People knew what was going on and cried for mercy, and the troops outside the cemetery turned toward the crowd with fixed bayonets. Among the well-to-do and the fashionable, however, public executions remained popular. The Parisienne, who faints at the sight of a spider, will push her way through dense crowds to see a criminal hanged.

1768—Elizabeth and I were dining at Trianon with the king and a few others, and the conversation turned to hunting and gunpowder, and the king admitted he did not know how gunpowder is made. At that, everyone competed to be found as ignorant as the monarch, and Elizabeth announced that she did not know where the rouge she puts on her cheeks comes from. The king asked a footman to fetch the *Encyclopédie*, and we opened those heavy tomes like the daughters of Lycomedes throwing themselves on Odysseus' jewels. The king read aloud the article on the divine right of monarchs, and everyone found the article he wanted. The prince de Conti said: "Sire, you are fortunate that under your reign there were men capable of knowing all subjects and transmitting them to posterity. Everything is here, from how to make a needle to how to make a cannon, from the infinitely small to the infinitely great." And this was the work whose editors were hounded and exiled, and whose very publication had long been banned. At court what is prohibited on Tuesday becomes fashionable on Thursday.

1769—Five years after Pompadour's death, a new mistress was presented at court, who called herself the comtesse du Barry. Du Barry was the name of her pimp, who sold her virginity twenty times at least. Lauzun knew her as an inmate of Madame de Rouxpoil's brothel. She impressed him with her skills and with her gifts as an actress. As a young girl, she married a man three times her age who brought her to the capital. She told Lauzun how she pretended to lose her virginity, which she seems never to have had in earnest, to that credulous old fool. "I cried," she said, "I tore my hair, I shouted, I scratched, I was as natural as a newborn babe. His frivolity was small and wilted, it looked like a bit of folded parchment, but I begged him to pity me and not tear me to pieces. Vanity convinced him that he had made heroic efforts."

The king, no less vain, believes that her only previous lover was Lauzun. He said she gave him pleasures he had never before known. Lauzun told him: "Sire, that is because you have never been to a brothel."

She was as pretty as if she had been made with a paintbrush, with long blond hair, a perfectly oval face, tiny feet, a heart-shaped mouth, and skin as smooth as cream, but she was no more a comtesse than I am Pope. Everyone snubbed her, and it was finally Elizabeth who agreed to present her at court, feeling sorry for this tarnished lamb astray in a forest where wolf packs lurk. Elizabeth's good deed made her the victim of slanderous rumors that the king had paid her debts in exchange for the presentation. However, when du Barry began to receive in her own apartments, there were precious few who turned down her invitations, particularly since at the bottom, written in her untutored hand, were the words: "His Majesty will honor me with his presence."

1770—The dauphin was married in great pomp that year to the daughter of the Austrian emperor Francis I. The fifteen-year-old princess Marie Antoinette crossed the border at Strasbourg, where she was given a complete change of clothes on a small island in the middle of a river. The king sent a secretary to watch and report back to him, for he was impatient to know what she looked like. "Does she have big breasts?" the king asked. The secretary replied that she had a charming face and beautiful eyes. "That is not what I am asking," the king insisted. The secretary protested that he had not allowed his eyes to take in that particular part of her anatomy. "You are a fool," the king said. "That is the first thing one notices about women." Her face was found pretty, except for a Hapsburg lip, that is a thick, pendulous lower lip. She was a sprite, gay, fun-loving, disdainful of court formalities. She was assigned a duenna, the comtesse de Noailles, whom she called Madame Etiquette. She brought with her the slapdash usages of the Viennese court, which were not without charm, and formed an agreeable contrast to the great lumbering lout that is her husband. It was reported that he was incapable of achieving the principal object of marriage, owing to a foreskin so compressed that it would not pull back at the moment of introduction and caused a sharp pain where there should have been pleasure, which obliged him to moderate the impulsion for the accomplishment of the act.

1771—The king banned *trente et quarante* after it was played at Marly for ten consecutive hours. A third *frotteur** was named to control the consumption of candles in the palace. An altogether uninspiring year.

1772—I was invited that year, with a great many others, to a ball in Marseille given by a madcap fellow, the marquis de Sade, who knows the inside of the Bastille as well as any man, having been sent there to ponder his assault on a fourteen-year-old girl, during which he subjected her to all the transports of a depraved imagination. There was a lavish supper, and the sweet consisted of chocolate candies laced with the powder of cantharides flies, the medicinal properties of which are well known. Those who partook of the chocolates began to burn with an immodest ardor, and abandoned themselves to all sorts of excesses. The ball, a formal affair until then, turned into one of those licentious assemblies made popular by the ancient Romans. Women of proven propriety were unable to resist the uterine rage. Monsieur de Sade, who likes to be different, enjoyed his sister-in-law. I was pursued by a lady

* The *frotteur* was a functionary who watched over the lighting and snuffing of the thousands of candles used in the palace and who was allowed to keep the stubs for resale.

who seemed to have taken more than one helping of the sweet. I could not see her face, for everyone wore masks, and I accompanied her to a room where she wasted no time stretching out on a silk settee. When she removed her domino, I saw a face as pockmarked and wrinkled as a painted garden chair left out in the rain.

Dropping to my knees, I said: "Madam, forgive my effrontery. I am a miserable scoundrel to have thus lacked respect toward you. Please have the generosity to attribute my rashness to the intoxicating atmosphere of the ball. I am not worthy of a single glance from you, and I came here to offer you my most humble apologies."

And with that, not giving her the time to reply, I turned on my heels and left. The pleasures of the flesh, pushed to this degree of frantic rutting, almost cease to be enjoyable. Several persons died of their priapic excesses.

1773—The dauphin's marriage did not make him less listless. Lauzun, believing that the court was forgetting the old values, found him playing lawn croquet one day and showed him a pamphlet defending patriotism. "What is the gist of it?" the dauphin asked.

"It's about an old word we have almost forgotten," Lauzun said, "and you are the right man to remember it, sire, for the word is patriotism."

"I don't like pamphlets," the dauphin said.

"You love the truth too much not to read this one," Lauzun said.

"I never read new things," the dauphin said. "Only the classics."

1774—Was the year the king died, on May 10, at 3:20 in the afternoon. He was exhausted by his pleasures, and told his doctor: "It is time to put the drag on the wheel," to which the doctor replied: "Sire, you would do better to unharness completely." One morning he awoke covered with red sores, and although everyone knew it was smallpox, no one dared pronounce the word. His own children would not enter the sickroom. He was attended by six doctors, five surgeons, and three apothecaries, who took turns feeling his pulse, and looking at his tongue, and commenting on the fine color of that royal organ, and telling him he was almost cured.

I tried several times to see him, but his head doctor, a charlatan of obscure trans-Dnieper origins named Jansen, would not let me into the darkened chamber. The only treatment he knew was bleeding, and when I remarked that to rob the king of his blood was to rob him of his strength and therefore lessen his resistance to the malady, Jansen gave me the patient look the man of science gives the student who, although willing, is slow to understand, and said: "Nothing pullulates like blood, and yet we need so little to subsist. Smallpox, you see, is an effervescence of the blood produced by a sour and corrosive yeast that threatens the brain. This yeast must be evacuated through the opening of the saphena. The blood is drawn from the trunk of the artery to the part of the body that is being bled, that is what we call derivation, and this at the same time draws to the most removed parts of the body new blood, which is what we call attraction."

Thus the king was made three times to suffer derivation and attraction, and on the third, weak from loss of blood, begged the doctors to desist, for he knew that it meant the last sacraments. An English doctor named Sutton, famous for his method of inoculation, came to Versailles, but was kept from seeing the monarch by the tribe of official doctors, who would rather have had their patient die than see him cured by an outsider. The king grew so weak they had to keep putting vinegar under his nose to revive him. There was a kind of justice in the fact that the king, who loved to make unkind remarks about the health of his courtiers, and announce their imminent demise, was now being given the time to savor his own. If the smallpox had not been enough to kill him, the bleedings would have done the rest. His body stank so that it had to be placed inside a double-lined lead coffin. It was carried through the streets of Paris in a heavy fog, though not as heavy as the fog of intrigue that surrounds kings when they are alive.

As soon as the news was out, what remained of the court left for Choisy. Rare were the tears shed for the monarch. I had served him but not loved him; he was too unstable and self-indulgent, and never outgrew a streak of childish cruelty. Those who, like myself, were often in his presence, grew increasingly conscious of his faults. What would he have been had he not been born a king? A petticoat-chaser, an idle dreamer, a general who wins battles on maps and loses them in the field, a merchant whose employees rob him, a minor functionary corrupted by women, he could have been any of these. It was our misfortune that instead he was king.

His death removed the rug of patronage from under the feet of those who enjoyed his favor. The first to fall was Madame du Barry, who on the night of the king's funeral was banished to the Pont-aux-Dames convent, where the nuns, expecting a horned and fork-tongued female demon, were astonished to find a soulful beauty who could have posed for a portrait of the Annunciation. As for myself, I had neglected to prepare a path of retreat, for the king's death was unexpected, and I had trouble masking my contempt for the gross dribbling fellow who succeeded him. All cabinet members were expected to hand in their resignations, and he would keep on those he wanted.

Also, Elizabeth, by presenting Madame du Barry at court, had alienated the old guard, which was already gloating over the royal mistress' disgrace. The new queen, for all her gamin ways, could be stubborn and even vindictive, and made no secret of her loathing for Madame du Barry. She surrounded herself with her own group of adulators, whereas Elizabeth was contaminated by her contact with the fallen mistress. At court, such reversals are the coin of the realm, and one has to learn that today's prince can become tomorrow's pauper.

1775—The new king rejected my resignation and told me he had the same trust in me his grandfather had. I replied that my attachment to him would be just as strong. Elizabeth escaped following Madame du Barry into exile but was overlooked on the list of ladies-in-waiting for the new queen, although her birth and position at court made her an obvious choice.

Elizabeth and I consolidated the friendships we had left, and to that effect, went to see the comtesse de Pastre, who had grown quite deaf, which made her no less talkative. She whispered as I left: "I have identified in the heavens of your amorous adventures sixty principal constellations, without counting the Milky Way of your ephemeral escapades."

Alas, I lived on my reputation. In my twenties, I vaulted out of bed each morning with a stiff pole that I endeavored to rid myself of by nightfall. In my fiftieth year, I found myself in that pleasant morning state perhaps once every two weeks. Elizabeth, on the other hand, whose loveliness was unfaded at forty, told me that she was growing more libidinous with each passing year, and indeed, she sought me out more often than in the springtime of our passion. A scientist should chart the rising and waning of passion in each sex, and the fleeting moment when they intersect.

1776—The crisis for the year was that one afternoon everyone thought that the king was spitting blood, but then someone remembered that he had been chewing cachous. In any event, a large bowl of leek soup cured him.

THE WAY UP

1777—The prince de Rohan took me that year to the Randon de Boisset auction in the Hôtel Aligre, on the rue Saint Honoré. About two hundred fifty paintings were knocked down, including Van Rijn's "The Pilgrims of Emmaus," which he bid on, unsuccessfully. Miffed, he bid more than he could afford for Rubens' "Descent from the Cross," and got it. I told him, in my pose as an art lover, that I would lend him the sum he needed. I must say that this painting is not without interest, for it tells a story. Christ's friends are removing His body from the cross before nightfall, in order that the Sabbath may be unpolluted. Two strong men have mounted ladders, and having released the body, are lowering it in a winding sheet. The body's weight is indicated by the bulging muscles of the older man, who holds the sheet in his teeth as he braces himself against the crossbeam. The body's inertness is shown by a hanging arm and a sagging head. The finality of death is utterly convincing, and the possibility of resurrection as utterly remote.

I Fall from Grace

1778—In August of that year, the queen approached the king and said: "Sire, I have come to ask for justice. One of your subjects has violently insulted me."

"What is that you say?" the king asked. "Why that is impossible."

"Sire, I can affirm that I even received blows," Marie Antoinette said.

"Madam, you must be joking," replied the king.

"Certainly not, sire," said the queen, "there was someone bold enough to kick me in the stomach."

News of this happy event contrasted with my own fortunes, which resumed their former uncertainty. My life was never a straight line, but a zigzag, with depths that matched the heights. Things that last are not worth having, and things worth having do not last. A man's will is a paltry thing, pitched against the outside forces that pull the strings of the wooden marionettes we are. The wheel turns, and one finds oneself, as in a race on a slow horse, one lap behind. To the observer, nothing has changed, for he sees the horses running together, without knowing that one among them has fallen so far behind that the others are overtaking him for the second time.

So at first did I not notice that my position at court was in jeopardy. When I could not see the king, I attributed his absences to his natural listlessness. When I was not consulted, I thought I was being given my rein. When I was not invited to the daily hunts, which constitute the king's only passion, I took that as a tribute to the urgency of my work. When the king appointed the comte de Saint-Germain to take my place on a long inspection tour of border fortifications, I felt he was freeing me to carry on more important tasks. Alas, we have an infinite capacity for self-delusion. Like the husband who invents subtle arguments to find his unfaithful wife faithful, or his faithful wife unfaithful, I tailored the evidence to fit my needs. But finally, the sword of Damocles, which I had mistaken for a laurel wreath, fell.

On Saint-Germain's return, I was told that I needed a rest, and he was appointed Inspector General of the Army in my stead. I asked to see the king, but he was always occupied, and transmitted his wishes through intermediaries. Everywhere he went, there were screens around him. He had changed the court ceremonial so that courtiers were no longer able to approach him when he rose and retired, and at half a dozen times in the course of the day. The previous king, his grandfather, for all his faults, had the courage to tell one unpleasant news himself. This one was an oversized, quivering jellyfish. I felt like a piece of unwanted furniture, which the new owner of a house, having brought his own, stores in the attic. My only fault was my years of long and faithful service. I felt I was entitled to a bill of particulars, for even a common criminal is told the charges against him. Apparently, in my case, there was none, and I was dismissed without a word, of either praise or displeasure. I could understand that the king did not wish to retain his grandfather's collaborators, that he wanted to surround himself with men he had chosen rather than men who had been chosen for him and with whom he felt, because of their experience and long friendship with the previous king, at a disadvantage. But then why not say so, in a forthright manner, instead of skulking around corners? The coward's way is ruthless.

The bad news kept coming in unsigned slips of paper marked with the royal seal. My Inspector General's pension was discontinued. This I had expected. My maréchal's pension was cut in half, an economy measure decided by the comte de Saint-Germain, who had already begun undoing the patient reforms I had spent years to achieve. This obscure provincial nobleman, who had once exiled himself to serve the Danish court, now turned the army back into a private preserve for the well-born, excluding all others from commissions. This, I knew, was the path of military decline. It sorrowed me to see the king manipulated by men who set their own interests above the nation's. The next blow came when I was told that Elizabeth and I were no longer welcome at Marly, where we had previously gone on every royal weekend as a matter of course, not waiting to be designated.

I could not tell whether Elizabeth was the victim of my disfavor, or whether she was still under the cloud of her association with Madame du Barry. She too was suffering the pains of exclusion. She was repeatedly snubbed by the queen and her two constant companions, the duchesse de Polignac and the princesse de Lamballe. As in my case, there was nothing overt. But when Elizabeth came into the queen's gaming room, the queen would stop the game. And at chapel, when the queen chose different ladies to take up the collection, Elizabeth was never among them. Thus, by a thousand tiny discriminations, Elizabeth was made to feel that her presence at court was unwelcome. She had always been one of the court's principal ornaments. When she entered a room, it seemed that an additional chandelier had been lit.

She was without malice, which made her the single member of a unique species, and thus had no enemies. Her very kindness made her vulnerable, just as a man who has no thoughts of harming anyone does not think to carry a weapon to protect himself. The wind-sniffers sensed that to be rude to Elizabeth was a way to ingratiate themselves with the queen, and she suddenly found old friends avoiding her. She did not have my defense against misfortune, a skeptical nature that leads me to expect the worst from people and accept their failings as natural. She was a rare flower unconscious of her rareness, and unaware that she blossomed alone in a garden overrun with crabgrass and nettles. Rare flowers are delicate, they only thrive in friendly soils, and the chill air that now blew about Elizabeth affected her health. She took to her bed, lost her appetite, and spent long melancholy days, relieved only by my visits. Her loss of weight was alarming, and when I suggested she see a doctor, she asked me whether doctors had yet invented a medicine to cure the heart's sadness.

I decided to consult my brother Alfred, for he had, through shameless fawning, remained on good terms with Marie Antoinette. He made her laugh, and she said that no man at court, and few women, knew as much about fashion and hairstyles as he did. When the queen decided on a Christmas ball with the theme of winter, it was Alfred who devised her coiffure of white-powdered hair adorned with flowers in tiny flasks half-filled with water, which he called "spring in the middle of the snow." Alfred knew how to be as attentive as a lapdog, and when he could not see the queen, he left her messages in which he made himself appear ridiculous. "Your little gibbon came to throw himself at your feet and make you laugh, but seeing you were not there, went away in tears," is a sample of his epistolary style.

Alfred was now in his late forties, and his efforts to look young involved immoderate quantities of rouge, which, instead of having the desired effect, looked like the comic disguise of a *commedia dell'arte* Pierrot. But a fat Pierrot, for he loved sweets, while the most strenuous physical exercise he allowed himself was petit point. I found him sitting in front of his mirror, removing curlers from his dyed hair, the slack folds of his jowly face covered with talcum and rouge, his waistcoat of scarlet brocade straining over the bulge of his stomach. This soft, corpulent symphony in red reminded me of an enormous candied cherry. In the corner behind him, on a yellow satin settee, sat a morose young man of the sort who have been told once too often that their face is their fortune.

"Dear Ax," Alfred said, "what favorable wind brings you here? You find me inconsolable. My old and dear friend, Sir Richard Titwell, has killed himself in London. I think you met him here once. He was no longer young, but he was rich, and had no reason for sadness. But he was bored with life. It is a common illness in this season, for it is indeed seasonal. He wrote out his will, called the notary into his study, and fired the gun in front of him. It is the malady they call spleen. But enough of that." Alfred rose, pirouetted, and tousled the hair of the boy in the corner. "What do you think of my new acquisition?" he asked. "Ah, those eyes, full of Utopian dreams."

The boy shook himself loose, threw Alfred a contemptuous look, and said: "Keep your hands to yourself, you big piece of lard."

"My dear," said Alfred, "he's a real street urchin, so temperamental. But so beautiful . . . Isn't he the very image of Praxiteles' Hermes?"

And like that young god, I thought, he administers to both sexes, for I could see from the way the boy was treating him that

Alfred had reached the watershed of pederasty, when you only get what you pay for.

"At last I've found true love," Alfred told me. "He fucks me silly every night and doesn't look at another man."

"Where's the twenty louis you promised me?" the boy demanded. "I have to leave for Paris in an hour."

"But you'll be back tonight?" Alfred asked, handing him a jingling doeskin bag.

"I'll be back when this is empty," the boy said, as he gave the bag a shake, and left without any further civilities.

"He's shy," Alfred said, "he doesn't like to show affection in the presence of strangers." I told him I quite understood, and mentioned Elizabeth's illness. "I'm sure it's not the queen," Alfred said, "for she is kindness personified. There's not a mean bone in her body. Why, she can't see a cat without wanting to give it milk. It's those two dyke bodyguards of hers, they keep her from old courtiers. Do you know she's given la Polignac four hundred thousand pounds to pay her debts, and la Lamballe two hundred thousand pounds a year? One thing you can say about dykes, they don't whistle while they work."

"But can't you put in a good word for Elizabeth?" I asked. "I'm not asking for anything for myself, but you are on close enough terms with the queen to make her look more kindly on someone who wants nothing more than to serve her."

"Well, I suppose I could try," Alfred said, "although one reason the queen tolerates me is that I never ask her for anything. I leave that to her two acolytes. She doesn't like to be told what to think about people. She looks like a piece of Viennese pastry, but the filling is concrete, not whipped cream. The king can do nothing with her." Alfred mused for a moment, tapping out a beat with two fingers on the edge of a table, then said: "Before I go to the queen, I'm going to take you to see the most marvelous man, a German healer on the rue du Coq-Héron who works wonders. Believe me, he could raise Lazarus from the dead."

"That's already been done," I said.

I Meet an Old Friend and Make a New One

As we rode to Paris in Alfred's mauve-upholstered carriage, he explained that this German healer, an *emeritus studiosus* from Ingolstadt University, was doing wonders with a method called magnetism. "He is making as much noise as Figaro," Alfred said. "He is making millions." The fellow claimed that he had channeled a primeval agent of nature, a superfine fluid that surrounds all bodies. He sold it by the bottle and made his patients bathe in it. "These magnetic applications are truly miraculous," Alfred said. "In one session I was cured of an intestinal obstruction." Magnetism was only the visible part of the treatment, and there were other, more occult cures reserved for the initiated, Alfred said.

I caught a slight odor of charlatanism that made my nostrils quiver. So this is where the power of science has led us, I thought, to making credible the most farfetched experiments. Science and magic, magic and science, one can no longer separate the two. The enlightenment has run wild. This century of light, of Newton, Leibniz, Montesquieu, Voltaire, Kant, Diderot, and so many other torchbearers, has become the century of superstition. Because of the shock to faith and principles that followed the acceptance of gravity and the Copernican universe, there has grown, parallel to the age of reason, an age of unreason. The custodians of ancient superstitions are only too willing to update them, since they are no more extravagant than the discoveries of science.

Thus are the advances of science used to advance superstition, which is, like medicine, merely a matter of convenience. If we must believe in the devil to obtain an honor, enjoy a woman, exterminate a rival, find a treasure, collect an inheritance, or know the future, we will believe. Which is why I am in this carriage on my way to see a man who cures people with magic magnetic fluids. Which is why one sees duchesses, when the night bows in, drive to the edge of a suburb, climb to a dingy fifth floor, and, under the tiles, question an aging harridan, who will convince them that past, present, and future are as yielding to their eyes as the lawns of their gardens. The mind's anxiety, bounded by the limitations of its knowledge, shops for new goods in every back-street secondhand shop. If there is one proven historical fact, it is the existence of vampires. All the evidence is there, trials, lawyers' certificates, doctors' reports, autopsies, and victims bled white in front of three witnesses. No event has been more fully documented. What a pity there are no more witches since we stopped burning them. Ah, but now we live in an age when people no longer believe in God but still believe in the devil. They no longer go to mass, but they seek out mysterious rites. They do not pray, but they evoke spirits. They no longer believe, except in the ludicrously unbelievable, in fortune-tellers, in Friday, in tea leaves, in the gospel according to Thomas, in the year two thousand, in magnetism, in everything but king worship, which is these days the most wretched religion of all.

I was shaken from my reverie by the bump of carriage wheels over uneven cobblestones in the courtyard of the Hôtel de Coigny, where the healer presided. In an antechamber, a quartet played Viennese waltzes. We were greeted by a liveried majordomo who led us into a larger room with drawn curtains. The floors were covered with thick carpets and arcane astrological decorations hung from the walls. Here a few patients drank potions and touched various parts of their bodies with metal rods. They paid no attention to us, so absorbed were they in their cure. I saw an emaciated young man poke his chest with a rod and spit up a large quality of phlegm into a bottle. We waited some minutes in this room, as Alfred explained that the healer had first realized his magnetic powers when he attended a bleeding and saw that the blood flowed faster the closer he came to the patient. I said I would believe it when I saw it.

"You will," said Alfred, so excited by the prospect that he jumped up and down on his chair and clapped his hands. "Why, he can even do it through walls."

Curtains were drawn, doors were flung open, and the majordomo led us into a very large room resembling a sort of bathhouse, for its principal ornament was an oval tub in which men and women sat with ropes looped about them. The windows were shuttered, and assistants sat on chairs around the heavy oak tub, which was filled with iron filings and bottles of water arranged like the spokes on a wheel. The main activity of the robed bathers was to swirl the water with their hands, drink potions containing iron, and then apply magnets to various parts of their bodies. An assistant regulated the atmospheric conditions with a thermometer, and in a corner, a musician pounded a pianoforte to provide the bathers with a rhythmical accompaniment. The patients seemed listless, and moved slowly, and their eyes were dull.

But they stood up expectantly as the curtains in an alcove rustled and were separated by two attendants. Through them strode a tall, strongly built man in a bright suit of lilac silk decorated with Malines lace. He had high Teutonic coloring, marcelled silver hair, a nose like a cannon, eyes like blue bullets, brows like thickets, and a mouth with a pursed upper lip. The overall effect of his face was angular, a bit like the wooden sculptures Swiss mountaineers carve on feast days. But this particular carving was so expressive that it would have stood out like a beacon in a crowd of a hundred.

Alfred nudged me and said: "There he is. That's Mesmer." After bowing like an orchestra conductor, Mesmer began massaging the temples of a man in the tub. "You see," Alfred explained, "he heals by touching the site of the complaint. He turns his back on the north to obey the laws of universal polarity, and applies pressure to the parts in pain. Each of his hands represents a magnetic pole. See him treating that young woman, and placing his thumbs on her epigastric crevices, while he pivots his other fingers to describe parabolas over her thorax, as he stares deep into her eyes."

"All those passes seem to me in the nature of unsolicited caresses," I said.

The patient responded to Mesmer's laying on of hands with increasingly violent tremors. In a moment she was shaking uncontrollably, rocking from side to side, her hair in her eyes, her mouth open and dribbling, her arms waving, muttering unintelligible phrases. Then she collapsed, with her arms around Mesmer's neck. Mesmer called out: "Roger, take her to the crisis room."

And then, for the first time since my arrival in this temple of magnetism, I was genuinely surprised, for the person who came to retrieve the stricken patient was none other than Roger la Trompette. I left Alfred's side to embrace him and tell him how glad I was to see him alive. The years had not spared him. He was stooped, and had lost his impressive corpulence, so that he looked like a dried fig, wrinkled and brown where he had once been plump and pink. But his eyes were still shrewd and merry, and he walked with the same beadle's gait. I told him how often he had been in my thoughts and asked him to forgive me for leaving him on the *Rôdeur* alone with the slaves.

"You did what you had to do," he said. "I don't hold it against you." I congratulated him on his new position. "Best job I ever had," he said. "People reserve their seat in the tub as if for the theater. They feel better when they leave, and it makes them less stingy. Quite an improvement over looking up slaves' assholes, eh?"

We made plans to have a quiet chat, and Roger had to carry off the young woman who was having convulsions. Mesmer was on the other side of the room, embracing a stout woman, who, from her beaming expression, was cured. "Go forth, touch, and heal," he told her, for every former patient became a disciple. Half a dozen other patients were waiting to talk to the great man.

A man in the black robes of a lawyer pushed through, holding his wife by the arm, and told Mesmer that she was leaving for England by ship and was afraid of seasickness. "Hug the mast," Mesmer told her. "It will act as a gravitational pole."

The husband shook his head, turned away from Mesmer, and muttered: "How can she hug the mast? It's as thick as she is, and covered with tar."

Mesmer, like a high ecclesiastical dignitary, went from one to the other, waving his hand in blessing, with a smile and a soothing word for everyone. He shook the hand of a wigged and powdered courtier and said: "Now remember, no snuff, it upsets the nose's magnetic balance."

"Ah," Alfred said, "what an extraordinary man, he knows the secret place where the material and the spiritual meet."

"They seem to meet on the tip of his finger," I said, "and I can imagine him perfectly with his hand up a woman's dress, asking: 'Does that feel better?' "

Mesmer now joined us, excused himself for having left us so long to our own devices, and led us into his private study. Alfred introduced me as the duc de Gramont. "My first name is Anaxagoras," I said. "Please call me Ax."

"Ah," said Mesmer solemnly, as if I had given him a piece of important information, "Anaxagoras, a name that is Hellenic, Hebraic, and Samaritan, full of precipitation and nitrate."

I explained that I had a very dear lady friend who was in need of treatment. Whatever one told Mesmer, one was entitled to a discourse in return.

"You have come to the right place," he said. "I cure dropsy, gout, paralysis, scurvy, blindness, deafness, vaporous melancholy accompanied by vomiting, obstruction of the spleen, St. Vitus' dance, putrid fevers contracted in America, tapeworm, hookworm, angleworm, snakebite, and the general degeneration of the organs of perspiration. I was recently in Africa, where I cured the entire seraglio of the Emperor of Morocco of a disease that attacks the sexual parts and reduces them to the consistency of applesauce. With the same amber liquid I employed there, I will cure your friend."

"But that is not at all what she is suffering from," I said, "and I resent the implication."

"Then it must be glandular fever," Mesmer went on, with a wave of his healing hand. "The cure is simple. What do you do when ink is too thick to write? You add water. Well, do the same thing with lymph, it will flow freely instead of piling up in the glands and pituitary membranes, which block the artery whose pulsations ruffle the sympathetic nerve cluster and are causing your beloved so much pain. To every cause there is an effect, as my good friend Aristotle used to say. Inside her nose, there is a tiny cavity which we doctors call the frontal sinus. It is a tissue of minuscule glands, as fine as an oak leaf. It is gorged, and the thing to do is relieve it, tell her to drink as much good Burgundy wine as her head and stomach can stand."

"It's nothing to do with glandular fever," I said. "How can you diagnose her illness when you haven't seen her?"

"There is a hand guiding my hand," Mesmer said, raising his blue eyes toward heaven, which made his broad brow furrow like a plowed field.

Credat alter, I thought to myself. "The lady in question is suffering from melancholy," I said, "not fever."

"I have just the thing," Mesmer said, "electrical stimulation of the brain, untouched by human hands, unseen by human eyes."

"Does it cure?" I asked.

He laughed, as though my question was funny, and his face flushed the color of a strawberry. "Oh, no," he said, "it merely occasions a little . . . change of direction."

"Is it difficult?" I asked.

"It's no trick at all," he said, "for those of us who have it." I said I was willing to suggest it to Elizabeth. "We may not even need it," Mesmer said. "My method is not based on medication. I can see I'm among friends. Forget the iron rods and the magnetic water, that's for the man in the street. My principle is that you must not fight your illness; you must adopt it until it becomes an integral part of you. Sometimes a word is enough, if it is believed. A mother brought her son to me because he stooped. There was no physical malformation. I told him: 'Do you ever think of yourself as Atlas bearing the burdens of the world?' The fellow went through a little epiphany right there in front of me. 'Ah, well,' he said, 'you don't think, could it be?' He never stooped again. He brought a friend to see me. The fellow habitually rubbed his eyes, until they were red and watery. I told him how Oedipus scratched his eyes out after Jocasta's death, and he stopped. Not that I had found the explanation; the thing is to make it embarrassing for the patient to continue his curious behavior by providing, not *the* reason, but *a* reason."

"There is no mystery in this lady's case, my dear Mesmer," Alfred said. "She is melancholy because the queen excludes her from court affairs."

"Perhaps we should treat the queen," I said.

"Ah," said Mesmer, "I see it. Air will be enough." He caught my puzzled expression and raised his hand to be allowed to proceed. "Not a woman in a thousand knows how to breathe. You must fill your lungs like a dervish to give them a big stock of oxygen, until you get a bright flash of light on every exhalation. If you close your eyes you see the jewel of the lotus, which is neither a block of gold nor a block of crystal, but both, and varies between green and magenta aftereffects. Of course it takes time. If you want something more expeditious, I have many specifics: The use of deadly nightshade, in tiny amounts, relieves the pressure on the spleen, the dried leaves of foxglove soothe the heart and cause the tissues to retain body fluids, monatomic alcohol sends a great rush of heat and clears the phlegm-laden bronchial tubes. I can cure sciatica with a compound of nitrate, sulfur, mercury, and copper. I'm also working, but this is strictly *entre nous*, with the wild psychosomatic crisscrosses that cause asthma, an unwanted bride, a peremptory husband, a cloying mother, ungrateful children. Asthma, you see, is a strain of the virus called love. Come, let me show you around."

"He's taken to you," Alfred whispered. "He doesn't show many people the inner sanctum."

"I expect he sees a fat fee on the horizon," I replied.

"I am not interested in money," Mesmer said, as if he had overheard. "I have been working for forty years, and I won't mention the expense, not a word, nor the anguish, the study, the dead ends, the sleepless nights. I offer the results voluntarily, for mankind."

"We have never doubted it," Alfred said.

Mesmer led us into a long corridor, tapestried in soothing-green velvet, with four or five doors on either side. "In each of these rooms," he said, "men and women are being saved from themselves. Here, for instance"—and he tapped on a door—"I am preparing an emolument that can give the most wrinkled crone a skin

like a baby's bottom. Can you guess what the secret ingredient is?"
We shook our heads, and Mesmer turned a key in a tiny panel in
the door so that we could look in undetected. I put my eye to the
opening and saw an attractive young lady doing something in-
delicate to a gentleman seated on a bed with his breeches around
his ankles. At the moment of culmination, nothing was lost, all was
deftly caught in a small flagon. "Two birds with one stone," Mesmer
said. "The gentlemen are being treated for inflammation of the
prostate, and at the same time provide without knowing it the
secret ingredient for my emolument. But on to more serious
matters."

He showed us another room that was furnished with a sofa and
a chair. "This is a new technique I am developing," he said,
"which consists in letting the patients talk without interruption. In
telling about themselves they disclose clues concerning the nature
of their illness. I am of the opinion that many personality disorders
have as their origin some sexual problem, such as the suppressed
love of a young boy for his mother. You may look skeptical, but
this is more common than one might suppose. One thing my biological and astrological research has shown is that everything has a
sex, microbes have a sex, stars have a sex, planets have a sex; you
can imagine all the fantastic galaxies, from the planets to the
germs and back again, all sexed up, and somewhere among those
swarming cells there is man, the creature of forces he doesn't even
suspect, homosexual microbes messing things up and swishing
around, frigid microbes, oversexed microbes, all competing for
attention inside his body."

"Very interesting," Alfred said, indicating by the coldness in his
voice that he was ready to pursue the visit.

"I first tried my couch treatment on Cleopatra," Mesmer said,
leading us again into the corridor, "but without much success, I'm
afraid. She was on an ego trip, and I couldn't get her over her
foolish infatuation. She was a little bit of a woman, thin, frail,
sparrow-chested, with black eyes and skin as brown as a berry.
What an amusing contrast between the fat and jovial Anthony,
with his barracks talk and officers' mess manner, and this tiny
black pearl of the Nile. Ah, how I loved that time of luxury and
misery, when Humanity was going backward, passing through vice
on the way to slavery. She was desperately in love, she crossed
Alexandria on a palanquin to meet him, and the night over, secretly returned, her cheeks still warm with the night's kisses, her

hair in amorous disarray, her clothes thrown on in haste, and one pearl earring missing."

I gave Alfred a bemused look and shook my head. "Reincarnation," Alfred whispered.

Mesmer extracted a small velvet case from his pocket, and opened it to show a large irregular-shaped pearl mounted on a gold loop. "Here, gentlemen, rescued from the abyss of history," he said, "is Cleopatra's missing earring."

"If you knew Cleopatra," I said, "I must say you look young for your age."

"My dear friend," Mesmer said, "I was born in 1734 on the Lake of Constance, in Iznang, so that I dare say I may be younger than you are, though you are very fit. However, I have learned that one can travel through time as well as space. As a young man, I visited a land where the air smelled of jasmine, where the woods were filled with birds of bright plumage that laid green eggs, scented fig trees, and lizards that changed color according to their surroundings. I met the Tulkous, the living Buddha, and I learned from him the first principle of reincarnation: We have within us not only our own but many lives of which we are the custodians. The fasciculus of disincarnated forces is united to a living being, whose physical and mental dispositions have been acquired in former lives, allowing a harmonious union of the spiritual functions."

"Now you've lost me," I said. "Do you mean that you can move back and forth in time the way I drive my carriage from the palace to Paris?"

"Not at will," Mesmer said, "for I have not reached what is called the ultimate Dan. But I have known many of the great of this world. I hunted boar with Charlemagne, I drank Munich beer with Luther, I threw darts with Henry VIII, I knew Christ intimately, he was the best friend a man could have, but romantic. He took his wishes for realities. And he put all his eggs in one basket. I used to tell him he would end up badly. Although a Jew, he was a very honest man. But he had an irresistible penchant for martyrdom."

"And can you project yourself into the future?" I asked. "That could be even more interesting, for one could see the mistakes one is going to make and avoid them."

"Alas," Mesmer said, "the future is still a closed door to me, but

I have been informed that I am to disappear at the end of this century and that I will not reappear for eighty-five years."

"And where will you be in the meantime?" Alfred asked, taking it all in like a child listening to a bedtime story.

"My body will be stored in a slab of ice, immune to the ravages of time, in a state of suspended animation, according to a technique I have developed. Tissue below freezing does not decompose, as we have learned from recovering the bodies of shipwrecked sailors near the Arctic Circle, or those of mountaineers caught in Alpine blizzards. Life does not end when the heart stops beating. I will simply be thawed out at the opportune moment."

"I would hate to leave so much responsibility in someone else's hands," I said. "They could decide to leave you on ice."

Mesmer shrugged and led us into a large room, bare except for a high-piled white rug. "This is where we have our group sessions," he said. "Another technique I developed, after spending a year in a Tibetan monastery, where vows of silence were observed except for one hour a day, when the monks discussed each other's failings with great frankness. I duplicate the experience here. It is a way of making each one of us his fellow man's doctor. I bring together a group of strangers, and soon they know more about each other than their parents or their closest friends. It is a form of collective confessional, without penance or absolution. The venom sacs empty, and the soul is cleansed. In this room, there are no disguises, such as position or wealth. One enters like a newborn babe, and it is up to each individual to decide whether he is entering a lion's den or a perfumed garden. Often it becomes a perfumed garden inhabited by lions. Why, I have seen duchesses break down and cry like unhappy schoolgirls. I congratulate them on reaching catharsis. Not everyone can."

Mesmer next showed us into his private study, a large, well-lit, paneled room with curtains of Genoa velvet. Two walls were taken up by a library dealing mainly with occult sciences, and the other two were covered with paintings hung over Flemish tapestries. On Mesmer's desk stood an inkstand made from a human skull. "He writes letters with both hands to save time," Alfred informed me, pulling me over to a large painting over a door. "Don't you think his Holy Family by Murillo is the equal to the Raphael in Versailles?" It was indeed a fine work, the first genuine thing I had seen in Mesmer's clinic. I congratulated him, bracing myself for the lecture on art I knew would come, for he was an inexhaustible torrent.

"I came to medicine after exhausting art," he said. "I abandoned music, being able to go no further, having discovered a twelve-tone scale far too advanced for my time, as I abandoned writing, rubbing and rasping the words against one another until I had seized their innermost meaning and all of literature was on the tip of my pen. It was too much, the glare was too strong. These canvases were given to me by the artists after I had shown them that painting is based on a number of optical tricks. As one grows older, the sacks of fluid in one's eyes begin to shrink, one's point of focus changes . . ." He stretched out his arm . . . "Here's your field of vision, where that fleck is, and you can't see anything else, it's exactly like the bubble in blown glass, all those little things are called rods and cones, they're not mixed properly, either there are too many rods or too many cones, little glassy clusters with filters running down the middle of them. This is what explains art.

"The painter is born with a greater perception of depth and distance. Remember the Molyneux premise: Distance of itself is not to be perceived for 'tis a line presented to your eye with its end toward us, which must therefore be only a point, and that point is invisible. A blindfolded man touched by a rod cannot tell how long it is. A painter's vision is a composite of the accidents of birth and eye defects. Painters are like saints, they have visions. Everyone knows that Saint Hildegard's visions developed from scintillating scotomy at the onset of a migraine attack. El Greco suffered from astigmatism and elongated the human form, and Chardin's colors are just as clearly due to faulty cortical coding, the result of a cataractic condition. So you see, my friends, art is the result of a faulty lens, the human eye."

"A novel theory," I said, prodding Alfred, for I felt we had overstayed our visit.

Mesmer saw us to the door and shook my hand warmly, saying: "We must see more of each other, I feel we have so much rapport."

"In this world or the next?" I asked.

Alfred hurried me off, and when we were in the carriage, asked me what I thought of my visit. "He is one of two things," I said. "Either he does not believe what he is saying, and he is a charlatan. Or he does believe it, and he is a madman. In either case, he should be locked up."

Alfred sulked for a while, then said: "That's always been the trouble with you, Ax, you only believe what you see, you can't accept mystery."

"It's a mystery to me why you bother with the fellow," I said.

"He has cured a great many people," Alfred said, "me among them."

"Everything he says is based on the irrational and the mystical," I said. "The man is a high priest of unreason. But there is no disagreeing with reason. Euclid was a greater tyrant than Tamerlane, for everyone must agree that from a point outside a straight line only one parallel to that line can pass."

"If only human behavior could be charted as precisely as geometry." Alfred sighed. We finally decided that I would take Elizabeth to see Mesmer, for it could do no harm, and I agreed with Alfred that the power of suggestion can work wonders.

I Gain an Entrée to the Queen

Upon returning to the palace, I was on my way to Elizabeth's apartment when I was intercepted by Lauzun, who wore the frown of serious days. "My dear Ax," he said, "come into the garden, where we can talk without being overheard." We crossed the Hercules drawing room and stepped off the stone terrace into the pebbled paths flanked by beds of white irises planted to form fleur-de-lis. "I overheard Saint-Germain tell the prince de Conti that you were a thistle he was having pulled so it would no longer sting him."

"But on what grounds?" I asked.

"On whatever grounds they have invented," Lauzun said. "Look around you and see how few are left of the courtiers who were loyal to the former king. One nail drives out the other. Pretexts are easy to find: You are seditious, you are plotting against the ministers, your eyes are the wrong color, anything will do."

"But the king . . ."

Lauzun did not let me finish. "The king," he said, "does not know his left hand from his right, nor his liver from his heart. He can be made to agree to anything. Like his grandfather, he is always ready to believe accusations of disloyalty. When he returns from a hunt, he drinks so much Burgundy wine that the next morning he cannot even remember what he agreed to the night before."

"And Elizabeth?" I asked.

"She is to join you in exile."

"And when are we to hear of this?"

"In a week's time, I should think," Lauzun said. "Saint-Germain was discussing which of his protégés would get your apartment." I thanked Lauzun warmly, and told him he was the last true friend I had at court, for we had over the years become as inseparable as an ass and a shirttail, and he replied, as if to lighten my burden by sharing it, that he expected to be banished not long after me. In fact, however, he had taken the precaution of forming friendships with several of the new ministers.

My first instinct was to go to the king, anticipating my banishment order, and offer to exile myself voluntarily as a mark of my loyalty. But I was unsure I could clear the obstacles that were placed between the king and his courtiers, and even if I did, it was too great a risk to take, for he might agree. And what of it? I thought. Why insist on remaining in a court that had lost much of its splendor, where mediocrity was rampant and men of obscure birth made the laws, where a frivolous Austrian queen broke down court usage until the palace resembled a country manor on the Danube? This was not the court I knew. I should be glad to leave, and turn my back forever on the whole business.

I was now fifty-three, although vigorous and healthy, and ready to lead a more secluded life and ponder the meaning of my existence among the country acres I had rescued from my brother's profligacy. Elizabeth could join me. I could see my daughters (Thérèse had never managed a son, not even the time I returned from Africa), who had all married dull, square-headed members of the provincial nobility. I could make my peace with my wife, who doubtless had many good qualities I had never taken the trouble to discover. As mayor of Bayonne, I could become an important regional figure. There were frequent border skirmishes with Spain to keep an old soldier busy. It would be a smaller arena, but with all the excitement of the larger one. It is pointless to remain where one is no longer wanted, I thought, when one can be useful elsewhere.

And yet . . . my very marrow rebelled at this solution. To plead *nolo contendere* was to admit the charges that had provoked my banishment. It was not in my nature to flee before an enemy. I had no real wish to remain, and under any other circumstances would have left the court gladly. But to be expelled as the victim of a machination, this I could not do. It smelled of resignation and cowardice. It was a denial of the qualities to which I owed everything, for it was not by fawning and complying that I had become maréchal of France and held a position of responsibility under the former king. A good strategist can turn a position that seems desperate to his own advantage. I would not go to the king. I would find some way to influence him indirectly. Since I was being obliquely attacked, I would defend myself obliquely. I had nothing to lose. Either I would avoid banishment, reserving the right to leave court voluntarily when I chose to do so. Or I would be banished, but only after showing my enemies that I was no palace relic, to be thrown out with the candle stubs on the morning after a great occasion. Either way, it would teach them a lesson. They would learn the difference between a fly and a wasp.

I decided not to tell Elizabeth about the king's decision, for she had already been laid low by the court's cruelty, and the news would only make her worse. I was appalled at her gauntness, at the deep shadows under her eyes and the points of her collarbone visible through her nightdress. She had left a tray of food untouched by her bedside. I tasted a dish, commented on how good it was, and suggested she try it. "I can't keep anything down," she said. "I want to, but my body rebels." Five doctors had sworn they could find nothing wrong with her. Her illness was a subtle, intangible thing. There had to be a soul, for there was a sickness of the soul. This at least Mesmer recognized, for he claimed that he could cure it. I told her I had found a man who would restore her to health. She smiled, as if to thank me for making an effort that was destined to fail, but nonetheless agreed to accompany me to the Hôtel de Coigny on the morrow.

The next morning I rode forward with the coachman so that Elizabeth could lie down more comfortably in the carriage, and we reached Mesmer's establishment in the afternoon. I led her through rooms where patients disported themselves in various stages of delirium, and she asked me in a trembling voice whether she would have to join them. "No, no," I told her, "he will give you private treatment." I found my old friend Roger, who again clasped me warmly to his bosom, for each time we saw one another, after so many years, neither of us could quite believe the other was real. We had so much to tell, and in the meantime, our embrace was a sign that we had to be patient. Roger went to fetch the great man, who was conducting one of his group sessions. We waited in the long corridor, and could hear mixed sounds, crying and laughing, behind the doors.

Mesmer emerged, more soberly dressed this time, in a suit the color of Spanish tobacco, with blue gold-braided cuffs and twelve large glass buttons representing each of the twelve Caesars. When I commented on the buttons, he said: "Julius was the best of the lot, and a close personal friend. I accompanied him on his Gaul campaign and told him not to kill Vercingetorix, but to put him in a cage like a wild beast and show him to the populace of Rome. That was the principal reason for his immense popularity, for the Romans loved *circenses* more than *panem*."

I introduced Elizabeth. Mesmer held both her shoulders, then touched her brow with one of his fingers. "I see what it is," he said. "A migraine located directly behind the eyebrow. You feel each beat like a knife blow that cuts you to the quick."

"Why, yes," Elizabeth said, surprised.

"Someone has cast a spell on you," Mesmer said. "Someone envies your beauty and your gentle heart. Someone has written your name on the skin of a stillborn lamb." Elizabeth shuddered. "No matter," Mesmer said, "I know the antidote. You are the victim of cheap parlor tricks. You only suffered because your heart is pure. Conscience is an organ of infinite sensibility for those who have it. The loveliest flowers are the most fragile. You, my dear, have an orchid conscience."

Mesmer took Elizabeth into one of his private consultation rooms, and remained there with her for roughly ten minutes less than an hour. During that time, I had a chance to chew the rag with Roger. Between us, we finished a good bottle of claret, for thank God, Mesmer's travels through time and space had not made an ascetic out of him, and his larder and cellar were well stocked. It was like old times. Roger told me how he had escaped from the clutches of Lumamba and the slaves, and made his way across Africa, to a port where he was captured by pirates, whom he eventually got to agree to let him return to France. His account, more fascinating than those of the most celebrated adventurers, such as Munchausen or Cagliostro, I will include in a later installment of this journal, for the amusement of adults and the instruction of youth.

We were interrupted by Elizabeth, who threw herself in my arms and exclaimed: "Your Mesmer is a wizard. He has done wonders for me." The change was astonishing. Gone was the veil of sadness that had covered her face, gone the penitent eyes, the pallid skin, the tight lips. To a waxen doll, Mesmer had restored the breath of life. Even Elizabeth's appetite had returned, and she announced that she was hungry.

"How foolish I was to spend so much time feeling sorry for myself," she said. "My darling Ax, you complained that you saw too little of me. From today on, you will be complaining that you see me too much."

"What medicine have you taken?" I asked. "It would be a good idea to keep a supply on hand."

"That is our little secret," Mesmer said, rubbing his strong, square-fingered hands with satisfaction. "A good chef never gives away his recipes."

"There is nothing I need take with me," Elizabeth said. "It is all here," and she kissed Mesmer lightly on his massive brow.

"Madam," he said, showing that he could be gallant and was used to dealing with ladies, "you have given me the most precious reward a man could wish for."

Impressed by Mesmer's success, I decided to consult him about my own problems. I still had my doubts, but it would have been foolish not to make use of such a resourceful fellow. I took him aside and briefly summed up the situation. "I think I have the solution," he said. "Come into my study." He led me in, rummaged among his books, leafed through several heavy tomes, and announced: "Yes, the conjunction of the stars is right. Venus is in the ascendant, and Mars is on the cusp." I waited for an explanation. "You must approach the queen," Mesmer said, "for she governs the king. She has more power than Pompadour. The monarch's life is a daily capitulation. In this way he atones for his physical inadequacy." I could see that Mesmer was well informed, and I told him that the king was now said to have submitted to a minor surgical intervention that made him a normal man. "No matter," Mesmer said, "for even if he has stopped stuttering, he will never be able to speak up. He is too weak-willed and apathetic. This is the first reign where the queen, not the king, has favorites. It will be a simple matter for you to become one of that number and put an end to this threat of banishment."

I told Mesmer that I had always treated the queen with respect, which had been returned in kind. "I am not talking about respect," he said, "but about disrespect." He removed some books from a shelf and unlocked a panel concealed behind them, withdrawing a bottle no higher than my index finger. "This will endear you to the queen's heart," he said.

"But what is it?" I asked.

"Merely a potion that will dispose her kindly toward you," he replied.

"So you deal in love potions?"

"I used to," he said, "but I stopped. Too many lovesick young men were back in less than a year asking for an antidote. People never know what they want." I asked Mesmer how one was meant to use the little bottle. "The contents are tasteless and colorless," he said. "All you have to do is add a teaspoonful to a glass of champagne, for instance, to obtain the desired effect. But you must make sure that you give the glass yourself, and that you are facing her when she drinks it, for the charm will operate on whomever she is looking at."

"And what exactly is the effect?" I asked.

"That," said Mesmer, "I leave for you to discover."

In the days that followed, I paid my court assiduously to the queen, looking for a chance to administer the potion. It was not as easy as it looked, for whenever she wanted anything, there was instantly a footman at her side with it. I joined the queen's entourage wherever it went. I followed her on walks in the garden in the morning, and in the afternoon, I followed her into the chapel for vespers. When she gambled, which she did nearly every evening, I stood close by, with discreet words of encouragement. The queen became accustomed to seeing me. Each day, I complimented her on whatever dress she was wearing, and I was careful also to flatter the principal members of her entourage, the sloe-eyed princesse de Lamballe and the honey-haired duchesse de Polignac. I was always ready with a cheerful word or a quip, and my brother Alfred helped by sometimes telling me what the queen's plans were. With any woman, and queens are no exception, attentiveness is the secret of success.

Marie Antoinette became more accessible, engaging me in conversation and banter. I learned from Alfred that on one musical matinee she had arranged, which I had been prevented from attending, she asked where I was. The next day I told her that only the most extreme circumstance could have kept me from her side, and I invented a story about a cousin's sudden death. She looked at me with such warmth that I began to think I would not need Mesmer's potion. But time was pressing, the news of my banishment might come any day, and the potion was no more than a shortcut for what I could, with time, have obtained without chemical assistance.

The queen told me she would that afternoon visit her hamlet, and asked whether I would like to join the party. I had heard about this hamlet, for it was often the object of court jests. Because of it, Marie Antoinette was vulgarly referred to as "the farmer's wife." The hamlet was a miniature farm she presided over in the Petit Trianon, where all the animals were pampered like princes. The veals were fed only egg yolks and orange juice, and their coats were said to be as white as snow. The hens were given the most extravagant care. A quartet of musicians played in the hen house to make the laying of their eggs more soothing. An egg from the hamlet was considered a great prize, and was said to taste like no other. The cows wore pink ribbons around their necks and were fed a special fragrant grass that was supposed to give their milk a jasmine flavor. Of course, huge sums were spent to keep up this bucolic fancy of the queen's.

That afternoon, with half a dozen of the faithful, we drove the short distance from the palace to the Petit Trianon, and were greeted by young shepherds and shepherdesses dressed like the figures in a Watteau painting, each one lovelier than the other. The queen delighted in showing us the spotless white barns where the animals were kept, far better housed than many of her subjects, and had us taste the bread that was baked on the premises and the butter that was churned from the milk of her cows, which was in fact delicious. Then, turning to me, she said: "Monsieur de Gramont, I know you think I am a frivolous, useless woman. I will show you that I was brought up like the simplest peasant girl."

She took my hand, and laughing merrily, led me into a long barn where the cows were kept, each in its own immaculate stall made of pink and blue ceramics from the Sèvres porcelain works. "Have you ever seen a cow milked?" Marie Antoinette asked me. I replied that was one of the joys life still held in reserve. "Well," she said, "now you are going to see it."

I must say that the sight of the queen of the most powerful nation in Europe sitting on a stool like a common dairymaid with her legs spread and her flowered sunbonnet thrown back, pulling on a cow's udders with a rhythmical motion that sent thin streams of milk spurting into a silver pail, was one of the most incongruous I had ever witnessed. I risked a pleasantry: "Your majesty is so

expert, one would think she had done nothing else all her life."
The rest of the entourage was still in the hamlet's model kitchen,
eating bread and butter. For the first time I was alone with the
queen.

"And I will wager," she said, "that you have never drunk warm
milk fresh from the cow."

"The fact that it was drawn by your majesty's hand will make it
precious," I said.

Here was my chance. We were alone. The attendant had ab-
sented himself. I helped her to her feet and pulled out the silver
pail half full of foaming milk. I detest milk; to me it is not fit for
human consumption, and since I suckled at my mother's breast, I
have refused to touch it. But this was a case of *force majeure*. Two
silver goblets stood conveniently on a shelf behind me. I poured
milk from the pail into each, and while the queen was examining
her prize cows, making sure each one had its pink ribbon on straight,
I opened the small bottle Mesmer had given me and measured out
a few drops in the goblet I intended for the queen. I handed it to
her, proposing a toast: "To the tenth muse, who combines the
qualities of all the others." She drank her milk in little sips, commenting on its exquisite flavor, and I had to drink some of mine,
as I tried to keep my face from wrinkling in a grimace of disgust.
I also made sure that while she emptied her goblet, she looked
at me and not at the cow.

Her acolytes now came running and chided us for hiding in a
corner together. "I was showing the duc de Gramont how to milk a
cow," the queen said. "It seems that is one of the few talents he
does not possess." And everyone laughed, but not unkindly. The
queen was more animated and witty than I had ever seen her. The
potion seemed to have liberated her fancy. She said she was delighted with her afternoon, and I concurred most sincerely.

Everyone returned to the palace in the best of spirits, and that
evening, I heard the queen repeat the milking incident to the king,
who grunted and moved uneasily in his chair, and looked at the
clock on the mantelpiece (which the queen sometimes set an hour
ahead), for his greatest pleasure was going to bed early.

In the days that followed, I watched for signs that the potion
had worked, but none was forthcoming. Indeed, it seemed to me
that the queen was more distant than before. Sometimes when I
spoke to her she pretended not to hear, and she laughed at the
sallies of other courtiers more readily than at mine. I began to fear

that the potion's effect was not what Mesmer had promised. I was also having trouble with Elizabeth, who complained that I was following the queen about like a toy poodle and making a fool of myself. Now that she was cured of her apathy, she wanted to see more of me, and felt she was competing with the queen. "Trust me," I told her. "What I am doing is for both of us, on Mesmer's advice."

"You can give your queen your days, if you must," she said, "but I reserve your nights."

And indeed, I spent nearly every night with Elizabeth, taking the same delight in her that I had first taken more than thirty years ago, for the women we love do not age; they crystallize in our minds at a moment of their youth, and never leave it. I saw Elizabeth now as I had seen her as a girl, and our lovemaking was no less a pleasure for having become a habit. For, as I have said, I sometimes experimented with the new, only to return to the familiar.

One night after attending a representation of Molière's *Le Malade imaginaire*, I returned to my apartment after midnight, too tired to join Elizabeth, although she had promised to wait up for me. I was removing my clothes by candlelight in my bedroom, when I noticed something shining on my night table. It was a beautifully worked, embossed gold snuffbox. I opened it and unfolded a message that had been placed inside. It was unsigned and said only: "You will soon know who gave this to you." There was nothing for me to do but wait for the mystery to unravel.

The next day I accompanied the queen and her entourage on a picnic in the woods beyond the formal gardens. It was called a picnic, although it was like bringing the royal dining room outdoors, for folding tables were set up and covered with damask tablecloths, and dozens of footmen brought dishes under silver cupolas, hot from the Versailles kitchen. I paid particular attention to the queen, but she ignored me, and did not invite me to sit at her table. I tried several times to catch her eye, but in vain. My mind was filled with doubts and uncertainties. I wondered whether I was the butt of some practical joke. By this time I was sure that Mesmer's potion was a hoax.

I retired early that evening, depressed by the little headway I was making, and expecting at any moment to be told to evacuate my rooms. A second snuffbox lay on my night table, more beautiful than the first, and inside it was a message that made my blood quicken: "At midnight you will go to the Hercules drawing room," it said, "and you will open the doors giving on the terrace and step outside, where you will find a footman wearing a black cloak whom you will follow." The note was signed: "Someone who cares." I had two hours to wait, and I was in such a state of nervousness that I could not read a book, or nap, or play solitaire. I kept turning over in my mind the possible meanings of the note, and wondering where it would all lead. I dressed very carefully, and sprinkled on some lavender water, and at the stroke of midnight I was where I had been told to be.

A cloaked figure stepped out of the shadows and beckoned for me to follow. We walked through the garden to a forest path where a carriage waited. The night was cloudy and black; there was no moon to give me an idea of where we were headed. We drove for ten minutes before passing through a gate, and we were in another garden, where the carriage stopped. I was asked to get out, and I followed the cloaked figure to a water-lily-covered pond, at the end of which was a moss-covered grotto I could dimly make out in the obscurity. I was helped into a rowboat that waited at the edge of the pond, and when we reached the grotto my cloaked companion tied a rope at the end of the rowboat to a short post on a ledge above the water, and hopped adroitly onto the mossy rocks.

I followed, and as he lit an oil lamp that cast a lambent light over the grotto's dark walls, we reached a narrow ledge. The coachman groped along the ledge until he found a tiny metal wheel, which he turned. Part of the rocky wall began to groan and slowly revolve, making an opening large enough for a man to slip through. My guide motioned for me to step across the secret door and made it clear that he was not permitted to follow. I waved farewell and stooped low enough to fit in the opening in the stone. As soon as I was through, the stone door shut behind me with a thud.

I found myself in a small, low, badly lit, unfurnished alcove, closed at one end by the secret door, and at the other by a spike-topped iron grille through which I could see a corridor lit by wall torches. I could go no farther, and I began to wonder whether, instead of the assignation I had been expecting, this was not a trap set by my enemies. I waited several minutes in the gloom, and was about to shake the grille and call out, when it began to rise, and I ducked under it as soon as I could. I progressed warily along the hall, my footsteps echoing in the empty passageway, and, rounding a corner, came face-to-face with two masked, motionless, white-robed figures. I instinctively put my hand to the pommel of my sword. "The lady is waiting," one of the figures said. They turned their backs on me and walked down the hall with slow shuffling steps, and I followed, feeling foolish that I had been so quick to take offense.

A door opened, and they ushered me into a spacious bathroom, where a large copper tub full of steaming water stood ready. They removed my clothes, and as absurd as I thought the whole scene was, I was determined to see it through. Soon I was naked as Adam, and they motioned me into the tub, and scrubbed me thoroughly with hard-bristled brushes until my skin was pink. I was then powdered and perfumed like a courtesan, and the two masked figures, whose hands were as soft and gentle as a woman's, beckoned me into another room.

This room had one low light and no furniture of any kind. Its singularity was that it was upholstered from floor to ceiling in black velvet, and the floor itself was as pliant as a mattress. I had to adjust my eyes to the dim light and the strange effect of the black velvet covering everything, and I realized that in this room no shadows were thrown, owing to the blackness of the walls and the lack of any contrast. I then noticed four short gold stakes planted in the floor and forming a rectangle. I was asked to lie on my back and stretch my arms and legs, which were tied to the four stakes. I found myself spread-eagled and immobile in this strange room, expecting the worst, when, as silently as they had come upon me, my two attendants vanished.

I pulled at my bindings, but only succeeded in slightly chafing my hands and feet, for the attendants had done their job well. I decided the only thing to do was wait. Less than three minutes later, the door to the velvet room opened and I saw the folds of a muslin nightdress and a head of ashblond hair. I could not see the lady's face, for she turned her back as she removed her nightdress, and I beheld one of the loveliest female forms I have ever seen, a perfect hourglass, with softly curving limbs and a back that the caryatids of the Erechtheum would have envied. When she turned to face me, I could not suppress a gasp of astonishment, for it was the queen. Marie Antoinette faced me, as naked as Eve, and twice as lovely. I expected her now to untie the knots that bound me, but instead, she knelt at my side and began covering my body with quick little kisses. In my position, I was unable to reciprocate.

"If I could move a little more freely," I suggested.

She shook her head with a toss of gold ringlets. "I love you to despair," she told me, "and I must make love to you. But I cannot bear to be touched. My first experience was too revolting." I understood what she meant. It was enough to disgust any woman, and had left terrible traces.

I did not insist. However peculiar the circumstances, Mesmer's potion was a success. I submitted to the experience of satisfying a woman without touching her, except with those parts of me she singled out, and I was glad that I was able to rise to the occasion. I will not go into details, for any man who has made love to a queen must above all remain discreet, and there have been enough calumnies spread about Marie Antoinette without my adding to the pile. But I will say that even queens have their moments of abandon, when the words that escape their lips have nothing to do with crown or scepter, and when their behavior makes them indistinguishable from any other woman in the kingdom. I did my utmost to please the queen, lending myself with good grace to all the fancies she did devise, and in return, I can say that she pleased me beyond all expectation, although that too may have been a result of the potion.

When pleasure had exhausted us both, the queen disappeared behind the velvet door, and soon my two attendants unbound me and returned me to my clothes. I left the subterranean love nest the way I had come, through the grotto, and over the pond. I had remained longer than I thought, for the first light of day was scattering the dark, and as I climbed into the carriage with the cloaked footman who had brought me, I was surprised to see that we were in the hamlet I had visited a few days ago. The grotto was part of a garden that had been pointed out to me as a place where the queen kept ducks and other aquatic fowl. I wondered how many in her entourage knew what else went on there.

I also wondered how the queen was able to leave the palace at night without the king's knowledge. It was true that he was a sound sleeper. The queen had used his sonorous snoring as a pretext to ask for separate rooms. Finally, I asked myself how many others had known the bizarre delights of the velvet room. It seemed to have been designed with but a single purpose in mind, and it had not been designed for me. The hamlet had been built two years before, and the queen's secret chambers must have been part of that construction project. Whoever had been bound to the gold stakes was not going to talk about it. We formed a club whose members were unaware of one another's existences.

The next day I saw the queen on the way to chapel, but she was haughtier than ever, scarcely acknowledging my reverential bow. I realized that this was the way it would be. In public, she would ignore me. But several times a week, I would receive a message, left by unseen hands in my apartment, and I would return to the velvet room and reenact the charade of my Prometheus-like love-making. That the potion had succeeded was certain; I had so much proof that I had to take naps in the afternoon, and complained of anemia to Elizabeth to explain my absence from her bed.

I was, however, no more advanced in my project to remain at court. Finally, one afternoon when the queen was at Fontaine-bleau, I was able to chat with her while the carriages waited. She was with two of her ladies-in-waiting, and I lingered by the door and paid her several compliments. She replied with kindness, encouraging me to speak up boldly, and I told her I greatly feared that my days at court were numbered. She found errands for the two women in her carriage, so that we could be alone for a moment. My arm leaned on the window, with my hand hanging loosely inside. No one saw her clasp my hand and no one heard her say: "As long as I am here, no one will dare ask you to leave."

I was filled with joy, for the queen had given me her word, and I knew the king would not dare dispute it. "I am forever obliged to your majesty," I said. It was odd to play the formal and obedient courtier before this woman with whom I had lain naked in the transports of lust.

"But there is one condition," she said. "I want you to remain at court. There is a certain lady, however, toward whom you are overly attentive. I want her to leave court."

So that was the terrible bargain. I could stay, but Elizabeth had to leave. I had noticed the queen's coolness toward Elizabeth increase since she had taken the potion. On several occasions I had seen fury in the queen's eyes when Elizabeth entered a room on my arm. I realized that the potion had done its work too well. The queen was not only infatuated with me, but jealous of Elizabeth. And now that I had asked for her help, she saw the chance to keep me and rid herself of Elizabeth. I could not agree to such an exchange. The main reason I wanted to stay at court was that Elizabeth seemed happier there.

Nor could I offend the queen by turning down her offer. "The lady in question means nothing to me," I lied. "There is no need to call attention to her by sending her away. I will stop seeing her, if that pleases your majesty."

"Indeed you will," Marie Antoinette said, "for she will be some hundred leagues removed from your presence."

I did not know what to reply. My only thought was to reach Mesmer and find out when the potion would wear off.

I Am Undone

I left for Paris the next day and was greeted at the entrance of the Hôtel de Coigny by Roger, who told me the great man was not feeling well and had remained secluded in his study all day. "What, the healer not well?" I asked. Mesmer looked despondent, his ebullience gone. He stood staring out a window, toying with an astrolabe. "I rushed to see you," I said, "for the potion has worked . . . too well. The queen has grown jealous, and has turned her wrath on Elizabeth."

"Oh, these damned potions," Mesmer said, "something always goes wrong."

"Yes, but when does it wear off?" I asked.

"Unpredictable," Mesmer said, "sometimes they last as long as six months."

"What am I to do?" I asked.

"You think you've got problems," Mesmer said, "take a look at this." He handed me a letter with the seal broken. It was signed by the king and ordered Mesmer to present himself to the Paris police lieutenant, who would have him taken to the Bastille. "The work of envious rivals," Mesmer said, "a sealed letter. I can't go to the Bastille. What would my patients do without me?"

"But the Bastille cannot hold you," I said. "You can move in time. You can escape through a keyhole."

"I prefer not to have recourse to a miracle," Mesmer said. "They should be used sparingly."

"But what are you charged with?" I asked. "Surely the influential persons you have cured can come to your defense. I will be glad to do so myself."

"No, no," Mesmer said, waving the sealed letter like a burning rag he was trying to put out, "this had nothing to do with magnetism. This goes back to the days of my arrival in Paris, when, returning penniless from an extended voyage to the twelfth century, I was forced to live by my wits to amass the necessary capital to open my clinic."

"But what did you do?" I asked.

"Things of no consequence, now magnified by my enemies. I did what any man does who has his back to the wall. I sold saffron-colored water in half-ounce glasses against malignant fever. I turned hemp into silk. I slept for a week, after which I claimed I was younger, lifting hollowed-out weights as evidence. I read a letter without opening it, having previously memorized it. I don't mind telling you, for you know my real cures work. I gave an ancient lady a filter to make her young and paid one of her friends to say he did not recognize her. I sent the king a bust of Caesar, remarking on the resemblance. But ill-intentioned palace bootlick-ers told the king the bust was false, and wiped off the patina with a cloth."

"That is what did it," I said. "You should have stayed clear of the king."

"Well, dear friend," Mesmer said, "we are both in a fine fix. I will have to close my clinic and take up residence in the Bastille, and you are about to be separated from the woman you love. We must leave potions behind and think of more drastic remedies."

"You could petition the king," I suggested.

"Nothing like that," Mesmer said. "You are off the mark. We must think in terms of centuries, in terms of eons. Liberate your mind, make the quantum jump. We are faced with a great prob-lem, and we must find a great solution, a solution to make nations shake. They will learn that when they touch Mesmer, they tamper with the cosmos." He turned to his desk, looked into the sockets of his skull-inkstand, and muttered words in a language that was unintelligible to me. He seemed to have worked himself into a trance. His eyes rolled back until I could see only the whites, and he said: "I see it now, I see it. Now is the time for monarchies to die out. I have seen republics expire, Greece wilt like a flower, Rome burn like a dab of sulfur, destroyed in the midst of noc-turnal revelries, with its orators, skeptics, generals, and vestals. Ah, Babylon, Nineveh, they thought they were immortal."

"Get hold of yourself, my friend," I said. "This is not Babylon or Nineveh, this is France in the final quarter of the eighteenth century."

"It is all the same," Mesmer said. "The overripe fruit is ready to fall from the branch."

"If I interpret your thoughts correctly," I said, "I want no part of them. Instead of the Bastille, you will end up on the Place de Grève."*

"Hear me out, dear friend," Mesmer said, "for mine is a voice that echoes with the ruins of lost civilizations. My nose is trained to sniff out the reek of decline."

"Things are far from perfect, I grant you," I said. "Discontent is widespread and the queen is publicly vilified. But the king's authority is solid, and the army is loyal."

"Ah," said Mesmer, "but what if there was no king?"

I shrank with horror at the implication of his words. "Do you mean . . ."

Mesmer cut me off. "I don't mean kill him," he said, "although that would be no great loss. But I abhor violence. I can't stand the sight of blood. I can't even stand to see a chicken killed. No, I mean, make him . . . disappear. The way a magician makes a lady disappear."

"As for that," said Roger, who had been following our conversation with eyes agape, "I have seen his lordship do it with my own eyes. A bill collector came to the door, and went up in a puff of smoke."

"It is a method I learned from the Sufi mystics of Persia," Mesmer said, adding with modesty: "I take no credit for it. It is a question of willing the particles of an individual to be reassembled in some other form, in some other place, even, although I have not yet reached that stage of perfection, in some other time."

"Do you mean you can make someone vanish and show up elsewhere as something else?" I asked in disbelief.

"It is all based on a scientific law of cellular mutation. I told you that we have within us several previous existences. This is merely a way of causing a regression to an earlier life."

"And what if the king does vanish?" I said. "The crown then goes to his brother, the comte de Provence. Surely you are not going to make the entire royal family disappear."

"Ah, but there is the beauty of my plan," Mesmer said. "For by getting rid of the king, we get rid of the queen, who is responsible for a great deal of the unrest at court and in the rest of the nation. That alone would be an immensely popular move. And it would solve our own modest problems."

---

* It was on the Place de Grève that criminals were publicly executed.

"I must admit that from my point of view it would be an improvement," I said. "For I count the comte de Provence among my friends. He detests the queen, and he is as different from the present monarch as dawn from dusk."

"There, you see," said Mesmer, "it suits us all. And it is nothing so serious as a *coup d'état* or a revolution. Merely a little . . . change of direction. The monarchy is preserved, and our own hand is strengthened."

"I dare say that with Provence on the throne I could regain my former influence," I said.

"But how are you going to make the king disappear?" Roger asked. His practical mind always cut through to the "how" of things.

"I must have a brief moment in the king's presence," Mesmer said. "That is all. The next morning, the courtiers come to attend his *lever* will peek through the closed curtains of his bed and find it empty."

"Can you imagine the consternation?" I cried. "Why, it will be the most startling event since the conversion of Henri IV."

"And there will be no explanation for it," Roger said.

"People will say he secretly abdicated or vanished to escape his nagging wife," I said. "Perhaps the church will say he had supernatural powers, and elevate him to sainthood. That will make the second Saint Louis. They will have to call him Saint Louis *bis*."*

"Or they will suspect he has been killed," Mesmer said, "but no *corpus delicti* will ever be found."

"The main problem as I see it," I said, for I had rallied to the plan, which seemed to afford a multitude of advantages for a minimum of risk, "is how to approch the king privately, for he is always surrounded, and in the evening guards stand outside his apartment."

"Does he sleep in the same room his grandfather, the previous king, employed?" Mesmer asked.

"He does," I said, "for more than most men, kings are creatures of habit."

"Then there must be a secret staircase we can use to reach the royal bedroom. It matters not whether the king is awake or asleep, the spell is effective in either case."

"Splendid," I said. "I will make inquiries about the location of

---

* *Bis* means twice, or in theatrical terms, encore.

the staircase and find out whether it is guarded. The king rarely retires after ten and sleeps so soundly an army on the march could not wake him. I see no reason to wait. You should be able to perform several days from now."

Roger wanted to come with us. "I've never seen a king vanish before," he said.

I returned to Versailles that evening and informed Elizabeth about our plans. She thought we had gone mad, and spent hours trying to dissuade me from carrying out what she called "a jest in the poorest taste." For she could not believe Mesmer was serious. I had the potion as proof of his wizardry, but I could not tell Elizabeth that. I vaguely referred to demonstrations that had convinced me of Mesmer's powers. "But do you realize what you are exposing yourself to if anything goes wrong?" Elizabeth asked.

"Nothing can go wrong," I said, for my mind was made up. I was tempted by the marvelous incongruity of the whole project. Elizabeth came into my arms and pleaded with me to give up the scheme.

"Oh, Ax," she said, "you say you are doing this for me, but you pay no heed to what I want. I want a life away from plots and artifices. We have been at court too long. It has thinned our blood. We are no longer capable of following the inclinations of our hearts. I don't think you realize how little it would take to make me happy." She was right, of course. I had convinced myself I was helping Elizabeth, whereas in fact I was drawn to the adventure for its own sake, and I also wanted to settle a score with a king who had shown me nothing but the back of his hand. I promised Elizabeth that when this was over, I would do whatever she liked, but to trust me this last time.

"After all," I said, "why should we allow ourselves to be evicted from court like servants caught pilfering?"

"Is that more important than our life together?" she asked.

Women are forever placing emotions before honor. In their eyes, the worst scoundrel, guilty of the most abominable crimes, can redeem himself by turning himself over to the custody of the woman he loves. I told Elizabeth we would have our life together, but on our own terms. She said I was wrong to trust Mesmer. She said she trusted her instincts, and that our plan made her feel more uneasy than anything I had ever done. She knew it would end badly. I promised that in a few days it would all be over, and she would be wondering what could have prompted her anxiety.

I learned that the secret staircase the former king's mistresses had used originated on the ground floor of the palace, beneath the bedroom, behind a secret panel painted by Boucher with an allegory representing spring, at one end of a small drawing room used by the queen as a music room. A latch under the mantelpiece sprung open this panel, and the narrow corkscrew staircase climbed to a hidden door that opened to one side of the king's bed. This door was kept locked, for the present king had no use for the staircase. I was able, through my friendship with a retired footman who had been privy to the former king's nocturnal escapades, to obtain a key. I told this old fellow, who lived in a tiny attic in Versailles, that the present king, who liked to play at locksmith, wanted a copy of the key to the secret door in order to study and duplicate it. He was only too glad to give it to me and I rewarded him handsomely.

That Thurdsay the queen had arranged a masked ball, and I chose the day to bring Mesmer and Roger to the palace. When one arrived with a group at a masked ball, only one person in the group had to unmask for the guards at the door. It was a habit left over from the days of the previous king, who liked to spice the attendance with ladies of doubtful reputation, who otherwise would never have been admitted to Versailles. In any case, thanks to this custom, Mesmer and Roger would have no trouble entering the palace, where they could mingle with the other guests in their disguises. Furthermore, the king, as was his habit, would retire after watching the first quadrille, and leave the queen to the waiting arms of a multitude of courtiers only too happy to dance with her in the absence of her lump of a husband. The ball was the perfect diversion to draw attention away from our plans.

On the appointed night, I waited for Mesmer's carriage as footmen in blue livery holding torches escorted the guests up the steps of the palace. I was costumed without affectation as a musketeer, a domino mask hiding the upper part of my face. Mesmer arrived as a Roman emperor, in a toga, a laurel wreath atop his head, and a parchment scroll in his hand, his face covered with a mask intended to resemble one of the Caesars, which made him look as if he were suffering from the disease that abnormally enlarges the features of the face. He was followed by Roger, ridiculously clad in a short pleated skirt, leather apron, short boots with knee-high leather thongs, and a rusty helmet on his round head, in the guise of a centurion.

"How do we look?" Mesmer asked, obviously delighted with his disguise.

"As though you had just left the Capitol," I said, to please him.

We came to the curtained doors of the ballroom entrance, and I dropped my mask and said "Duc de Gramont." The guards dressed as footmen bowed and stood aside to let us through. We waited on one side of the room for the king and queen to arrive. Soon the royal couple appeared, the queen resplendent in a dress of pink organdy covered with precious stones, her hand held aloft by the king's, who with his other hand was stifling a yawn, and seemed bent under the weight of the powder in his wig.

The king asked the prince de Conti to open the ball. Conti was dressed in the black robes of a member of parliament, his tiny head all but invisible under his mortar hat, and when he took the queen through the steps of the quadrille, she seemed to be dancing with a wing-flapping crow. Soon enough, the king disappeared, and the ball became more lively. Mesmer had engaged the attention of a small group and seemed to be making a speech on the customs of ancient Rome. I drew him aside and begged him not to call attention to himself. "Just getting into the spirit of things," he said. He showed not the slightest trace of nervousness. I asked him whether his spell-making powers were in good form. "At their peak," he said. "Why, tonight, I could make myself disappear." I told him and Roger that we would wait another hour to give the king a chance to fall asleep. Roger spent most of his time at the buffet drinking champagne as though it was water and sampling the *pâtés* and meats. I danced several times with Elizabeth, who was lovely in a white satin gown set off by a ruby necklace. She had come as Héloïse, and while complimenting her on her beauty, I protested that I was not suited for the part of Abélard.

When it was time to carry out our plan, I kissed her lightly and told her we would be back in twenty minutes. She raised her white satin domino to show me that there were tears in her eyes, which she said she could not explain. I beckoned to Mesmer and Roger, and led them through the dark and empty drawing room to the Boucher panel. I pressed the secret latch and it sprung open.

We closed it behind us, taking candles to light our way up the tiny staircase, which creaked, having been designed for lighter traffic. Upon reaching the door of the king's bedroom, I put my ear to it, and it seemed to me I could hear snoring. "Now is your chance to show your true colors," I whispered to Mesmer as I fitted the tiny gold key into the lock. It was rusty, and took coaxing to open, but we finally entered the bedroom. Alas, the king was not snoring in his bed but fully dressed and standing in the center of the room, surrounded by guards and several of his ministers, including the one who had replaced me, Saint-Germain. They looked as though they were about to call a cabinet meeting. The king affected a stern expression, which only made him look constipated. Saint-Germain wore a thin, knowing smile. Guards moved to block the secret staircase and the main, double-doored entrance to the king's chamber. Mesmer and Roger found a dark corner on the far side of the canopied bed and huddled there like mice.

Sprightly as an acrobat, I regained my poise and said, bowing low: "Your obedient servant, Sire."

"What is this, sir," Saint-Germain asked, "forcing your way into the king's chamber at midnight with two cohorts?"

"I felt it was my duty, sir, to warn the king of a plot against his life," I said, for in truth I could think of no more convincing reason to explain my presence.

"To warn or to surprise, sir? Mark well your choice of words."

"The insinuation is odious, sir," I replied, finding refuge in indignation.

"No more odious than your back-stairs wandering, sir," Saint-Germain said.

"I have brought with me a man well known in Paris and throughout Europe for his prophetic powers," I said. "He can give you full particulars of the danger to the king." And I stretched my arm in Mesmer's direction. But instead of taking the cue, he shuffled in his corner.

"We are acquainted with Herr Mesmer," Saint-Germain said, "and have already had the benefit of his prophecy."

The light dawned. I mockingly said, "And now, great man, I will show you how *I* disappear." At the same time I bent to pluck the dagger from my left boot and held it to Saint-Germain's pale throat. He tried to wave my arm aside as he would have an irksome petitioner's, but when he felt the blade's cold point, his arm dropped to his side, and he shook his head at a guard whose half-unsheathed sword remained in its scabbard.

The king, who had dropped his obesity onto an upholstered stool and seemed to be watching actors in a picaresque drama, spoke up for the first time: "Ministers are as interchangeable as forks and spoons," he said, as he stifled a yawn with the back of his hand, for he was unaccustomed to keeping such late hours. "Kill him and I will have twenty postulants at my door tomorrow," he added, and I felt Saint-Germain's Adam's apple bob. "You will only make your own cause more desperate."

I could not see how my cause could be more desperate than it already was. My goals, my ambitions, my plans, all were now reduced to the essential simplicity of survival. I thought that with Saint-Germain as a shield, I could withdraw down the secret staircase and take advantage of the agitation of the masked ball to escape from the palace. But I had to make sure the staircase was not guarded at the other end.

"Roger, old friend," I said, "Bastille companion, *Rôdeur* shipmate, one final favor. Make sure the way we came is still open."

Roger bowed his head to avoid meeting my glance. There are no friends, cardinal de Noirot had told me years ago, only moments of friendship. Roger was in Mesmer's pay. I turned again toward the transalpine mystifier, who raised his bushy eyebrows and said, "Just like life, baby." The mustard rose to my brain. "German swine," I thought, "at least I'll put an end to his double-dealing." I left Saint-Germain's side and lunged at Mesmer, who shouted out some Eastern imprecation. "More of his damned rot," I thought, but though my mind continued to proceed, my body no longer followed. I found that I could no more move than Lot (or was it his wife?) after looking back at Sodom. I called out Elizabeth's name, but could not hear my own voice. A mineral heaviness immobilized me, and I knew that a man is never such a total charlatan that he cannot transform a friend into a quarry to feed the yelping curs of circumstance.

The memoirs end at this point. It seems evident that they were written while Anaxagoras languished in whatever royal prison he was taken to. How they reached the Gramont family archives is not known, but the most plausible explanation is that Anaxagoras smuggled them out of jail to Elizabeth, who passed them on to another member of the family, possibly his brother Alfred. Anaxagoras' fate remains a mystery to this day. Most historians believe he was put to death within a year of plotting against the king, which would have left him just enough time to write his memoirs. There is, however, one interesting piece of evidence to show that thanks to the efforts of Elizabeth de Villiers, Gramont was saved *from execution, but condemned to remain for the rest of his life in a remote provincial prison, where he was made to wear an iron mask, so that the other inmates would not be able to identify him. The device of the iron mask was commonly used in the seventeenth and eighteenth centuries to preserve the anonymity of prisoners whose identities would have been a source of embarrassment to the king. I have seen the evidence with my own eyes on the wall of a tower cell in the fortress of Angers, which is now used as a museum where the tapestries of the Apocalypse are exhibited. There, faded by the years but still visible on the damp gray walls, are the following words scratched into the stone:* Combien de temps encore?* *Followed by the interlocking initials AG and the crude drawing of a mask underlined by ten crosses. If the graffiti was indeed made by Anaxagoras, it indicates that he lived ten years in prison, which means that he died one year before the French Revolution, in 1788, at the age of sixty-three. Had he endured a few months longer, he would have been freed with the other inmates of royal prisons. Admittedly, a scratch on a prison wall falls somewhat short of conclusive proof, and yet it is more than a straw in the wind. I offer it for the reader's judgment. In any case, Anaxagoras de Gramont was never heard from again, and his body was never returned to his family.*

---

* How much longer?